PRAISE FOR THE HOT IN CHICAGO SERIES

SPARKING THE FIRE

"The many instances of a family sticking together through it all are more than enough to tug on the heartstrings, but the steamy sex and sentimental pillow talk make this book a must-read."

—*RT Book Reviews*

"WOW. . . . Amazing, beautiful, and tissue-worthy. That is what this book is."

—*Harlequin Junkie*

"A sparkling, sexy, second-chance romance . . . a story of fighting for both yourself and your family."

—*All About Romance* (Desert Isle Keeper)

PLAYING WITH FIRE

Winner of the RT Book Reviewers' 2015 Award for Best Contemporary Love & Laughter

A *Publishers Weekly* Best Book of 2015

A *Washington Post* Best Romance of 2015

"Meader packs the flawless second Hot in Chicago romance with superb relationship development and profane but note-perfect dialogue."

—*Publishers Weekly*, starred review

"Steamy sex scenes, colorful characters, and riveting dialogue . . . a real page-turner."

—*RT Book Reviews*, Top Pick Gold

"A smart, sexy book."

—Sarah MacLean, *The Washington Post*

"Hot, sexy, wonderful."

—Beverly Jenkins, The Huffington Post

"I absolutely love Meader's voice and the easy flow of her dialogue, the growth of the characters, and the actual plot of the story. And, oh my God, is Eli Cooper one sexy alpha male."

—Heroes and Heartbreakers

"When it comes to writing hot, sexy heroes and strong, independent women, no one does it better than Kate Meader. Her Hot in Chicago series is a scorcher."

—Harlequin Junkie

FLIRTING WITH FIRE

"Sexy and sassy. . . . I love this book!"

—#1 New York Times bestselling author Jude Deveraux

"Sexy, witty, and hot, hot, hot. Kate Meader will make you fall in love with the hunky firefighters at Engine Co. 6."

— Sarah Castille, New York Times bestselling author

"Get your fire extinguisher handy—Flirting with Fire is HOT and satisfying!"

— Jennifer Probst, New York Times bestselling author

"This book is everything you want in a romance: excellent writing, strong characters, and a sizzling plot that keeps the pace up throughout the story."

—RT Book Reviews, Top Pick

Irresistible YOU

KATE MEADER

Pocket Books

New York   London   Toronto   Sydney   New Delhi

Pocket Books
An Imprint of Simon & Schuster, Inc.
1230 Avenue of the Americas
New York, NY 10020

This book is a work of fiction. Any references to historical events, real people, or real places are used fictitiously. Other names, characters, places, and events are products of the author's imagination, and any resemblance to actual events or places or persons, living or dead, is entirely coincidental.

First Pocket Books paperback edition September 2017

POCKET and colophon are registered trademarks of Simon & Schuster, Inc.

For information about special discounts for bulk purchases, please contact Simon & Schuster Special Sales at 1-866-506-1949 or business@simonandschuster.com.

The Simon & Schuster Speakers Bureau can bring authors to your live event. For more information or to book an event, contact the Simon & Schuster Speakers Bureau at 1-866-248-3049 or visit our website at www.simonspeakers.com.

Interior design by Alison Cnockaert

Manufactured in the United States of America

10 9 8 7 6 5

ISBN 978-1-5011-8088-0
ISBN 978-1-5011-6855-0 (ebook)

To Jimmie,
thanks for taking this road with me

ONE

A bucolic bedroom community with easy access to Boston, only thirty miles away, West Bridgerton looked like a typical New England town as Harper Chase drove her rental car through its family friendly streets. This late, she was surprised they didn't roll them up after dark. On her left, she passed a gazebo in War Memorial Park, on her right a steepled white church. Two Dunkin's. No Starbucks. Farmland, a rail trail, a river, and a state forest spoke to its pastoral character.

Hard to believe a lughead of a hockey player would feel at home amid such peaceful surroundings.

The lughead in question? Remy DuPre, or Jinx, as he was better known with the Boston Cougars, a nickname earned because he was considered the unluckiest guy in the NHL. A little bird—in the form of his agent—had told her the Cajun was ragin' about his trade out of Boston and would need a dab of soft soap to smooth his transition to the Chicago Rebels.

Harper sighed. She had never met a bigger bunch

of divas than hockey players. For all their supposed rough-and-tumble-warrior credentials, they were nothing but whiners when it came to their contracts.

She had made this trade fair and square.

Was it her fault DuPre was a bargain? Paying out the last year of his contract—a contract that should have been better negotiated by his loser agent when he came up for renewal with Boston two years ago—had cost her a pittance compared to what she'd have to pony up for someone younger. So he was thirty-five, positively elderly for hockey. And *maybe* his chances to go deep in a season were running out.

There's no room for sentimentality in this game.

That was the mantra of Clifford Chase: three-time Stanley Cup champion, Hall of Famer, hockey franchise owner, notorious asshole.

And Harper's lately departed father.

Two weeks ago the maverick owner of the Chicago Rebels had died following a massive heart attack at the age of sixty-two. A week later, Harper's life was upended again with the reading of the will, leaving her to negotiate the rubble of her father's final wishes for the team. Their relationship had been combative, to say the least, but she had never expected this.

Over the past decade, the Rebels, once the most popular team in the city, had become a laughingstock, named "the worst franchise in sports" by ESPN, with the second-lowest attendance in the NHL. Having made the playoffs only once in the last fifteen years—an abysmal record considering half the teams qualify each year—the organization was also suffering through the longest championship drought in the league. Sure, they had a few good players—their poor results put them in prime position for the best draft picks—but not enough. Her father's grip on the team had been tight enough to bruise. Harper, despite her official title of vice president, was his right-hand woman in name only.

Now they needed to rebuild. And that rebuild began with the acquisition of veteran center Remy DuPre, who could take her band of talented misfits and make them shine.

However, DuPre had decided he didn't need to follow the rules. He didn't need to hop on a plane within twenty-four hours of being traded and haul ass to Chicago. He didn't even need to speak directly to Harper, as acting general manager, about his absence.

The moment Coach Calhoun had shared DuPre's travel plans, she had called and left a message. Fortunately—for DuPre—she'd missed his returned call, so he didn't get the full brunt of her wrath. If he truly understood how pissed she was that he had chosen not to show for practice in Chicago, surely he would not have fobbed her off with a casual "See ya for the game in Philly, Harper."

She had played his message several times. Not because she enjoyed that syrupy New Orleans drawl that crept over her body like a thief and made every hair stand at attention.

No. She had replayed it to assure herself that she was indeed hearing the words of a man who thought he had some say in his to'ing and fro'ing. DuPre appeared to be under the impression that the Chicago Rebels' organization did not own his ass. She was here to set him straight.

A midnight visit to his home in Massachusetts had not been part of the plan. She'd intended for this smackdown to happen earlier. Fly in. Lay down the law. Fly out. But her flight had landed late and she'd been on her way to her hotel when she decided to drive by DuPre's house first.

She pulled into the drive of a classic Colonial—behind the eight million cars already lining the path. The steady thump of a distant bass echoed through the air. Blazing lights from the house set the October night sky aglow. All that was missing was a spotlight shooting upward announcing Here Lives Remy DuPre!

Harper's teeth, already in danger of being ground to dust, were now set on edge. Instead of getting acquainted with his new team in Chicago, her new acquisition was throwing a party.

Sitting in the car, she considered her options. She would prefer not to get into a mud-flinging match with DuPre in front of an audience. It could wait until tomorrow. She checked her watch: 12:02 a.m.

Past curfew.

Hockey organizations implemented strict rules about how much sleep players should be getting. Their diets were regimented, workouts monitored, every aspect of their lives recorded to ensure they remained valuable assets to the team.

Harper had invested considerable money in DuPre, and the man was throwing a party when he should have been sleeping off a hard practice and preparing for the game against the Philadelphia Liberty in two days.

Lost in her indignation, she barely noticed that she'd left her car and reached DuPre's front door. It rose before her, a barrier to her doing her job, and her mouth fell open at the words stenciled on the red-painted wood:

Laissez les Bons Temps Rouler

Let the good times roll, the motto of spring breakers everywhere. And Remy DuPre had it indelibly fixed to his door.

Oh, God. Panic edged across her skin, making her heart pump madly.

She had made a huge mistake.

This was not the man she needed to lead the Rebels to a top-three finish in the Central Division. She would find a way to back out of the trade. Cite irreconcilable differences, buyer's remorse, having her GD period. Anything!

Ready to retreat, she turned away, but something popped in her chest.

The news that the Rebels had been divided up

among Clifford's daughters like a Shakespearean trag-
edy was still a hot topic in the sports media. Add to
that the team's terrible start to the season—0 and 4—
and the idea that a woman, or women, knew jack about
running a professional hockey team was still getting
plenty of airplay. Usually with jokes along the lines of:

*How many women does it take to screw up a sports fran-
chise?*

Just one. But three sure is prettier.

Anger at her father evicted her panic. What had the
man been thinking, leaving the team to be jointly run
by a trio of estranged half sisters? Clifford had promised Harper the team. Not in so many words, no, but
they had an understanding.

No one expected him to go so soon, but she had
hoped he'd involve her more and would recognize the
value she could add to the organization. She'd majored in
sports management, interned at Rebels HQ, made damn
fine coffee, given a knowing wink and a smile while her
ass was ogled by her male coworkers and those horn-
dogs on the team. She'd sat in on every negotiation from
player to equipment to concessions. And yes, all the ultimate decisions came from on high, but at thirty-one years
of age, she was ready. Clifford had known she was ready.

Yet he still hadn't trusted her to do the job herself.

She steeled her spine and stood as tall as her Cole
Haan wedges would allow. She should have worn the
Choos, but she was practical to her core, and the Cole
Haans with the Nike Air insoles were perfect for traveling.

She refused to let a dead man, two sisters who were practically strangers to her, and an overgrown frat boy named Remy DuPre dictate how she ran her team.

Who's the boss, Harper?

You da boss!

Determination in her sway, she pivoted and searched for a doorbell. Nothing. The knocker would have to do, but as she curled her fingers around it, the door gave way like something out of an old Hammer horror film.

Of course. The good times would have a hard time rolling through a locked door.

The music increased in volume. Hoots and hollers tinged the air. She moved forward, trying to force her feet to match the indignation in her chest. A few steps more, and she wished she had gone with her first instinct and turned tail the moment she read that door inscription.

A woman was removing her clothes.

Harper hadn't just walked into a party, she'd walked into an orgy.

Okay, cool it. It wasn't quite as bad as all that. No one was having public sex . . . yet. But it looked increasingly likely.

A curvaceous brunette in red hot pants was in the process of peeling off a teeny-tiny top, *aaaaand* there it went, revealing a sparkly bra with tassels. Really? She swung those tassels like a sixties burlesque queen.

Everyone cheered. All of them men.

A blood-chilling creep frosted over Harper at the

sight of this woman surrounded by so much testosterone, powerful machines with more strength in their forearms than in that woman's entire body.

The burlesque queen straddled a man, her body hiding his face, her obvious self-confidence a direct repudiation of Harper's fears. The man's massive hands, as big as ham hocks, skimmed her hips and drew her flush over muscular, jean-clad thighs.

"Tonight, Remy," the woman said in a smoky purr, "you're gonna get a send-off you'll never forget."

She raised her hands to the back snap barely containing all that flesh ready to spill forth. The cups sure did runneth over with this one. Was she actually going to—

Harper couldn't stand it another moment. "DuPre!"

Twenty-five sets of eyes turned on her, cold, accusing. So much for slipping in under the radar.

Moving his head to the side of his "gift," Remy DuPre raised the eyebrow of a rogue. She had never met him in the flesh, but seeing this warrior battling it out on the ice—both in person and on TV—should have prepared her. Every day in her job she dealt with mountains of muscle with the honed and sculpted bodies of gods. Some of them were good-looking. Some of them had faces only a mother or a woman looking to score with a million-dollar athlete could love.

Remy DuPre's face compelled her attention. Not classically handsome, instead he was all brute angles and solid planes that indicated both hard work and the ability to enjoy life. His was a lived-in face, that of a man who laughed often and knew pleasure. A sensualist.

And those piercing blue eyes, brutish hands, and tree-trunk thighs were sensualizing all over the place.

He tapped the woman's ass once, twice, and issued a husky order. "Up, *chérie*." She obeyed—of course!—turning to face Harper as she stood.

"Who the hell are you?" Tassels demanded. Really, she should be thanking Harper for putting a halt to this demeaning display.

"Chérie, don't be rude to my guest. This is Harper." Creases formed at the corners of DuPre's cobalt-blue eyes. Incredibly attractive creases that reaffirmed her earlier impression of a man who enjoyed life. He nodded in her direction. "Glad you could make it."

As if he had invited her.

At six and change, Remy towered above Harper's five feet one and a half inches. Those hands, those thighs . . . everything about him was supersized.

"Come on back to the kitchen." He headed off, leaving her no choice but to follow.

Suspicious eyes set in familiar Cougar faces bored into her as she marched through. Although her identity was well known, no one nodded in recognition. A basketball game on a huge wall-mounted TV riveted the attention of the crowd in one room, men so inured to strippers that they hadn't even bothered to move next door for the show. Not even the skimpily clad women perched on the arms of sofas and armchairs could compete. A few tried their best, shoving surgically enhanced breasts into bearded faces, only to be met with cries of, "Baby, I'm tryin' to watch the game!" Men.

No sign, thank God, of the one person she'd prayed would be absent.

Skipping ahead faster than her feet, her gaze collided with DuPre's broad shoulders. Then traveled down a well-muscled back that tapered to slim hips and an ass that even Harper, who was on a strict man embargo, could appreciate. Purely from an aesthetic point of view, mind you. What woman wouldn't like the sight of taut buns filling out a pair of jeans with such authority? She assumed DuPre worked lunges into his routine to get those perfect globes.

The bastard should be working those lunges in the workout room at Rebels HQ.

Nearing what must be the kitchen, her nostrils flared in anticipation. Something smelled wonderful— not DuPre, who probably smelled like an unwashed gym bag—but something hearty. Her stomach growled, annoyed with her for allowing it to subsist on that half-stale bagel at O'Hare seven hours ago. Don't even try to tell her that hungry was not an emotion, because, like every woman, she felt that shit in her soul. However, the delicious scent of cooking was soon ruined by a more potent sensory experience: DuPre draped over another woman in front of the stove.

Poor guy couldn't go more than a couple of minutes without female company, it seemed.

His tanned forearm, sprinkled with dark hair, curled around the waist of a woman in a vagina-length Cougars hockey jersey and high heels. His other hand held a wooden spoon at a tempting angle to her pouty red lips.

"Remeeee! You know I don't do spicy."

A low rumbled chuckle, laden with sex and menace, mocked her protest. "Now, I happen to know that's a lie, Doreen, 'cause a little bird told me you like it plenty spicy. My mawmaw taught me how to make the perfect jambalaya and you ain't even gonna give it a shot?" He squeezed her waist in encouragement, and she leaned in closer, brushing her breast against DuPre's substantial chest. Harper could almost hear the sigh of pleasure Doreen's hormones released at that touch.

Time to get down to business. Harper coughed. And went unnoticed.

This rarely happened to her.

"Mr. DuPre."

Both of them turned, Doreen's pirouette guaranteeing she touched an entire hectare of boobage against Remy's thick bicep. DuPre's expression was one of mild annoyance that Harper was still here.

"Doreen, go see if the boys are hungry. Tell 'em we got po' boys and jambalaya."

With a world-class pout, Doreen tottered out.

"You hungry, Harper?" DuPre asked with that lazy-as-shit drawl. She didn't like the flutter in her belly when he said her name. Know what else she didn't like? His inky-dark eyelashes, almost as though someone had painted them on around those blue eyes. Harper was immediately suspicious of a man with prettier eyelashes than her.

"No," she lied.

He ladled a serving of jambalaya into a bowl. "Surprised to see you here."

"You're on my dime, now, Mr. DuPre."

"Call me Remy. Didn't you get my message? I told you I'd meet up with the team in Philly." He gestured with the bowl, and at her moue of discontent, he grabbed a fork. In a display that threatened to turn her annoyance into apoplectic, hangry levels, he teased a piece of shrimp in rice and raised it to his lips. After a chew, a swallow, and a look of near ecstasy that had Harper's mouth watering—because she was hungry, she insisted—he spoke again.

"The boys wanted to throw me a party, so I figured one more day wouldn't hurt. Been here a long time."

She knew that. Five years was an age in hockey, which by its very nature required men to be ready to upend their lives at a moment's notice as soon as a trade came in. DuPre had been traded six times since he was the number one draft pick seventeen years ago. His file said he'd never married, had never even come close, so he wouldn't have the comfort of a wife or girlfriend to smooth over his move to Chicago. Unless Tassels or Doreen had her bags packed . . .

"It's important you bond with the team sooner than later. There's no time to waste."

"Not sure what you're expecting here, Harper." The easy tease that had laced his voice was gone. His accent was punchier than she remembered from postgame TV interviews, Brooklyn by way of the Bayou. "You could have brought on anyone."

"I need a leader. Someone who's seen everything and can make something of—"

"Nothing? You need a miracle. It's gonna take two years to rebuild. Minimum. You need money, because good players don't come cheap. You need patience."

Patience was for winners. She would lose everything if she didn't employ drastic measures, because not only had her father screwed her over by not leaving her the team to run solo, he'd put another obstacle in her path. A time-sensitive requirement.

"I've been patient."

"Would it have killed you to exercise that patience for another year? Because your lack of it has fucked me over royally. You saw how close we came in May. The Cougars have the makings of a dynasty, and I planned to inaugurate it this season. What you've done is rip that chance out of my hands." He slapped the bowl down on the counter with a bang.

Harper jumped, an involuntary reaction to his little temper tantrum. It was nothing, of course. Understandable, even. Every day she watched men fight over a rubber disc, violence seething from their pores, but she had always kept her distance from the players. She knew that would be impossible as acting GM. That she was going to have to face her deep-seated fears about being up close and personal with war-making machines that could break a woman in half.

Those demons set to gnawing in her chest, so she inhaled a deep breath and used an old therapy trick: act normal until the panic "gets bored." She looked around. Normal, even homey, kitchen. Normal stock-pot on the normal stove. Normal employee with normal muscles and normal . . . hair. Pretty awesome hair, actually. Mahogany brown and perfectly mussed, but not trying too hard. So many hockey players wore their hair long—salads, they called it—but not Remy DuPre. No straggle for him, just enough on top to allow for a decent finger rake. Not that she was in the market for a decent finger rake.

The monsters went silent.

Well done, DuPre. Your awesome hair has just helped fight off my imminent panic attack.

He was watching her curiously. "Okay there, Harper?"

She squared her shoulders. "I'm fine. Just tired after my flight was delayed, the one I shouldn't have had to take at all. I want you in Chicago tomorrow, and you'll fly out with the team on Thursday. You won't be swanning in like some diva in Philly. This isn't how it's going to work. You're a Rebel now, and you play by my rules."

TWO

Remy couldn't help congratulating himself: damn, he made a great jambalaya. Not too spicy, bursting with flavor, each mouthful a perfectly self-contained meal.

He raised his eyes from the bowl in his hand to the woman before him. Not too spicy and far too skinny. Barely an ounce of flesh on her, only a couple of inches above five feet, she stood before him like a pissed-off toothpick. Her blond hair was pulled back in a bun, a move one of his old girlfriends told him women employed to remove wrinkles. It had the effect of drawing attention to her eyes, big sea-green saucers that flashed silver when she got emotional. And boy, was this woman emotional.

Her rage waved from ten feet across the kitchen, so he took another bite and chewed slowly, because he suspected Harper Chase wasn't used to delays. Everything would be *Now, there. No, there!* Bet she was bossy as all get-out in bed.

His cock stirred. No idea why—okay, it was probably

because it'd been a while since he'd gone sheet diving. However, Harper Chase was not his type in the slightest. He liked his women with meat on them, unafraid a laugh might give them lines around their eyes or reveal a side they'd rather remain hidden.

A crying shame, because she had that husky, sex kitten voice he knew men mistook for a bimbo's. Harper Chase was no bimbo. She was a savvy businesswoman. But she would need to lower that voice by several octaves before anyone took her seriously in the NHL. Barely weeks since Clifford Chase's death and the subsequent reveal of how he'd given the middle finger to everyone from the grave, and the jokes were still flying about how the Rebels' estrogen influx would likely send them from second last to bottom.

Didn't help that they'd just lost their general manager, Brian Rennie, and already had an open position for an assistant.

If it was just Harper, Remy might've given them a shot. It was no secret that she'd been itching to get her hands dirty and turn the org around. The woman had balls of steel, but having to rule by family committee when by all accounts said family couldn't stand to be in the same room together? Hell, he had four sisters he *liked* and he wouldn't have wished that on his worst enemy. Now, with no GM or assistant, the Rebels were up *merde* creek, paddle in smithereens.

"Did you hear me, Mr. DuPre?"

Mon dieu, the flavor in that tone, like a sweet blues

ballad. He bet she could serenade his cock to full mast if he let her. Marveling at where his brain had already gone, he shook his head. Women should not be running hockey teams.

"I was sorry to hear about your father." Guy was a complete *fils de putain*, but he was also a helluva center back in the day.

She inhaled a short, sharp breath, and for a moment looked young. Vulnerable. "Thank you."

Doreen finally must have made an impact, because the next sound was a herd of wildebeest pounding the antique Java hardwood flooring he had installed a year ago.

"Let's talk outside, Harper."

He stepped out onto the deck he had built with his own hands last summer, irked by the constant reminders of how much he'd invested in his life in Boston. Once she'd joined him, he closed the door. This conversation was not for the ears of his teammates.

Former teammates.

Fuck, that stung. After five years, these men were his coworkers, his friends, the guys he'd lay down everything for. The Cougars had started to come together last spring, getting as far as the semifinals, and had just missed the big time by a lucky goal in double overtime.

When it came to Remy, fortune always seemed to favor the other side.

He'd been saddled with the label of unluckiest

guy in the NHL. Made three finals, each run ending in heartbreak. Traded six times, and in four of those instances, the team he left went on to win the Cup the year after. Matt Stein, Boston's GM, had laughed his head off when he acquired Remy five years ago.

No one's that unlucky, DuPre. A guy who works as hard as you eventually has to get the right call.

Not even Remy's agent knew that he'd planned to retire after this season, and he had high hopes of going out in a blaze of glory. This was supposed to be the Cougars' year. *His* year. Finally, he'd get to hold the Cup, not gaze at it in the fucking Hall of Fame like some drooling rookie. But the only certainties were death, taxes, and that you could be traded at the drop of a hat. Sure it was a business, but he didn't enjoy Harper Chase's methods.

"Have a seat," he said, gesturing to the Adirondack chair he liked to kick back in with a cold beer on his days off.

Her eyes widened briefly, a flicker of something unnameable in them, and he could have sworn she took an incremental step toward the door. Did he look like the sort of jerk who'd make an unwanted move on a woman? This *femme* sure thought she was the shit.

"Don't worry, Harper, you're not my type." If she wouldn't sit, then neither would he, 'cause that's how his momma raised him. He leaned against one of the deck's wooden beams.

"Mr. DuPre—"

"It's Remy."

"Remy," she said, clearly exasperated. "Leaving a voice mail to say you'll make your own way to Philly for the next game is not how you conduct yourself on my team. If I say you need to be in Chicago, then you need to be in Chicago."

"I don't take orders, Harper. I barely take suggestions." He sighed, realizing that was not terribly respectful. Time to let the facts speak for themselves. "The Rebels' record this season already sucks. Oh and four. Whether I show for practice today or tomorrow is not gonna make one blind bit of difference to that game. Hell, two months of practice and team building and whatever horseshit you have in mind to make this crew work is not gonna matter."

Earlier she'd said she needed a leader. Well, baby-sitting was not part of his job description. Move forward on the ice or die—that was his job. He'd put his time into being an inspiration after he won the Cup.

If he won. Because now that was looking less and less likely.

She fisted her hands at her hips. Skinny bones in skinny jeans that looked like they'd been ironed. Everything about her pissed him off.

"You're already giving up?"

He was too old to fall for that reverse psychology bullshit. "You've got injured players, guys with low morale, skaters that don't give a crap, and last season's worst record in the league."

"Second worst."

"You just lost your GM—"

"I fired him."

He closed his eyes. This was worse than he'd thought. How could this be worse than he'd thought?

"Damn, when you step up to the plate, you swing for the fences, don't ya?"

"I need you to take us to top three in the division by the end of the season."

Remy had met a lot of women in his life, and in his younger days, he'd gravitated toward crazy. Ginny Calderon in the ninth grade, who jumped into the St. Louis Cathedral fountain because the Virgin Mary told her to. Sharon Townsend, whom he hooked up with the night of his first game with the Sharks, barely nineteen years old and three days into the league. She called him every day for a week afterward because she thought he was going to lose if he didn't wave to her on TV. Total whack job. They dated for five months.

But he didn't do crazy anymore. He wanted to knuckle down in what would likely be his last year in professional hockey and win a fucking championship. Standing on his deck listening to Harper Chase spouting off about her pie-in-the-sky dream of making top three in the—*hold up*.

"You're talking about making the playoffs."

"I am." Calm as a clam.

"Now I know you're nuts." He was all for can-do and visualizing an endgame, but hockey players were far too superstitious for that kind of corporate goal setting. "There's nothing about the Rebels that can take them from a bottom two to a top three in one season. Even a wildcard spot is a long shot."

She smiled, and fuck him sideways, wasn't that something? That no-shit demeanor was completely transformed. "That's where you're wrong, Mr. DuPre. This season, we have you."

Anger boiled up, swift and sharp. This was his dream she was stepping on with her crazy ambition. She might be within her legal rights, but she knew the minute she made that call to Matt Stein she was screwing him over.

"What's your game, Harper?"

She looked taken aback. "My game?"

"You know what's on the line for me. You know what you've done in bringing me on." That this year was his swan song might not be common knowledge, but he was thirty-five and on the downside of his career. Everyone and his aunt Lucille knew the Cup was the last thing Remy needed to scratch off his bucket list to finally retire in peace. He shouldn't have to explain it.

"This is a business—"

"Yeah, I know. There's no cryin' in hockey. Okay, let's talk business. You want my help whipping your team into shape, then I need something from you."

She bristled, on the defensive again.

"Already told you you're not my type, Harper, and

frankly, I'm insulted you think I'd sell my body for a shot at the Cup."

No smile, not even a hint. So, humorless in the extreme. Just perfect.

"Nothing surprises me," she said. "Most people will do anything to win."

True that, and Harper was certainly giving off that vibe. A curious energy twanged between them, which could be labeled only one way: affinity.

She felt it, too. They recognized something in each other. Now, wasn't that interesting.

Seeming to realize that she had revealed too much, she rolled her shoulders back in an obvious attitude adjustment. "What can I do for you, Mr. DuPre?" All business again.

Remy, minou, *call me Remy in that sex-bomb voice of yours.* "Trade me."

Her face crumpled in disbelief, then she broke into laughter. Soft and musical, that laugh hit him right in the balls. "Tell me who your dealer is, because that's some mighty fine product you're smoking."

He remained silent, a tough proposition for him because he liked to talk. Ask him the time and he'd build you a watch.

Those big eyes of hers widened. "You're serious."

"Completely." He held up his hand to stall her inevitable protest. "Now, I'm not expecting you to dump me purely because I ask you. Neither am I expecting you to do it tomorrow—"

"How about not at all?"

"If you want my cooperation, I'll need certain assurances."

Pure incredulity sizzled off her. "Assurances? How about you do the job I'm paying you to do?"

"I could do that, I s'pose. Play the puck, put in what my body will allow. Not sure how much I have to give at this point."

"You need incentivizing, DuPre?"

"I need the Cup."

Four little words, clear as the New England night sky above their heads.

"There are no guarantees," she said. "We can try—"

"I don't mean with the Rebels. I know that's not happenin'. *You* know it's not happenin'. But I'll give you half a season. I'll light a fire under your team, do everything in my power to get them in a good position for a playoff spot. Can't promise anything, but it'll be my mission for the next three months. I'll play every puck like it's my last. Then you trade me to a team that's in with a real shot of going all the way."

"I can't do that. You can't lead, then rip the ice out from under them."

He snorted. "They're adults. Most of 'em, anyway. They'll get over it, especially if they've got some wins under their skates. This is your rebuild year, Harper. Don't even pretend you can get any further than a half-decent showing in the conference. I'll help, but only if you help me."

"I won't be blackmailed so you'll agree to do your damn job!"

Fair enough, so endeth the fun and games. He moved in, towering above her, but she seemed to draw herself up to twice her height to go toe-to-toe with him. Admiration almost beat out his annoyance.

"Guess I'll see you in Philly, then," he said, easy as can be.

She didn't like that, not one bit, but then neither of them were in this business to be liked. If Harper wanted war, he'd bring the artillery. She'd get his feet on that ice, but the rest of him would be in the locker room.

"I'll walk you out, Ms. Chase."

"No need. I wouldn't want to deprive your *chéries* of the pleasure of your company for a second longer."

As she headed back into the kitchen with a switch in her hips that now looked pretty damn fine from this angle, he realized he might have been wrong about Harper Chase.

She wasn't crazy. She was certi-fucking-fiable.

THREE

One week earlier...

Harper leaned against the doorjamb of one of several guest rooms in what she half jokingly called the West Wing at her house in Lake Forest. The stone and cedar mansion, designed in the Hamptons style, boasted six bedrooms, four bathrooms, and stunning views of Lake Michigan. Left to Harper outright fourteen years ago when her mother died from ovarian cancer, it had always been far too big for one person. Now it looked like its population was about to double.

Her sister Isobel sat on the bed, as if testing out its firmness. "You really think this is going to work?"

What? Running the team together? Getting their little sister on board? Or the fact that Harper had just invited Isobel to stay at her place whenever the Rebels played at home?

"I don't see why not. This place is huge—"

"And we never have to see each other," Isobel finished. Named after Lady Isobel Gathorne-Hardy, the daughter of Frederick Stanley, Sixteenth Earl of Derby and donor of the Cup, Isobel was tall and dark compared to Harper's fair and petite. At twenty-five years old and topping six feet, Isobel had a strong frame that echoed their father's sporting prowess.

Today she looked tired, dark circles under her green eyes, her chestnut hair lank and lifeless. Of all of them, she was the one taking Dad's death the hardest, and Harper resolved to be gentler with her. Harper, on the other hand, knew the old man too well to be sucked into a grief she did not feel.

"I know you don't want to give up your coaching position in Montreal," Harper said. Keeping Isobel invested in her other life as an assistant coach in the minors had an additional benefit: little sis wouldn't mind if Harper handled the day-to-day operations at Rebels HQ.

The terms of the will had shocked everyone. Harper could have tolerated the joint rule requirement with her usual bullheadedness but for the real sticking point: the team had to make the playoffs by the end of this season or would be sold to a consortium waiting in the wings. The revenue from the sale would pay each of his three daughters a sizeable inheritance with the rest funding a scholarship at the University of Wisconsin, her father's alma mater, though he'd never shown them any particular loyalty before.

In other words, playoffs or bust.

It was outrageous, but then so was Clifford, a man who lived life mowing down everything in his path.

Her father obviously didn't think Harper could run the team. He didn't think *they* could run the team. And now he was watching from below, because he sure as hell wasn't viewing from on high, laughing his head off at the havoc he had wreaked.

Faced with an almost impossible situation, Harper was offering an olive branch to Isobel. Unsurprisingly, Isobel viewed it as a thorn-studded twig. Harper couldn't really blame her. At one time, Harper had legitimate reason to dislike Isobel, but those reasons were the reedy complaints of a little girl. Isobel couldn't help being Clifford's favorite. The blame for Clifford abandoning Harper's mother when Harper was six years old could—and should—be laid squarely at the feet of the man himself.

One of the will's stipulations was that Isobel attend all home games. "This way, you could fly in when needed and not have to worry about keeping a place in Chicago for the next year."

"Until Montreal fires me when a Rebels game clashes with what's happening in my real life. I worked really hard for that job." A furious hurt tightened Isobel's face. The only female coach in the AHL, her hockey pedigree was impeccable. NCAA champion, Olympic silver, a promising career in the new women's league before it was cut short by injury.

"Of course, I could coach anywhere." Isobel must have seen Harper's look of horror. "Yeah, Dad would have loved that. A woman coach for his precious team."

As he was on board for a female triumvirate of power, it seemed anything was possible, though this cluster had all the hallmarks of a cruel Clifford Chase joke. Besides, Harper had too many targets on her back right now; rocking the coaching staff with a new appointment that smacked of nepotism would not go over well.

"One fire at a time. Did you read his letter?"

At the will reading earlier that afternoon, they were each given a personalized letter from Clifford. Harper had hoped it would explain her father's thought process.

"It didn't shed much light," Isobel said cagily. "You?"

"The same."

Harper had already read it enough times to recall it word for word.

Harper,

I know this isn't what you expected, but it's what you deserve. I've always had my doubts about your fitness to run the team—you know that already and you know why. But you've hung in there for so long that I'm going to give you one more shot. Maybe this test of your mettle will reveal some real balls on you.

Clifford

As last letters to the fruit of your loins went, this wouldn't win any warm-fuzzies awards.

"So what do you think?" she asked Isobel, wondering what was in her sister's letter. Should Harper invest in Kevlar to defend herself against the coup Isobel might have in mind?

"Sure, let's play happy families, Harper. But as soon as it threatens my job in Montreal, we'll have to figure out my place in the Rebels' organization. And I don't mean rolling me in for contract-signing parties purely so we can meet the will's requirements."

"We'll cross that bridge when it's shoved in our faces. For now, we need to work on our bigger problem."

Meaning Violet Vasquez, their "new" sister. Unsurprisingly a no-show for the funeral, she had made an appearance at the office of Kenneth Bailey, lawyer for both the Rebels' organization and their father personally. After the reading of the will, Violet said she needed some "space away from you crazy bitches," but agreed to stop by the house in Lake Forest later that evening.

Isobel stroked a finger along the Laura Ashley coverlet, her expression musing. "There was a time I would have done anything to have my big sister invite me to this house for a sleepover."

Heart punch. Oh, God, what a bitch Harper had been. Isobel had done nothing wrong except be on the receiving end of the love Harper had always assumed was hers and hers alone.

"Isobel, I—" The doorbell rang, cutting off whatever stilted apology was on her tongue.

"Forget it, Harper. Water under the bridge. How about we present a united front?"

Okay. Save hockey franchise dream now, repair fractured sister relationship later.

Isobel trailing her, Harper headed downstairs and answered the door. Violet stood on the threshold, five feet five of ink and attitude.

With raven-black hair, flawless olive skin, full red lips, and their father's green eyes, twenty-three-year-old Violet rocked a Jessica Jones meets JLo vibe. Tonight, the most recent addition to the Chase Mental Asylum wore a skin-tight tee bearing the slogan "Men are like beer: Some go down better than others" above a short leather skirt and ripped tights with tattooed roses playing peekaboo. Every time Harper saw her—and this would be the fourth time since learning of her existence two years ago—Violet had a new round of ink adorning her skin.

"Hey, thanks for coming over."

"Didn't think I had a choice. You made it clear it was life or death." Probably a defense mechanism, but she sounded amused, which put Harper's back up. This might be a joke to her, but it was everything to Harper.

Seeming to realize she'd spoken cavalierly, she added, "Look, I'm sorry, but this is pretty fucking awkward all around."

"It doesn't have to be," Harper said, glancing at Isobel for support. "It's only for a season, nine months at most. We can do this."

"Rah-rah, go team," Violet muttered.

That's the spirit! "Would you like a glass of wine?" Harper asked. Wine made everything better.

Flourishing a hand that said *pour away*, Violet followed them into Harper's salon and accepted a glass of Malbec. The air was thick with tension. Harper had done her best to dissipate it in the last few years, but her father had appeared to relish the fact his daughters did not get along.

Exhibit A: Violet Vasquez.

Two years ago, almost to the day, Harper had found out that Clifford fathered another child from a one-night stand with a hockey groupie and had elected not to share this with either of his ex-wives or his daughters. Covering up his marital indiscretion with money and lies made much more sense.

"What proof is there?" Isobel had asked before Harper could. *"How do we know this isn't just some scam? Women are always accusing Daddy of knocking them up. He was a famous hockey player."*

But Clifford had already done the legwork and confirmed it with a DNA test—then proceeded to shove the problem into the Chase family closet. As soon as Harper found out, she did the decent thing: she immediately contacted her new sister.

Violet had ignored her.

Harper tried again. Sent her gifts on her birthday

and at the holidays. Visited Violet at the Reno tattoo parlor where she worked as a receptionist. Violet tolerated her for an awkward lunch where Harper played unsuccessfully at older sister and Violet played successfully at bored. That she had shown up for the reading of the will was a surprise in itself, but then there was a lot of money in play.

No buyouts or transference of assets were allowed. If they refused outright to run the team jointly, it would be sold. If they didn't make the playoffs this season . . . shit, Harper couldn't think about that now.

One foot in front of the other. They had to convince Violet to wait a year before she took her cut.

"The way I see it," Harper said after Violet had taken a sip, "is that you guys need to trust me to make this work. Sure, that's asking a lot, but I know what I'm doing here. I've been preparing for this moment all my life."

Violet frowned. "If it was just a matter of showing up at a couple of meetings every few months, I'd say, screw it, let's do it. But I know zilch about hockey. As for these terms, the ones that say we have to make the decisions together and I have to live in Chicago or commute here for the home games—I mean, what the hell was he trying to prove?"

Harper heard more pain than annoyance in her voice. Clifford had learned of her existence about ten years ago and had handled the news terribly. Blaming Violet's mother took precedence over making any effort to connect with his newfound daughter. Better to send hush money. Better to ignore this girl who must have been so hurt and confused.

"I think this is his way of saying sorry," Isobel said. "For being somewhat lacking in the daddy department."

Harper whipped her gaze to Isobel, who had never once criticized their father in her presence. He was a hero to her, a powerful counterpoint to Harper's failed relationship with him. Was it possible he'd been less than perfect in Isobel's eyes?

Violet slumped in her chair and folded her arms, all sullenness. "By forcing us into this make-or-break arrangement? It's bad enough I don't know either of you, but now we're supposed to play at sister-besties while trying to turn this crappy hockey team around. In what universe does that qualify as an apology?"

Harper sipped her wine. Gulped, rather. Hell, she knew it was nuts, but didn't crazy beget crazy?

"It's unorthodox, but then he was an unorthodox man. He wasn't in this business to be loved. He wanted to leave a legacy."

Isobel shook her head. "By playing cheapskate and undermining every coaching decision? Ask any player if he's happy with his contract, and I'll bet the answer is *hell, no*. Ask any ex-coach if they'll work for the Rebels again, and you'll be laughed out of the room. In the last five years, we've lost at least twelve high-caliber players—Martin, Rios, Tenkinov." She counted off on her fingers. "And don't get me started on Brian Rennie, our glorious

GM. Did he do anything to argue for a new way forward with Dad? Three years in a row, voted the worst franchise in the league, and that's down to our managing executive who couldn't stand up to the great Clifford Chase." Isobel frowned at Harper. "What's so funny?"

"I've never heard you say a single word against Dad."

Her sister colored. "I'm just frustrated to see all that talent go to waste. This team had some great players and now it has a bunch of lazy fatties."

Violet looked skeptical. "I've seen some of those guys, and 'lazy fatties' wouldn't be the first thing that springs to mind."

Isobel returned the skeptical expression with interest. "Cade Burnett is holding the defense together by a thread," she went on, "but Dixon is a total sieve in goal. We need to offload him—"

"And start with Erik Jorgenson. I know." Harper's body lit up with that familiar tingle in her blood when something good was building. Like a plan. Or an orgasm. Although it had been a while on that last one, or at least one that benefited from a man-made assist.

Isobel waved a hand in frustration. "But Brian doesn't want to spend—just like Dad—and he spends more time micromanaging Coach Calhoun than working on player development." Most owners and GMs trusted their coaching staff to make the roster and game calls, but not Cliff or Brian. "Then there's the elephant in the rehab facility."

Violet perked up. "Rehab facility?"

"Bren St. James, our captain," Harper said. "He's coming off a three-month stint of drying out." The broody Scotsman had relapsed last season, and management had ordered him to get his act together or risk being let go.

Truth be told, Harper had ordered it. Both her father and Brian wanted to send him packing, but Harper had fought for him. He was a damn good center and deserved another chance.

"I remember him. Looks like Jason Mamoa, talks like Ewan McGregor?"

"Thought you knew zilch about hockey," Isobel said with a barely stifled grin.

"True, but I know plenty about men." Violet looked thoughtful. "Worried you can't trust him to be a team player?"

Harper touched a finger to her lips, considering. "Right now, the players are the least of my concern. As for being a team player . . ." She let the insinuation hang in the air between them.

Violet sat up straight. "Look, I have a life that does not revolve around hockey. I have a life in Reno."

Harper was unconvinced. She'd paid someone to run a background check on her sister. Not cool, but she had to know what she was dealing with. Violet lived in a shady part of town, was barely making rent while she worked two part-time jobs in a tattoo parlor and a biker bar. Her mother had moved back to Puerto Rico a year ago.

"Are you telling me you couldn't do with a little extra cash?" An understatement. If Violet agreed to the will's terms, she'd get a generous stipend now and a cool half mil in a year just for signing a few contracts and watching a few games. If the team succeeded, Harper would buy her out, assuring her of a huge windfall.

So she had to up sticks and move to a new city. Hang with the sisters she'd never met. Surely, no big deal.

"Do you have a boyfriend?"

"No one special."

Isobel cocked her head. "Plenty of manwhores in Rebel Land."

Nah-uh. Discomfort tightened Harper's heart in a fist. "That's not happening," she snapped. "The players are off-limits. No fraternization whatsoever."

"You're no fun." Violet pouted while Isobel delivered a curious look at Harper getting her knickers in a twist about hockey romances. Harper was only too aware of the perils of traveling down that road.

"I'm not supposed to be fun," Harper chirped, trying to blow off her overreaction with a blithe comment. "I'm the oldest and I will give my right tit to make this team work."

She turned to Violet. "We have a chance to do something extraordinary here. There've been women team owners before, but none of them have taken a failing franchise and turned it around into something phenomenal."

Professional sports was a boys' club from the top

down. The rough-and-tumble world of major league ownership was a trying business, requiring deep pockets and hard work, and it was extremely difficult for a woman to ingrain herself. But three women working toward a common goal? Just think what they could achieve.

"So you're saying the fact that it's so damn hard should be its own reward?" Violet grinned and, damn, it was like seeing her father smiling back at her.

"It's either this or we give up. I'm not giving up, so this is what we're doing."

Isobel raised an eyebrow. "Just like that."

"Just like that." Harper leaned toward Violet. "We could help you find an apartment or . . . there's a coach house on the property. It's small"—*but bigger than your hovel in Reno*—"and we'll figure out your place in the organization's structure. Isobel and I know hockey, so we can handle the bulk of it. You're here to rubber stamp the paperwork and collect the checks."

"They could all do with someone to listen to their whining," Isobel said. "There's your salary right there."

"Okay," Violet said, suddenly the picture of cheer. "I could do with a change of scenery and some new material for my novel."

Presumably that was a joke, but the moment Violet spoke, Harper knew. She'd made up her mind before they'd even had this conversation.

Now, wasn't that curious. She wondered what Violet was running from.

Aren't we all running from something? Still, Harper would take the win and worry about the why later.

"What's first?" Isobel asked.

More like, who. "I want to bring someone in who can lead on the ice. I know that's St. James's job, but I can't rely on him to pull everyone together if he's Lord Jonesing-For-A-Drink. We need someone who's been around the block, who can knit this team together." She had an idea. A glittering *hell yeah* idea. "But before we do that, we need to make a few changes in the front office."

Izzy's mouth dropped open. "You're not wasting any time, are you?"

Relieved that her sister understood without her needing to say it aloud, she asked, "Do I have your backing, ladies? This is our first big decision, and we have to be united on it."

"You'll get no argument from me," Isobel said.

Violet frowned. "You're going to have to explain it to the knucklehead in the room. What's the big decision?"

Harper smiled, and anyone who didn't know her might have thought that smile was downright evil. "Time to lop off the rot."

FOUR

"He doesn't look like he's even trying."

Harper hated to agree, but Isobel was right. The Rebels might as well have been bleeding instead of sweating, because that's what she was witnessing. A bloodbath.

Unable to stand it a moment longer, she jumped up from her seat in the visitors' box and walked to the window, as if those few feet could improve the view of the Philly Liberty's rink.

It could not.

Down four-zip and there were still two painful minutes left in the second period. Meanwhile, her newly acquired star center, Remy DuPre, looked like he was sauntering on a Sunday skate in Millennium Park.

"Coach needs to pull him," Isobel said, now with a smidgen of urgency.

Harper remained silent, watching as DuPre was slammed against the boards by a Philly defender and . . . laughed it off. Again. Where was the ragin' Cajun she'd hired to create solidarity and push the men to the limits and then past them? This version of DuPre might as well be playing for the other team.

She certainly did not need any more reasons to be furious with him. A reporter had snagged DuPre for a pregame interview and asked him how he felt about moving to Chicago. *Good food town*, her star and savior had said in that laid-back twang. *At least I have that to look forward to.* Social media exploded with speculation on DuPre's cryptic comment, though the conclusion was clear to anyone with half a brain: poor li'l Remy was not a happy camper.

Harper shot laser-eyed heat rays of disgust at the spot where Remy now stood, sharing a joke with one of the officials. Maybe if she stared for long enough she could melt the ice and send Remy DuPre to hell where he belonged with Clifford. But before she could will his descent to the fiery depths, the man did something she wouldn't have believed if Isobel hadn't made a slight noise of surprise behind her.

He tipped the butt-end of his stick to his forehead and saluted the box. Saluted Harper herself.

Her blood in a scrambled fury, she turned to find her sister grinning. "So, how did that meeting with DuPre in Boston go again?"

After the second period blessedly came to a close, Harper stood outside Philly's guest locker room and drew the deepest breath of her life. Her father had played a very hands-on role, (over)stepping on coaching territory, always thinking he knew best. Harper's preference was to let Coach Calhoun and his team do their jobs. There should be no need for her to get into the dirt, and besides, such close proximity to so much muscle made her nervous. With good reason.

Six years ago, the last time she had stood in an NHL locker room, her then-boyfriend had punched her hard enough to bloody her lip.

The moment that fist connected, she had lost more than her self-confidence around the brawn that was her bread and butter. She had lost her legitimate shot at the team.

But she needed to stand tall. Brian Rennie was gone, and she was in charge until they found a chief executive brave enough to take on the Rebels challenge.

You can do this. Remember, you own every single one of their asses.

Stepping inside, she expected to hear the gruff tones of Coach Calhoun berating or encouraging, so imagine her surprise when her ears were violated by the languorous drawl of the devil on skates himself.

"So he was the number one draft pick that year," DuPre was saying, "but hell if he wasn't the most ornery nineteen-year-old you'd ever met. Twitchy and overcaffeinated and always in your face if you so much as cut a look his way. And that was him on a good day."

A few chuckles filled the air, enough to encourage DuPre to continue.

"One moody sonovabitch, all right. And he had that weird winking tic. Remember?"

More chuckles of agreement, and someone shouted, "Yep!"

"You'd think he was makin' everything out to be a joke. '*Where are my shin pads?*' Wink. '*Anyone got tape for my stick?*' Wink. And people were always hidin' his shit because he pissed 'em off. Of course I didn't know about his eyelash battin' problem, so we're sittin' on the bench after practice and I think he's winkin' at me because something's funny, y'know?"

The team's low laughter graduated to deep chortles.

"And then he says—"

Harper didn't have time for this. "Coach," she called out.

Coach Calhoun turned around, surprised at Harper's appearance in the locker room. She had considered getting rid of him during the purge along with Brian, but he was good at what he did, provided he had the right raw materials. He would be dealt with later. Tonight she had come for DuPre.

Coach coughed as embarrassment caught up with him at last and he turned back to the team. "Now I know you have it in you to do better. Let's try to get out of here without conceding any more goals."

What? On the wrong end of a four-goal deficit and

they were worried about looking bad? *Oh, boys, that puck has sailed.*

A swarm of pissed-off bees was buzzing in Harper's head and the situation was not helped by her gaze clashing with DuPre's blue-eyed stare. On seeing her, he had immediately stood—a gesture of chivalry, she supposed. The dichotomy disconcerted her. That scene she'd come across at his house back east seemed so at odds with this polite Louisiana boy. But there was no confusion about her feelings toward him and his toward her, which was fine, because she was not here to be liked.

"Mr. DuPre, would you mind giving me a moment of your time?"

That surprised him. It surprised them all, even Bren St. James, the Rebels' captain, who offered an imperceptible eyebrow raise in her direction. She saw something else there. An unspoken question about her mental well-being.

"Mr. DuPre?" she asked again, adding a shot of bitch to cover the tremble in her voice.

"Final period's about to start," he drawled, those long, lazy vowels sending a bolt of unwanted heat through her. No man should look like that *and* be blessed with that panty-dropper voice. God's quotas were definitely off with this guy.

She stood her ground. Held his gaze.

He sighed as if she were the difficult one. "Where would you like to have this moment, Ms. Chase?"

"Out. All of you."

"They've got five minutes left," Coach whined.

Harper shot him a look that would've had him clutching his balls if the man had any to protect. "Then they can use that time to learn how to put a fucking puck in the net." She arced a withering gaze over the team. "Now, gentlemen. Don't make me say it again."

Amid a chorus of grumbles, they trod out, with Coach taking up the rear.

Leaving her alone with DuPre.

He looked uncomfortable standing there, balancing on his skates, ready to spring for the door. But she knew he wouldn't sit while she stood, because his mother had raised him to respect women. Something fluttered in her chest at that notion. DuPre might be a lot of things—ladies' man, good ol' boy, thorn in her side—but she suspected he would never hurt someone weaker than himself.

"You've got three minutes, Harper."

"Do you remember what I told you in Boston, DuPre?"

"Somethin' about needin' me to instill leadership and help these boys get to the playoffs." Warm honey flowed through her veins at the timbre of his voice. She could have sworn her panties slipped an inch.

"I did say that. I meant it. And I thought you understood."

He rubbed his chin, the scrape against stubble delicious to her ears. All he was missing was a Stetson, a blade of grass, and some flighty piece in a cropped tank and Daisy Dukes. "I understood the words because you'd put them together in a highly entertainin' way, and to certain ears, they might make sense. Then I told you what needed to happen to ensure my cooperation."

This nonsense stopped here. "Is that why you're playing like you can barely walk, much less skate? What's wrong, old man? Feeling a touch of arthritis in your joints?"

For a brief moment, she thought she might have found his weakness: vanity. But no. He merely threaded his arms over his chest—over the Rebels' logo of a big C with a hockey stick and a cutlass crossed behind it— and cocked his head.

"You're gonna have to use a little more finesse, Harper."

More surprising than the fact that Remy had used the word *finesse* correctly in a sentence was that he didn't seem annoyed with her. He seemed . . . amused. As if she were a toy he could happily bat around like a kitten would a semiconscious mouse.

Applause sounded, signifying the beginning of the final period. Neither of them moved, hands metaphorically hovering at their hips like Old West gunfighters.

"The trade deadline," she said, feeling livid and helpless. "Give me that."

"The all-star game."

Three months. The all-star game, held in late January, was traditionally viewed as the halfway point of the season. On the cusp of the busy trade period, it led into a month of bartering and haggling as everyone lined up their teams for the big push to the playoffs.

At her hesitation, he leaned in, those cobalt blues flashing. It wasn't enough to unholster her gun; she should have already taken her shot, and that delay was her undoing.

"Would you rather three months of my full effort or a whole season of my skatin' like I'm playin' squirt hockey?"

"You can't seriously be reducing this to a game of 'would you rather'?"

His voice dropped to an intimate tone, her panties another inch with it. "If you shake on it now, I'll begin that full effort tonight."

The siren blared in the distance, followed by the home crowd's roar. Five-zip. Harper didn't enjoy being blackmailed, but she enjoyed losing even less.

She thrust her hand forward impatiently. He took it in his firm grasp. That electricity setting her skin aflame was her body telling her she'd made the right decision. Nothing else.

"You have a game to finish."

He held on, and now he inclined his head so close she could count each and every one of those pretty-boy eyelashes. Her pulse rate spiked, and she was certain he could sense it. Sense her heart thumping rabbit kicks, her vein pulsing in her throat.

"We've shaken on it now, minou, so don't you dare think about welshing. I might sound like I spend my spare time spitballin' from the rockin' chair on my porch, but don't let my accent fool you none. I'm not the kind of man you want for an enemy. We clear?"

She might have rolled her eyes if she wasn't just a wee bit impressed by his chutzpah. Still, he needed to be informed that while he might have won this battle, the war was far from over.

"Try not to trip on your way to the rink, DuPre."

He laughed, deep and robust, clearly delighted with himself. Idiot. His thumb pressed against her inner wrist, and a crackle of energy leeched from him into her body.

"You feel that, Harper?"

She snatched back her hand. "If you mean my good-will evaporating with every second you're standing here, then, yeah, I feel it."

"I think we're havin' a thing."

They were. Oh, God, they were. "Why are you still here again?"

His mouth curved. "Lady, I got the distinct feelin' these next few months are gonna be fun."

He picked up his stick and, with more grace than a six-foot-two brute wearing skates on dry land should possess, he left the locker room.

FIVE

The Rebels' miserable season continues with a loss last night in Remy DuPre's first home game. The veteran power forward has made no secret of his displeasure with his trade, a surprise acquisition in a year when the beleaguered organization should be bringing in fresh legs while it rebuilds instead of relying on old-timers in the last flush of their careers. Also not a secret? How Clifford Chase had little faith in his eldest daughter, and it seems adding more estrogen is not improving the decision making at Rebels HQ. Put the city out of its misery, Ms. Chase, and hire a GM!

—Curtis Deacon, *Chicago Sun-Times*

Boxes, boxes everywhere, and not a single coffee mug to drink from.

Remy surveyed the cell—okay, very nice apartment—the Rebels had leased for him in Riverbrook, a three-minute walk from the team's arena, and about thirty minutes north of Chicago. Two bedrooms, two baths, decent kitchen, nice balcony where he could grill. Furnished, per his request, as he had no intention of relocating entirely. Not for three months.

He'd had a few things sent over, though. His gym equipment, because he liked to put in extra time away from prying eyes at the team facility. That was frowned upon by trainers, but he knew his limits, and no way did he need the judgment of his younger teammates who didn't have to train as hard as he did to stay at level.

He'd also packed up a coffee machine, a stockpot, flatware, plates, and mugs. Plural, because he was ever hopeful he might get laid one of these days, and he'd like to be able to offer a cup of coffee to any lovely chérie who stayed the night. Damn, he'd like to be able to offer a cup to himself.

Should've marked the damn boxes before they were loaded in the U-Haul. Lesson learned: never pack angry.

Morning skate would start in about ninety minutes, so he should probably get rolling. Typical practice was to visit the trainers for a check-in to get taped, rubbed, and assessed for play. Hockey was hard on the body, and it only got harder the older a man got. He pulled up Yelp on his phone and checked the location of the nearest Starbucks. Five minutes in the opposite direction from the stadium, but not a problem.

A knock on the front door cut into his coffee daydream.

Some well-meaning neighbor probably, because it sure as hell wasn't Bren St. James, the Rebels' captain, who happened to live in the same building. Yesterday, Remy had spotted him in the elevator, sporting bags of groceries, a grim expression, and a stay-the-fuck-away attitude. The guy had to have seen Remy heading toward him, but he didn't even make eye contact, just let the damn doors close in Remy's face. Rehab must have stripped the man of all his charm.

Remy hadn't met anyone else yet, but he imagined news of his arrival might have spread through the halls of the building. Steeling himself for a blue-haired little old grandma carrying cookies (if only), he opened the door.

It *was* St. James, and he wasn't alone. Beside him sat a giant black-haired mutt as tall as his hip.

"Hey," Remy said after a good five seconds passed with St. James keeping his own counsel.

"I need a favor."

Not one for small talk, then. Remy didn't know the guy well, but he recognized that he seemed agitated, and his Scottish burr only emphasized it.

"Does the favor involve your friend there?"

St. James looked down at the dog, then back up at Remy. "I have a family emergency and don't have time to get him to the kennel."

"Yeah, of course. How long you need?"

The grim Scot ushered the dog in and handed off a leash and key. "A couple of days. My eight-year-old broke her arm and she lives with her ma in Atlanta, so—"

"Hey, not a problem." *Next time, lead with that headline, why don't you?* Remy looked at the key. "Food and stuff at your place?"

St. James was already backing away. "Yeah, 3B, one floor down. Closet right inside the door." He looked mighty uncomfortable, as if the notion of asking anyone for a favor didn't sit well with him. Guess when a man's been apologizing to people about his drunken behavior for months, it begins to wear on him. He moved off and turned at the last second. "Thanks, DuPre. I owe you."

"If your dog shits all over my hardwood floors, I'll piss in your next postgame beer."

Shit. Don't make beer jokes to the alcoholic.

A slight nod was his reward. Tough crowd. St. James was already at the elevator when Remy remembered something. "What's his name?"

"Gretzky."

The Great One. Why not? Remy shut the door and stood with hands on his hips, assessing his guest. His guest returned the favor by assessing Remy's crotch with his slobbery tongue.

"Buy me dinner first, big guy."

The dog replied with a tail wag and a loud fart. Real charmer, this one.

Another knock, and Remy pounced on the doorknob, ready to demand the name of a local kennel, but it wasn't St. James (or anyone with cookies, dammit). Filling Remy's vision was a big blond Viking, bearing a gift that, on reflection, was better than baked goods: two large cups in a carrier tray. Liquid gold steam whorls rose from the lids' holes as the coffee's aroma hit him like a semi to his senses.

Above the offering, the face of Ford Callaghan, the Rebels' right-winger, lit up with a doofus grin. "Thought I'd walk you to class, newbie."

Remy opened the door wider. "I would ask how you got into the building, but I'm guessing you smiled at someone."

"One of your neighbors held the door. I'm extremely nonthreatening." He grinned again. "Off the ice."

Never a truer word. Guy was a beast on skates. "Come in. Just need to grab a jacket and boots."

Ford nodded at Gretzky like he was an old friend, put the tray down on the counter, and removed both cups. "Figured you for a cream-and-sugar guy." Said in the tone of *don't really care, just be thankful*.

Remy took a sip and the day suddenly started to look a whole lot better.

Ford turned his attention to the dog once more. "What's Big G doing here?"

"Our captain had to skip town suddenly." The dog let another one rip, which Callaghan found to be hilarious.

Despite sharing an agent, Remy had met Callaghan only three or four times off the ice. He'd always impressed Remy as driven, professional, and way more mature than the average twenty-six-year-old. Or, that was Remy's opinion before news erupted a month ago that Ford was dating the ex-wife of his boss at the New Orleans Rage, last season's Stanley Cup champions.

Awkward.

For his pains, he was traded to the worst—second-worst—team in the league, all because he couldn't keep his dick in his pants.

"Our fearless leader appoint you head of the welcoming committee?"

"My girlfriend thought you might need someone to hold your hand. I said guys don't really need that kind of support system, but she insisted, so here I am."

Totally pussy-whipped, then, except Remy suspected Callaghan had his own agenda, and for some reason, he'd rather let his woman take the fall. Remy remembered reading somewhere that Harper Chase was BFF with Callaghan's girlfriend, lingerie model and designer Addison Williams.

While Remy's brain cycled through what that might mean for this visit, Callaghan took in the sterile surroundings and the not-yet-unpacked boxes. His eyes lit up on seeing the PlayStation Remy had set up first thing. Priorities, he had 'em.

Callaghan picked up the disc case for *Hockey All Stars* sitting on top of the console.

"How the fuck do you have this? It's not out until December."

The kid turned over the advance copy of the game and read the back cover. *One, two* . . . Remy let him get there all by his lonesome.

"*You're* in the game?"

"Sure am."

Ford shook his head, disgusted. "Perks of your veteran status, I s'pose."

"Perks of my awesomeness."

Remy sat and pulled on his hand-crafted Luccheses. Gretzky ambled over, climbed onto the sofa at the other end, and curled up. Not his furniture, so hell if Remy cared, but the farting might be a legit problem in such a small space.

"Callaghan, if you could change anything about the Rebels, what would it be?"

"Better leadership." At Remy's look, he clarified. "Not Harper. On the ice. That's what she's trying to do. She thinks you're the linchpin."

"That what you think?" Is that what they all thought? An NHL pro for seventeen years, Remy was known as a hard worker, a team player, a guy who went to any lengths necessary to get the job done. He'd never worn a captain's band. Had never had that kind of expectation thrust on him.

He should have wanted the responsibility. Thrived on it.

Instead he was . . . worried. This wasn't how he imagined his final year playing out. His body was in a state of collapse, the speed of which had increased these past twelve months. There was only a finite amount in reserve that he could draw on during the playoffs. Not that he'd expected to coast to the finals, but he *had* expected to be part of a well-oiled machine, an organization where he was a cog, not the engine.

Striking that bargain with Harper in the Philly locker room had energized him, though. Not just the bargain, but the negotiation of it. Ms. Chase sucked ass at hiding her feelings, and boy was she pissed to the Almighty at him. That night, they'd clawed two goals back, one scored by Remy, another he'd laid up sweetly for Callaghan. Not a win, but better than a shutout. Remy definitely preferred giving it his all to half-assing it like he'd been during the first two periods.

Good thing Harper hadn't called his bluff, because he respected the game and his teammates too much to keep up that shitty level of play. But in this sport—hell, in any professional sport—the owners and management held all the power, and they knew it. They'd use him, chew him up, and then spit him out when they no longer needed him, without a care for his hopes or dreams. He had to use what little leverage he had.

Ford was making his case. "I think we have a captain, but he's not there mentally. We have guys who've been beaten down and would give their shooting arms to be playing for any other team in the league. We have an owner-slash-GM who needs every person in the org to be contributing one hundred percent."

"Sure she didn't send you?"

There was that blinding grin again. There'd be a whole lot of feminine wailing and teeth-gnashing the day Callaghan put a ring on his woman's finger.

"I won't pretend I'm not a fan of Harper's. I am. New Orleans wanted to punish me big time. They'd rather have held on and benched me for the two years left on my contract than let me play or trade me out to a decent team. Now I'm here with the woman of my dreams and my family nearby. That's down to Harper."

The sainted Harper. "You made a decision with your dick and paid the price. And Harper got a pretty good bargain. A great right-winger from a Cup-winning team."

"She gave up her top draft picks for the next three years."

"Shit, you're not *that* good, Callaghan."

He chuckled. "If I had a center who played as hard as you did in the last period against Philly, then I could be that good, DuPre. *We* could be that good."

"I'll pay you for the coffee if you cut the pep talk."

More laughter. For a guy whose career had taken a precipitous dive by his going from a champion team to the dregs of the league, he was remarkably sanguine.

"What's on your dance card tonight, DuPre?"

Digging out his coffee mugs. Playing himself on *Hockey All Stars*. Deciding how he was going to make his time in Chicago count.

"You tell me."

"Celebrating my birthday." He picked up his coffee and headed toward the door. "But now, we skate."

Later that evening, Remy walked into Jimmy's Tap, an Irish dive bar in Chicago's Bridgeport neighborhood on the South Side, and succumbed to an acute pang of longing for New Orleans. Maybe that was why he'd been so antsy. He rarely went this long—an entire month—without seeing his family, but in two weeks they'd have an away game in NOLA and he'd get to check in with them all.

The hardest thing about hockey was not being able to put down roots, and that was especially hard for a Cajun boy like him. Family was important, and as soon as he was done with the pros, he'd get busy making one of his own. Sure, he could be working on that during his player days, but damned if he was going to miss a minute of his kids growing up. Neither did he want to inflict his moods on the people he loved the most, and hockey players were moody fuckers at the best of times. No woman should have to put up with his shit every time he came home after skating within kissing distance of the Cup and failing yet again.

Nodding his way through the crowd, he headed for the birthday boy and his knockout girlfriend. Addison Williams was an amazon of a woman who'd made her

fortune showing a lot of skin. Remy had no problem
with that, though he had to wonder how he'd feel if it
were his femme walking the runway in sexy lingerie. He
guessed as long as his hands, and his hands alone, got
to touch her skin it'd be all right.

"DuPre," Ford said, his goofy grin stretching wide.
"Have you met my girl, Addy?"

"Not had the pleasure, chérie." He raised Addison's
hand and kissed her knuckles, adding a cheeky wink.

Addison laughed. "Oh, it's all true, then."

"What is?"

"That southern charm that gets the ladies warm."
She drew her hand back and fanned her face. "My, my,
Mr. DuPre, have pity on my sensibilities."

"No quarter given, not where a pretty lady is concerned."

"Told ya he was trouble," Ford said good-naturedly.
Remy appreciated that he wasn't some asshole who
felt threatened whenever a guy flirted with his woman.
Sign of confidence right there.

"Oh, babe, there's Harper. I'll be back in a second."
Leaving him with the kind of kiss no woman should
lay on her guy in public, Addison sashayed off toward
the door of the bar. Remy would have watched, but he
didn't want to look like he was ogling the very fine ass
of his teammate's girlfriend.

"How'd a goon like you end up with a quality
woman like that?"

Ford blew out a breath, his eyes still on Addison

over Remy's shoulder. "I ask myself that question every fuckin' day. She's something, isn't she?"

Remy took that as permission to look so he could verify that Addison was indeed something. Of course, his gaze leapfrogged over the future Mrs. Ford Callaghan and landed right where it meant to go.

On Harper Chase herself.

Mon dieu.

She'd let her hair down. Literally. Until now, he'd only seen it tied back in a Wicked Witch of the West bun that looked like it caused a perpetual headache. Tonight it fell past her shoulders in a cascade of corn silk waves. A red top slashed across her collarbone, one shoulder covered, one exposed. It gave her fair skin a luminous, almost translucent quality. He imagined that if he touched her, his hand might pass right through. She had on dark jeans and black shiny heels that gave her a few inches, but he'd still need to lift her up to align his favorite parts with her favorite parts.

This was not where his head should be going—either of them. But sometimes it was okay to give the little head some leeway as long as it remained in the depths of fantasy. Nothing wrong with thinking about a beautiful woman and the dirty things he'd like to do to her. He could just as easily transfer that mental action to Addison Williams. Hell, he'd seen a lot more of her skin.

Something dark clawed in his chest. Harper was not alone.

A vaguely familiar guy was hovering at the bare shoulder that needed Remy's lips on it now. Right. The Rebels' lawyer, Kenneth Bailey, who had his hand on the small of Harper's back. Remy couldn't actually see that for sure, and neither should he care, but the proprietary nature of that arm's positioning sparked something greedy inside him. He needed to stop looking before these forbidden thoughts became easier to read on his face than the pout on one of his nieces' faces when she didn't get the ice-cream cone she'd begged for.

Turning back to Ford, he asked, "You still underage, or are we actually celebratin' something here?"

Ford's mouth curved into that pretty-boy grin.

"Sure. I'll let you buy me a drink, DuPre."

SIX

"So. Kenneth." Addy sipped her soda, her sharp eyes on the attorney as he tried to cut a path through the mass of pro-hockey muscle to get Harper a drink at the bar.

Harper played coy. "What about him?"

Her friend raised an eyebrow.

"Don't give me that eyebrow of disapproval, Addy Williams. I practically dislocated mine two months ago when you hooked up with Callaghan."

"Which is why I'm being a good friend now. I know you're not sleeping with him, and I can't believe he's still here playing at perfect little lapdog."

"So men only stick around if the promise of sex is in play?"

Addy tilted her head. "You've had him on a string for a year, Harper."

"Kenneth knows the score. I've told him I'm not interested in a relationship right now, and we're happy to be each other's plus-one for various events. No expectations, no complications."

And no chemistry. Still, it was nice to have someone to rely on for a dinner date or an armrest for a charity gala. She'd told Kenneth he was welcome to date anyone he chose; he'd told her he was happy to be her "support" as she went through this difficult time. Far be it from her to disabuse him of his mission to feel useful.

Her gaze arced over the bar, looking for . . . oh, no one in particular. Before it landed on no one, though, it collided with Violet in combat boots and a tutu. Lord, give her strength.

Her youngest sister held court with Cade Burnett, Erik Jorgenson, and the rest of the defensemen. Since moving into the coach house on the lakefront property two weeks ago, Violet had kept a low profile. Per the will's stipulations, she'd attended three home games so far and signed everything that was put in front of her. Tonight she was enjoying the unwritten perks of hockey team ownership: immersion in the pool of sports' fittest specimens. Harper would have a little chat with her later about management/labor boundaries.

She refocused on Addy, who looked positively gorgeous. Was it possible the boobs that made her fortune were even bigger than usual? "What did you get Ford for his birthday? Lemme guess. Anal?"

Addy flushed. Gun. Fish. Barrel.

"Knew it."

"*Nooo*. I haven't given him his gift yet." The slightest

vestige of doubt fluttered over her face for the briefest moment. Pinning on a smile, she said, "Your savior's a real charmer, by the way."

"My sav—oh, right." Inevitably, Harper's gaze was drawn toward the man who was supposed to solve all her problems, Mr. *No One* himself. He had his back to her, but his shoulders shook with laughter at something Ford was saying. Big, strong shoulders, as wide as an ox, topping back muscles she could swear she saw defined through the gray T-shirt drawn tight across his body. As for what was happening below those trim hips . . . Yet again, she was staring at DuPre's ass and imagining what that warm slab of marble would feel like beneath her greedy fingertips.

A tingle started up in places that had not tingled in a very long time. Of all the people for her libido to toggle on for, why did it have to be Remy DuPre? She longed to be attracted to Kenneth. So much easier. Much more suitable. But annoyingly, her lizard brain insisted on elbowing its way to the fore and screaming, "Me want Cajun!"

Perspective, Harper. She was still furious at how he had outfoxed her in Philly, and her fury was clearly tied into her attraction to him. Just an unhealthy case of sexual loathing, nothing more. She shouldn't be having any feelings of the kind for her employee, but the tingle, and the lizard brain, and—gah!—her damn nipples were all reinforcing this inappropriate draw.

"I wonder why he's not married," Addy mused. "Or in a relationship."

"Some men aren't cut out for it." Case in point, Harper's father. "You probably found the last magical unicorn in the NHL."

Addy squinted. "He's had girlfriends. Plenty of girlfriends."

Harper had witnessed that Big Easy charm of DuPre's when she did the mom pull on his ear a week ago. That woman straddling him, her pert breasts positioned at the perfect angle for his mouth, his big hands cupping her half-exposed butt cheeks, ready to spread them for his pleasure. No doubt Remy had received the sendoff he deserved that night in Boston. And tonight there were any number of women present who would be happy to welcome him to Chicago.

Ugh! Harper was jealous of some puck bunny she hadn't even laid her disapproving eyes on yet. This was so beneath her.

But you wouldn't mind if Remy was beneath you . . . or vice versa.

She blinked at the image that conjured up. The taboo of it. She wasn't looking for a fling. She wasn't looking for anything. Harper had plenty of reasons for not wanting a relationship: too busy, career focused, no one had yet caught her eye. But the real reason never took long to cut through all those excuses.

She was a broken bird, and she would never allow a man to hurt her again.

"Sweetheart, I missed you," Harper heard, and she turned in time to see Ford throw his arm around Addy and pull her in for a passionate kiss. Despite her own reservations about true love, she couldn't help but appreciate the happiness Ford had brought her friend after her difficult marriage to the owner of the NHL franchise in New Orleans—and Ford's former boss.

"Harper," came the whiskey-laced voice of the Rebels' messiah.

Peace had broken out, so it was only right that she should play along. "Remy, so nice to see you bonding with your teammates."

He grinned, just a flash, but it really worked for him. "You need a drink?"

"Someone's getting one for me." She'd forgotten about Kenneth, her pillar in her time of need, and now she sought him out in the crowd three deep at the bar.

"You've been here five minutes and you've not got a drink in your hand? What the hell kind of party is this, Callaghan?"

A private party, apparently, as Ford was now busy getting his birthday present early from his girlfriend. The two of them had slipped away into the crowd, like the horny little devils they were.

Without missing a beat, Remy put his hand at the base of Harper's spine and led her toward the bar before she had a chance to protest. Protesting would have been silly; they were surrounded by people, after all. The tingles returned, this time in a shock wave that danced all over her skin.

"What's your poison, Harper?"

"Van Winkle Reserve, but really, there's no need . . ."

Remy had already made eye contact with a bartender. He must have telepathically given her order, because the barman pulled the Pappy from the top shelf and started to pour.

The Cajun's big, blunt hand was still positioned at the small of her back, feeling perfectly natural, strangely belonging there. It felt like her body was an extension of that hand and he was her puppet master, the slightest twist of his fingers enough to control her limbs. A couple of steps forward in these heels and she could graze her breasts along that perfect spot below his pecs. Of course, if they were lying down, their nipples could meet and get acquainted . . .

She blinked at the sound of a deep rumble. *Sigh*. The man was speaking, ruining a perfectly good fantasy.

"Sorry?"

"Water in your whiskey?"

"Just a splash." Keep the rest to put out the flames igniting all over her body.

The drink appeared, and in no time at all, Remy had pulled her strings again and steered her to a less-trafficked spot—a romantic might call it an alcove— away from the growing crowd. He handed off the drink and then unhanded her completely. Her body roared its disappointment.

"Some skills you have there," she said. "Learn those in New Orleans?"

"New Or-*leens*? Wash that mouth out, minou."

Minou? What did that mean? It sounded like an endearment, at least the way Remy's devil mouth shaped it. His lips looked soft, and she wondered how they would feel on hers. On her everything.

"Uh, what did I say?"

"It's pronounced New *Orr*-linz. Not N'awlins, and certainly not New Or-*leens*. Now say it right, Harper."

"New *Orr*-linz." The words spilled from her mouth, shaped and pronounced correctly.

His hot gaze fell to her lips as she said it, his expression tightening with each syllable she enunciated. "Better," he said in a low tone, though he didn't sound all that pleased she'd gotten it right. He stood tantalizingly close, the scent of freshly showered man making her a touch dizzy.

Cleansing breath. She took a sip of her drink, relishing the burn and the reality it ushered in.

"How are you settling into your new place?"

"*Bon.* I need to buy some new coffee mugs because I can't find the ones I thought I brought, but other than that, *c'est bon.*"

He was speaking French. Christ on a Ritz cracker, if that wasn't the hottest thing she'd ever heard out of a man's mouth. And now she was thinking of his mouth again. Whispering French endearments, grazing her heated skin, exploring private, needy places.

Remember who he is to you. What *he is to you.* "Players often live in that building while they get situated."

"Yeah, I ran into St. James. Would've thought he had something more permanent."

It was no secret that her captain was going through a rough time. A split from his ex-wife—a split that was a long time coming because the woman was a soul-sucking vampire—had left him in need of temporary accommodation postrehab. Harper had hoped that placing Bren and Remy in close proximity to each other would yield results. Time was of the essence, so nurturing their bond was one of her ideas to move the team forward.

"Now that his girls live with their mom in Atlanta, he thinks a big house is too lonely." Living in a mau-soleum of her own, she understood exactly where Bren was coming from. "He needs good people around him."

"Right. I'm the official team baby-sitter." No longer sounding pissed, he projected resignation to the role he'd been given. She'd take that for progress. "Mind if I ask you a question, Harper?"

She gave that the eyebrow hitch it deserved.

"A decent GM shouldn't be hard to find. Why make it so hard on yourself?"

"Worried I'll take on skating drills as well? Owner-manager-coach, the triple threat?"

He studied her, maybe trying to puzzle her out. Good. She liked keeping him on the tips of his blades.

"I've seen your sister hanging around the coaching offices, so I guess she's your designate."

Over Harper's dead body. "Minor-league coaching isn't quite the same ball game."

"You need a GM," Remy said definitively.

Fighting for serenity, she swirled her drink in her glass and counted to five so she wouldn't scream her head off. "When my father died, I saw a chance to make changes. Brian Rennie was part of the old guard, and I knew he'd be reluctant to go in the direction I needed. Sure, I could persuade him, but I'm already in an uphill battle trying to get the team back on track. I don't have time for infighting."

"Not when you're too busy pickin' fights with your players, huh?" He smiled to soften the jab. "How's joint rule working out?"

"My sisters understand that I'm in the best position to make this work. My whole life has been building to this." Her voice was almost as steady as her gaze, but then she had to ruin it with the slightest crack when she added, "This year is make or break."

He looked curious. Probing. What was it about Remy and his blue-eyed burn that saw right through her?

My father screwed me over, and not for the first time. No one thinks I can do this. I need you to think I can do this.

He could have pushed and she would have caved, but any imminent confession was derailed by a screech and a cloud of perfume that made Harper's eyes sting.

"Remy!" A tall redhead wearing what looked like a band of gauze lassoing two Goodyear blimps threw her arms around his neck. "I can't believe you're here!"

The new arrival practically knocked Harper out of the way, pretzeled her stacked body around Remy's, and sucked on the Cajun's lips like an anteater. It took him a good three and a half seconds—but who was counting?—before he drew back.

"Have we met, chérie?"

"We have now, Jinx," she purred. "I just wanted to welcome you to Chi-Town. Properly."

His mouth hardened slightly. "Well, it sure is a pleasure, but right now I'm kind of in the middle of something, so I'll have to take a rain check." His eyes flickered over the woman's shoulder to where Harper was sipping on her whiskey, enjoying the show. She had a perfect view of the woman's tramp stamp—the positively poetic Get Some with an arrow pointing down—along with her above-the-waistband leopard-print thong.

Goodyear Blimps speared a look designed to put Harper six feet under twice over and then quickly recalibrated her smile for Remy. From her cleavage, she extracted a (crumpled, undoubtedly sweat-stained) business card and placed it in Remy's jeans pocket. It took a few moments to ensure that it was safely secured.

"The welcome offer is open-ended, Jinx."

Another wince crossed Remy's face, though Goodyear missed it as she was too busy trying to maintain her center of gravity on her totter toward the bar.

"*'The welcome offer is open-ended, Jinx,'*" Harper mimicked in her most breathless gush, adding a bout of vehement eyelash batting into the mix.

"Don't be jealous, now, Harper. I sent her away, didn't I?"

"That 'Jinx' business must get tiresome."

"Just a name. Don't bother me none." He rubbed his mouth of any remaining lipstick, a man without a care, but she knew better. "So where's your date?"

"My date?"

"The guy you came in with."

She had completely forgotten about Kenneth, again. The moment Remy entered her awareness, the rest of the world faded. This was not good. She refused to be distracted by her attraction to this man.

Admitting the problem freed her mind. So she was attracted to Remy—crazy, lights-out attracted—but her hormones were not the boss of her. She could have affirmed that she and Kenneth were just good friends, but it seemed easier to use him as her buffer. Kenneth did so enjoy being useful.

She looked over Remy's shoulder, seeking out the lawyer's blond head and Teutonic good looks. There he was. Somehow he'd been waylaid by the biggest attraction in the room: the fantastic breasts of supermodel Addison Williams. Her friend caught her eye and winked.

Hell, that's all she needed. Addy playing match-maker. "He's around here somewhere," Harper said to Remy. "I probably should get back to him."

In the last few moments, the Cajun had moved closer. Or maybe she was closer? Either way, her lungs were filled with him and her eyeballs were filled with that painfully gorgeous mahogany brown hair and those cobalt blues, a little darker now than before.

"If you were my woman, I wouldn't leave you alone for a second."

Her heart—and somewhere lower—gave a delighted skip. Had he really just said that? It was just so . . . out-rageous. She opened her mouth to tell him so, but a chorus of "Happy Birthday" whooshed into the sex-drenched pause. Some impatient well-wisher pushed her from behind, sloshing her drink so that a sizable portion of it landed on Remy's chest.

"Oh, I'm sorry." Her hand went to his chest because of course it did. That's what happened when you spilled a drink on a chest that looked like Remy DuPre's.

Damp pecs, therefore grabby hands.

She snatched her hand away. "Sorry, I shouldn't . . . let me get you a napkin." Acutely aware of the heat flooding her cheeks, she searched her immediate sur-roundings for napkins, but nothing entered her field of vision.

Her purse! "I'm sure I brought tissues . . ." Needing desperately to compose herself, she gave him her back and opened her Kate Spade (Cobble Hill Ella in emerald forest), only to feel a warm pressure at her waist.

"'S okay, Harper." His breath blew sweet against her ear, his body a wall of heat behind her. Long, strong fingers indented perfectly above her hip. "It's just a little splash. Next time you want to touch me so bad, just ask, minou."

That word again. It sounded deliciously intimate and entirely inappropriate. Resisting the urge to whip her phone out and Google it right then and there, she delivered a tacked-on smile over her shoulder to let him know she appreciated the joke.

"Funny, DuPre."

"You think so?" He didn't think it funny, she could tell. Not with the way his eyes burned her alive. Not with the way his mouth turned harsh with desire. The world around them had further receded, leaving only this bubble, this sensual space built for two. Distant echoes of "Happy Birthday" tried to intrude, but nothing could penetrate.

"Hilarious," she said, going with the flow while aiming for her boss voice. Rusty at best. His hand curled around her waist was the only thing keeping her standing.

No response from him, unless you counted those fingers of intent digging into her hip. Holding her up, dragging her under, and *oh God, oh God, oh God he's going to kiss me*. Right here, in front of the whole damn world.

Worse, she wanted it. Those lips on hers, the surrender, the fall, after trying to stand tall on her own for so long. Never mind that she'd be a laughingstock or that every accusation about being unable to manage the team because she was a woman would be thrown at her. Meet Harper Chase, team owner, acting GM, and her sidekick, VP of player relations—aka her vagina.

"Remy," she whispered. *Please don't do this even if every cell in my body is telling you I need your mouth on mine. Please be the stronger person here.*

"I know." And then he bent his head and grazed her bare shoulder. Just a whisper of those full, surprisingly soft lips on her exposed skin. It could have been an accident. Surely it was, because, again, inappropriate.

But then everything about him and what was happening here was so, so wrong.

A light squeeze to her waist—filled with want and a hint of regret, if that was possible—and he disappeared into the crowd.

SEVEN

A week after Ford's party, Harper's shoulder still tingled where Remy's lips had touched her. She'd gone through several emotional reactions since, and had settled on irritated.

The sheer gall of the man, kissing her shoulder in, not exactly broad daylight, but atmospheric bar light. She'd spent several nights tangled up in sheets, analyzing his behavior. That kiss had been no accident. His lips had not grazed her exposed shoulder as he leaned over to grab his beer. His hand on her hip followed by his lips on her shoulder, a straight line from A to B. The evidence was clear.

Her star center had made a pass at her in front of the whole team.

In what universe was Remy living if he thought that was acceptable? Perhaps she had encouraged him when she splashed her drink on his hard, sculpted chest. That was it. She had given off mixed signals and he'd gotten the wrong end of the stick. If anything, it was her fault. She should talk to him about it. Moving forward with that thick tension between them would be detrimental to the team dynamics.

Adding to her discombobulation, she was also shaky after a pregame interview ten minutes ago. One would think that a month into the season, the sports media would have found another story to latch on to. It wasn't as if anything had changed since last year. The Rebels were still unlovable losers, only now they were unlovable losers being led by their dicks to last place. The notion of three women "ruining" a franchise already in tatters was considered a huge insult to the proud testosterone-soaked bastion known as the NHL.

Curtis Deacon of the *Chicago Sun-Times* hadn't asked her a single question about acquisitions or the strategy for tonight's away game against Boston. All he and every other analyst cared about was when she would hire a new GM. Translation: *You need a man to make the tough decisions, little lady.*

First DuPre, now the rest. Every single one of these motherfuckers really got on her tits.

On her way to the executive-box level in the Boston Cougars' arena, for their third game in a row on the road, Harper inhaled yoga-quality breaths. Tonight's game was important, and she wondered how Remy felt being back on his old turf. He had to have mixed feelings about it, but she hoped his desire to prove himself to his old crew was the overriding emotion. Round-ing the corner, with one path leading to the stadium tunnel, the other to the elevators, she spotted Isobel in conversation with someone big, wearing full player gear in Cougars colors. At first Harper didn't recognize him with his back to her, but as she moved closer, a deep, booming laugh chilled her blood.

She looked down at her peep-toe Franco Sarto booties because she realized her feet had stilled. That's what his laugh did to her. It halted function. Excised joy.

There had been no sign of him at Remy's going-away party in Boston, a blessing she hadn't fully appreciated at the time because she was so furious with her new acquisition. Maybe he and Remy weren't all that friendly. That notion was a bright spark in the midnight of her mind.

"Get away from her." It was out of her mouth before she had a chance to bite it back.

Billy Stroger turned at the sound of Harper's voice echoing loudly in the hallway.

Isobel frowned. "Harper?"

On jellied spindles, Harper marched over to her sister and stood between her and the Cougars' defenseman. Anyone viewing the scene would think two towering athletes were crushing the pygmy in their Harper sandwich, but she didn't care. She would not have her sister flirting with this pathetic excuse for a human.

Billy grinned. It used to make her stomach flutter. Now it nauseated her. "Harper. Long time no see."

Ever original. "Isobel, go up to the box."

Isobel's mouth dropped open. "Harper!"

Harper almost stomped her foot and pointed like she was sending her sister to her room. Realizing that she risked sounding like more of a nutjob than usual, she changed tack to conciliation. "Please. I need to talk to . . . Billy for a moment." His name on her tongue tasted like ash.

She watched as Isobel walked away, worry on her face, her long stride making short work of the trip toward the elevators. Hauling in a deep breath, Harper turned and faced Stroger. He would never be Billy in her head, only on her lips to cover her dislike of him.

Almost six years ago and against her father's express wishes that she stay away from romantic entanglements with the Rebels' players, she had fallen into lust with Billy Stroger. He was so cocky, so assured, a demon on the ice, a danger to anyone near him. For six weeks they'd snuck around, meeting on the sly, stealing moments together. He had a temper, but he usually reserved it for play, channeling it into the martial atmosphere on game night. Until on one of those nights he was ejected for high-sticking, a deliberate move because he had a grudge against a forward on the opposite team.

Stroger nursed grudges like a miser would a top-shelf scotch.

She had slipped away from her father's side in the viewing box and sought him out, needing to soothe this wild beast because that's what a woman did for her man. She absorbed his pain, supported him although he was in the wrong. It's what her mother had done, even with soul-crushing evidence of her father's affairs. Even when he didn't come home at night.

Harper was self-aware enough to know there were limits, but she was still figuring out where to draw the line. Billy was sometimes rough during sex, which she put down to his uncontrollable desire for her and the fact that they rarely had more than moments to spare. Just a dirty little fling with the owner's daughter. All those times she'd let him inside her body for a quickie that barely lasted sixty seconds, and Billy was the only one getting off.

She had known the minute she entered the locker room that night that his fury was different. Mean and twisted, it tainted the air around him.

Babe, it's okay. I'm here.

Shut up, Harper.

Billy, just talk to me. Let me help you.

Her soothing hand on his shoulder.

His hard knuckles across her mouth.

That had shut her up.

He was sorry—later—but then, men invariably were. She knew the reason for his remorse. He was worried about losing his place on the team, being tagged as a man who hits women, being charged with felony assault. He was worried his career would be over.

This man had struck her, busting her lip and drawing blood. Just once, though, because Harper wasted no time kicking that human trash fire to the curb. Off the team and out of her life.

Back in the present, he towered over her, his padding making him look taller and more menacing than ever.

"Hey, honey."

The taste of vomit replaced the ash in her throat. "I can't imagine what you'd have to say to my sister."

"We know each other."

Her heart jerked violently. That had better not be in the biblical sense.

Stroger smiled, a malevolent slash in his stupid face. "We worked on a charity gig for the Olympics together a few years ago. Got along pretty well. She sure didn't have a whole lot of nice things to say about you."

Harper couldn't imagine Izzy airing the Chase dirty laundry in public. If they were alike in any way, it was that. Harper's throat had constricted, words struggling to emerge and dying in the grip of her fear.

Stroger appraised her, sniffing out weakness. "So you got what you wanted, Harper, your own team of puppets to play with. Bet you were pissed to find you had to share it."

"Don't think you know me," she snapped. "A few weeks of whatever you want to call what happened between us doesn't give you an all-access pass into my head. Now I'd appreciate it if you didn't bother Isobel anymore."

He leaned in, an ugly twist to his mouth. The years had not been kind, but perhaps kinder than Stroger had been on himself. He'd always liked to party hard, a pattern she saw now was so similar to her father's that she almost slapped her forehead with *duh*.

The guy's brand was asshole.

"Still jealous of your little sister? Some things don't change. You never got enough attention from your old man. Poor little Harper, begging for someone to love her. We have a fight and you go sniveling to him with your woes. '*Billy was mean to me, Daddy. Get rid of him, Daddy.*'" He sniffed. "I didn't like it at the time, but you did me a favor. Got me off that hellhole team that was going nowhere. And then you did it again, acquiring DuPre. That beat-up old has-been was dragging us down, so here you are doing me all sorts of solids. It's like you're working for me, honey."

Anger flared, fueled by her whip-smart recollection of hockey stats. "And as soon as he left, you lost your next three straight. Sounds like DuPre was holding things together in Cougarland. *Honey.*"

Stroger loomed closer, stealing her personal space by a few more scary inches, but Harper remained still despite the clatter of her heart. A therapist she'd seen briefly not long after the incident had told her: *Forget what hurt you but never forget what it taught you.* That punch had taught her she was strong. She would not be bullied. Not by Clifford Chase, Billy Stroger, or any asshole who said *no, you can't*.

"God, you were always such a coldhearted, frigid bitch."

Achievement unlocked. Her day was not complete until someone had called her that heartfelt endearment.

"Have a good game, Stroger. Make sure that old has-been Rebels' center doesn't get by you, but I expect that'll be tough seeing as how Remy DuPre is ten times the man you are."

Stroger's arm twitched, and instinctively she took a step back. Looked like she could be bullied after all.

"Everything okay here?"

Harper turned to find a god in Armani standing behind them. Dante Moretti. Boston's assistant GM— and pro hockey's first openly gay managing executive— assessed the situation with cool detachment.

"Just fine," Harper managed to get out. While she didn't know Dante well, they were often drawn together at hockey PR events, their "otherness" in this sport they loved enough to create a bond of affinity.

Now he held her gaze for a beat, then swiveled his strong, shadowed jaw to Stroger. "Puck's about to drop, Billy."

With one last glare at Harper, Stroger pivoted and stalked back to the locker room around the corner.

Dante stepped in, giving her all his attention. "You all right, Harper?"

"Y-yes, thanks! I should be—" She waved in the direction of the elevators that would take her to the visitors' box. Every bit of her shredding willpower was currently being spent on not falling down.

"I can walk you up." His tone was so gentle she cringed. Could he tell that her internal organs were currently switching places inside her chest cavity?

"No need! I should find a—a restroom first. Is there one on this floor?"

"Sure. Just down the end of this corridor." Unease danced across his handsome Italian features, but she helped him deal by curving her mouth into something that resembled a smile. So what if she looked unhinged.

"Enjoy the game, Dante. But not too much!" *Ha-ha.* A hysterical stress laugh spilled from her mouth, and she left him nodding in concern. Conscious of his sharp eyes on her back, she escaped in the direction of the nearest restroom.

Stay calm. Don't run. One foot in front of the other. You've got this.

One-one thousand. Two-one thousand. Thr—

She barely made it to the stall before she threw up her pork tacos.

Back in Beantown.

Remy skated onto the ice, his legs as heavy as waterlogged sandbags. Might've been his age, but he suspected it was the prospect of playing against his former team in front of his former fans, who gave a raucous cheer at the announcement of his name. Nice, but that didn't make it any easier.

Six times in his storied, luckless career, he'd come back to an old stomping ground and faced his previous comrades. But there was something different in the air tonight. Maybe it was the fact that Boston was the team he'd expected to see out his golden years with, or that these were the guys he'd once felt were brothers but were now strangers to him. A desperate cut sliced through his chest, and he knew its cause.

This was truly his last year on pro ice.

His body was shot, and he'd run out of chances. It was now or never, every fucking cliché you could think of to signify the sands in the hourglass running out. He needed to fight—not for the Rebels and certainly not for Harper Chase—so he'd be prime trade material come January. Beating the shit out of his former teammates would let everyone know the score, and he figured it'd be easy enough as soon as he clashed sticks with Stroger.

While every one of Remy's former crew had welcomed him back like the return of the prodigal when the announcer called his name, Stroger had merely sneered that ugly-ass grin of his and skated away. Billy was one guy Remy wouldn't piss on if he were on fire. The love between them? Not lost for sure.

So no open arms. Fine. The only conversation Remy had to have with that mofo was stick to stick on the ice.

Warming up before the game, Remy absorbed the sound of the crowd, the swish of the blades, the gentle *tap-tap* of wood against puck. These were the sounds of his childhood, his adolescence, his entire adult life. This was the soundtrack of his life, and hockey gave his life meaning. He would miss it like hell.

Someone checked him from behind, pretty much a no-no during the warm-up, and lo and behold if it wasn't his old friend Billy, here to give him that Cougars welcome after all.

"How's being on the same menstrual cycle as your bosses workin' out, Jinx?"

"Four sisters, remember? I'm still on theirs."

Billy spat close to Remy's left skate. "You make Harper cry yet?"

Remy let that fly over his head. He didn't have any problems with a woman being in charge, and if he did, he sure as hell wouldn't be sharing his concerns with the likes of Stroger.

"She's tougher than she looks. Not sure you are, though." He shoved his former teammate and skated away. "Let's see who's cryin' at the end of the third."

Less than two minutes into the first period, it was as clear as the Plexi walling the rink that Stroger was on a mission to pound Remy ten feet below the ice. Tough checks were expected. This was the most physical of pro sports, not even pansy-assed football with its extravagant padding and constant stop-and-go could compete. But Stroger was acting like someone had a bounty out on Remy and dead was worth twice as much as alive.

Ten minutes gone, Callaghan had possession and was working his way down the ice. The Rebels' right-winger was a beast when he was in the zone, great at cutting angles and sliding into scoring position. Tonight he was on fire, had already bagged a goal that slid under the tender's body as easy as honey. Now he was on the break again and Remy was wide open because for the barest second, Stroger was not magnetized to his ass.

Remy was about to call for it, then realized he didn't have to because he and Callaghan had suddenly reached that point, that magical moment when words were more likely to hinder than help. Where the connection between two players was so damn fluid the pass was already done before it even happened.

The puck was on his stick and he was twenty feet from the Cougars' goal. Fifteen. Ten . . .

Stroger was coming for him, his eyes like burning holes behind his mask, and then—fuck, he slammed Remy right against the boards, making no effort to play the puck whatsoever.

Beyond provoked, Remy pushed back, and apparently that was all the encouragement Stroger needed to get Remy in a headlock and lift him two feet off the ice and into the Plexi. His fist connected with Remy's chin and something crunched.

Stroger was on him, his mask almost interlocking with Remy's, his breath labored with hate.

"Word of advice, Jinx. Show her who's boss, early and often." *Slam.*

What the fuck? Awakened from the fugue state he seemed to be drowning in, Remy finally managed to push Stroger off and down on the ice. Then he pulled back, ready to lay the fist of New Orleans on him.

"What's your problem, asshole?"

Stroger spat, but the loogie didn't get past his mask, just hung there from the shield. *Connard* couldn't even do that right.

The zebras pulled them apart, and Remy's one consolation was that Stroger's stretch in the sin bin and the resulting power play gave them the goal they'd take as advantage to the end.

Game Rebels.

EIGHT

After close to twenty years of regular commuting by plane, Remy still hadn't figured out how to fall asleep on one. All around him on the chartered flight, the rest of the team snoozed soundly, except for St. James five rows ahead. The guy had growled at anyone who came near him, covered his ears with headphones, and lost himself in the beat of something loud, violent, and possibly composed with the death of puppies in mind. Remy had to admire the guy. Piecing your life together after rehab and doing it under the full glare of the press and your team was something he wouldn't wish on his worst enemy. Remy liked to think that if he was in that position, he'd also keep his head down and bury himself in work. St. James had played well tonight. They all had.

A win on the road at last.

Remy wasn't used to acting like a win was the best thing to ever happen to him. Sure, a win was better than a kick to the head, but his whole life was about winning. Yet while tonight's victory felt good, especially with the bonus of seeing Stroger in that penalty box, funny how it didn't feel half as good as the two goals he'd clawed back in Philly two weeks ago. They'd lost that game, but those goals had meant something.

They were the first steps on his road to the Cup and his exit off the Rebels' roster.

He turned back to the worn paperback in his hand. Not his usual diet, but he'd promised his niece Sophie he'd do a read-along. With her parents in the middle of a contentious divorce, he'd been checking in more frequently. The book was about five sisters who needed to get hitched and a bunch of crazy rules about who could talk to whom and in what order. Sophie had to read it for AP English, and while he'd die before admitting it to anyone, it was better than he expected. Slyly funny, despite the main dude being a complete ass, insulting everyone left and right. A real catch.

A shadow darkened his peripheral vision. Now, wasn't that nice. Just the lady he wanted to play hide the puck with.

"You're reading *Pride and Prejudice*?"

The surprise in Harper's voice should have been an insult, but he couldn't blame her.

"Well, I was grabbing some reading material on my way out yesterday morning and accidentally picked this up instead of my copy of *Hustler*."

"Would've thought you'd be more a *Juggs* kind of guy."

"That's my other subscription."

Her mouth quirked, but in a flash, it was gone. He looked around. *Anyone, anyone?* Surely someone could corroborate that Harper grin sighting, but alas, he was alone in this.

He took a good ol' gander at her, unsurprised that even now she was impeccably dressed in a sleeveless dark pink dress that matched her glossy lips and high-heeled gray boots with cut-outs showing pink-varnished toenails. Sexy as hell. He'd venture to say *travel-casual* was not in this woman's vocabulary. The tightly coiled image she presented turned him on and pissed him off in equal measure. He tried to imagine her unspooling. Overindulging in dessert, shimmying on a dance floor, losing herself in bed.

Screaming out his name when she came.

His cock stiffened at the notion of drawing this woman's inner vixen to the surface, provided that there was anything to draw.

"So what's the deal, DuPre?" She waved at the book in his hand. "Is this some elaborate ruse to conquer the nonstripper demographic? Did one of your ex-girlfriends say you weren't sensitive enough?"

"Just a poor boy tryin' to better myself." He laid his accent on brick-thick. "Figured I'd start with this fascinatin' insight into the female brain. Did you know that accordin' to this, all women wanna do is get married?"

Another twitch of those pouty pink lips. Her Majesty was amused. "Not all women. Back when that was written, females didn't have much control over their own financial futures. Things have changed, and now we don't need to rely on a man for a single thing."

She emphasized those last three words, probably so he wouldn't make some dig about the reasons why a woman might need a man. Like that could stop him.

"What do you ladies call it? The battery-operated boyfriend? There's only so much BOB can do for you."

"At least it doesn't talk back."

"Oh, you like your men quiet. Noted." Like the lawyer, he supposed. They probably fucked each other like very respectful mice. *Was that okay, dahling? Yes, Kenneth, that was perfectly pleasant.*

Best not to think about that because, one, he didn't much enjoy thinking about people he knew having sex, and, two, he *especially* didn't enjoy thinking about Harper having sex. Or, having sex with anyone who wasn't him, which was crazy cakes, as his niece Sophie would say.

"I like them doing what I pay them to do."

"Hell, Harper, when you get snippy about something you sure don't let up. I said I'd play my heart out for you—"

"After you blackmailed me."

"After I negotiated the terms of my departure." He lowered his voice. "Now I know you don't wanna talk about this right here."

She leaned in at his soft tone, a proven strategy

to get a woman within kissing distance. Not that he wanted to kiss her.

Remy, you wanna bang this pretty lady without laying lips on her? Now, that ain't nice.

Okay, he wanted to kiss her. He wanted to kiss her so badly the only thing keeping him from doing it was the damn seat belt strapped across his hips. He glanced down. No seat belt.

Shit.

Looking up, he found something close to concern in her eyes. "How are you? After your run-in with . . . Stroger?"

That hesitancy before she said Stroger's name set off a four-alarm in his head. His best guess? Ms. Chase didn't quite have the stomach for the violence inherent in the game.

He rubbed his jaw where Stroger had gotten him good and pondered how he'd allowed a punk like that to get the jump on him. *Gettin' old, DuPre.* Remy supposed that could be it, but bad blood between them notwithstanding, there was still the fact that Stroger had come at him all night with no provocation whatsoever.

"I'm all right. Just boys bein' boys."

Her look pronounced that to be bullshit, so he tried again.

"Billy and I weren't exactly bosom buddies when we played on the same side."

"That right?"

"He's one mean fils de putain—that's Cajun for

sonovabitch—and while I could put up with that if he had a streak of decency in him on occasion, he's never shown any evidence that he's worth my time. Kind of guy who aims at puddles and pisses in front of you in the team shower, y'know? One day I came across him hazing a rookie, making him down hot sauce until he puked. Not sure what set him off tonight, though."

She bit down on her lip, a supercute lip snag that got him more than a little hot and bothered. Jesus, he had seen women looking nervous before and it hadn't turned him on faster than a lamp. So why did the sight of Harper Chase running her orthodontist-bought teeth along her plump bottom lip, and leaving that same lip looking wet and luscious and ready for his mouth to taste—

Where was I again?

Oh yeah. Why would this relatively common sight get him hotter than a short-order cook in a Lafayette diner in July? Looking to divert his brain and other interested parts of his anatomy away from how she was making him positively swoon (fucking *Pride and Prejudice*), he went on the offensive.

"Got somethin' to say, Harper?"

There it was again, another lip bite. Another nervous dart of her tongue. What the hell was going on here?

"Do you mind if we . . . ?" She gestured toward the galley behind them.

He stood and followed her, not trying all that hard to ignore the switch of those trim little hips and that cute little ass in that tight little skirt. Hadn't he already decided she was too skinny for him? Yes, he had. Yet somehow his cock had gone rogue and was staging a coup to overthrow the governing faction.

He passed Burnett, snoring his head off and sounding like a damn buzz saw. Jorgenson had his mouth dropped open, a touch of drool dripping from the corner. The youngsters had done well tonight. They deserved their rest.

Back in the relative privacy of the galley area, Harper reached for a bottle of Dewar's and splashed a couple of fingers into a glass. He could have sworn her hand shook a little.

She didn't drink, but she was definitely working up to saying something. Seconds passed, then close to a minute. He leaned in, a move he usually used to get answers from his sisters or nieces. It rarely worked because he was pretty much whipped when it came to his female relatives, but he was confident that one day he might strike gold with this particular strategy.

"Harper?"

Still nothing. Instinctively, he cupped her upper arms. She trembled under his touch, and that just made him grip harder and pull her closer.

"Minou, you're scarin' me."

Those green eyes seemed to implore him. Soothe her. Keep her warm. Make it better. Unbidden, one of his hands coasted up to the beautiful rounded shoulder he'd brushed his lips over a couple of nights ago.

Stop me, Harper. He curled a hand around her neck and noted with satisfaction how she seemed to relax into his touch.

Shut me down, baby. Holding her at the nape, he let his thumb wander to her jaw. Was it his imagination or did she fold into him ever so slightly?

"Tell me what's goin' on." Really, he meant why she'd invited him back here for the private tête-à-tête, but her breathing had picked up, and her moist lips were parted, and it was all he could do not to push her to her knees and demand she put that tart mouth to better use.

"Remy, I—" She let loose a breathy moan, likely because his thumb had glanced across that pouting bottom lip. He couldn't help it. His hands didn't care about her motives for bringing him here because his body couldn't survive another second without knowing how that mouth tasted.

With his palm anchoring her head, he angled her up and sucked on that fleshy lip. She gave a little squeak, but she didn't back off, so he took that as invitation and covered her mouth with his.

Dumbass hands, running the show, because now he was fucked. No woman should taste this incredible. Harper Chase's mouth could tempt a man to forget everything that was good for him.

Her hands pressed against his chest, holding him

at bay, yet somehow pulling him deeper into this madness. She kissed him back with all that passion he'd seen her put into their contract negotiations. A little angry, a whole lot desperate, both of them winners. Their tongues touched, then tangled in a manner that might be considered workplace inappropriate.

He was happily drowning in the hottest kiss of his life.

She broke away, eyes wild and blaring her confusion. "That—that's not why I asked to speak with you."

He licked his lips, needing one last taste of this Class A drug that was Harper. His heartbeat would take longer than his erection to subside. "No worries. I won't tell anyone the real reason you acquired me."

Her lust-dazed eyes focused in annoyance, and she slipped his grasp.

"I might have had something to do with it."

"With what?"

"Stroger going off on you."

Not expecting that. "And you know this because?"

She took a slug of the whiskey she'd poured earlier. "Before the game, I ran into him near the locker rooms. He was talking to Isobel, and I told him to leave her alone."

"What was he saying to Isobel?"

"I don't know. Apparently they worked on some charity thing during the Olympics, but seeing them together—well, he's bad news. And I don't want my sister to have anything to do with him."

With any other woman, Remy might have suspected a distinct case of the green-eyed monster. Add the innately tricky relationship between sisters, and that female jealousy theory went for double. But Harper didn't strike him as the jealous type, so seeing her all bent out of shape because of Stroger made him hella curious.

"Stroger used to play for the Rebels," Remy said, accessing his memory bank for the details. "Five years ago?"

"Six. One and a half seasons, and then we traded him to LA."

Recollection kicked in hard. "Not a great trade if I recall. Kind of unexpected."

"Do you remember the details of every transaction in the league?"

"Just the ones that look funny." *Aw. Shit.* He got it now. "Something happened with you and Stroger?" Tonight. Six years ago.

"I told him to stay away from Isobel, and then we traded the usual smack talk. He mentioned something about how the Rebels were down so bad there was no getting up and not even a . . ." Her voice petered out.

"Not even a what?"

"Not even an old has-been could bring us out of our slump."

He'd heard worse. "And?"

"I might have mentioned that you were ten times the man he was."

Remy's heart reared like a wild beast in his chest.

Not ten times the skater. Not ten times the player. Ten times *the man*. That could be interpreted in any number of ways, but if he were Stroger, he would have read it one way, and one way only.

Harper had used Remy to win points against a man she'd once been involved with.

"When you traded him out six years ago, you did that because you were . . ." His pulse had skyrocketed while his brain hurtled toward the shittiest conclusion imaginable. "Dating him?"

She darted a tongue over those luscious lips he'd just tasted. "Dating is a stretch."

Oh, so much better. She'd been . . . *fucking* Stroger. Neither did she see fit to contradict this as the reason for Stroger getting canned.

Remy wasn't given to emotional outbursts either on or off the ice. He was known for his laid-back, suthin' way of approaching everything, even hockey. Some people thought he was *too* laid back and blamed his easy temperament for his failings in the final stretch. But the thought of Stroger touching Harper had him ready to do considerable violence.

"So you told your daddy to banish your ex. Must be nice to have that power, princess."

She bristled, and cool ice-queen Harper returned, but not before a flash of something in her eyes alerted him that he might not understand fully what had happened between her and Stroger. Whatever occurred, it ended badly, with Harper hurting.

But this woman fixed her pain by screwing with a guy's career. Never in his life would he have thought he'd feel a smidgeon of pity for a shithead like Billy Stroger. The message was clear: do not get in Harper Chase's emotional crosshairs.

For a moment, her cool facade cracked, and she looked as vulnerable as she had in that split second before he kissed her. "I just wanted to make sure you were okay and apologize for setting him off. I never expected he'd go that far."

"Don't worry, Ms. Chase. All's fair in love and hockey, right? But next time you want to use me in some grudge match you have with Stroger, give me a heads-up so I can protect my oh-so-pretty, *Juggs*-readin', stripper-lovin' face."

Furious, and not just because he felt like an idiot for thinking his boss might have his back, he stalked to his seat.

NINE

You're my princess.

For most little girls, hearing those words spoken by their father would have made them feel like the most special daughter in the world. But not Harper.

Sure, she'd bought it at first. Birth to age six, the pre-cynicism years. She was the apple of Clifford's eye, his precious bundle of joy after her mother had suffered so many miscarriages. Harper burst onto the scene, promptly breaking her mother's womb in the process. (A fact former runway model Lorraine never failed to remind her daughter of every single day of Harper's childhood.) Because of Harper, there would be no more children. No chance of sons.

But Clifford had her, Harper, his princess.

It should have been enough, but like Henry VIII, he decided his first wife was no longer living up to her end of the bargain—to produce male heirs—and it was time to move on to a new and shiny model.

You're my princess, Harper—until something better comes along.

When Harper first heard about Isobel, she was too excited to be jealous. She'd always wanted a little sister, a live doll she could dress up, someone she could boss around, an ally who understood how hard it was to be Clifford Chase's progeny. And when she saw week-old Isobel, with her too-big-for-her-little-body head and her dark, silky hair, Harper had fallen in love for the first—and only—time.

In the living room of her father's new house near the Rebels' stadium, Harper asked if she could touch her.

"Of course you can," her father had boomed, his voice so loud that Harper worried he'd frighten the newborn. But Isobel didn't even flinch. She was already that tough. Her eyes opened wide, big, blue, and impossibly heartbreaking, and she grasped Harper's finger. Its strength shocked her, but what shocked her more was her father's unconditional love for his new daughter. She hadn't even done a thing to earn it yet!

"She's strong," Harper murmured, while her stepmother, Geraldine "call me Gerry!," looked on indulgently. A former Olympic ice-skater, she had clearly been chosen for her perfect gene pool. At six and three quarters, Harper was old enough to recognize her father's end game here.

"She's going to be a champion," her father affirmed. "When women go pro, she'll be right there." Even now, she remembered the desperate tinge to his voice. He hadn't yet achieved his ultimate reproductive goal— a son—but he'd remake this child in as close to that image as he could.

As if sensing her father's lofty aspirations for her, Isobel gripped Harper's finger tighter. *I've already won*, that grip said. *I'm better, stronger, a million times more lovable.*

The melodrama of a child, perhaps, but kids have a sixth sense about these things, don't they? And while Isobel might have been Harper's first love, that passion burned to a fiery death in the face of Clifford's boundless adoration for his newborn baby girl. (Children, so fickle.) With first love, Harper also experienced bitter jealousy, and it consumed her in its totality.

Why, twenty-five years later, was Harper even thinking of this? Remy DuPre, that's why. *Must be nice to have that power, princess.*

No one had called her that since she was a little girl. Neither time had she deserved it.

Trust the dumb jock to jump to conclusions about how she'd used him to win points with Billy Stroger. As if that piece of shit was worth Harper getting in a feminine snit about. Remy had no idea, just assumed the worst.

Let him. She didn't need his good opinion. Neither did she need him to act like she had lured him to the plane's galley for that hot, sexy kiss. Her intentions had been benign, only wanting to check on him after all those hits he took from Stroger during the game. Even

Isobel had commented that it was more egregious than usual. But when Remy mentioned his burning dislike for Stroger, something had cracked open inside her.

Vindication.

It wasn't your fault, Harper. Billy Stroger is an asshole to everyone!

Alone with Remy in that tight galley space, she had come *this* close to spilling every secret and fear. Stroger, the "playoffs or bust" stipulation, how in over her head she felt every minute of every day. It was so easy to melt into his arms, to forget her problems for a while, especially with that drugging kiss. Why couldn't he be bad at that?

The cold light of day put a gloss of reality on it. To let him burrow further under her skin would be a huge mistake. He had caught her in a weakened moment and used his lips to reestablish his dominance in their war. There would be no more of that!

Bleary eyed after no sleep and her body still reeling from the DuPre Smooch Attack, Harper came into the kitchen just as Violet was walking out, wearing a pair of tiny shorts and an off-the-shoulder ripped tee.

"Hey, there." Violet had lain low since their last home game four days ago. Before heading to Boston yesterday, Harper had knocked on the door of the coach house at the end of the path, but there had been no answer, just Stevie Nicks's "Rhiannon" blasting at decibel levels not usually heard, or tolerated, in the tony enclave of Lake Forest. There wasn't a whole lot

Harper could do to force her sisterly devotion on her, short of banging down the door like a crazy person.

Violet held up a plastic bag of ground coffee, still on a slide for the exit. "Ran out, so took the liberty."

"Sure!" Harper said a little too brightly. "Maybe you can stay for breakfast, and we could talk." After her spat with Remy, she wanted company. She hadn't realized how lonely this big old house was until people had moved into the hood.

Her sister looked like she'd rather have a root canal with a rusty screwdriver than talk, but she wasn't completely without class, so she walked back to the kitchen island. Slowly.

Harper bit her lip. "Problem is, I lied."

"Oh yeah?"

"I usually just do coffee for breakfast."

Violet's lips quirked ever so slightly. "Coffee's fine."

As Harper busied herself measuring out grounds for the coffeemaker—her Keurig was on the fritz—Violet took a seat at the island. This was nice. They could catch up, and maybe Harper could give Violet some big-sister advice and fashion tips, because Lord knew she needed it, just look at those shorts, and—

"How's the sexy Cajun?"

Harper spilled the grounds she was about to pour into the filter.

She couldn't say "who?" because that would be stupid, so she responded with, "You think DuPre's sexy?" and prayed to the gods of nonchalance that

Violet didn't notice how her voice dropped a couple of octaves.

"Sure. All that lazy menace. Sleek like a cat. Could do with working on his reflexes, though, with how that asshole came at him last night."

"You watched the game?"

Now it was Violet's turn to take the awkward baton and run with it. "I need to learn what it's all about so I can earn my inheritance," she muttered.

Harper suspected that Violet knew a hell of a lot more about hockey than she let on.

Isobel walked in just then, dressed in Hello Kitty PJs and stifling a yawn. "Hey." She noticed Violet. "You guys plotting against me?"

Violet smiled. "Sure are, and all dastardly plots require caffeine. If Harper could get around to making the coffee."

"Oh, right." Harper returned to the task that had been derailed by Violet's mention of the sexy Cajun. Her words. Harper would never think . . . ah, who was she kidding? He was both sexy and Cajun, and she didn't enjoy Violet's leer.

"Curtis Deacon at the *Sun-Times* is still being a jerk," Isobel said, tapping her phone. "We won last night, yet the grief continues."

Violet leaned over to catch whatever was on Isobel's phone screen. "Is that the guy who called us the Spice Girls?"

Harper rolled her eyes. "I'd take it if they kept the

original names. I remember dressing up as Scary Spice when I was a kid, and I totally rocked it." Instead Deacon had labeled them as Incompetent Spice, Middle-Child Spice, and Latina Spice. Hilarious.

Isobel snickered. "I should be Sporty Spice. I mean I'm actually good at freakin' sports!"

They laughed, though it wasn't all that funny. Wanting to take advantage of the *us versus them* vibes, Harper chose her next words carefully.

"I've been thinking. Maybe we should set aside a night each week to spend time together. Watch dumb movies, eat ice cream, drink wine."

The others stared at her as if she'd grown two heads and one of them looked like a creepy clown's.

"Or not."

Isobel squinted at her. "You never seemed all that interested before."

That smarted, but Isobel was right. All her life, Harper had refused to let her younger sister in when she wanted to be closer. Why should she have played nice with the girl responsible for her parents' broken marriage and her mother's descent into depression and alcoholism? Circumstances placed them on opposing sides, and Clifford as referee always made the calls in Isobel's favor.

Harper recalled how her father had forced her to invite Isobel to her thirteenth birthday party. As if a seven-year-old could have fun at a party with big girls! On reflection, locking Isobel in the utility room was harsh, but it was the only way to ensure her father's undivided attention. It wasn't every day a girl became a teenager.

Shame at how she had acted all those years ago crept over her now. It was why, once she'd heard about Violet's existence, she'd pushed for a relationship with the newest leaf on the Chase family tree. Too little too late, perhaps, but she wanted to give it a shot and steal her own chance at sisterly redemption.

"Things have changed, haven't they? It seems strange to be practically living together and acting like strangers."

Isobel looked unconvinced.

Violet spoke up. "So you want to do Awkward Girls' Night In, emphasis on *awkward*?"

Harper turned away, feeling foolish for having tried. She watched the drip-drip of the coffee filling the glass pot, willing it to move faster.

"We'll do it," she heard behind her from Isobel, "if you do something for us."

"What?"

"Tell us what's going on with you and Remy DuPre."

"You two looked pretty cozy at Ford Callaghan's birthday party," Violet hummed in agreement.

Facing them, Harper opened her mouth to deny it. Closed it again.

"And last night on the plane," Isobel said with a devilish gleam in her green eyes, "you both went to the galley, and Remy came out looking like his nuts had been stomped on by size five Choos."

"I knew it." Violet wagged a finger. "After all your apocalyptic warnings about getting involved with the players."

"There is no involvement. We just rub each other the wrong way"—*deliciously wrong*—"and last night I screwed up." By almost dragging him into an airplane bathroom to finish what that kiss started.

The girls waited, and realizing that partially fessing up to her sins might increase her stock in the good-sister market, Harper told them the shortened, abuse-free version of her run-in with Billy Stroger, how that likely contributed to his vendetta for Remy out on the ice, and how DuPre hadn't quite appreciated her retelling of the tale.

She kept that spine-dissolving kiss with Remy to herself. *I didn't think it was relevant, Officer.*

"So that's why you're so opposed to boning the players?" Violet asked. "Because you had a bad break-up with this Stroger guy?"

Today, children, we're learning all about shame! Another round coursed through her, the memory of how low Stroger had made her feel an alternately hot and cold front in her chest. Not even 8 a.m., and this day sucked donkey balls.

She refused to elaborate. "We are the first women to own and run a professional sports team. The world is watching how we handle this. If we let our hormones get the better of us, what does that say? That we're slaves to our desires—"

"So you admit you have the hots for DuPre?" Violet was like a dog with a bone.

"I admit nothing!" Complete with finger point. "He's an employee who I happen to not get along with particularly well. But I don't have to get along with him. I just have to ensure he plays to the best of his ability. The same with all the players. We can't do anything that puts that in jeopardy. So no flirting, fraternization, or—or smirking! Okay, Violet?"

Violet threw up her hands. "Why are you looking at me?"

Isobel laughed. "We've all seen you getting cozy with Cade Burnett. Heads huddled, whisper-whisper, et cetera, et cetera."

Harper blinked. "I thought you had your eye on St. James."

Violet smiled serenely. "I'm equal opportunity when it comes to these hunks of brawn. This is the year of the V, *chicas*—and I mean that in all the ways it can possibly be taken." Her brow crimped, some other thought taking over for the briefest second. "But you can strike Nessie off the list."

"Nessie?"

"Loch Ness," Violet said. "Because he's Scottish and gives off the still waters of mystery vibe."

Harper had heard plenty of names for the broody captain of the Rebels: Laird of the Puck, the Gentleman Enforcer, and the team nickname, Highlander. Nessie was a new one.

Violet chuckled. "I might have thrown that one at him, and he looked at me like I'd asked what was under his kilt."

Harper had no problem imagining Bren's reaction. Not exactly known for his cheerful disposition, since emerging from rehab he'd been as dour as a rainy day in the Scottish highlands. She grabbed a few mugs and started pouring coffee.

Isobel coughed slightly. "Nice diversion, Harper, but I think we need to also talk about the fact you had a fling with Billy Stroger."

Her blood turned to ice. "It was years ago. Dad said I shouldn't, so that was like cock nip. The thrill of the forbidden and all that."

Isobel looked sympathetic, while Violet studied her more closely. "Yeah, but what exactly happened?"

No amount of sisterly bonding would help loosen her tongue on that topic. "He wasn't performing well so we traded him out. He took it personally. And that, ladies, is why hockey and sex do not mix."

Better they see her as a hard-ass who'd happily trade a lover. No sentiment because, dammit, there's no crying in hockey.

Isobel poured cream into her coffee. "He doesn't seem your type at all."

"What's my type?"

"Kenneth," they both said in unison.

Boring, staid, wouldn't-hurt-a-fly Kenneth. She supposed that wasn't entirely wrong, but why did it sting to be filed away so quickly? Although she had been holding Kenneth at arm's length, perhaps it was time to let him off the bench. Spending time with him would crowd out all thoughts of a certain Cajun ice warrior.

She was almost sure of it.

This was not how Remy imagined spending his first free Saturday night in a month, but then Chicago had been just one long cavalcade of surprises so far.

Cade "Alamo" Burnett sat on Remy's sofa, whupping all comers at *Star Wars Battlefront* on Remy's PS4. Alamo was from, you guessed it, San Antone, and was about as arrogant as you'd expect from someone born in the Lone Star State. His fingers feverishly worked the controller as he played Boba Fett, the badassest bounty hunter in the galaxy, against a bunch of anonymous online players.

After about two minutes, he twisted his wrist, unleashed a weird war cry, and smashed the Rebel resistance back to wherever the hell they'd X-Winged in from.

"Yeeeessss!"

"Congratulations, dude," Callaghan said. "You just beat a bunch of twelve-year-olds."

Burnett smirked. "Are you kidding? Those little fuckers play this 24/7. You bet I'm proud to crush their spirits."

An hour ago, Erik Jorgenson had led several of the

players into Remy's apartment, saying they'd heard Remy had "the video games." Remy liked their goalie, Erik, or "Fish" as the team nicknamed him. He came from O-Vik, a small town near Bumblefuck, the Arctic Circle. Considered the holy city of Swedish hockey, it had produced more NHL players per capita than anywhere in the world. People said it was the air, the water, the northern lights. Remy assumed there was only so much sex you could have during all-dark days in winter; if you were surrounded by that much snow, hockey would be your life.

"So none of you guys have your own PS4?"

"Uh, we're worth fucking millions, DuPre," Ford said. "Of course we have our own PS4. But we figured you were lonely, not knowing anyone, so we came over."

"Your woman was sick of you fussing around her, right?"

Callaghan grinned. "Bingo."

Ford's girlfriend was pregnant, which he'd learned the night of his birthday party. He wouldn't shut up about it in the locker room, so lord only knew how annoying he was at home. Remy guessed Addison had pushed him out the door tonight with instructions to stop hovering.

In truth, Remy was glad for the distraction. After that fight with Harper two nights ago, he'd been irritable. Not even a ten-mile run today had cast off visions of her wounded expression.

Like she had a right to be hurt. Jesus.

He wasn't enjoying that guilt curdling in the pit of his stomach. Neither did he enjoy that this morning's in-shower fun times with his right hand only caught fire when the memory of how she'd tasted popped in for a visit.

"How long for the food?" Burnett asked. As soon as the guys arrived, Remy had done what he always did when his teammates came over: he dragged out his stockpot.

"You could've ordered pizza."

"Pizza in Riverbrook sucks, man. They don't know what they're doing this far from the big smoke. Besides, we heard you were den dad to your last crew." He grinned big. "Can't wait to try that gumbo, Jinx."

Taking that as his cue, Remy headed into the kitchen, with requests for more beers and "something salty" from Jorgenson, who apparently thought sodium was a food group. A knock on the front door redirected his journey.

St. James stood on the threshold, looking as awkward as, well, an alcoholic at a party. He held up a six-pack of Sam Adams Octoberfest, which did not make it any less uncomfortable. Gretzky, who'd been sitting at the petulant Scot's feet, pushed past Remy with a loud toot to announce his arrival.

"Heard we were playing video games." That gruff brogue challenged Remy to disagree.

"Sure," Remy said, "accepting" the beers shoved in his midsection as Bren walked by.

"Highlander!" Erik called out cheerily while the rest of the gang joined in.

Bren waved and waited for Remy to move into the kitchen. They hadn't talked much in the few weeks since Remy's arrival, though the team seemed to have his back. That's what your hockey family did, even when you fucked up royally. Remy didn't know all the details beyond the guy's need for detox after he apparently showed up for a game drunk out of his tree in the final days of the regular season.

"What'll it be?"

"Water would be good."

While Remy grabbed a bottle of water from the fridge, Bren approached the stove like a bomb sat on it. "Smells good."

"Seafood gumbo. Old family recipe."

Bren took the water Remy offered. "You still pissed?"

How in hell had St. James heard about his fight with Harper? He played dumb. "About what?"

"Your trade."

Oh that. He guessed he had been a bit sullen about it. "I'm coming around. Winning always helps."

"You played a blinder in Boston. I guess you had something to prove against your old team."

Bren took a slug of his water while Remy considered his next move. Time to get down to brass tacks. "Apparently we're headed to the playoffs."

St. James's smile was about as lively as Remy had ever seen it. "Harper's not given to hyperbole, but it won't happen without us coming together. I was surprised she asked me to wear the captain's band again, but I've always trusted her. She had my back when the rest of 'em were ready to bail on me."

Bren's burst of honesty was as unexpected as that pretty picture he painted of can-do-no-wrong Harper. First she's bringing Ford and his woman together by trading him in, now she's holding St. James's hand on the road back to recovery. None of it squared with the ruthless woman who didn't allow for sentiment.

He considered himself a pretty good judge of character, so he didn't enjoy being wrong about anyone. Harper had already demonstrated she wasn't making the best calls: going for broke toward the playoffs. Firing her GM. Fucking Stroger.

Next.

Harper didn't act like any manager he'd ever worked with. Though it wasn't required, she usually came into the locker room before the games to wish them all luck in that stilted way she had. The guys didn't know what to do with it, not because she was female—though he guessed that could be part of it—but because she seemed so ill at ease with them. Like she was holding her breath every time. For a woman who had grown up around professional sports, she sure didn't act like it.

Weird, because she knew her stuff and had no problem giving as good as she got from Remy. She could reel off stats, had an eye for talent, and clearly ate three square meals of hockey a day, but when it came to the intangibles of running a team, Harper Chase knew shit.

He wondered why she was so desperate to force the issue this year, and why that desperation made her sound so human. *Don't get all caught up in her schemes, DuPre. You're out of here in ten weeks max. The Rebels are not your problem.*

"So what else you got to prove, DuPre?"

Remy stared at Bren, trying to interpret that question amid the undercurrent of tension that'd existed between them since Remy's arrival. That he was here to knit the team together had to get Bren's back up. Ensuring that they acted as a cohesive unit should be the captain's job.

"I know how to win."

"Up to a point," Bren returned with challenge. Evidently he was wondering what sort of deal Remy had with Harper. He'd witnessed that run-in in the Philly locker room. He'd seen Remy's effort levels increasing since. A man as astute as Bren St. James would be rightly suspicious of Remy's endgame.

While he could assure the man his captain's spot was safe, now was not the time to mention that Remy's stay was short term. He might not agree with Harper on much, but he recognized that ripping the rug out from under them would interfere with the mission.

"You believe I'm jinxed?" Remy asked, turning the challenge around.

Bren rubbed his mouth, a resigned gesture if ever Remy had seen one. "We're all jinxed in one way or another."

TEN

Home at last.

Remy breathed in the scent of jasmine, fried food, and horse manure, with top notes of tourist vomit, and thanked the Lord for the glory that is New Orleans. Coming in a day early gave him a chance to catch up with his family, who lived in the Garden District about twenty minutes from the French Quarter. There'd be a big meal tonight with everyone on hand to tell him what needed fixing with the Rebels' game. His family never let the fact they knew fuck all about hockey get in the way of giving advice.

He loved them anyway.

No doubt he'd have to suffer through the usual chatter about how he needed to settle down, as if the seven nieces his sisters had bestowed on the DuPres weren't enough. As the only son, he felt a special responsibility to carry on the family name—and he would, in good time.

He cut from Royal onto Pirate Alley, heading for the

speakeasy where he was scheduled to meet his cousin Henri for a midafternoon drink. How much would he have to down to exorcise thoughts of Harper Chase? Talk about latching his fantasies on to the wrong woman. Nothing could come out of developing an attraction for his boss, never mind that she was the reason Stroger had a hard-on for doing Remy a serious injury during that game.

Even with all these God's-honest reasons not to think of Harper in that way, putting that No Trespassing sign on it guaranteed that was the one place his mind would go.

When he was with her, he wasn't thinking that she was the owner of his team. He wasn't thinking that she was his employer. He wasn't thinking at all. His dick was taking over, throbbing to the beat of man-wants-woman.

This man wanted *this* woman.

He needed to get laid. This shouldn't have been a problem, because he had any number of opportunities to get laid. Women threw themselves at hockey players, even older past-their-prime jokers like him. Easy should have been his speed, yet all he wanted was hard. The one woman he couldn't have, because that's the way the bitch of a universe liked to operate.

New Orleans had always been a quirky town that thrived on difference, and Remy enjoyed his walk through the narrow streets steeped in history, especially as the weather was warmer than usual for early

November. New retail establishments had sprung up in the Quarter, fancy boutiques, aimed at affluent locals and well-heeled tourists. His sister Martine probably shopped down here regularly; he could imagine her flitting in and out of these high-priced shops spending all that cash she got from the lawsuits she usually won in her job as a personal injury lawyer. Like most DuPres, that woman could persuade anyone to do anything, and the proof was in her expensive shoes.

Speaking of . . . a large plate glass window showcased a display of colorful heels designed to cut off the circulation of any woman who wore them. He was musing on whether he should risk buying a gift for his sister—and had decided against because he'd have to spend the rest of the day buying something for all of them *and* his nieces—when he spotted the last person he'd expected to see.

The boss in the honey-toned flesh.

She sat on a sofa in the store, her bare legs stretched out before her, contemplating the shoes on her feet. Red ones that had to be at least four inches tall and sparkled to the point he was dazzled. Or maybe it was just the sight of Harper with that serious look on her face. She looked sad, a little lost, and a whole lot younger than her thirty-one years.

He really shouldn't, but by the time he'd finished that thought he was already inside the store. The saleswoman caught his eye, and evidently recognizing him as a native, gave him the traditional New Orleans greeting. "Where y'at?"

"All right."

Harper snapped her head up at the sound of his voice.

"Remy." A fiery blush crawled up her neck, and to say that pleased him would be the understatement of the millennium. "In town early for some R and R?"

He sat in an uncomfortable-looking armchair across from her. "I have family here, so I thought I'd take the opportunity to spend some time with them."

That was her cue to tell him why she was here ahead of schedule. A romantic getaway with the lawyer, perhaps?

She didn't take the bait, just dropped her gaze back to the shoes, which sent his gaze there, too. Damn, those legs were fine. She wasn't a tall woman, but all her height was in those killer pins. She wore a black-and-white-checkerboard dress in some drapey material that clung lovingly to her breasts and thighs. The hem would have hit above her knee if she were standing, but hitched a few inches higher since she was sitting down.

He approved of the sitting down.

Several boxes lay scattered about. "Need help deciding?"

"One of your many talents?"

"You'd be surprised. Four sisters."

She shot him a look of understanding. "I didn't know that. Younger than you?"

"Worse. Older. I'm the baby and they never let me forget it. We're all about a year apart."

"Your poor mother."

He flashed a grin. "Well, with four girls, it very soon became 'my poor father.' But yeah, after me, Momma ordered Poppa to get the snip. Five was plenty." He leaned forward, elbows on his knees. "So, let me see."

"See what?"

"The shoes. Stand up and walk over there a ways."

It was a risk. She could interpret it as the inappropriate come-on that it was and shut him down, or she could respond to his opening salvo in a way that would please them both.

He watched her wrestle with that dilemma a moment. Finally, she stood.

So did his cock.

Thankfully, her attention was on the shoes, so she didn't notice that. He leaned forward so *no one* would notice that.

"Take a spin, minou."

That baby frown came back, and she was again weighing the pros and cons. She angled her right toe in such a way that it drew focus to the smooth line of her leg. He almost groaned.

"Let's see how they look from the back," he encouraged.

Still frowning, she walked a few feet toward the front of the store, and the sway of her hips spiked his pulse. How had he ever thought her too skinny?

Baby, gimme that look. You know the one I mean.

She turned her head and threw a pout over her shoulder. "They're a little tight."

So were his jeans. *Bada bing!*

"You need another size?" the sales associate Remy had forgotten about chimed in.

"Five and a half," Harper said.

While the saleswoman went back to retrieve another pair, Harper did a catwalk strut to the door and back. Was that for him? He liked to think so. Just as he liked to think of this woman wearing nothing but high heels while he drove into her to the hilt.

Was this really where his mind should be going the day before a game? Anytime whatsoever? This was Harper Chase he was thinking of spreading wide, pumping deep, and—he needed to get a grip.

Nothing like a little reality check to force his mind back on track. "Think you and me should clear the air, Harper."

"We should?"

"You seem to have made up your mind about me. Like Elizabeth Bennet."

She stared at him for a good five seconds. He liked how her no-filter gaze made his skin burn.

"From *Pride and Prejudice*," he explained unnecessarily. "She makes up her mind pretty damn quick that Darcy is an unsociable moron with a stick up his ass—"

"Well, we'd never call you unsociable. You're a friend to all, unclothed and barely dressed."

How did such a tiny thing produce so much vinegar? "See? There you go again, deciding what kind of man I am based on our initial meeting."

Oh, that had her spittin'. Ms. Chase did not like to be wrong about anything, something they had in common.

"You mean when I had to track you down because you decided to follow your own schedule and not join the team for practice? Or maybe you're talking about that time when, instead of obeying the terms of your contract and doing your job, you blackmailed me. Your hands all over a stripper's ass seems like the least of your sins."

"You missed that pass I made at you in that Irish bar and that kiss I laid on you on the plane ride from Boston."

She blushed to the roots of her corn silk hair.

"Or maybe they don't count as sins in my long list of transgressions?"

"I was giving you the benefit of the doubt, assuming that first time was accidental."

He scoffed. "I don't do accidental kisses, minou. And I pretty much confirmed that when I tasted you properly the other night."

Growling in a way that went straight to his balls, she passed over that. "You pulled your own Elizabeth Bennet on me after the Cougars game. Jumping to your own incorrect conclusion." Her gaze fell to the too-tight shoes. She was clearly uncomfortable bringing this up.

Good. This was his real destination, but he preferred coming in using the back roads.

"You mean you didn't use me to needle Stroger and
make him"—he waved a hand—"jealous?"

"Of course not!" Checking that they were alone,
she stepped closer, hands on hips, and peered down at
him. He liked closer and he liked how she smelled. Flo-
ral, sexy.

"He and I didn't end well. He blamed me for getting
traded out when really he was going anyway because
his plus-minus sucked and his attitude wasn't much
better. He was never the most reasonable of people."

On that they could agree. He still couldn't believe
that a quality woman like this had spent a minute on
that waste of humanity, but then lust made people do
the strangest things, didn't it? Case in point: Remy
DuPre sitting in a French Quarter shoe store drooling
over his boss.

He could tell it was killing her to admit this weakness she'd had for Stroger. Could she tell it was killing
him? He should step in, end her misery, but she had
more to say, and he enjoyed watching her unravel.

"I shouldn't have let Stroger poke at me, but he's
always pushed my buttons and—I'm sorry you got
caught in the crossfire."

Aw hell, he felt as dumb as a box of wet mice for
making such a fuss of it. In truth, his anger stemmed
from knowing she'd given Stroger the time of day. He
was man enough to admit that—to himself.

"That's okay. We all make mistakes. Judge without getting all the facts."

She gusted out a breath. "We do."

He stood, suddenly needing to be closer to her. To touch her, take her into his arms, show her how truly sorry he was. He compromised by balling his hands into fists to stop from reaching out.

"I'm not some sort of manwhore, Harper. What you saw when you came to Boston, that was just high jinks that frankly I'm far too old for. That's not what my life was like there and it's not what it's like in Chicago."

Why the hell was he telling her this? Why was it so important that she knew he wasn't this nail-anything-that-moves kind of guy?

Why the hell couldn't he shut up?

"I'm not interested in bimbo trophies looking for a good time. My tastes run to women. Real women who have a little more life experience than suffering through a hangnail."

Judging by her parted pink-glossed lips and that snatched breath, she liked the sound of that. Hell, *he* liked the sound of it. Harper wasn't a girl. She was all woman.

She was starting to feel like *his* woman.

She lifted her chin and murmured, "I guess we got off on the wrong foot."

Maybe, but it sure was sexy balancing on that wrong foot. That spark between them was fueled by how much they bugged the hell out of each other.

He'd hate to think it might vanish now that they were BFFs.

No better place to get back on the right foot than in a shoe shop, *n'est-ce pas?*

~

When Harper spotted Remy DuPre standing before her like a god of sex she'd conjured from her fevered imagination, she'd almost had a heart attack. Just dropped and died on the spot. Addy had instructed her to go to New Orleans early for a little Harper time. Spa day, mani-pedi, shopping. Just try to relax amid all the stress of this season on which her entire future was riding.

She'd hoped Addy would make the trip with her, but her friend was reluctant to travel in her first trimester. Harper had been right about the woman's amazing boobs looking even more fantastic than usual, but what she hadn't expected was her own emotional reaction to the news: ovary-busting envy. So strange, as she had never considered herself the maternal type. Or maybe she'd let her problems with men overshadow some profound need to share her love with another human being.

Keep your love for the Rebels, Harper. That's where she needed to expend all her effort and emotion. Which led her back to her current problem. What the hell was she doing modeling shoes for Remy DuPre?

Somehow it seemed to suit the intimate conversation they were having, the *air clearing* as he labeled it. He could be blowing smoke up her ass about what she'd walked in on during his send-off in Boston, but he seemed to be taking her explanation about Billy Stroger at face value. The least she could do is give him the benefit of the doubt. It would make things easier if they got along.

She sat and slipped off the shoes, which while beautiful, would likely produce blisters the size of Volkswagens in the first hour of wearing them. DuPre retook the seat across from her, that easy manner of his not putting her at ease in the slightest. He unnerved her. Unhinged her. This extra day in New Orleans was supposed to be the opposite of stressful, but not with the sexy Cajun around. She would try on the other size, make her purchase, and run out of here.

The sales associate returned with the other pair. As she knelt, Remy stood.

"I got that, chérie."

The woman straightened and split an *oh-I-see* glance between them. "Sure." She moved to greet another customer who had just entered the store.

I got that, chérie. Did he mean—?

He folded to his knees, right in front of Harper, and held her right foot. No rub, no massage, merely a cup of his hand to her heel, and she practically had a mini orgasm.

"Remy, you don't have to do that."

He peeked up through those criminally beautiful lashes framing sparkling eyes. "Happy to serve, minou."

That word again. "What does that mean?"

"Serve? Oh, y'know. Perform duties. Fulfill obligations. Be of use."

She cocked an eyebrow. They both knew that's not what she'd been asking, but the explanation was not unpleasant. Especially the "be of use" definition. Remy kneeling in front of her in supplication sent her thinking in another direction, to another meaning. Serving up her body. Parting her legs to let him taste her.

Hell. Moving from loathing to understanding was supposed to eliminate this pesky attraction.

She swallowed. The moment stretched between them as his thumb moved along the arch of her foot and pressed lightly. Neither of them spoke. Neither of them drew breath. She'd already had a foot rub this morning during her pedicure and it had come nowhere near this level of pleasure. Her panties dampened.

Because it's an unseasonably warm November day, right?

Sure, that tingle is weather related. Like rheumatism in your crotch.

"Ready to try on those shoes now?"

"Yes." Barely a whisper.

Prince Charming unboxed the shoe and slipped it on Cinderella's foot. *It fits!*

Would he fit? He was so, so big, and it had been a long, long time.

Nope. The only fitting happening here would be shoes. She let him finish, enjoying the possessive cup of his palm around her ankle as he gentled the shoe onto her foot. In all her years of retail therapy, she had never associated shoes and sex. Now she would never think of shoes again without thinking of Remy DuPre.

His palm lingered on the back of her calf. "How does it feel?"

"Feel?"

"The shoe."

The shoe. She stood, wiggling her toes while Remy leaned back on his haunches, giving her room. Looking down at him, she had a shocking temptation to place a foot on his chest, a stiletto over his heart, claim him like a Victorian hunter who had taken down big game. A thrill rippled through her at what might come next. She would think she was in control—that she had bagged the king of the jungle—but this huge, dangerous beast would have been faking it. He'd turn the tables, leap from his position of supposed weakness, and overpower her. Before she knew it, she'd be conquered, all because she had underestimated this man.

Such drama. She blinked away that foolish meandering of her mind. What she did know is that Remy DuPre fascinated her in a way that threatened everything she was trying to build. She refused to let him— or her hormones—drag her down.

ELEVEN

Remy held the door of the shoe store open for her and she stepped outside. The clear azure sky had given way to rain-heavy clouds while they'd been doing . . . whatever they'd been doing. No one in their right mind would call it shoe shopping.

"Well, thanks for your help with . . . that."

"What are you up to now?"

"Heading back to the hotel. I have some calls to make about scouting prospects, and tonight I'm taking a walking tour." *Yes, I'm so busy. Don't even think about asking me out for a romantic candlelit dinner.*

He squinted at her. "A walking tour? Fake history and faker ghosts?"

"I'm a tourist in the most haunted city in the U.S. That's what tourists do."

"Which one are you doing?"

She fumbled with her purse and withdrew the brochure given to her by the hotel's concierge. "This one. It meets at the cathedral at 6 p.m." She did *not* say that to encourage him to join her. Of course, he wouldn't want to do some tourist trap ghost tour in his hometown.

"I'd recommend a different one. Put your phone number in there, and I'll send you the name of it."

He handed off his phone, still warm from the heat of his jeans pocket, where it had been close to his—no, no, no. Not thinking about her employee's penis. Not at all.

"Oh, it's already in here," she said with a touch of saccharine. "Probably from when you called to fill me in on your travel plans post-trade. And look, I'm listed as Big Bad Boss. How appropriate."

"Now, Harper, would you rather I called you Incompetent Spice?" His grin was unrepentant as he took back the phone, plugged in a text, and returned the device to its penis-heated cocoon. "Are you staying at the team hotel?"

She nodded, but he'd already taken the shopping bag from her hand, cupped her arm, and steered her a few steps. "I'll walk you back."

"There's no need. It's perfectly safe."

"I'd feel better if you'd let me do this for you."

There was that gentlemanly streak again. The way he stood whenever she entered the locker room. The shelter of his body the night of Ford's birthday party. His obvious concern when she tried to work up the nerve to tell him about her run-in with Stroger.

He removed his hand from her elbow, but remained

close enough to keep her in a state of sexual aggrava-
tion as they weaved by slow walkers and clumps of
tourists.

They didn't talk as they headed toward her hotel.
There was so much unspoken between them, this curious energy that was a language all its own. Making
small talk would ruin it. Trying to explain it would
burden it with too much significance. She let him lead,
but within three minutes recognized that they were
heading in the wrong direction.

"I think it's that way."

"Wanted to show you something first."

A half block later, he stopped at an intricately
wrought iron gate and pressed a code into a keypad.
With a wave of his hand, he sent her ahead into a
cramped passageway. About ten feet in, they came out
into a clearing framed by a brick arch.

One of the Vieux Carre's secret courtyards.

History and atmosphere assailed her from all sides.
The courtyard's focal point was a brick-framed central
garden with a fountain urn that tied into the blue window shutters above. Cast-iron balconies covered with
ferns and late-flowering blooms that had managed to
survive the fall looked down on them. Sasanquas, holly
ferns, sweet olive, and agapanthus along with colorful annuals welcomed her into a relaxing and fragrant
atmosphere. They'd stepped through a portal into
another world.

"It's beautiful."

"*Oui, ça l'est.*" He was closer than she'd thought. "A lot of these places have hidden courtyards, secret spaces for the natives to get cool."

"So we're trespassing?"

He hesitated slightly before answering. "This belongs to a friend of mine, but he's out of town."

In her four-inch Louboutins, she picked her way over the cobblestones, imagining she was a lady of a previous century with a parasol and petticoats. The rain clouds had cleared, though the sun's brightness appeared muted in the courtyard. No street sounds intruded.

Her heart's *th-thunk* more than made up for that.

She turned to find him watching her. Gone was the playfulness he'd displayed at the shoe store; now he gave off an intensity that knocked her sideways. His beauty pained her in a delicious way. Those blue eyes had deepened to navy; his mouth had tightened in a grim seal. He looked how she felt.

Hurting with lust.

A few drops of rain fell from a cloudless sky, soon followed by more in steady succession. Chicago wasn't known for sun showers, but New Orleans was like a foreign land. Exotic. Erotic.

"C'mere," he said roughly, his hand gesturing to a doorway on the courtyard's west side. The rain fell harder as she click-clacked quickly to shelter, and she expected him to stand to her side, but instead he faced her, protecting her from the inclement weather like a human umbrella. He moved his forearm up along her cheek, a beefy bicep straining against his long-sleeved Henley. She wanted to take a bite out of it.

"I've never understood sun showers," she said, suddenly nervous. Suddenly more nervous than she had ever been in her entire life, even during the worst of times when fear had ruled. These nerves were borne of excitement, though. She knew he'd never hurt her.

"It's the devil beating his wife."

"What is?"

"The sun shower. That's how the saying goes. Like the devil's the sun's rays and his poor femme is crying her eyes out as he beats her." His eyes dropped to her mouth.

The devil beating his wife. She knew it was just an expression, but she didn't like the ball of hurt it knotted behind her breastbone.

He continued to stare at her, his gaze flickering between her mouth and her eyes.

"You cold, Harper?"

She'd started to shiver. Those memories, the damn memories.

"Your back—it must be getting wet." This apparently gave her an excuse to grip his arm and pull him a few inches closer out of the rain. It seemed the polite thing to do, even if her fingers enjoyed the hard muscle they encountered a little too much. She imagined steam rising at every droplet that met his warm skin.

"Better than you getting wet," he said.

"Such a gentleman."

He grunted, a very male sound. "If you only knew."

"You've been nothing but since the moment I met you. Mr. Polite when I enter the locker room. Protecting me when I walk down the street. Your mom raised you well."

He moved closer. Nothing gentlemanly about it, yet it was Remy, so it was protective, and she wanted to think of him this way so she wouldn't think the opposite. Of what his strength could do to her. How it could be as much a weapon as a shield.

His kiss would be protective. His body covering hers would keep her safe.

So strange to think that. So ridiculous to want it. She had been looking after herself for years, had weathered everything thrown at her, attacks both physical and emotional. She had only herself to rely on, yet Remy DuPre inspired in her something she couldn't deny.

A womanly need to be cared for.

Those blue pools still wavered between her eyes and mouth. "I'm gonna kiss you now, minou."

She might have nodded. She might have blinked. One for yes, two for *hell yeah*.

The kiss started soft, heartbreakingly so. On either side of her face, she was caged by his forearms, yet she didn't feel trapped. She felt liberated with his mouth on hers, enough that she parted her lips to drink in more of his taste, his essence. Drops of rain dripped off the gable, splashing her hands, which had risen to shape his back and pull him closer.

His kiss became more thorough, inching into her. Stealing entry, cell by cell. Or perhaps it was all her, dragging him closer, needing his heat while she claimed her freedom.

The devil's wife's tears continued to fall and so did Harper's resistance. She felt his touch, a gentle graze of his knuckles, along the jersey fabric clinging to her ribs. Her body shivered in pleasure; her nipples popped against the lace of her bra; his mouth smiled against hers.

The chain reaction of a kiss in the rain.

He cupped her ass and squeezed, bringing her closer to the erection now jutting into her belly. He wanted her to know how aroused he was, how much he wanted her.

The dress she'd worn today draped over her thighs, its loose fit making access easy, but he didn't take the easy route. He just kissed her and fondled her rear, like he was learning her shape. Making plans for later.

His tongue tangled with hers, a deliciously sensuous dance. A small moan escaped his throat and set her on a path to wildness, giving her permission to enjoy this intensely physical connection. She was wet, and not from the rain. Between her thighs, heat she'd not felt in forever bloomed, all because Remy DuPre was slowly seducing her in a secret courtyard.

Forget his name. Forget who he is. Forget everything.

She rolled her hips into his erection because she was a modern woman and pleasure was hers for the taking. The action unmoored something in him. In them both.

Suddenly they were clawing at each other's clothing below the waist, fighting to be the first to go hand to skin. Zipper down. Briefs tugged halfway off. *I'm winning!*

He refused to give her the lead. Large, rough hands hiked up her dress, kneaded her ass, and delved into her panties. Finally, finally he was touching her. *He's winning!*

But it wasn't enough, because she needed to feel all that hard perfection. She wrapped her hands around his cock and stroked.

He grunted. "Fuck."

She did it again, this time sliding from root to tip. Controlling his pleasure, and the man with it, felt so damn good. Her mouth dried up and her pussy gushed, both clearly jealous of her hand.

"Harper—dammit—let me—"

His fingers stroked through her and it was amazing, but she couldn't let him get ahead. Why should he dictate the terms? So it was expected that the woman should disintegrate first, but what if she couldn't and why should she feel that performance anxiety and—

He pushed inside her, one finger, then two, the stretch amazing, and all the while his mouth devoured and destroyed, breaking her down pulse by shivering pulse. She loved and hated what he was doing to her. The pleasure she demanded that would only be her ruin.

She cupped his invading fingers and pushed them away, out of her body. Anything to get her bearings. Then she reapplied herself to breaking him with a hard, rough stroke, her fingers circling and pumping, using his pre-come to smooth her glide.

"Merde, Harper. This isn't a fucking contest." Oh, this dangerous man had her number, and to prove it, his fingers resought her heat, outside, inside, to the depths of her soul. Just a couple of strokes sent her flying. She came apart all over his hand, a victory for her damn hormones and a defeat for Clifford Chase's daughter.

She needed revenge. She needed to see him on his metaphorical knees, because if she had to feel so weak, she wanted company on this ride to hell. Harder and harder, she pumped, stroked, raided.

"Oui, juste comme ça. N'arrêtez pas."

His gaze was sticky hot on her hand, his groans louder with every stroke until he finally let go. Unlike her reluctant orgasm, Remy's was wild, noisy, and joyful. She would expect nothing less.

She jerked back, thumping her head against the wall behind her. "Ouch." Good. She needed the jolt to sanity.

His hand was splayed across her ass, now the other cradled her head. "You okay, minou?"

Tears sprang into her eyes, and not from her argument with the wall behind her. "I'm—I'm fine." But she was far from it. She felt as if she'd lost some piece of herself, though she couldn't say what.

"Hey, it's okay, baby." He wiped a tear that had escaped despite her best attempts to restrain it. "A kiss from me shouldn't hurt." His eyes crinkled with laughter, a joke in there about how they'd done a damn sight more than kiss.

His humor froze the blood in her veins. Kisses shouldn't hurt. Men shouldn't hurt. But the devil beat his wife, and that was the way of the world.

"I—I have to go."

The rain had stopped, but even if it hadn't she would have run through floods to escape him.

He watched her with a wariness that wasn't there before. "I'll walk you back."

TWELVE

Three hours later, Harper felt a little silly for her behavior this afternoon. Things had gotten out of hand and she had acted like a frightened virgin.

That's what happened when you'd gone so long without. You panicked. Her real concern should have been this attraction she had for an employee. She'd crossed a line and it wouldn't, couldn't, happen again.

She blinked back to the tour in time to catch the tail end of a story about the ghost of Pere Claude, whose robes could be heard swishing over the mist-shrouded streets near the cathedral along with his muttered prayers. The woman leading the tour had an animated way about her—a frustrated actress, no doubt—and she clearly relished her work.

"Antoinette, mistress of a wealthy Frenchman in the early 1800s, made the mistake of falling in love with the man who kept her in great style in this fine home on Royal Street." The guide flourished a hand toward a beautiful building, dripping with history. "The

Frenchman was also in love, but marriage to a woman with one eighth Creole blood was unthinkable at that time. He asked her to prove her love—if she spent the night outside, naked as the day she was born, he would marry her. It was a cold December night, much like this one"—tonight was actually quite warm and it was November, but the crowd went with it—"and the beautiful girl's lover was sure she would come inside. But he hadn't reckoned on her desire to prove herself good enough for him. In the morning, he found his beautiful Antoinette nude and lifeless outside on her balcony."

She paused for effect, then pointed at the roof. All eyes followed her condemning finger. "Now on the coldest December nights Antoinette can be seen walking the roof, naked, wailing her love for the Frenchman who insisted she pass his harsh test."

Harper repressed an eye roll. Typical man, who couldn't appreciate his woman while she was here.

The women in the group huddled closer to the men they'd dragged with them on the tour. Typical women.

You sound like a jealous shrew, Harper. Granted, she wouldn't have minded a strong male body to curl into on a winter's night in New Orleans. If he whispered French in her ear, all the better.

"*Bonjour*, minou."

The streets were filled with ghosts, and they sounded like hot Cajun hockey players. She turned, surprised to find the fantasy wasn't of the spirit world at all. Remy stood before her like the result of some spell.

"Is there a GPS tracker in my purse?"

Eye crinkling ensued. "Just thought you might like some company."

He wore a Jimmy Buffett Fun Run 1997 ball cap pulled low over his forehead, a tan leather jacket that smelled almost as good as him, cowboy boots, and very worn jeans. Probably the same ones he'd filled out so well earlier. You know, when he was feeling her up.

More than feeling you up, naughty girl. Her star center had kissed her senseless, fondled her ass, and given her an orgasm that left her knock-kneed. In truth, she'd be a damned sight safer if she stayed the hell away from Remy DuPre. Tonight she should have just changed into her PJs, mainlined a bottle of wine, and settled in for a *Real Housewives* marathon.

The group was moving. She was not.

He gestured to the slowly departing backs. "After you."

Was it so wrong to take pleasure in his company? It so was. But if she never expressed it aloud, then it would remain her dirty little secret.

She let the group move away because frankly she wanted him to herself. Each thought in her brain was getting more wildly inappropriate by the minute. She wanted to pull him into an alley and finish what they'd started earlier. She wanted him to lift her skirt, slip a finger—two—no, three—inside her, stretching her in readiness for that thick, fat cock she'd stroked with such abandon earlier.

"Harper?" he asked again, eyeing her like he knew

exactly which lewd thoughts were running on the hamster wheel in her brain.

This was insanity. He was—oh, God. She hurried to catch up with the chaperones her untrustworthy mind and hands so obviously needed. He caught up with that easy, ground-eating stride of his.

"What brings you out on this fine evening?" she asked, endeavoring to be sociably distant.

"I haven't done one of these tours for a while. Thought it might be fun. And educational."

His presence was certainly educational for her. A warning about how she was in serious danger here.

The tour guide stopped outside a bar. "Now we have a tale that'll appeal to all you lovers out there. This former speakeasy was owned by the New Orleans mob, and the mob boss's daughter fell in love with a musician." She arced her gaze over the group, alighting briefly on Remy. Her squint said she recognized either a native son or a mooch bumming a tour. "Every night the musician would bring his lover flowers, until one night he didn't show. The mob boss had put a hit on him for daring to touch his precious daughter."

"What happened to the daughter?" one of the ladies near the front asked.

The answer surprised no one. "She killed herself. Now her spirit haunts the balcony of the club and the sweet scent of flowers lingers on the stairs."

Remy cleared his throat loudly. "Funny how all these ghosts tend to be women with an ax to grind."

The tour guide—Josette was her name—glared at Remy. "Women who've been wronged tend to be pissed off."

"Even in death, apparently," Remy said laconically.

"Wouldn't stop me," Harper said.

"Precisely." Josette pointed at Harper, as if this were a very insightful thing to say instead of a rather cheap shot at Remy's observation.

Laying a withering glare on Remy, the guide continued. "Let's move on. We've got at least three angry lady ghosts to cover."

The crowd laughed at her good humor, and as they moved away, Harper slid a glance at Remy, who was grinning outrageously. It hit her right in the lady parts.

"Happy, DuPre? You've pissed off a live woman who's probably in touch with the spirits."

"Don't you worry none. I've got a way of charming the ladies, both alive and dead."

Forty minutes later, the tour ended about two blocks from her hotel, and Harper's nerves set to a jangle again. She was going to have to negotiate an extraction from this situation, because Remy had made no move to abandon her.

Damn his manners.

As the tour guide smiled and accepted tips, Harper

fished in her purse for her wallet and plucked out a twenty-dollar bill. So it was almost as much as the tour itself, but she imagined the guides lived on gratuities, and the tour had been entertaining.

She offered the money. Josette took it and thanked her, but bristled when Remy coughed significantly.

"Problem, *couyon*?"

"Still gouging tourists, *bébête*?"

"Better than chasin' a stupid piece of rubber for forty-five minutes."

Harper split a gaze between them just as Remy stepped in and pulled the woman into his arms. "I chase that stupid piece of rubber for *sixty* minutes," he said, then added loudly, "You've put on weight."

Josette thumped him hard in the shoulder. "Is it any wonder you're still single if that's the best you can do?"

Remy turned to Harper. "My pain-in-the-ass sister Josie."

"My ugly Irish twin, Remy," Josette countered. She held out her hand to Harper. "Hope you enjoyed the tour, and if you didn't, I'd rather not know."

"She doesn't take criticism well," Remy said. "I have the scars to prove it."

Harper smiled. "Bet you deserved every one, what with your tactful tongue and all." She shook Josette's hand. "I'm Harper Chase."

Josette's eyes—cobalt blue just like Remy's, Harper now realized—flew wide. "You look taller on TV."

Harper gestured to her walking-tour-friendly wedges.

"I'm usually in heels. Besides, I think everyone looks short next to your brother."

"True. We're pretty sure the Loup Garou left him on our doorstep. Momma took pity and raised him as her own."

"The Loup Garou?"

Remy bared his teeth in a snarl. "Cajun werewolf."

Josette's phone pinged and she checked it. "Speak of the woman herself. We'd better get going. You guys need a ride?"

Remy shook his head. "I drove Dad's truck in, so we're good."

"He doesn't let me drive it!"

"Because you've crashed three cars in as many years, sis."

"It's the ghosts. They follow me around." She grinned at Harper. "Okay, see you guys soon." Off she went, leaving a gust of ghostly wind in her wake.

Remy's hand moved to her elbow, spreading warmth through her like molten lava. "Dinner plans?"

"I'm not sure it's a good idea."

He remained uncharacteristically silent.

"After what happened this afternoon," she explained. Patiently.

"When we went shoe shopping together." A cheeky lift appeared at the corner of his mouth.

She fought a smile. "Right. Shoe shopping."

"Thought I did a good job, tending to your needs." He leaned in. "Serving you."

"Stop. It."

"What?" He blasted her with that do-me grin. "Just talking about shoes."

"Remy, I can't do this." She lowered her voice to a desperate whisper. "I can't kiss you, be seen with you, have anything to do with you." Especially orgasmic things.

"Hell, Harper, we went for a walk in the historic French Quarter, took shelter from the rain, and the steamy NOLA heat got to us."

"It's November."

He ignored that. "This is a passionate town and it makes people lose their heads."

True. The phantoms of women who'd allowed their hearts to trounce common sense haunted the streets around her.

"So that's all it was? A moment of New Orleans–inspired madness?"

"Told you, it's New *Orr*-linz. I'd like to say it snuck up on us, but it's been building since we met. Somethin' had to blow."

Relief loosened her locked-up muscles. He understood. "Yes. We've let off some steam and now we can forget all about it."

He rubbed his chin, as if pondering a great question. "I dunno, Harper. It's mighty hard to unring that bell, especially now I know how goddamned beautiful you look when you come. That's kind of like locking the stable door after the orgasm has bolted. Like trying to shove the orgasm genie back in the bottle. Like—"

"Yeah, I get it." But she wasn't so sure *he* got it. This afternoon was a mistake—a sensual, erotic, crazy mistake. "Just because it happened and it felt good does not mean it has to happen again." That sounded far too encouraging, so she finished with a definitive, "And it won't."

Harper Chase had decreed it.

"Okay, I hear you," he said with a blitheness she didn't believe for a second. "Now, about dinner."

He still held her arm, and his touch was starting to burn a path of surrender all the way to places that needed to be fortressed. She refused to be another ghost statistic.

"Remy—"

"There will be chaperones present. My parents, my sisters, my nieces. So many nieces, Harper. You wouldn't believe the level of estrogen I've been contending with my entire life. Now I refuse to sit by you at the dinner table. That way, you won't be tempted to cop a feel." He held up a hand as if she'd protested. "I'm serious, femme. No more harassment. You're gonna have to find some other guy to work your sexual frustration out on."

"You're an idiot."

"A hungry idiot. Let's roll."

THIRTEEN

Sitting in his momma's parlor, Harper looked a little overwhelmed. Remy liked that look on her. Liked it a lot.

Of course it wasn't hard to be overwhelmed at a gathering of DuPres. They sure knew how to shock and awe. Take his nieces—five of them between the ages of four and eight—who were crowded around her in a horseshoe of admiration.

"Do you use rollers in your hair?"

"What color is your nail polish?"

"Do you have a boyfriend?"

"Are you as rich as Uncle Remy?"

To which Harper had answered: *Sometimes; it's called Rip Your Heart Out Red; several; and no one is.* In that order.

He was already thinking of how to use his chatterbox nieces to pump Harper for intel later, but for now he recognized that it might be a lot for their guest to take in at once. He handed her a glass of wine, to which she muttered something that sounded like, "Thank Christ."

"Mignon," he said to his seven-year-old niece, touching her freckled nose. "Would you rather hold a snake or kiss a jellyfish?"

All his nieces *ewwed* at that. It was a fun game he played with them on the road, checking in on the important issues of the day through FaceTime.

"A snake!" So pronounced Diane, who had just turned six last week and was getting mighty opinionated in her advanced age.

"All right, this question is for everyone. Would you rather be invisible or be able to fly?"

A chorus of competing answers made that one a draw. His sister Elise put her head around the door. "Would you rather set the table before dinner or clean up after?"

"Neither!" Mignon replied, the cheeky little monkey.

"You have to choose," Remy said. "Remember what I told you?"

"God hates a coward," they all sang.

"Sure does," he said. "No fence sitting allowed. How's about y'all set the table and your aunt Josette will do the dishes?" He loved nominating Josie for chores.

Happy with this arrangement, they left the room, though Diane pulled Mignon's braid on the way out, making her younger cousin squeal. He'd mention it to Elise later. Best to nip that in the bud.

"Sorry, they like to latch on to the new and shiny," Remy said to Harper.

"That's fine. I've got plenty of experience dealing with little divas, running a hockey team. And I see that 'Would you rather?' isn't limited to your contract negotiations. All part of your charm offensive?"

He studied her for a few extralong beats and cheered the watercolor bloom that crept over her cheeks. "Do you find me charming, Harper?"

"You're growing on me. Like fungus."

Evidently embarrassed by her admission, she walked over to the built-in shelves near the fireplace, weighed down with all manner of trophies. His momma kept everything he'd won from the age of nine, even his medal for placing first in debate in the tenth grade. Never try to beat a Cajun in an argument.

"Did you buy a house for your parents?"

"Come 'gain?"

She hand-waved around his family's home, a stately Greek Revival in the heart of the Garden District. "A lot of players do that. Buy a dream house for their parents or little old grandmother."

With fourteen-foot-high ceilings, floor-length windows, marble mantels, and a beautiful staircase, the house sure made an impression on any visitor. "Sorry to burst your bubble, Harper, but this house has been in the family for generations. I'm a redneck who was born into money. Then I worked my ass off to make sure I never went without the latest iPhone again."

"My deepest apologies. I didn't mean to imply you were a disadvantaged kid who fashioned your skates from old tires and trudged ten miles to hockey practice."

"It was only five miles, but uphill both ways." He grinned, and she returned his smile with interest. Something lurched in his chest. "This house was passed down through my momma's family, though they'd probably be turning in their graves if they could see her in it now. They didn't approve of her marriage to my poppa. Love across class lines, you see."

"You jest."

He leaned in. Damn, her scent, her smile, her everything made his body haywire. "Haven't got a funny bone in my body, Harper." But another bone in his body had some serious intentions toward this woman.

With an exhaled breath, she turned to the trophy display. Slender fingers, those same fingers that had milked him to release a few hours ago, reached for one of the awards.

"Is this a fucking Grammy?" She covered her mouth and looked around furtively. "Sorry, I didn't mean to say that so loud, but . . . is it?"

"Sure is. My poppa's kind of a big deal in the bluegrass-Zydeco world. Actually, he's won six, but he stows the rest in his studio."

"Wow, I've never met a Grammy winner before. Does he still make music?"

"He's been out of it for a while. When he's not touring or recording, he makes classical guitars. Real beauties. With Momma a musicology professor, Poppa always composing and playing, and my sisters being their extraspecial selves, this house has never known quiet."

He'd had the best childhood, despite the Four Horsemen, aka his sisters. Pains in his ass, every last one, especially as they'd insisted on dressing him as a girl until the age of five.

That overworked spot between Harper's eyebrows crimped. "I like the sound of that. Noisy and rambunctious, filled with music and laughter and love."

He knew enough about her situation to recognize yearning. He knew enough about his own not to allow her to reel him in with those beautiful eyes. Thankfully, his sister Martine's shout of "Dinner!" meant he didn't have to think on that too much.

Harper was usually a whiz when it came to names, but she was having a hard time remembering all of Remy's nieces. *Monique. Mignon. Diana—no, Diane.* Three of his four sisters were present; the absent one lived in Zurich with her Swiss lawyer husband. The man had not been kidding when he said he was raised by she-wolves.

But Remy DuPre pumped more than enough testosterone to compensate, and despite his promise— threat?—to sit across from her and not beside her, so she wouldn't be tempted to cop a feel, she was completely and utterly aware of him.

God, how she wanted to cop a feel.

Especially as right this minute he was involved in what had to be the hottest transaction she'd ever witnessed: speaking to his deaf fourteen-year-old niece, Sophie, using sign language. At this rate, she'd need a ciggy and a pregnancy test instead of dessert.

With great reluctance, she dragged her gaze away from Remy's fast-moving hands, the ones she imagined pulling even faster moves on her body, and applied her focus to the food. The chicken gumbo had been excellent, the bouillabaisse even better. As for the corn bread? She could live on that for the rest of her days.

Remy called out to his father. "What's this month's haul looking like, Poppa?"

Alexandre DuPre was an incredibly handsome man, though Harper suspected he was recovering from a recent illness. His features bore a hollowed gauntness she recognized from that last year nursing her mother through her ovarian cancer.

He rubbed his chin just like Remy did. "Twelve-month supply of Egg McMuffins, a case of Snapple—"

"What flavor?"

"Diet raspberry tea."

Remy made a face while his father went on. "And tickets to a Rage hockey game."

"Hell, I could get you those." Remy grinned at Harper. "Poppa likes to enter radio contests. Tenth caller wins a vacuum cleaner and lifetime supply of ShamWows, that kind of thing. He's been keeping the family in useless crap for years."

"Sounds entrepreneurial," Harper said.

Martine said, "Sounds like a cheapskate Acadian. I want in on the Egg McMuffins, by the way. You can keep the Snapple." According to Remy, she was a recently divorced lawyer and mother of Sophie, Mignon, and Milly. Or was it Molly?

"So, Harper," Mr. DuPre said, his expression suddenly grave. "What are we going to do about the Rebels?"

"Poppa, not the time," Remy said.

"Seems this is the perfect time. We've got the main stakeholders here, and as a family, I'm sure we can sort this out."

Harper might have been a touch annoyed at his presumption if Remy's mother, Marie, hadn't caught her eye and shared a conspiratorial smile. Now her DuPre-blue eyes sparkled with the same mischievous twinkle her son had down pat.

"Harper, this is standard at our table. We can't help but be in each other's business, and as we only get to see Remy once a month—"

"Twice last month," Josette said with a long-suffering sigh. "He visits more often than the Acadian relatives."

"We have to ensure his problems are resolved the best we can," Marie finished.

"Not sure Harper needs anyone to tell her how to run her team," Martine said.

Remy's father would not be so easily diverted. "Must be tough being the owner and the general manager, Harper."

"I've been your owner and general manager for forty years," Marie cut in, to which everyone shouted their agreement. "Tough ain't the word for it."

"So how did you two meet?" Harper asked, eager to throw the pack off the scent. Remy's comment about them being from different social classes had stuck with her.

"I could tell you," Marie said, "but the rest of the family tell it so much better."

"A romance for the ages," Josette offered in her tour-guide voice. "Momma was doing her PhD on Cajun music and she went to stay in Broussard while she researched her dissertation. She wanted to interview Poppa because he was a fifth-generation Acadian musician but—"

"Any time she tried to talk to him," Elise picked up, "he wouldn't say anything to her. Not a word." Elise was a stay-at-home mom, married to an oil driller who was currently stationed on a rig in the Gulf of Mexico.

Marie slid a smile of such love to her husband that Harper went a bit gooey herself. He muttered something—it sounded like French—and his hand curled around his wife's.

"Why wouldn't he talk?" Harper asked. *How rude, Harper, the man is right there.* "Why wouldn't you talk to her, Mr. DuPre?"

"Well, Ms. Chase"—a little dig because he had already asked her to call him Alexandre twice—"she was too beautiful. Every time she stood before me with her notepad and pen, my vocal cords melted."

Remy chuckled. "But his fingers worked just fine. Whenever she asked a question, he would answer with a few chords on the guitar. That's how the interviews went. Momma asking questions, Poppa answering with music."

Marie laughed, the sound youthful and filled with remembrance. "It added an extra year to my PhD. Finally, he told me all his secrets. And now I'm a grandmother, seven times over."

Everyone groaned. Harper looked around in confusion. "What?"

Martine laughed. "This is the part of the evening when Momma talks about how she loves being a *grandmère* but her life is a failure if Remy doesn't settle down soon."

So Baby DuPre was upsetting Momma's life plans.

"Well, Remy," Harper said in mock sternness. "Why are you disappointing your mother by not being married?"

"Gotta give my femme one hundred percent."

Harper raised an eyebrow. "What does that mean?"

"It means that life as a pro hockey player is not that conducive to a good home life. Am I supposed to leave my woman with a passel of rug rats at home while I get my head pounded every other night, half the time in another city? When I marry, I want to commit to it properly."

Surely that wasn't true. Plenty of players married and supported families, and none of them worried that being a road warrior made them any less of a husband or father. Remy's statement indicated a single-mindedness she would never have suspected below that easygoing facade. Neither could she help noticing he'd said *when*, not *if*.

Josette grinned. "Remy's the only guy I know who's looking forward to being pussy-whipped."

"Language, young lady," Alexandre said.

"Sorry, being a house husband and stay-at-home dad."

"Got a good role model." He shared a smile with his father. "Momma went and earned the bread playing professor while Poppa did all the real work at home."

"This is true," Alexandre said wisely. "Best years of my life whipping you kids into shape. Had to make sure you turned out sensible like me instead of flighty like your *maman*."

Harper laughed. "So that's it, Remy. You want to mold your kids in your own image."

Remy winked at her, and while normally she despised winkers, Remy DuPre could make her change her mind on that score. On a lot of scores.

"It's a pretty good image, don't ya think, minou?"

Josette had a brief coughing fit. "You're calling your boss minou?"

Harper perked up from her wink-induced lust fog. "What does that mean?"

"Kitten," Mrs. DuPre said with a curious look at her son.

"Kitten? Yeah, sometimes," Josette said. "More often it's—"

"Language, young lady." This time, the admonishment came from Remy himself. What had Josette been about to say?

Sophie nudged Remy, seeking a translation of the dinner table talk. Remy launched into a recap, using sign language again.

Harper was mighty confused, and not because she didn't understand sign language. Remy DuPre had a lot more going on than she'd previously suspected, and it was making her dangerously attracted to him.

As if she needed another reason.

FOURTEEN

"I could've taken a cab back," Harper said for the sixth time since they'd left his parents' place. "There's really no need."

"Told you, Harper, I'm staying in the Quarter."

She was nervous around him, he could tell. Well, her instincts were spot-on. He wanted to take a bite out of that luscious skin at her neck, mark her up with his werewolf fangs, and sink into her heat until he lost all sense of time and place. But he wouldn't because he was a gentleman, just like his momma raised him. And there was that annoying boss-employee problem.

"Your family's lovely." She hesitated before asking, "Is your dad ill?"

"Colorectal cancer. He had surgery last year and the prognosis is looking good. Five-year survival rate is about sixty percent." The bottom had fallen out of Remy's world when he'd heard that about Alexandre's diagnosis. Watching him deteriorate over the course of his treatment had been hell, just like seeing how he was slowly inching back to the life he knew gave Remy hope that anything was possible.

But what if his father was in the 40 percent? What if he took a turn for the worse and never saw his son hold the Stanley Cup above his head? Every pass that failed to connect, every biscuit that missed the basket, every mistake in every finals game had haunted Remy for the past twelve months. *Should've worked harder, fool.*

"They seem very happy together."

"They're lights in each other's darkness." She looked impressed, so he fessed up. "My dad wrote a song once with that lyric, and Momma likes to quote it at him during arguments."

Harper chuckled. "She plays dirty, huh?"

"Never been afraid to hit below the belt, my momma." He decided to stay on Caliborne heading back into the city instead of hitting the highway. A little longer, though he cursed the light traffic that made the journey pass too quickly.

Curiosity tickled him. Bren had mentioned Harper's mother died of ovarian cancer when Harper was seventeen. "What was your momma like?"

"Ever hopeful."

"Of what?"

"That my father would come back to her. She was a real pillow soaker." At his frown, she explained. "Cried a lot into her multiple G and Ts. That's the sound I remember most from my childhood. Quiet, desperate sobbing."

Jesus. "And you? Did you cry?"

"No," she said too quickly. "Crying over things you can't change is pointless."

Don't tell him she didn't care. She worked her ass off to make sure she'd inherit the team. There had to be some sense of wanting to impress her father there.

The moment ticked over. "I'm sure you have something to say, Remy. You always have something to say."

"Get that from Marie." He considered his next words. "Your father left your momma and married another woman. Had Isobel when you were . . . what, six?"

"Right."

"Did you see him much?"

"Barely. He wanted a son and Isobel is the closest he got. I wasn't good at sports or singular enough to win his attention, but Izzy made him proud."

"I'm sure he was proud of you, too," he said reflexively, though really he had no idea. How could any man not be filled with pride at raising a kick-ass daughter like Harper? Hell and damn, Remy was proud that this woman was *his* boss.

"He felt guilty about how he treated Mom and me, and I used it."

"His guilt?"

"Yes. Even though I wasn't an athlete, I loved hockey as a kid. I won every fantasy league I entered, knew the sport inside out, knew I'd make a great scout or GM. My father felt guilty about abandoning me for his new family, so he let me intern during summers in college and gave me an entry-level job after graduation. He hoped the all-male environment would chill my enthusiasm. But it didn't. I thrived because it's what I was meant to do. And now I'm going to fix the mess he made and get our team to the playoffs."

He laughed. "Go, Rebels."

"You don't believe me?"

"I believe you think you can. But I have to wonder what your dad had in mind dividing the team in that way."

She made a small noise of disgust. Clearly still a sore spot. "My father had a twisted sense of humor. He never believed I could run the team, and this was his way of setting me up to fail."

Remy's experience of Clifford Chase was of a gruff, overbearing ass who had the best head fake in the game. Expertise often substitutes for personality in professional sports.

"It'll take time to get the team there, and in the meantime, it might bring you closer to your family."

Harper did that frowning thing again. "Or destroy us."

Or that.

He rounded the corner at Royal Street and pulled up into the alley behind his place. "The hotel is a couple of blocks from here. I'll park and then we can walk if you're up for it."

"Think I can handle that."

Within two minutes they were back on the street after parking the truck. A few steps in, and she looked around. "Hold up, isn't this the same street we were on earlier? Where the secret courtyard is?"

"Where I"—teasing pause—"kissed you?"

She turned her head slightly. "I thought we agreed not to talk about that."

"I don't remember agreeing to that. And yes, this is the same street. That's my place in the city."

She stopped and faced him. "You never said. Why not?"

"Because then I would have been obliged to invite you inside, seein' as how I'm a gentleman and all, and we both know where that would have led."

"With you boring me with your hockey stick collection?"

He smiled, enjoying her take on it. "Yep, you'd have been bored senseless, Harper."

The look she gave him was a full-on smolder. *Baby, do not look at me that way. I cannot be responsible for my actions.*

As much as he wanted to fuck Harper Chase—properly—he recognized that she had a whole lot more to lose than he did. She had a hard enough time getting respect as it was; add rumors of a fling with one of her players into the mix and she'd be crucified.

Unless they could keep it to one night . . . but Remy suspected that one night with this woman would never be enough. He was already a horny wreck from feeling her clamp on his fingers, her hand loving his cock. A taste of more would fuel a fire he might not be able to put out.

They continued on in silence, a foot or so apart that felt like a mile. He wanted to hold her hand. Dumb as dirt, he knew, but that's what he wanted. The underlying current of energy was thick and charged.

Something was building in his chest, a tightness that wouldn't be eased until he took action. Just before they turned the corner onto Canal, he grasped her elbow and steered her into the shadows. Her breath hitched, her breasts with it, and he bent in nice and close. Big mistake. That heady scent of Harper and the forbidden invaded his nostrils.

"What are you doing?"

"I need you to know something, Harper."

She didn't respond, just stared up at him with those big storybook-character eyes, and he got so lost in them that this thing he needed her to know fled his brain.

What the hell was it? Oh, right. The words took a moment to form, stuck in his throat with his heart. "I need you to know that if you weren't who you were and I wasn't who I was, this would be happening."

"I understood about every third word there."

For Chrissakes, DuPre. Explain. Better.

He tried again. "We should be in my bed right now. I should be kissing your breasts, sucking your nipples, tasting your honey. I should be sinking inside you slow and hot and so deep that you'll be begging me to make it fast, then make it last. I should be feeling your sweet grip on my cock, and I bet you grip hard, Harper, 'cause you're the kind of woman who takes no prisoners. I should be squeezing that gorgeous ass of yours while I pump in and out, looking for that spot that'll light you up. I need you to know that in another universe, this would be a done deal, and the only thing stopping me from making you mine is that in *this* universe, my current employment situation stops me from making good on all the dirty things I'm dying to do to you. You understand?"

She opened her mouth but nothing came out. Seemed about right. Nothing she said could make this better.

With great difficulty, he removed himself from her space. "Let's get you back."

What he really meant was "Let's get you safe." Safe from the chill that was moving in off Lake Pontchartrain. Safe from the standard drunken revelry of a French Quarter evening. Safe from him.

At the entrance to the Marriott, they stopped.

"Well—"

"Thanks—"

At talking over each other, they both smiled, a little ruefully.

"I had a lovely time at dinner, Remy."

Was that regret shining in those big eyes of hers? More likely, that was wishful on his part, but he preferred to think not. She should come home with him. All those things he'd told her they should be doing—well, they *should* be doing them. He opened his mouth to tell her so, to hell with the consequences. "Harp—"

"—per!"

Another voice finished Remy's rusty utterance of her name. He turned to see Kenneth Bailey walking toward them with a sweater over his shoulders, the sleeves tied together. Remy didn't think anyone did that outside of *Archie* comics.

Harper inched away from Remy, subtle to anyone else, but blindingly obvious to him.

"Kenneth, I wasn't expecting you."

The lawyer had the balls to kiss her right in front of Remy. Only on the cheek, but still. His inner werewolf bared his fangs, but somehow Remy kept his snarl on the down low.

"Thought I'd surprise you. I'd hoped to get here in time for dinner but my flight was delayed." He looked at Remy, immediately dismissive in an oh-right-just-one-of-the-jocks kind of way. "DuPre, how are you?"

"Just fine, Bailey."

"The bar is nice and cozy, Harper," Kenneth said, having decided Remy was no longer worth his consideration. Remy had to give it to him. Guy was smooth as slime. "How about a nightcap?"

That should have been Remy's cue to leave, but a perverse part of him waited for a dismissal. Not from Bailey but from her.

Harper turned to Remy, super cool. "Thank you for walking me back, Remy. Like I said, I had a lovely time tonight."

That's right, Bailey. Stick that in your four-hundred-dollar loafers and kick it.

But as nice as it was to hear Harper affirming she'd spent the evening with him, it didn't quite make up for the fact she would not be spending the rest of it in his bed. Bailey had her now—for a nightcap.

Maybe more.

Christ.

Before his inner werewolf could go berserk, Remy gave a curt nod and headed off into the ghost-ridden shadows.

Remy slammed the door to what his Realtor had called a pied-à-terre and threw his keys on the foyer table.

Fuck.

Fuck fuck fuck.

He stalked to his liquor cabinet, whipped out the very expensive Willett Distillery bourbon he kept on hand for when he lost the Cup, and poured a triple. No wonder she'd looked at him like he had a million heads and every one of them belonged to a couyon: he had just made a pass at his boss, the same boss who was in a relationship with someone else.

Fucking Kenneth Bailey.

But she let you do more than make a pass this afternoon, DuPre.

Probably just caught up in the moment. He'd cornered her in a secret courtyard. He'd strong-armed her into coming to dinner. He'd pretty much told her she was a constant on his mind.

She was with someone else. It should have been a relief, because he couldn't have her anyway, and this was just the universe affirming it. How petty would it be to begrudge Harper's happiness with another man when she was so out-of-bounds to him?

Petty didn't even *begin* to describe it.

Remy wanted her. She was already *his* in his head, and but for the employment situation—and her current relationship status with the lawyer—he would be making good on his claim. He sure as hell didn't want Kenneth Bailey to get what was rightfully his.

He took a deep slug of his drink, barely noticing the burn as it trickled down his throat.

This was not how Remy approached the fine art of wooing. Truth be told, he didn't usually have to struggle because he'd always chosen easy. Likewise, his natural talent on the ice meant he didn't work as hard as he should have in his youth, and maybe that was why he'd come up short so many times in the late season. After the first close-but-no-cigar, you always assume there'll be another shot or else you couldn't get out of bed in the morning. Remy'd had another three shots. With each passing year and no joy, he had to wonder if there was some truth to that "unluckiest guy in the league" label. The Susan Lucci of hockey, the sports media joked. But even Susan had eventually won an Emmy.

Getting older meant he had to put in the extra hours to keep up, to make his dream come true. But that didn't mean he had to work harder for a woman, did it?

What was he doing setting his sights on a woman who was his boss and, at the same time, so unlike his usual diet? Harper wasn't one-night-stand material. But neither was she the kind of woman he had in mind for his posthockey life. He needed a femme who wanted a family and was ready to be part of Team DuPre. Harper didn't fit that description. Her own family was a mess and her teamwork skills were somewhat lacking.

So not one night, not the long haul. Some happy medium, perhaps? Not that it mattered, because she was with the lawyer *and* she was his boss.

Fuck.

He needed a shower. He needed to wash the failure of this day away and he needed to get drunk.

Stripped, he stepped under the tepid water with a bottle of booze while he fisted the tile and slugged away. The water and the bourbon should have put a significant damper on his hard-on, but alas, no. He could still feel the imprint of her sweet body against his, a memory stamped on his brain from this afternoon's orgasm in the rain. His rain-forest shower head was reminding him in the worst possible way, and her sexy scent haunted him like the ghosts of the Quarter.

But the phantoms weren't done with him yet. Harper's bombshell voice echoed, whispering sweet, filthy orders in his ear.

I don't care that you're my player. I don't care that I'm your boss. It's all wrong, but it's the best kind of wrong. I need you inside me now, Remy.

Another slug of bourbon and his hand found its way to his cock.

But the grip felt inadequate, a pale imitation, because it wasn't hers. Fantastic. Jerking off, the last thing he had going for him, and she'd ruined it. He turned off the shower and stepped out, grabbing a towel to swipe at the body that had decided to betray him.

Give me an orgasm. It's the least you can do.

Neck deep in his misery, he barely heard the buzzer. One of the hazards of living in the Quarter was how revelry quickly became bedmates with idiocy. Drunks out on the town. Ding, dong, ditch, NOLA style.

It went again, more urgent this time.

He took another slug and pushed thoughts of Harper Chase from his mind. He'd get drunk. Very drunk . . . and play like shit tomorrow. That'd teach her.

Buzzzzzz!

After making short work of the few feet to the intercom, he slammed the talk button hard. "If you know what's good for you, you'd better be gone by the time I get down there."

A slight pause, then a barely audible, "Okay."

His heart exploded in his chest, just upped and boomed.

Harper. That was Harper.

He pushed the entry button, then the talk one again. "Harper? Don't leave. Merde . . . just don't, okay?" He threw open the door and sprinted five steps down, then twenty feet through the courtyard toward the gate.

Harper was framed in the passageway with some sort of halo above her head. So it was the security light shining right down on her blond waves, but his fevered imagination saw an angel descended to earth.

Lord, take me now.

Two things happened simultaneously: Harper's eyes went wide, and Remy realized he was cold. Both of these things were related.

He'd answered the door completely naked.

And his boner was back, urgent as ever, though he wondered how long that would last because it was pretty fucking chilly out here.

"I've interrupted something," she said, her gaze greedily roving his still-damp body.

"Only a pity party in my shower."

She swallowed audibly, and just that sliver of vulnerability had him ready to fall to his knees for her. She was here, yet he had the distinct feeling that rushing her would be bad. This woman was like a highstrung filly that needed gentling and every ounce of TLC he possessed.

"Minou, talk to me."

A shallow breath was followed by . . . another shallow breath. Before he could worry about which would happen first—Harper's panic attack or his dick dropping off like an icicle—she spoke, her voice scarcely above a whisper.

"I shouldn't be kissing you. I shouldn't be touching and licking and stroking your hard body. I shouldn't be begging you to take me all night long. I shouldn't be fantasizing about the player I signed to save my team and career because this could be the very thing that tanks my team and career."

His sexy little minou was hurting, and the only cure was the thing that might destroy them both.

She snatched a breath. "I can't give more than what you see. I can't give more than a few hours. So, Remy DuPre, would you rather have one night exploring this thing between us or a whole lifetime never knowing what it was like to feel so good?"

"Harper," he ground out. And then she was in his arms, the way it wasn't supposed to be, but the only way that made sense. Greedy lips met in a torrent of hunger as they melted into each other, her mouth on his so amazing he could die. His hands strayed to her ass and bound her close to make sure she was real and could never, ever leave.

She had come to him. Made the decision, and that meant more to him than every goal he'd ever scored.

He drew back an inch. "What about Bailey? As much as I want you, Harper, I won't trespass on another man's territory."

"Bailey?" she panted, her eyes glazed, her lips puffy from his kiss. "Oh, Kenneth. That's nothing."

"Nothing as in 'we have an agreement' nothing, or nothing as in 'we're not together' nothing?"

"Nothing as in 'in no universe would I ever date or sleep with Kenneth Bailey' nothing."

"Thank fuck." He picked her up, hitched her around his hips, and covered her mouth with his.

"You're wet," she said.

"Not as wet as you'll be soon."

"Already there, DuPre."

Sweet Jesus. With a deep groan, he carried and kissed her into his pied-à-terre, but the whole situation might very well be Harper-à-terre, because there was a fair to middling chance he was going to do her on the floor of his living room. He slammed the door shut with his foot, still kissing, still marveling that she had come to him. She'd left the hotel and walked the streets—*shit.*

"You should have called me to pick you up."

"It was only a few blocks." She licked her lips. "All

the ghosts of New Orleans had my back. This is a town that roots for forbidden passion, you know."

That it was.

"You taste of bourbon, Remy. Top quality."

A woman who knew her liquor. How did the unluckiest guy in the NHL suddenly have fortune shine on him so brightly? "I'd planned to get shitfaced and made a head start in a cold shower. Leaving you behind did not sit with me well."

"Already driving you to drink *and* pneumonia?" She grinned, pleased with herself. "Sounds like my job here is done."

"Your job here is far from done. Got plenty of tasks in mind for tonight."

She licked the corner of his mouth and made a little moaning sound. Oh, Christ, he was not going to last. "Give me the tour."

He was definitely not going to last.

He spoke as he walked—very, very quickly. "You saw the courtyard. Front door. Living room. There's probably a kitchen and a couple of bathrooms." At the door of the most important room in the house tonight, he halted. "Bedroom."

"Nice. I'd buy."

He placed her sitting on the bed and jackknifed to his knees between her legs. "You sure about this?"

"Looking for an excuse to back out, DuPre?"

"You, here, in my bed, Harper. Never wanted anything more in my life." Shit, that sounded way more serious than he'd intended. But it was true. She didn't need to be *as* into him, but he needed her to be sure.

She looped both hands behind his neck and brushed his lips in a tease. "I could be curled up in my hotel room with an indifferent scotch, scouting reports, and tapes of last week's game, but I'm not. I know this is crazy. I know this is dangerous. I'm not a crazy or dangerous person. But I want you. I want to feel what I suspect only you can give me."

That was all—no, more than—he needed to hear. He would give her a night she'd never forget, and then tomorrow . . .

Best not to think of tomorrow. Assume this was a one-shot deal, a product of crazy NOLA-inspired passion. Assume they were different people, inhabiting the bodies of strangers.

Strangers who wanted to fuck each other raw and senseless and forget the world outside their courtyard.

FIFTEEN

Crazy. Dangerous. Apt words for this situation, more than apt words for Remy. But Harper couldn't stay away. Kenneth's surprise visit had toggled something on in her brain. The man clearly wanted more, and here she was sitting on the fence, letting him think she would eventually come around.

She wouldn't, not to Kenneth, so she needed to be straight with him. Straight with herself. What had Remy said to his nieces? *God hates a coward.* She was so tired of sublimating her desires, throwing herself into the team instead of taking something for herself. As Kenneth tried to persuade her to go to the bar, all she could think of were Remy's words about how things would be different if they were different people. And then there were all those gloriously filthy things he wanted to do to her.

She thought she could withstand the sensual onslaught that was this man, but it turned out she was only human after all. She could no more deny herself this than stop her heart from beating. And she wanted it to beat in unison with Remy's . . . while they got down and dirty. .

"I need to see you properly," she said. "Stand up."

He stood, a tower of unrepentant masculinity, unclothed and unabashed. Seeing him rush out his door naked, his fear of her leaving overriding his worry about public decency, she had almost collapsed in a puddle of lust. And now? His absolute beauty awed her. Every ridge defined. Every muscle hard earned.

As her gaze moved south, she swallowed.

Whoomp! There it is.

Though she'd felt him in her hands earlier, seeing the full package attached to this huge bear of a naked man gave her pause. He was big, both as big as and bigger than she expected. Something must have flickered in her expression, because he rested a finger under her chin and tilted her gaze to his.

"You okay, minou?"

A little stalling was in order. "Why do you call me that? Kitten?"

"Because I love that voice of yours. It's a bombshell voice, the kind that makes a man itch to touch and rub himself all over the body it belongs to. When I heard you first, I thought 'sex kitten,' and I guess the name stuck."

"I speak and you think of sex?"

"You exist and I think of sex."

Holy whoa. Her eyes dipped to his cock, which was

showing no signs whatsoever of flagging. Not that she wanted it to, but maybe if it was less brazen . . .

"Your sister said it meant something else."

Another wicked grin. "Kitty or . . . pussy."

"Oh." Every time he'd said it, that was on his mind. And he'd said it a helluva lot of times.

"That's not very appropriate."

He lifted her off the bed by the upper arms and pulled her flush against him. All of him. "No, but then none of this is, now is it? It's a little bit wrong and a whole lot forbidden. Let's not pretend the taboo ain't part of the rush." He tilted his head. "Like I said, you can back out anytime . . . minou."

He rolled his tongue over it, extra-Frenchifying it, making it sound as dirty as the word's intent. Now that she knew what he meant by that seemingly innocuous endearment, she was a complete goner.

The two men she'd slept with in the past three years were slight in build, as far as you could possibly get from a powerful, muscled athlete. One of them had packed a peanut below his belt; the other guy's enthusiasm didn't quite make up for his lack of skill. After the disaster that was Stroger, she'd chosen with deliberation, careful to avoid men who could overwhelm her.

So much for that pattern, because Remy DuPre defined overwhelming. Every feminine sense flared, hyperaware of his blatant virility. Blood rushed hot and needy through her veins, neurons tingled in anticipation, and cells exploded from dullness to glitter.

"I'm not backing out, but it's been a while and I'm—I'm out of practice."

What if she was as frigid as Billy Stroger had accused her of? If she couldn't live up to the bombshell-sex kitten voice? Remy moved his lips to the curve of her neck, raising gooseflesh in the trail of his kiss. "Fine by me. We can discover each other at a pace that'll work for both of us. Now I assume your lack of practice is the only reason I'm naked and you're still wearing clothes."

"Clothes usually come off?" she teased, enjoying his humor as much as his touch. She'd never really considered sex fun, but with Remy she might emerge from this with a new worldview. "Is that how it's done these days?"

He chuckled. "I'm not a 'quickie with my pants on' kind of guy. A night in my bed is usually sweaty, deep, and very hands-on." He demonstrated hands-on by unzipping her Tory Burch dress, his finger pads touching each inch of skin he revealed. She felt like a treasure under his care. He slipped the dress off her shoulders and held her hand as she stepped out of it. She kicked off her comfy wedges.

"Next time, wear the heels, Harper. The ones you bought today."

Next time. As this was a onetime event, it was easy to agree and at the same time make him just a little bit wild. "Heels and nothing else."

He groaned and captured her mouth with his, stealing her nerves, mating his tongue with hers in a way she knew mirrored how it would feel with him moving deep inside her. Unlike this afternoon in that court-yard, she met his invasion with no resistance, just a ready acceptance. Within seconds she was lying on the bed in her demi-bra and satin thong with this huge hulk leaning over her. Remy's cock pulsed against her thigh, though he remained on his knees, keeping his weight off her.

"You're so tiny, minou," he murmured, his ravenous gaze taking stock of her body clad in rose-blush lace. True, she was petite everywhere—small breasts, slim hips, an ass he could likely cover with one vast palm. Nothing bombshell about her figure, yet she felt so desirable while his eyes stoked fire all over her body. He followed up with his hands. First the side of her breast, then the flare of her hip. Coasting a palm over her ass, he squeezed, like he was assessing her ability to take him deep inside her.

As he continued his erotic scrutiny, his erection appeared to surge, growing inch by mouthwater-ing inch. It tapped against her thigh, demanding her attention.

"You know how I hate to give you any encourage-ment whatsoever, DuPre, but that cock of yours is . . ."

"Keep goin'."

"Slightly above average."

"'Slightly' ain't a word ever used in the same sen-tence as my dick." He notched in between her legs, the only barrier the satin shield of her panties, and stroked along every sensitive nerve ending.

"You were sayin'?"

She grasped for the power of speech. "I'm—I'm trying to tell you that it's been a while. I'm going to be tight, and this concerns me."

He stilled and gentled her jaw, holding her in place for his soul-searing gaze. "You understand that I'd never hurt you, baby?"

That's not what she'd been angling for, but the moment he spoke, she realized that maybe she'd been pushing for some small assurance. Of course he wouldn't hurt her. He was the perfect gentleman, a man with values and a devotion to his family, a guy who wanted to give himself 100 percent to a woman and his children further on down the road. And while all these things should have put her mind at ease, it was his soothing words she absorbed into her heart.

"Take my panties off, Remy. Now."

She made a move to help, but he gently swatted her hands away. "I'll take care of that. I'll take care of you."

Tears stung. *Stupid, Harper. Stupid, stupid.* Struck dumb, all she could do was nod and watch and anticipate as he unhooked her bra and threw it onto the floor. Here was the true test. She searched his face for disappointment.

His eyes darkened at the sight of her small breasts. Her Cajun werewolf growled.

"*Très jolie.*" Her nipples budded for him, straining to

be sucked, and his mouth drew one to an even harder peak. Licks and sips spiraled her pleasure while he removed her panties. Multitasker? She loved that. His wicked mouth trailed down to her stomach, her belly, her hips. Nothing was beneath his interest.

"We're going to take it slow," he whispered against her core. "So no rushing me, oui?"

"Are you talking to me or my . . . uh, minou?"

"Tonight, this is where your brain is gonna be, Harper." He heeled his hand over the neatly trimmed strip of hair between her thighs, spreading her wide, then dragged up in a dirty grind. The sensation of that rough palm was indescribable. "I get the impression you're kind of bossy, and while we can work with that later, for now you're gonna trust me to take care of your pleasure. No fightin' me like you tried earlier today."

"I'm—I'm not bossy." *I'm your boss.* And how sharp of him to understand what was going through her mind in that courtyard.

His grin was devilish, his fingers positively fiendish as he set up a soft, tantalizing stroke through her hungry minou. Then he pulled them away.

She rolled her hips, chasing the sensation. "Nooo!"

"That's what I mean. Impatient." A slight brush of his thumb against her clit crossed several wires in her brain. The man was an outrageous tease. "By the time I'm finished, Harper, you'll be begging my slightly above average cock to sink deep and give you what you need."

"There's always the chance I'll fall asleep first."

"Sarcasm won't make me move faster."

Both hands caressed her thighs and separated them. He watched her for an infernally long time as she slickened under his predatory gaze. *Please. Oh, please.*

The first touch of his tongue lifted her clear off the bed. She was levitating!

Strong hands pinned her hips while his mouth spared no expense in getting her primed. And those hands. So big, so coarse, so perfect against her sensitive skin. While his tongue explored all the ways to make her wet—dipping, licking, spearing, who knew there were so many?—his palms wandered over her slight frame. In no way voluptuous, she didn't possess the body type men went wild for, but that didn't seem to matter to Remy. His hands roved, finding curves she didn't know existed, his appreciation reframing everything she'd thought about how her body could give and experience pleasure.

Ignoring her female needs had been necessary before, but tonight she would revel in the feeling of being wanted in this primal way. Tonight she would revel in Remy.

Remy loved eating a woman out.

He loved her taste, her sounds, that squirm she got in her hips that told him she was digging it as much as he was. Mostly he loved the power he felt coursing through his veins terminating in a steel-hard dick, the euphoric rush that lit up every cell like he'd just top-shelfed a goal in a big game. *This mouth can take you places, chérie. This tongue can send you on a one-way trip to paradise.* Making a woman feel so good boosted him up.

But tonight felt different. Seemed he'd been playing for the farm team this entire time.

He'd never met a woman who needed to be fucked as badly as Harper Chase. Who needed to be kissed thoroughly, eaten out professionally, and screwed so deep she couldn't walk until playoff season. All that would happen; he just hadn't reckoned on how his own limits would be tested.

Opening her up kiss by kiss, lick by lick, Remy was not only feasting on the sexiest woman he'd ever tasted, he was learning what made Harper tick. Knowing her as he did, he couldn't help his awe at her coming to him. She was risking everything: her professional reputation, her ethical boundaries, that tough-girl mask she wore so well. And Remy loved unlocking her. Loved how every lick through her sweet, sweet *minou* had her panting his name and straining for more.

On the topic of straining . . . he was harder than a honeymoon dick. He'd never had problems waiting a woman out, but there was a real chance he was going to explode before she did, and the idea of that happening outside the snug confines of her tight body was a prospect he did not enjoy.

He needed in. He needed to feel that sweet suction, her orgasm milking him to release. But he'd also promised he'd take it slow.

Dilemma, table for one.

Lifting his head, he met her lust-stoked gaze. "Harper, I have to—" He licked his lips, needing one more hit of her taste. "Inside you. I need to be inside you."

Could you eye roll and keep those same eyes heavy-lidded with lust? This woman proved that indeed you could. "Then stop talking about it, DuPre."

Yes, boss. He grabbed a condom from the side table drawer, and when he turned back, the beautiful sight would have knocked him on his ass if he weren't already lying down. Against the pillow, Harper, glorious Harper, her blond waves fanned out, her hand resting on the curve of her abdomen—and creeping lower.

"Not sure I can wait," she whispered before stroking a finger through her glistening pussy. Holy fuck. Watching her part her folds, her swollen clit peeking out to say hello, almost undid him there and then.

"That's right. Keep good 'n' wet for me." He secured the condom and, leaning up on one elbow, lay between her thighs. "I'll go slow. I promise."

Desire clouded her eyes as he nudged the broad head of his cock at her entrance. He rubbed a little, enjoying the sleek glide of the sensitive tip as it met all that feminine softness. He dropped a kiss on her parted lips, and running his tongue along the inside, drew a rusty moan. Then the irresistible pull of that spot where they were almost joined won out as they both stared at her fingertips working herself in hot, sultry strokes around his cock.

"Take it, Harper. Take it all."

He could have done it. Notched, nudged, and plunged deep, but he wanted her to invite him inside her body, for this final decision to belong to her. Control was important to this woman, and he was happy to let her have it in this way that would bring them both higher.

One hand spread herself wide, and with the other, she gripped his cock and positioned it right where they both needed it. That wet heat sucked him in an inch, and then she was arching up and he was pushing in, and it was the hottest, sweetest fuck of his life before it had even started.

Two inches in and he thought his cock would explode. Three inches in and he thought he was going to die. Then this shit happened:

"Stop," she whispered.

He stopped. His heart stopped. The whole damn world stopped.

She squeezed and gave an evil, *your-cock-is-mine* giggle.

He should never have answered the door.

"Remy, how long do you think—?"

"Harper!"

Chuckling, she cupped his jaw, drawing a fingertip in a sensuous line along his cheek, before kissing him softly. "Thank you." And then she grasped his ass, locked her legs around his hips, and pulled him until he was buried to the hot hilt.

A loud groan echoed in the room, a heavenly chorus as the two of them became one at last.

"Jesus, that's—" He had no words to describe exactly what that was. Sweat sheened on her forehead and her eyes fluttered to half-mast, drugged on the sensation they were creating. He needed to move, but he needed to ensure her pleasure first.

He dragged out a few inches then pumped again. Slow, rhythmically, each thrust making his mark and focused on one goal.

Making this woman his.

Somehow he was still able to form sentences. "You with me, Harper?"

"If I was any more with you, I'd *be* you. More, please. More."

He raised his body and angled his thrusts so each return of his cock gave her the friction she needed.

"Yes! Oh, God, yes!"

But that wasn't enough. He'd promised her a slow, sexy screw, and though it killed him a little, he whispered against her mouth, "Stop," before he slipped out and rolled onto his back.

"Remy! What the hell?"

His cock throbbed and his balls felt as large as his

ego, yet he had an unaccountable urge to laugh his head off. "I'm not as young as I once was, baby."

She growled, setting off a vibration all over his body. "Do you need to take a break? Or maybe you're expecting me to do all the work?"

"I'm expectin' you to get that sweet ass over here and take what belongs to you." He was feeling more energetic than he had in years, but he liked the idea of a little tit for tat—not to mention switching up the power dynamic.

"You've got some nerve, DuPre," but she was laughing as she straddled him and held herself suspended over his body for a second. Then she sank down with a lusty moan.

Fucking A. "Now ride me, minou."

Oh, she liked that. Mesmerized, he watched as the last flickers of hesitancy fled those glittering green eyes. She started to move, slipping up and down his cock, loving it with every inch of her soft, sexy body. Harper on top was wild, uninhibited, a queen demanding her due. Making it good for her made it perfect for him.

With each rock into her body, his heart beat faster and his brain cells disintegrated in clumps until he was a mindless mass of muscle and sinew and skin. The sexy, sweet talk devolved to urgent demands as their bodies figured out the only way this conversation could end.

"Là . . . juste là . . ."

"Good, so good . . ."

"Plus vite, ma belle . . ."

"Oh, God, oh, God, oh—"

At last she screamed, not for God, but for Remy as her orgasm gripped her along with his hardworking cock, which in all actuality should've been destroyed by now.

Good thing he came from hearty sixth-generation Acadian stock, because his people knew pleasure in all its forms. How to create it, appreciate it, take it as their right. And that he did, letting it pull him hard and deep, using Harper's aftershocks to fuel a release so explosive he might have worried whether he'd recover in time to play tomorrow.

Except his boss would probably have something to say about that.

Wrung dry, his brain a lust-mush, he stayed lodged deep and pulled her down over his chest. He needed to feel the heat and heart of her close to his skin.

"Think you might've broken my dick." Gently, he kissed her temple and enjoyed the soft flutter of her laugh against his neck. "You remember what I told you back in the Philly locker room?"

Her voice emerged passion-rusty. "That I'd better not welsh on our deal?"

"The other thing."

"Oh, right. *'I might sound like I spend my spare time spit-ballin' from the rockin' chair on my porch, but don't let my accent fool you none. I'm not the kind of man you want for an enemy.'"* She recited it with a yee-haw twang that earned her a gentle pinch on that cute ass of hers.

"Hey!"

He stroked her cheekbone, loving her postorgasm dishevelment. "What I *said* in that locker room was, this was gonna be fun."

"When does this fun start, DuPre?" She grinned, and then they were kissing, deep and wet and sexy, having more fun than he could recall since he'd lost his virginity to Juliet Depuis in the St. Ignatius High art supplies room at the tender age of fifteen. And that had lasted all of fifty-four seconds.

"No regrets, minou?"

"Ask me tomorrow." She slipped off him, and he held on to every sensation to store away for later.

Ten seconds was all it took to dispose of the condom in the bathroom. Harper used at least seven of those to sit up and reach for her panties.

"Don't even think about it, femme."

"I should get back."

He cut off that ridiculous argument by wrestling her back under the covers. Thankfully, she didn't put up much of a fight. "I'll accompany you on your walk of shame before sunup. But for the rest of this night, you're mine."

With a sigh of acquiescence, she melted into his body.

SIXTEEN

"Why the fuck are there so many little girls in the locker room?"

Remy frowned at Cade's question, but because he was largely responsible for the presence of this gaggle of girls, he couldn't really defend himself. Fortunately, they'd invaded after everyone showered and dressed.

"My sisters and nieces."

Cade laid his hand on Remy's shoulder. "This explains a lot."

"Fuck you," he muttered, then turned on his noncursing mouth to smile at his five-year-old niece, Colette.

"Uncle Remy, you kicked butt on the ice!"

He cupped her freckled cheek. Damn, he couldn't wait to have little ones of his own. "I sure did, chérie. Glad you caught me on a good night."

More like an amazing night. The puck was as big as a dinner plate, his eyes tracking Grand Canyon–sized gaps through the defense, crafting perfect angles like he'd majored in geometry.

Waking up alone after the best sex of his life would normally have put a stutter in his skate, but not today. That great sex with a hot woman—who admittedly he should be skating away from—had left him feeling so good that not even her sneak-out this morning could dull the experience.

Sure, he'd been disappointed. Then he'd read her note.

That note had cheered him right the fuck up because in it he sensed her fear, and while that shouldn't make him happy, it did. She was frightened because it was that good.

Remy, the note had said. *Last night was wonderful, but I really need to get back to the hotel. Have a great game!*

See? Terrified.

Meanwhile, back in the real world, his sisters were currently ogling everything within ogling distance, never mind that two of them were happily married. Hardly an example to set for his nieces. He pulled on his suit jacket and entered the fray.

"Where's Poppa?" he asked Marie, who was trying to restrain Mignon from folding dirty towels. This was his niece's latest. Tidying up.

"You know he has to watch the game in the bar. He's probably buying rounds for everyone after your performance." His father drove his momma nuts when they watched the games together because he liked to shout at the screen. Marie touched Remy's cheek, and they shared something unspoken. The past year

had been tough on this woman, the DuPre pillar of
strength. Now that he had his mojo back, Remy was
more determined than ever to bring home that hardware.

"Bar? Did I hear a bar mentioned?" Jorgenson
stepped forward and held out his hand to his mother.
"You must be Remy's sister."

"Marie DuPre," his momma said, allowing Fish to
kiss her knuckles while Remy rolled his eyes. "And yes,
we're headed to a local bar. Good food, music." She
turned to Remy. "Your father will pretend he doesn't
want to sing."

Yep, that sounded like Poppa. The cancer had stolen
his joy in music, but in the last couple of months, it
had returned by bars and chords. Erik called out to the
team. "Guys, Remy is buying drinks at his sister's bar."
He cocked his head at Remy. "Lead the way."

Remy sighed. "I'll meet you outside." As soon as his
woman showed.

His skin tingled, awareness creeping over him. *About
time.*

She stood at the door in her usual hot-shit suit,
tonight's version a navy pinstripe over a pink blouse
that would look better on the floor of his apartment.
Her hair was piled up on her head, held together with
what looked like a chopstick but on closer inspec-
tion was a tiny hockey stick. There was a whimsy to it
he would never have associated with Harper. His gaze
took inventory, moving down, down—damn, she was

wearing those red shoes, the ones he'd put on her feet like some freaky-deaky Prince Charming.

Strutting in, she didn't spare him a glance. "Gentlemen, great game tonight. Coach Calhoun and I couldn't be prouder."

Murmurs of thanks floated through the locker room. As she walked in his direction, he braced with his best we-didn't-sleep-together face, but she did a fine job of passing over him, instead speaking to his momma. "Marie, you left your purse in the box."

"Oh, thanks, Harper," his mom said before she spied one of his nieces getting a little too familiar with a jock strap. "Jeanette, put that down." She took off to wrestle the offending garment from the girl's innocent hands.

Remy eyed the team's owner. "Ms. Chase."

"Mr. DuPre. You played well tonight." She slid a furtive glance left and right, and seeing they were unobserved, said, "We should talk."

"Or we could pass notes back and forth."

She grimaced. "About that . . ."

"It's okay, Harper. This is dicey and you have to be careful. We both do."

Relief relaxed her shoulders. "Thanks for understanding. A pleasant diversion that can't be repeated."

Before he could protest, one of his nieces popped up like a whack-a-mole and stared at Harper in awe. *Yep, know what that's like.* "Colette, go find your grandmère."

"Oh, she's fine right here," Harper said, placing her hands on Colette's shoulders and moving behind her.

Using his niece as a human shield? For shame.

Leaning in, he inhaled this woman's sexy scent and whispered, "I'd say it was a bit more than a pleasant diversion, wouldn't you?"

"Perhaps," she conceded begrudgingly.

"That will be repeated."

Her eyes flew wide in shock. "Are you kidding? We can't—"

He peered down at his niece. "Colette, chérie, do me a favor and tell that big guy over there that he played well tonight. He could do with some cheering up." He turned her in the direction of Bren, who was sitting on a bench tying his laces. Lately Colette had been obsessed with the parable of the Good Samaritan, and she skipped off, ready to do a good deed.

He lowered his voice. "Well, you see, Ms. Chase, we have a problem. For some reason, I've suddenly started playing better. It could be down to a growing cohesiveness with the team. Or the fact I'm in my hometown and the food makes me feel right. Or it could be I'm feeling inspired because the boss had her lips wrapped around my dick last night."

Her mouth fell open. "Did you just accuse me of being your . . . your . . . muse?" She hissed it like he'd said something truly filthy. For a woman as guarded as Harper, maybe it was.

He really should not be enjoying himself this

much, but Poppa was on the mend, they'd won a hard-fought-for game in his hometown, and he'd had a night of awesome sex with a gorgeous woman.

"Yes, I did. So if you want me to continue play-ing this well, you'd better figure out how to keep me happy."

"More blackmail?"

He grinned. "That's how I roll, minou."

<hr>

"What the hell is that supposed to be?"

Violet canted her head and took in the half-formed—penis? elephant trunk? nuclear reactor?—spinning like a top on Isobel's ceramics wheel.

"I call it *Wishful Thinking*." Isobel dipped her hands in water and applied another lascivious stroke to the phallic lump before her. "It's been that long that I truly don't remember what one looks like."

Harper grabbed her wineglass with clay-covered fin-gers. The Sister Bonding sessions had been continuing on as regular a schedule as they could manage. Indoor rock climbing was more fun than Harper expected. She'd vetoed trapeze (Isobel's idea), so this week they were doing something a little less active and a bit more . . . drunken. Pottery and Pinot, a class for people with no clue about ceramics and no intention of getting one, had seemed like a great addition to the rotation. Get dirty. Drink wine. Make clay penises. A laugh riot.

Of course Harper wasn't making a clay penis. She was—well, she was waiting for inspiration. Inspiration was choosing to stay the hell away, so all Harper had on her wheel was a disc that could possibly pass as a puck. Because she lived and breathed hockey, obvs.

But at least she had wine. One more gulp into the abyss.

The creative sort, Violet was crafting something that looked like a really nice mug that could actually be drunk from without producing an unladylike drool. The ceramics class was her bright idea. She'd claimed she'd never done it before, which was patently a lie.

"Why has it been so long since you saw a penis?"

Said just loud enough to draw Church Lady glances from their classmates as well as from Debbie, the instructor who preferred to devote her attention to the people who spent more time with their hands on the wheel than wrapped around a wineglass.

Uh, Pinot is in the class title, Debbie.

Isobel sighed. "Look at me."

Harper and Violet obeyed. Then exchanged puzzled glances with each other because looking at Isobel provided no enlightenment whatsoever.

"I'm six feet tall and have better musculature than any of the guys I've ever dated."

Violet frowned. "Not getting the problem."

"I'm a jock. Guys, or at least the guys I like, don't date jocks."

Harper took another pull of her wine. She wondered if drinking and ceramics was such a good idea. Throwing under the influence. "What's your type?"

"Guys who make me look like *I'm* not going to flatten *them*."

"So, tall and built." Remy made Harper look small, but she felt ten feet tall when in his arms. A week since that night in New Orleans, and her body was still on fire with want.

No wonder her ceramics efforts were garbage when all she could think of was his hard body sliding against hers. The halt he'd pulled when she asked, just testing his resolve and respect. His fun turnabout as he ordered, *Now ride me, minou.* The man had known exactly the right combination of words and actions to smooth away her nerves and turn her into a full-fledged sex bomb. With Remy, she felt like she'd reclaimed a missing part of herself.

She was now engaged in what could only be termed *anticappointment*. A week had passed with Remy not pushing for more, and though a part of her might have liked him to push, the sensible—team-owning, sexless— part was grateful that he respected her decision. So what if she wanted him? That was not the point. She wanted to eat cupcakes for lunch and lie in bed reading romance novels all day. That didn't mean she could just throw her responsibilities out the window and indulge.

"I also like guys who dress sharp," Isobel added to her list of exceedingly low requirements.

Violet chuckled. "So, a hockey player on game day."
She shot a pointed look at Harper. "But we all know
what a terrible idea that is. At least, according to no-
fun Harper."

If they only knew. Harper put the pedal to the metal
on the potter's wheel and applied herself to shaping a
plant pot.

"I've bagged a couple of hockey players in my time,
and frankly . . ." Isobel shrugged. "Overrated."

"Ooh, details," Violet said.

"I'm just saying, I lost my virginity to one who had—
who *still* has—a rep for being a god in the sack. And he
sucked."

"If he's any good he will." Harper giggled at her own
lame joke, then quieted on seeing that Isobel wasn't
laughing. "Sorry, too soon?"

Both of her sisters stared at her.

"What?"

"Ladies! How are we doing?" Debbie cut in, ready to
assess their progress with a critical eye. Her gaze was
first drawn to Violet's mug. "Nice! Wonderful jollying
technique."

"Thanks, Debs. I try."

She switched to Isobel, but before she could offer
a critique, Isobel spoke up. "It's the Stanley Cup." At
Debbie's blank look, Izzy elaborated. "The hockey trophy? Ice hockey? You see, it's broader at the base and
gets narrower until it blooms into the cup."

"Right," Debbie said, though she clearly thought

what she was seeing was all wrong. Evidently not an NHL fan. "And how about you?"

Harper looked down at the lump of clay, which had somehow become *something* in the last five minutes. All this talk of penises must have crossbred with her own X-rated reminiscences of Remy.

Her clay was now shaped like a long, thrusting appendage, complete with bulbous head. It even had a slight lean to the left, just like—oh, my God, what was wrong with her?

A shocked Debbie looked like she might have to ban someone for the first time in Pottery and Pinot's history.

"It's—it's—a mug tree," Harper said quickly. She pinched at the side of the inappropriately erotic sculpture, drawing out a nubbin. With a little massaging, she shaped a feeble clay branch you could hang a mug on. "See?"

Debbie saw perfectly. "Well—"

Someone called her over from the other side of the room, and with one last glare, she took her judgment with her.

The sisters broke into unrestrained laughter.

"Jesus, Harper, are you trying to get us thrown out?" Violet asked. "More important, though, is there something you want to tell us?"

"I'm not sure how it happened. One minute, it was a lump of nothing, the next I'm channeling *this*."

"More like channeling PornHub meets *Ghost*," Isobel muttered.

Harper cocked her head, taking in her new mug tree. "I'm going to call it *Well Hung*."

Instead of appreciating that for the comedic gem it was, her sisters exchanged a look.

"You seem . . ." Violet said, "different."

"Yeah, lighter." Isobel squinted at her, eyes filled with suspicion. "More relaxed."

She *felt* more relaxed. That experience with Remy couldn't be repeated, but it had been so liberating to let all the expectations she had for herself melt away, if only for a night.

"Wine. Three-game winning streak. And a spa day in New Orleans. It was a good idea to go out a day early." Harper raised her glass. "Did me a world of good."

SEVENTEEN

Harper hung up the phone in her office—formerly her father's office—and stared at it accusingly, thinking on what she'd just heard from Curtis Deacon at the *Sun-Times*.

Care to comment on the news that your sister Isobel has left her coaching job in Montreal?

Apparently it happened three days ago and Isobel had elected to keep it to herself. What the hell was wrong with her, letting the organization get blindsided like this? They had PR people who could have issued a statement and handled it much better than Harper, who had assured Curtis, after a five-second pause to collect herself, that Isobel's separation from Montreal was all part of the plan.

What plan, Harper? Curtis had pounced.

I'm not at liberty to say, Curtis. Just rest assured that everything happens for a reason.

Then she'd hung up and unleashed a yell she hoped Isobel could hear two miles away in Lake Forest.

"Now, that sounds like a mighty frustrated woman."

Well, the prodigal returns. Remy stood in the open door to her office, looking too sinfully delicious to exist. A brief flash of dread seized her chest. Sure it was after seven in the evening and everyone in the Rebels' front office would have left by now, but she was still very conscious that she and Remy in the same small space together was a PR sex-disaster in the making.

"Can we pretend you didn't just hear me screaming my head off like a banshee?"

He leaned against the door, all casual devil-don't-care. "That depends."

"Oh?"

"On how hungry you are."

Not falling for that. "I'm fine. I'll grab something on my way home."

She turned back to the reports Paul Carson, the Rebels' chief scout, had delivered earlier, her entire body in heightened awareness. How could it not be after coming alive for the first time in years in Remy's arms? Now it itched to be ignited again.

"Or you could have something now." He held up a bag she hadn't noticed before. "Muffuletta sandwich."

The mouthwatering scent of salami and olives hit her hard. Her stomach betrayed her and made its demand: *Feed me.*

"How did you know I was here? Or are you usually roving the halls of Rebels HQ, sandwiches in tow, on the off chance you'll find someone who needs feeding?"

He grinned, and clearly taking her question for permission, stepped into her office.

"Amazing what can be learned by sweet-talking the GM's assistant. I *might* have learned a certain team owner has been staying late every night there's no game this past week." He placed a sandwich at the edge of the desk, slightly out of reach. Such a tease.

"You shouldn't be here." She may as well have been talking to the food.

"Worried you can't resist me?"

"Remy—"

He held up a hand. "It's just a sandwich, Harper. Take a break, and then let me walk you to your car. Don't like the idea of you working so late."

There he was, playing at gentleman again. Not playing, though. Remy DuPre was the genuine article. She wished she didn't want him so much. But right now, she wanted the sandwich more. So sue her.

He unwrapped the sandwich, its tantalizing scents growing stronger with each unfurl of the paper. The man was using it in a foodie striptease—and it was working!

She picked up the roll and took a bite. Pleasure as the combination of olives, mayonnaise, meats, and cheeses hit her tongue drew her moan.

"You made this?" she asked after her first swallow. Jesus, it was amazing.

"Uh-huh. That there is my mawmaw's recipe, passed down through six generations of Acadians."

"I thought muffuletta was Sicilian."

"Italian immigrants made their way into the Bayou and left their mark. Like all good Louisianans, we take what we like and make it our own."

"Thieves and hoodlums."

"Pirates and poets." His gaze strayed to the reports. "So how goes it in the high-powered world of hockey franchise management?"

"Well, I'm always on the lookout for the next big thing. And I have to replace you."

"I'm irreplaceable, but do what you must."

She hoped that wasn't true, though she acknowledged that he brought a real coherency to the team that she'd have trouble emulating with someone else. He worked well with Callaghan, but they needed a stronger left-winger to round out the line.

"I'm looking at Brad Hogan. Rumor has it he's not too happy in Tampa."

"Who is? Place is a swamp."

"Says the man who was born in one."

He grinned, a heartbreaking curve of his lips that was like a stun gun to her brain. She hadn't realized how much she'd missed that smile until her body lit up in its presence.

"Louisiana is a swamp, but it's a swamp with culture. So who else is on your list?"

She shouldn't really be discussing it, but bouncing ideas off him seemed like a good use of those years around the block. Also, if they talked about business, she wouldn't be tempted to talk about why they weren't kissing or touching or . . .

Okay. She named a few players, and he offered honest and forthright opinions, most of which she agreed with.

"I've got a player for you." He was still leaning against her desk, his most excellent ass quite at home on her father's antique mahogany. "Vadim Petrov."

She frowned. "Out of Quebec? He's been benched more times than not this season."

"Yeah, he had a knee injury last year, but when he's on, there's no stopping him. Can totally clean up."

"He spent a summer training with the Rebels before he played for the Kontinental League about eight years ago. A lot of talent, but he plays on the right."

"Quebec doesn't know how to use him. He's so versatile that they keep moving him around on the line, but he's born to be a left-winger. All his power is off that side." He cast a glance at her laptop. "You got any tape?"

She returned an eyebrow arch at the stupidity of that question. Sixty seconds later, she opened her folder on Petrov, subfolder Power Plays, and chose a file from a game the big Russian had played against the Rebels last season.

That hitch on Remy's lips told her he was impressed. He pulled up a chair while the video opened, and there was that sizzle again. Proximity to this man was turning out to be a major problem.

Remy leaned in, his expression intent. "See how he's playing on the right—"

"He's right-handed, so that's his natural side."

"Sure, but his natural side is really his off side."

Harper thought on that. Most players preferred to receive the puck on their forehand. It was more innate, but there were always some who didn't fit that mold. She racked her brain.

"That early-season game against Boston last year. He played on the left side then—"

"And scored two goals that night." Remy looked rueful at the memory. "Quebec beat us 4–1. I think he'd work well with Callaghan and St. James."

"I'll talk to Coach about it." She felt warm inside, whether it was from her sated hunger or the company, she wasn't sure. More likely it was the ease of this discussion. No tension, no pressure, just a mutually respectful conversation about the work she loved.

"How are you and Bren getting along?"

Remy leaned back in the chair, those big orgasm-producing hands laced behind his neck, a pose that drew her attention to his Henley stretched tight over stunning pectoral muscles. "How are we *supposed* to be getting along, boss?"

This man, so astute. "Nothing like a little healthy competition. I gave him a chance. Now I want to see him earn it."

"By letting him think his captaincy might be ripped from him at any minute?" He shook his head in admiration. "Your daddy sure did underestimate you, Harper."

He wasn't the only one. She'd ensure it never happened again.

"He didn't suffer fools, that's for sure."

"Yeah, I got that. Great center, decent coach, so-so businessman."

She smiled at that accurate assessment. "So you weren't a fan?"

"I wouldn't say that." He took a deep breath, his expression softening. "In fact, your dad's the reason I started playing hockey."

She perked up. "You're kidding."

"Nope. How else was a swamp kid like me gonna come to it? It's not exactly popular down south. At least, it wasn't twenty-five years ago."

Already enthralled, she urged him to share. "Tell me."

"When I was eight, my family moved from Acadiana to New Orleans after my mom landed a job as a musicology professor at Tulane, but I wasn't having any of that. I hated the city. I missed home. Missed it so much that I kept running away back to it and my poppa kept chasing me down."

She giggled. "Bet you were a terror."

"Sure was. Made their lives hell. So one day, I wasn't running back home—must've been tired—and I was watching TV when hockey came on. It was a finals game between Chicago and Montreal, and your father played a barn burner. There was nothing he couldn't do on the ice. I was hooked and I begged Poppa to find me a way to play. Turned out there was a squirt league over in the Ninth Parish and *c'est l'histoire*."

"My father inspired you?"

"Cliff Chase inspired many a young player, Harper. Maybe he wasn't the best human being, but he was a legend on the rink." He tilted his head. "I met him once, y'know, much later after he'd taken over the Rebels. It was about ten years ago and I was with the—"

"Calgary Saints."

He smiled, pleased she had that fact so close at hand. "Right. We played a game here, and I remember it so well. Every pass, every play, the crowd singin' their hearts out. What was that song they used to play during the warm-up to every Rebels game?"

"'Wonderwall,'" Harper said. She'd forgotten about that, the team's unofficial anthem when they used to win more than lose.

"Yeah, 'Wonderwall.' After the game, I ran into your father in the tunnel and just *had* to tell him how he'd started my love of hockey. I was stutterin' like a woodpecker, *'Ex-excuse me, Mr. Chase, c-could I have a minute of your t-time?'*" His robust laugh warmed her inside out. "Well, that night the Saints had beaten the Rebels, with yours truly scoring a hat trick, and Clifford was hella pissed. He told me that if he could go back in time, he'd drown me in a swamp." He shook his head, still smiling. "Never meet your heroes."

Harper couldn't agree with that. She was starting to think she might have met hers—the man sitting in front of her.

Moving on. "You played well in Denver," she said, referring to their recent win on the road, the game she had elected to watch from home. He hadn't needed her as his muse, and she wasn't sure how she felt about that. She knew how she was *supposed* to feel. Thrilled that the team was finally coming together. Under no circumstances should she begrudge her center's excellent play because she had no part in inspiring it.

Try telling that to her mouth. "Seems you don't need to be kept happy after all. Winning tends to be its own inspiration."

Elbows on his knees, he inclined his head, assessing her with those knowing blue eyes. Her breath caught at the proximity. He was big and masculine and so, so present.

"Think I've forgotten all you've done for me, Harper? I'm letting those memories of our night together fuel every stride on the ice, every pass of the puck, and every shot between the pipes. And when I need to refill the well, I take myself in hand, remembering those sexy sounds you made when I was buried deep in the heart of you."

"You shouldn't say that," she said halfheartedly as heat rushed to her core.

"Now, you opened that door. I think you're annoyed I've been so respectful of your wishes."

"DuPre—"

"Remy."

"DuPre," she said sweetly. "What happened in New Orleans was very pleasant . . ."

He mouthed, *Ouch*.

"Okay, more than pleasant. It was good." *So good.* "And if you weren't who you are and I wasn't who I am, then maybe we could do it again."

"Seeing as how it was so pleasant and all."

"I said it was good!"

His grin was as wicked as they come. "You did. My mistake. So the only thing holding you back from a repeat is the employer-employee situation?"

Goddamn him, she'd walked into that. "It's not exactly surmountable."

"In a few weeks, I won't be your employee anymore."

She didn't want to think about that. Not just that she would have lost this important part of the team, but also because she liked having him around. He made a mean muffuletta.

"So all we've got against us, really, is timing. Listen, Harper, I understand your concerns. You have to present a certain image to the world. All eyes are on the Rebels and you, of all Cliff's daughters, are the face of the team business. I get that. I totally respect that. But that doesn't change the fact I want to throw you over this desk and fuck you until you scream my name, forget your own, and come so many times you practically pass out."

Good thing she was sitting down, because her whole body shook with those words.

Denial was on the tip of her tongue, starting with how she didn't want him that much (lie) to his words were inappropriate (truth). Instead she countered with the incredibly witty, "You made me a sandwich."

He grinned, that rogue's smile she remembered from steamy NOLA as he ravished her body with assurance and a slowness that killed her. "Can't be having you running your empire on an empty stomach."

He understood what she was going through. He respected what she was trying to do here. His honesty smashed through her, and she owed him the same, even if nothing could come of it.

"You know I want you, Remy. It's just—" She couldn't finish because it was too depressing.

"I know, minou." He leaned in, and with the slightest brush, touched his lips to her forehead. "Now pack up your reports and let me walk you to your car. I'm not leaving you here alone."

EIGHTEEN

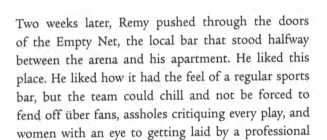

Two weeks later, Remy pushed through the doors of the Empty Net, the local bar that stood halfway between the arena and his apartment. He liked this place. He liked how it had the feel of a regular sports bar, but the team could chill and not be forced to fend off über fans, assholes critiquing every play, and women with an eye to getting laid by a professional athlete. Not that Remy would be wholly opposed to that latter option, but he also knew that shitting on his own doorstep would come back to bite him.

Kind of like with Harper. Gorgeous, off-limits, crazy-sexy Harper was resisting him with a lot more fortitude than he'd expected. Good thing one of them was making sense.

His game—and the team—had started to gel on the ice after New Orleans. He'd taken the sound of her voice, the memory of her skin, and the imprint of her body gripping him deep into every battle since. He was playing like a god, and they'd won four of their last five.

Coincidence? *Mais non*.

As he approached Callaghan, Jorgenson, and Burnett at the corner table, he heard this from the Swede: "The coconut would win. No contest."

"Do I want to know?" Remy asked Ford.

"These two"—he thumbed at Tweedledee and Tweedledum—"are arguing over which fruit would win in a fight."

"Assuming they were sentient," Burnett clarified before turning back to Jorgenson. "A dragon fruit would win, dude. It's got 'dragon' in the fucking name."

Jorgenson shook his head. "The coconut is the armored tank of fruits. It can fall out of trees and kill people even when it is not sentient."

Remy suspected he was going to regret this. "Pineapples, *mes enfants*. Spiky skin, hard as fuck, total badass. They've also got an enzyme that breaks down meat. If they're not winning one way, they're attacking through the back door."

The boys stared at him for at least ten seconds. Finally Jorgenson spoke. "This changes everything."

His work done, Remy headed to the bar and ordered a Sam Adams just as Violet Vasquez walked in and joined the group. Remy was having a tough time getting a bead on that girl. One minute she was the wild child, life of the party, the next she was looking like she'd had a shitstorm journey just to make it to the present day. He also suspected that Harper would not approve of her sister hanging with the players, because that sounded like a rule the Dragon Lady would make. No fraternizing.

A rule that Harper had broken with joyous abandon in Remy's bed, but had pledged herself to anew. He should have known one night wouldn't be enough with her, but he'd taken his shot, sunk the puck, and now was looking at being benched for the rest of the season. He didn't like the idea of warming the pine where Harper was concerned. He wanted in her, wanted the heat her body would give him. The taboo was a kick, but that wasn't just it. Harper excited him like no other woman. Period. She was smart and sexy and driven, and that combination turned him on big time.

However, she was also smart enough to know a hot fling with him was bad news for her. He was trying to respect her boundaries, the walls she'd built to keep him out. He wanted to take a sledgehammer to them, which was pretty selfish of him.

Stay away, DuPre. Don't fuck with her life.

St. James bookended the bar, giving off that morose force field he rocked so well, only his attention wasn't quite so glued to his phone as usual. Every few seconds, he'd throw sneaky glances toward the corner table group, then return to his phone with a storm-clouded frown.

Violet's shout of "What about bananas?" pierced the air, and Bren raised his head like he was scenting prey. Nothing furtive about it now. The man gave new meaning to the phrase "dirty look" as he glared at Violet.

Those Chase girls were nothing but trouble.

About to head down to Bren and ask him to join the woe-is-me party, he stopped short when he felt the vibration of his phone. Unreasonable joy flared in his chest at the sight of a kitten pic he'd found online to attach to the contacts entry for "Minou."

Minou: *I could so kick Katniss's ass.*

He smiled at the answer to tonight's burning Would You Rather? question: Would you rather get chosen for the Hunger Games or for the Triwizard Tournament?

Remy: *That president dude must be quaking.*

Minou: *Speaking of ass whuppin', you skimped on the peppers again, DuPre.*

He smiled, then shut it down because it would look suspicious.

Remy: *Spicy costs extra.*

Minou: *Sorry, I don't carry cash. I'm far too important.*

Remy: *We accept all forms of payment.*

Kisses, stripteases, hand jobs . . .

He blew out a breath to calm his racing pulse and rising dick. For the last two weeks, on each night there wasn't a game, Remy had food delivered to Harper's office, courtesy of a couple of Jacksons dropped on one of the bartenders at the Empty Net. Chez Remy's take-out menu consisted of gumbo, shrimp creole, and jerk chicken and rice.

He could have delivered it himself but (a) that would raise questions in the Rebels' front office and (b) he would have likely knocked, waited for her haughty *come in*, and then turned his porno fantasies into delicious, dirty reality.

Delivery, Ms. Chase.

Oh, hello. You're new . . . exactly how hot is the jambalaya tonight?

Before she could lick those plump, glossy lips, he'd have jumped clear across the desk and ripped off that sexy little skirt and see-through blouse she liked to taunt him with when she walked in before the game to wish them all luck.

So he had a snowball's chance in the bayou with her. At least he could make sure she was eating right. He looked down at his phone, worried that maybe he'd scared her off with his innuendo. The little dots appeared, signaling that she was composing a message.

. . . typing . . . typing . . .

"What up, Big Easy?"

Violet leaned on the bar, a smartass grin breaking her face in half. She wore a black minidress, a red cable-knit sweater, thigh-high argyle socks, and Converse. The only thing the Chase daughters seemed to have in common were those big green eyes hiding hurt, secrets, and indomitable will. It took a brave woman to handle being thrown into the lion's den, forced to navigate the worlds of pro hockey and dysfunctional family dynamics.

"Violet." Harper's name wasn't on his screen, but he still tilted the phone away from prying eyes. "How you doin' this evening?"

"Just fine, *Mon-soor* DuPre." She delivered a mock bow. "Can I give you a word of advice?"

"You're gonna give it anyway, I suspect."

She finger-pistoled her agreement. "I see how she acts around you. You make her nervous and, for Harper, that's a good thing. She needs to have her world shook up, y'know?"

Not much point pretending ignorance, and frankly, the secrecy was killing him. "You don't think her world's been shook up plenty these last few months?"

An old-soul wisdom haunted her eyes. "That's nothing. Right now, she thinks she has it all under control, but the reality is that you need to come close to losing everything to realize what's important. *Capisce?*"

He wondered what she'd weathered to reach that conclusion. For Remy, coming so close to losing his dad had refocused his game. No more *maybe someday*. No more screwing around, because someday was now.

Violet patted his arm, and Remy felt the frost of St. James's displeasure burning holes in his head. *Just add it to the tab, Highlander.* His phone buzzed, and Violet smirked again as she swayed off. Remy checked the latest incoming message.

Minou: *Get some sleep, DuPre. We need you tomorrow.*

The team. Always the team.

He threw down a ten on the bar, gave a wry salute to Bren, and headed over to the guys who needed him to skate his heart out tomorrow night.

Harper smiled at her phone. Thank God no one was in the office to see her acting like a lovesick loon. She wished Remy had made the special delivery himself, but they both knew where that would lead.

As amazing as the food was, it was the thought behind it that blew her away. And she had to admit to feeling a certain swooniness about the Post-its he'd taken to adding to each delivery, along with the backstory he'd created to justify their inclusion. Apparently, his nieces had questions about the "pretty lady with the sunshine hair."

Questions from the "nieces" so far had ranged from "Would you rather fight a hundred duck-sized horses or one horse-sized duck?" (That one horse-sized duck was going down!) to "Would you rather gain ten pounds or be banned from the Internet for a month?" (She was eating the damn sandwiches, wasn't she?)

As for tonight's question on the Hunger Games versus the Triwizard Tournament—he should really have asked how much resistance to Remy DuPre did Harper have remaining in her frail Katniss-whupping body?

Her phone buzzed again and she smiled, ready to

play along, but the caller ID wasn't who she expected. She answered, her heart in her throat.

"Tommy, how are you?"

"Peachy keen," Remy's agent said. "Yourself?"

After a moment or two of chitchat, he got to the point. "I hear you have an agreement with Remy to unload him before the all-star game."

"Which is more than two months off."

He ignored that. "I already have interest. He's been playing better than ever and any team worth its salt would be glad to have him to make that final push."

"Which is why I should be holding on to him. There's nothing in his contract that says I have to do exactly what Remy wants. We're running a business here, not the Make-A-Wish Foundation."

Tommy chuckled. "Damn, this world suits you. Your father should've let you get down in the dirt where you belong sooner."

"Why, that's the nicest thing you could have said to me, Thomas."

"Look, Harper," he said, serious again. "The Rebels' organization has had a good month, but you were never known for your consistency. I can't risk Remy being left with his dick in his hand come the trade deadline. I want to be sure he's topmost in every GM's mind when they look at acquisition."

But we need him, she almost whined. *I need him.*

Realistically, as good as the Rebels were playing, their shot was a long one. At least five other teams in the NHL had a better chance of taking him there. His legacy would never be assured if he rode it out with the Rebels.

With her.

If she didn't give him this, he'd never forgive her. Heart on a downward spiral to her feet, she managed, "If Remy still wants out, then I'm not going to stop him, Tommy."

And then she hung up before her hormones—and maybe something else—tried to override her common sense.

NINETEEN

~

Harper popped her head around the door of Coach's office. He wasn't here.

So it was unlikely on this snowy Wednesday before Thanksgiving, but Coach was a workaholic who lived close to the practice facility. Once she'd found him here inventorying equipment at 11 p.m. on the Fourth of July. But not tonight. She had hoped to talk to him about how best to replace DuPre.

The bargain she'd struck with Remy two weeks into the season was still their dirty little secret. Isobel was going to go apeshit when she heard, but Harper would deal with that later. Now it was time to bring Coach into the cone of silence so they could be in the best position come trade season.

Yet again, Remy had played like a demon at last night's home game against New York, scoring one goal and setting up two more. There was something about his ability to deftly surf the currents in both the locker room and the rink, a rock-solid strength of character he brought to bear on the team. Something they'd been sorely lacking in the last year as Bren wrestled with his addiction and the collapse of his marriage. She prayed the Scot could take up the mantle once they gave up Remy.

Frustration boiled beneath her skin at the thought of *having* to give him up.

The sooner she talked to Coach about it, the better. Discussing its reality would attune her to what needed to happen. It would also have an added side benefit.

She would no longer feel so itchy. So needy. *So horny.*

She might also lose some weight, because the food deliveries would finally end. Damn, she was going to miss that gumbo.

Her mind shied away from the lurch in her chest. Remy DuPre was just one piece in the plan, and so far he was fulfilling his end of their devil's bargain. The team was in its best shape in years, finally in the black—just—with this season's win-loss record.

Walking through the facility's backstage maze, she smiled to herself, thinking of the strides she'd made since her father's death. *All mine.* Isobel and Violet might have a say, but Harper was running this show. So she had no love life to speak of and she was leading the second-worst team in the league, but she was making it happen.

That's right, Dad, you old bastard. Here I am and here I will stay.

The heady sensation of power lifted her for a moment and she spun on her new favorite heels—the ones Remy had helped her choose in New Orleans—jumping in the air with a whoop that echoed in the empty corridors.

"Celebrating, minou?"

Ah, not so empty after all. Why did he always have to catch her at her weakest moments?

That streak of gorgeous male stood against the door to the player gym wearing nothing but shiny black shorts and a sheen of sweaty manliness coating a chest so sculpted Michelangelo would've smiled in approval. He folded his arms, and her body screeched its disappointment at the removal of those pecs from her sight line.

"I didn't know anyone was here," she said rather obviously.

"While you roam your kingdom, lady of all you survey?"

"Something like that."

He held her gaze. She wanted to look away but she couldn't. How ridiculous to be held in such thrall.

"I assumed you'd be off to New Orleans for Thanksgiving."

"My flight got canceled because of the weather, but I'm hoping to get out in the morning." He rubbed a towel over his chest, and her mouth reacted predictably: it grew desert-dry. "I was putting some time in on the elliptical when I heard this strange little squeak."

"I didn't squeak," she squeaked. Hell. She cleared her throat to get back on track. "I don't squeak. I just . . ." She trailed off, unsure how to explain it.

"You're feeling good about where you're at, Harper. No reason not to." The right thing to say, but then Remy was as skillful with the verbal as he was with the physical. With a nod, he walked back into the gym.

She followed, like her core was attached to his ass by a lifeline. She wanted to go hand over hand along that string until she reached that ass and grabbed on to it like her survival depended on it.

Back on the elliptical, he restarted his workout. If she didn't know him to be the straightest talker she'd ever met, she would think he was playing some game to showcase those amazing lats, how his trapezoid muscle pulled with every smooth motion. The man was simply sublime.

"How goes it in the Kingdom of Harper?" he asked, his voice not even strained from his exertion.

"Fine. Isobel's gone to visit her mom in Arizona, and Violet is headed to see some friends in Reno."

He frowned. "On your own for the holiday?"

"No. I . . ." She hesitated, not sure why she'd done that or even why she offered up her sisters' current locations. "I have plans."

He stopped the machine and turned to her, his forehead in an adorably sexy crumple.

"Do these plans involve you eating a granola bar and downing a bottle of wine?"

"You think so little of me."

"Harper . . ."

"Remy . . ." she sang back. She knew why she'd paused in telling him. She didn't want him to know because it felt like disloyalty.

He held her gaze for a moment, then seemed to shake off whatever it was about her attitude that was bothering him. She was relieved. Mostly.

He grabbed the towel and gave another swipe across his glistening chest. *Tongue right here, dude. I could so clean that off for you.*

"So, what are you doing down in the belly of the beast?"

"Worried about me?"

He inhaled a deep breath, his annoyance audible because she was teasing him for his chivalry. "You know I don't like you working here late."

She did know. He informed her constantly, usually with overbearingly protective texts checking in on her and making sure she was asking security to walk her to her car. Each message loosened her grip on sanity a little.

"I wanted to catch Coach Calhoun. Talk about new acquisitions." *Not a jot of hesitation now.* "I talked to Quebec about Petrov today. Told them we might be interested."

"Yeah?"

"Your name was mentioned as a possible trade."

There, she'd said it. Not that it was secret knowledge between them, but she needed to be clear—to him, to herself—that he was leaving.

He should have looked pleased instead of gorgeously grumpy. Quebec was doing well in the conference and had a great offensive line this year. This trade would put Remy on the best path.

But right now, she wasn't thinking of his shot; neither were Remy's dreams uppermost in her mind. Harper's fantasies were ruling. Harper's fantasies were *rioting*.

God, she wanted him.

"That's what we agreed, isn't it?"

His gaze dipped to her mouth as she spoke, then moved farther down. Her nipples pebbled and heat pooled deep in her belly.

"I'm giving you what you want," she said, reiterating her point when he didn't reply.

She was close enough to smell his scent, the spice of hard work. No player put in the effort he did, and was that ever a turn-on. Until he uttered his next words.

"Tell me who you're spending the holidays with."

He already knew, or he knew enough to ask.

"Kenneth and his mother."

"Kenneth and his mother," he repeated mechanically, as if she spoke another language.

For the last three holidays, she'd accompanied Kenneth to his mother's house in Winnetka. Mrs. Bailey was a sharp old dame who assumed Harper was trying to trap her golden boy into marriage. The first year,

Harper had interrupted them hissing at each other in the kitchen, the words *gold digger* and *trollop* being bandied about liberally. Never mind that Harper could buy and sell Kenneth—and his mother—ten times over. Harper attended the next Thanksgiving dinner out of spite, and tomorrow she would go to Kenneth's mother's house and endure Mrs. B's stink eye because it was better than being alone.

"I go there every year."

"You're still—I thought—never mind." He stepped off the elliptical, shaking his head.

This was about the sandwiches and the notes and how something had been building and was now crashing in rubble around them.

"Remy, it's just turkey."

"Sure, Harper. Turkey." Grabbing the towel, he turned and stomped off.

She had promised him nothing. *You have nothing to offer him.* Not the same thing, exactly, but productive of the same result. He understood this, or at least she had assumed he did, yet here he was getting in a sulk because she wouldn't be spending Thanksgiving alone like she had every year since the age of six.

Mom would start drinking while she stuffed the turkey, and by the time it was done, so was she. Completely lit and spewing hate at Geraldine and Isobel.

I hope she chokes on a wishbone, her and *the brat.*

Harper's father used to call the first couple of years after the divorce, but soon enough knew better not to.

He had no compunction about leaving Harper to pick up the fragments of her mother's heart and to try to glue them together again with tears and gin. Of all the crimes Harper should lay at her father's door, this one hurt the most. His callous neglect.

By the time Lorraine had died of ovarian cancer when Harper was seventeen, the holidays were fixed in Harper's mind as the season for dread. Even this year, with her sisters on site, nothing had changed. They had lives of their own, and while both of them had issued invitations, Harper had declined. She refused to be pitied.

Now Remy DuPre thought she owed him an explanation for how she would spend her holiday. Screw him.

She followed him into the locker room, and when she didn't find him there, she moved on to the showers. Indignation powered each step, because who the hell did he think he was?

Waltzing in, she immediately realized her mistake. There had been so many mistakes, but this one beat them all hands down. He was . . . naked. Gloriously so.

His back to her, he was kicking off shiny black shorts, the ones that made his ass look like two watermelons lashed together. And then he turned and she forgot all about the ass. She forgot a few other things, too. Her social security number. Her name. How to breathe.

He was semierect and . . . there he went, all the way to full-mast. Was that because of her?

"What do you want, Harper?"

Even if she knew, she'd be hard-pressed to get the words out. Her mouth had turned to sandpaper, her legs as wobbly as water. All the moisture she needed to lubricate her tongue was busy lubricating other areas of her body.

Just pretend his penis isn't there waving at you. This is just a regular old GM chat with one of your players in the showers. "I wanted to know why you're in such a huff."

"I'm not in a huff. I'm just sweaty and tired and cranky because I couldn't fly out tonight and I might not be flyin' out at all, which makes this the first Thanksgiving with my family I've ever missed."

"I'm sorry." Of course he wanted to get home to his perfect, loving family, especially with his father recovering from illness. Every moment would be precious. "Have you looked into a charter flight? I could call and see if anything—"

She broke off because something was happening here. His entire body had tensed, muscles rigid to the point that he bulged everywhere. Cords of sinew stood out in stark relief along his arms, and she tracked her gaze down his right arm to the big, dominant hand . . . that gave one long, blatant stroke of his erection.

She gaped. He could not seriously have touched himself in her presence. So she was standing there acting like she was one of the guys, gabbing with her star center in the shower room while he stood naked before her. Same day, different dick. But he had chosen to take it from five to negative one million on the appropriateness scale.

His hand was fisted at his side, as if it had never moved. Hand to God, she had to rewind her brain to check, and yep, the playback was not unpleasant. That had happened, all right.

Remy DuPre had stroked his cock in front of her. *At* her. Like a threat.

Or an invitation.

"You're angry with me."

"Harper—" He raked a hand through his hair. "I need a shower. I need a cold. Fucking. Shower."

He turned to reach for the faucet and as he did, she made a strangled sound, not even sure what she meant to say. Something like "talk to me" or "need a soapy hand?" or "why are you wasting that glorious erection?"

Stopped in his tracks, his left hand stretched out to the tile framing the shower. Seeking an anchor. He didn't turn to face her, just issued the starkest of rasps.

"Minou."

Maybe he meant to say more, but whatever it was never found air. His back muscles were clenched, and damn, they looked good, like he was holding every ounce of frustration inside his body. All his frustration with her.

She couldn't have that.

She moved toward him, a few steps that felt like a million miles, and when she reached him she touched his back.

He groaned. Animalistic, desperate. Beautiful.

The heat that sizzled on making contact fired through her like a furnace. Her fingers traced striations of muscle banking his spine, coming to rest at the indents of his hips. He held himself still, restrained power that could detonate at any moment.

Feeling brave, she brushed her lips across the lower part of his shoulder blade. Even in heels, she couldn't go higher.

Another groan, heavy with want, quaked the air.

The muscles in his right triceps bunched, and there was only one possible reason for that: he had taken himself in hand. She continued to kiss his back, the ladder of his spine, the breadth of his shoulder, anywhere she could reach, and then those kisses turned openmouthed and greedy. Licking, sucking . . . all while his muscle-corded arm worked, pumping his cock. Up and down, mean and rough.

But this wasn't a solo operation because she was right here with him, her kisses spurring him, his jerky tugs firing the want between her legs. He might have his back to her, but she was his fantasy. How powerful she felt to give him this.

This new knowledge forced a moan from deep in her throat, enough to split his attention. He whipped around, his face a torment of need. The hand not wrapped around his cock hooked her neck and brought her to his mouth to take the kiss that belonged to him and him alone.

This kiss. All she'd missed, every emotion she'd suppressed was unraveled with this kiss. His greed shouldn't have shocked her because it matched her own, yet his hunger told her a story no words could adequately express.

This kiss seared her. Not just on her lips but all over her body, which burned with maddening need. They were consenting adults. They wanted each other. He'd be gone soon, so why not enjoy these moments?

No one would know.

Panting, she pulled away. "Remy, let me touch you. Properly." She cupped his balls and stroked, watching as his face crumpled in ecstasy. He released his grip on his cock, dropped his hands to the hem of her skirt, and yanked it above her hips.

"Jack me, Harper. *Pleasebabyplease.*"

Gladly. But then he slipped his hand inside her panties and she forgot everything but the pleasure his fingers wrought from the slightest touch.

"Please, baby," he pleaded again, and her to-do list flashed before her. Meaning the one must-do thing on it: touch Remy and make him lose his mind. But first there was this, his fingers stroking through her wetness. Slipping inside her. Destroying her completely.

She tried but failed to focus, so he grabbed her hand and put it where he needed it.

"Here, in case you've forgotten what it feels like. 'Cause it ain't forgotten you. How good this is. How good we are."

We. She squeezed, relearning his shape, recalling the tempo that drove him crazy in New Orleans.

"That's right. *Ça c'est—c'est bon.*" And all the time he kept up that wicked slip 'n' slide through her folds, the exquisite pressure building. The tension was unbearable, a wave hurtling toward the shore, and one slight glance of his finger against her clit, and there.

Yes. There.

Gone.

She paused in her stroke to let the orgasm ride to every extremity, her body clenching, her mouth open, and sobbing at the indescribable pleasure. And then she fell to her knees and wrapped her lips around him in the shower room at Rebels HQ.

Bad, bad girl.

But nothing else seemed to matter, not after the release Remy had just given her, not after the sweet torment on his face when she confronted him, not after he'd pumped his cock at the sight of her.

She read a million things in that gesture, but the most important was this: *Look at how much I want you, Harper.*

Time to show just how much she wanted him.

TWENTY

Remy was beyond pissed at Harper Chase.

She'd waltzed into the gym . . . wait now, had she? Okay, he'd lured her in after coming across her being all cute as a kitten GIF in the hallway. Not just cute, but so damn sexy with her tight skirt and tailored jacket and high heels. Those fuck-me babies, the red ones he'd helped her try on as he bent before her in New Orleans, planning her seduction.

There he was minding his own business in the workout room, working off his frustration at not being able to return home for the holiday and the uncertainty surrounding his career and the ache in his balls whenever his dumb brain so much as strayed to Harper.

So yeah, he was pissed at her, and that was before she dropped her bombshell.

Your name was mentioned as a possible trade.

This information should have made him happy. Why didn't it make him happy? Maybe because it was soon followed by that little nugget about her holiday plans with Bailey and his mother.

Which of these things annoys you the most, DuPre?

All of it. The whole fucking lot of it.

Now he was trying to hold on to that anger, but it was too busy being crowded out by pure pleasure. Harper's pleasure coating his fingers. Harper's lips closed over his dick.

Harper's sounds as he tried not to fuck her mouth, because that's all he wanted to do. Roll his hips and thrust deep until his cock head touched the back of her throat and—

She moaned, a long hum of pleasure, and it vibrated around him. His hips flexed, pistoning forward with a momentum all their own, and he gripped her head gently to both hold her steady and hold himself in check. No slouch, she grabbed his ass (not so gently) and dug her nails in, taking him even further into the warm, wet heaven of her mouth. Like his cock was her last meal.

In the haze of lust, he almost missed her hand dropping to between her legs. Merde, was she—? Christ, she was. She was touching herself.

That's what sent him over. "Minou, I'm gonna . . . I'm gonna come."

In her moan he heard her invitation. *Give it all to me, Remy.* His balls filled, his spine sizzled, and he came with Harper's gorgeous lips wrapped around his cock.

She took it all, licking and sucking him clean like a good little sex kitten, and then released him, resting her head against his thigh. Meanwhile, her fingers worked herself furiously, her moans louder now that his dick wasn't muffling her sounds of pleasure.

He stroked her hair and cradled her head so she could watch him while she got herself off. From beneath hooded eyelids, those green eyes flashed silver. He pushed her lower lip down, revealing that pink flash of tongue, the weapon she'd used to make him mindless.

Watching her reach that peak had him half hard again. Never had it been like this with another woman, but then never had he met a woman like Harper. All that ice-queen armor melted as her eyes rolled to the back of her head and she lost herself to pleasure.

So fucking hot.

She sat back on her heels, her fingers still down her panties, panting herself back to normal. In a sated lust daze, it was almost as if he wasn't here.

"Harper," he murmured, just so she didn't forget him.

She looked up, a sly grin curving her swollen lips. "Still in a huff, DuPre?"

That made him laugh. "I'd say I'm the opposite of in a huff. I'm out of a huff."

She stood with his help and pulled her skirt down. He wrapped her in his arms, needing her close. Needing to cuddle.

Snap the fuck out of it, DuPre.

He chose not to. He chose to hold her tighter. Only his brain could tell he was a sap for her.

"You're staying with me tonight," he said.

"Hmm. How about trying that again with a slight lilt at the end of your voice to signify you're making a request?" She added a lilt of her own to demonstrate.

"No request intended. Only statement."

"What about your neighbor?"

He had her covered. "In Atlanta to see his girls. Now go get your things, but leave anything resembling work here."

"So damn cocky."

"That's why you hired me." He pushed the cockiest part of him to her belly. "Let's take these opportunities while we can, Harper. What happened in New Orleans was so good. What happened less than five minutes ago was even better. Don't tell me it's ever been this hot with anyone else because I won't believe it."

She blinked those big, sexy eyes up at him, and for a moment, he thought, *This is it*. Bon nuit, *Remy*.

"One more night. And then—"

He kissed her to cut off any talk of the future. He would take it one night at a time.

For now.

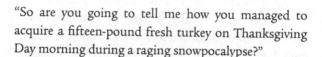

"So are you going to tell me how you managed to acquire a fifteen-pound fresh turkey on Thanksgiving Day morning during a raging snowpocalypse?"

Remy smiled. Some secrets were worth keeping,

especially ones that drove Harper a little bit loopy. It was amazing what could be achieved with the promise of Rebels tickets for the rest of the season.

This morning he'd caught her trying to leave his apartment at the gray crack of dawn—what was it with this woman and the sneaky slip-out?—and it had taken his A-game on the sofa, the assurance he was not flying out of Chicago today, and the promise of a real Thanksgiving dinner to keep her here for the holiday. That last part required that he tap into his Neanderthal ancestor genes to provide, hunter-and-gatherer style.

He added a couple more slices of white meat to her plate. Expecting resistance that would match his preconception of her as a woman who ferociously watches her figure, he was more than gratified when she smothered it in onion gravy, added a dollop of cranberry sauce, and loaded up on more dirty rice.

"A Cajun never tells his secrets. You can thank me properly later."

"Will blow for food?"

"Now don't sell yourself so short, femme. Never settle for less than a bottle of wine for that BJ."

She grinned, that know-it-all smile he loved more each hour he spent in her presence.

"Sorry I wasn't much use to you in the kitchen."

He'd set her to peeling potatoes. Ten minutes later, with one measly Idaho skinned, he'd relieved her of duty, but it had sure been fun to watch her hunched over, a look of earnest focus scrunching up her dainty features as she hacked away at the poor, defenseless tater.

"Your momma didn't cook?"

"She did, but she'd only cook for my father, and she never wanted me in the kitchen. She had to have everything just so. Once he left, it was like all her joy left with him. No more cooking. No more—" She bit off whatever she was about to say and took a sip of the nice Pinot he'd opened. "Clifford paid a personal chef to come in and make dinners so I wouldn't starve. It just seemed easiest."

Perhaps, but not exactly conducive to a happy home life. What kind of mother abdicated responsibility for her child because her husband couldn't keep it in his pants?

Remy could see how that all went down. A young Harper, old beyond her years, taking care of business in that big ol' mansion on the lake. Putting her tipsy, teary momma to bed before she did her homework. Making her own lunch before she caught a ride to school. All while Clifford Chase made a life with his spanking-new family.

Her phone buzzed and she checked the screen. A guilty lip bite told him who it was before she spoke. "That's Kenneth, hoping my migraine is better."

"Wow, a text. Guy's all heart."

She canted her head, a look of *subtle, aren't you?* illuminating her features. So he was jealous. He'd deal with that shit later.

Discomfort twinged in his chest. His greed had overtaken him, and because he was the kind of guy who needed to feed off the company of others, he'd kept her from where she really wanted to be today, with people she knew and cared about. Bailey and his mother.

As quickly as it had hit, the little red devil on his shoulder pushed the guilt away. That guy was A-okay with his decision to quarantine Harper. The storm was a rager, and no way was he letting her go out in it.

Not when she looked sexy as sin wearing his team jersey, a pair of tube socks, and a sultry smile as she ate the dinner he'd prepared for her. He had to be careful with the temp in the apartment—not too hot that she'd want to wear a tee instead (naked was too much to hope for), and not too cold that she'd need to cover her legs with sweats. A careful balancing act.

He reached for her hand and curled a finger around hers. "You're staying the weekend, Harper. We're gonna cook and talk and cook and kiss and—"

"Cook?"

"Yup."

"That sounds a little . . . domestic."

"Sure it is, with the amount of cooking I'll be doing. But don't you fret, I'll make time to keep you satisfied in all the other rooms as well, minou."

She looked down at their joined hands, a ministorm forming between her brows. "Let's play it by ear."

Hell and damn, this woman was one tough nut to

crack. He supposed witnessing your momma falling apart because of your asshole father's behavior had to have an impact. Made you gun-shy. Harper had grown up desperate to prove herself to the old man, that she was a worthy successor despite being born dickless— and hell if she needed to rely on anyone else to carve her path to glory.

Why the hell did he care so much? Maybe because it seemed like she could do with someone at her back. Someone taking care of her. Strong as she was, she had to be tired of making that trek alone.

"You know, it's okay to let people in a little, Harper. Lean on others. It doesn't make you weak."

She cupped her chin, scrunching up her brow in thought. "You mean, I shouldn't use my parents' marriage as a model for all relationships?"

Smart as a whip, this woman. "Look at my parents. Sure they've had their problems, and God knows my sisters didn't make it easy on them."

"But you were a saint."

"Sure was. I'm the reason that marriage is so good. They had me and realized, *We can stop now, it's perfect.*"

She mock-punched him in the arm. "So modest."

"Modesty doesn't win hockey games, Harper. Or get hot businesswomen in your bed." He sipped his wine. "When my dad fell ill, we all stepped up, but it was mostly down to my momma. I know there were times when she was ready to pack it in, because like most men, he's a big-ass crybaby when he's sick, but they soldiered through. I guess what I'm saying is that there are examples of marriages that work. Ones that take the vows seriously." *For better or worse, in sickness and in health.* Harper was seventeen when her mother died, and Remy would bet dollars to donuts Cliff was no help.

"I know. Take Ford and Addison. They're not married yet, but it's only a matter of time with the baby on the way. And they didn't even wait until he retired." She tilted her head and shot him a cheeky look. "You wait any longer and that sperm of yours will be worthless, DuPre."

He'd not intended to share, but if anyone deserved to know this, it was Harper.

"I'll be working on it sooner than you think." He hauled air into his lungs. "This is my last year in the NHL."

TWENTY-ONE

Harper jumped from her seat. "What? But . . . it can't be! I mean, I know you're not getting any younger, but surely you have at least two more years. Three, even."

"I'm no Jágr." The great Czech was still going strong after a thirty-year pro career, but to be honest, Remy couldn't imagine sticking around that long. Not when some lucky lady was waiting for him to rock her world. He palmed Harper's hip and pulled her into his lap, settling her with a soothing stroke along her thigh. "My body doesn't have much left in the tank, minou. I'm skatin' on fumes."

Her eyes shone glossy. "And I almost screwed up your chance."

"Baby, you made a business decision. You did what you had to for the team, and yeah, I was pissed at first, but I get it. No sentiment, oui?" He kissed her unsentimentally, loving that lusty moan she gave as she kissed him back.

"So." She curled a finger in his hair. "Win the Cup. Find a wife. Knock her up."

"That's about the right of it." A sudden image of Harper cradled in his body while he stroked her pregnant belly reared up so strong his heart clamped. Where the hell was this coming from? Harper as a momma? Harper as the mother of *his* child?

Cool yo jets, fool. He so happened to be cuddling a hot woman he wanted to impale with his dick 24/7 and they were talking cookie-bakin' and baby-makin'. Bound to get his wires crossed.

"Back to your opposition to the holy state of matrimony, Harper. What I'm saying is that it's easy to get spooked. Let past performance be indicative of future results."

"Who says I'm spooked? Maybe I just don't want to have to mollycoddle a husband because he'll object to where my true love really lies." At his querying frown she explained, "The team, DuPre. Most guys don't like playing second fiddle to a woman's career. I've dated guys who went into epic hissy fits because I texted them I'd be late for dinner."

"How late?"

Averting her gaze, she muttered in the cutest way imaginable, "A couple of days. The point is I'm not going to become soft, maternal, wifey material overnight. Or ever. I have an empire to run. A team to rebuild. A legacy to establish."

"And don't stand in your way?"

She blasted him with a smile that felled him before tacking on the sweetest "Get the fuck out of my way."

He loved her honesty, how it made her sound both vulnerable and strong. But Remy's thirty-five years on this earth had taught him that people were not built to travel through life solo. Harper had to crave something more than making a losing franchise a roaring success. Once she'd done it, then what?

His phone rang in FaceTime mode with a call from his momma. He'd checked in with his dad this morning but Marie had been unavailable. He raised his eyes to Harper, a question on the tip of his tongue, but she was already scampering away into the bedroom.

I guess that answers that.

He accepted the call. "Where y'at, *mon cher*?" Marie asked.

"Good, Momma. Sorry I couldn't make it."

"That's okay. We're just worried about you being all alone and starving in the frigid north."

Pretty warm where he was at. "I managed to scrounge up something. Is everyone there?"

"The house is full and starving. Your father's in the kitchen treating the turkey to some sort of wake to acknowledge all the pleasure it's going to bring us."

Remy chuckled. That sounded like Poppa. His heart panged, missing them, but not as much as he expected. Amazing what wonders having a sexy woman around the house will do for your frame of mind.

"Of course, if you'd just find a nice girl, I wouldn't

have to worry about you so much." Someone groaned in the background, either Martine or Josette.

"Ask him if he's banged his boss yet." Definitely Josie.

"Josette!" As his momma admonished his sister, he could feel his body warming and his cheeks flushing.

"How is Harper?" Which was mom code for "Have you banged your boss yet?"

"Bon, I guess."

"Do you think—" his momma started, then was distracted by someone off camera. Two dark heads popped up, and Mignon and Colette screamed, "Hi, Uncle Remy!"

"Hi, *mes chéries*. You hungry?"

"Starving!"

His momma repositioned the phone so his nieces were out of the shot. "I know you plan to retire soon. This year, as long as you bring home the Cup, but I think you need to get crackin' on the woo with a girl who's ready to marry quick and start a family."

Josette stuck her head over Marie's shoulder. "We're gonna put you on a dating site, Remy. 'Pro athlete seeks baby factory for immediate production.'"

Momma was not amused. "You're not really putting yourself in the position to meet the kind of woman who's ready for that, now, are you?"

All joking aside, he could hear the thread of concern in her tone. She worried he'd be too old and beat up for marriage by the time his career ended.

"Puck bunnies aren't my usual diet, Momma, and that's pretty much all I meet."

"Okay. Just don't go setting your sights on anyone . . . unsuitable."

"Like your boss!" Josette again.

Remy sat up straight. Did Marie think he had Harper in mind to be Mrs. Remy DuPre? Is that what they all thought?

The ideas women latched on to. He should never have brought her home to dinner.

Yet only a minute ago, he was imagining her carrying his kid. He was closer than two bugs in a rug with his family, and now there was some weird interstate telepathy going on.

"Momma, you do not have to worry. But it's Cup first, femme later. As soon as I have that trophy, the other's gonna fall right into place."

Who would turn down a champion? He'd have his pick of the pack, not that it guaranteed a connection or even the sizzling chemistry he had with Harper.

Unsuitable Harper.

Eager to change the subject and bat away crazy thoughts of a future with his sexy boss, he said, "Hey, Momma, take me into the kitchen so I can see what this turkey wake looks like."

Day two of the Thanksgiving Holiday Fuckfest, as Remy had termed it, and somehow they did not want to kill each other. This morning she'd awoken halfway to paradise as a gorgeous hunk lapped between her legs. Finally, an alarm clock she could get on board with! After an orgasm and a much-needed nap, she'd perked up again to the smell of bacon and coffee. Remy knew how to do snowbound right.

This shouldn't feel so good. The sex—well, that should feel good. It was what every girl deserved (Woman's Bill of Rights, testify). But the rest of it, the hanging out, how natural it was with him? That should have made her feel weird.

She was screwing around with a player on her team, a man whose whopping big checks she signed, and yet she couldn't find it in herself to feel wrong about it. Worse, she was resisting hard the notion it might feel a little too right.

Holed up in his apartment like survivalists (he had a fridge freezer and can-filled pantry worthy of someone expecting the End Times), she knew that this was an artificially created bubble of sex and comfort. Later this afternoon, she would return to her car, bribe someone in security to dig it out from the Everest-sized snowdrift covering it, and drive home to Lake Forest. For now, she'd pretend that this was real life. Where was the harm? It was just a fantasy.

Curled up on Remy's sofa, Harper checked email on her phone and surreptitiously sniffed the Rebels' jersey she'd borrowed from her host. That scent went straight to certain points south.

"Ready for lunch?"

Remy came out of the kitchen waving a spatula and wearing an apron with a blue ribbon and the slogan: Together We Can Help Fight Blue Balls.

"We just had breakfast." Homemade cinnamon rolls and a Brie-bacon omelette. The skills were ridiculous.

"That was two hours ago. I was thinking steak tacos with cilantro-lime salsa."

"Sounds passable."

He grinned, knowing full well her lack of enthusiasm was a tease. The man was a wickedly amazing cook, along with all his other talents, one of which was on full display when he turned away. Nothing on under the apron!

"DuPre, hold up there a second."

Standing still, he gave a coquettish twist of his head over his shoulder. "You see something you like, minou?" She loved how comfortable he was with his body, though if she looked like him she'd walk around naked all the time, too.

He clenched his butt muscles and she almost orgasmed. Words refused to form.

"No wow for this ass, baby?" He backed up, wiggling suggestively as he moved closer. "Come on, baby, you wanna take a bite out of this, don't you?"

Oh, he was a cheeky one, pun most definitely intended. Forcing her goggle-eyed gaze away from the Globes of Perfection, she picked up the PS4 controller. "Think I'll play a game while you cook."

That got his attention. "You play the video games?"

"*The* video games?"

He sat, all thoughts of lunch clearly forgotten, though she was having a tough time forgetting that he was naked underneath that apron. "That's what Jorgenson calls it. Usually when he's getting his ass handed to him by Alamo. Now that kid can play."

She'd heard rumors that the team spent occasional nights off over here. It did her heart good to know that Remy was taking them under his wing.

She turned on the console and asked casually, "Are you any good?"

He skewered her with a look. "*Am I any good?* There's a reason *Hockey All Stars* based one of its characters on me."

"You mean apart from the check they wrote you for the privilege of using your likeness and name?"

He whipped the controller from her, indignant. "Yes, apart from that. They based a player on me because they know I'm a fan and I'm damn good at *the video games*." Less than a minute later, *Hockey All Stars* had loaded up. "You ever play this one, Harper?"

"An older version, though not in a few years. I'm sure I can get the hang of it."

She let him show her how the controller worked while he explained the objectives of the game (uh, score more goals than the other side). She even asked a few stupid questions.

Then she proceeded to wipe the rink with him.

"Playin' the ringer, huh? Pretty sneaky." He regarded her with new appreciation. "I like it. I was letting some goals in there at the beginning because I didn't want you to be humiliated, but now it's on."

"It's on?"

His mouth creased into a dirty DuPre grin. "Like Donkey Kong. Let's make it interesting."

"What did you have in mind?"

"How about a game of strip PlayStation?"

"As you're only wearing an apron, it'll be over before I can say 'she shoots, she scores.'"

"One piece of clothing versus"—he pulled at the neckline of the hockey shirt she'd been wearing like a Remy pelt since yesterday morning—"four. My shirt, your panties, and those sexy tube socks. That's a considerable handicap, Harper. I'm already three points to the bad, which means you can lose three games and still be in with a chance of winning the war."

Interesting. "What are we playing for?"

"If I win, you stay another night."

"And if I win?"

"Anything you want."

The possibilities. "Do I have to state it up front?"

He thought on that, likely seeking a trap. "You can call it in at any time."

Did he realize what he was saying? The things she could ask of him.

Stay in Chicago. Stay with the Rebels. Stay with me.

He mistook her hesitation for something else. "I'll even handicap myself further. You can sit on my lap, little girl."

"Losing turns you on, DuPre?"

"You turn me on, minou. Only you." He kissed her. Slow, sweet, a preview of coming attractions, or more likely part of his strategy to jumble her brain before they started, which was confirmed when he inched up the apron in a slow tease. Every beautiful muscle was on display, including the fast-growing one between his legs. Foxy fast, he pulled her into his lap with her back to his chest.

As her already slick center met the silky steel of his cock, he hissed. "No panties? And there was I thinking you had that extra piece of clothing to give you an edge."

She sat back on his erection, loving how hot he already was for her. Then she peeled off her socks, one at a time, and dropped them to the floor. "I don't need to be handicapped in games with you. Level playing field. One game. Winner takes all."

They were already even in every possible way, and God, she loved that. How they matched each other, quip for quip, stroke for stroke, orgasm for brain-destroying orgasm.

"You think you can beat me in this position, DuPre?" He'd have to reach around to hold his controller, plus she could easily block his view if she wanted. She wriggled in his lap to let him know just how hard this position would get for him.

"Bring it, Chase." He licked the inner shell of her ear, sending shivers through her.

A few minutes later, she realized that Remy had indeed been downplaying his skills in the first round. Practically handcuffed, blind, and under assault every moment she squirmed against him, he was still putting on an amazing show.

Time to up the stakes. She slid her damp crease along the rigid pressure beneath her. His thumb slipped on the controller—and she slipped a goal past his tender.

"That's how it is, huh?" His voice was low. Dangerous.

"Got to use all my weapons and wiles." She pushed back, angling to deliver further interference, but only got pleasure in return as his hardness found a perfect spot in her softness. They needed to be careful, because the temptation to let him slip a goal past *her* tender was near irresistible.

"Remy—"

"Got it, minou."

At the sound of a music-to-her-ears crinkle of foil, she lifted off him to allow access. "Do I want to know where you were hiding that?"

"Seat cushions," he rasped. "After yesterday, when we came close to fucking on the kitchen table only to have to move to the bedroom because of the condom situation, I've taken the necessary precautions. Here, shower, cookie jar in the kitchen . . ." And then he slipped inside her, his reach deep, his girth filling her to the point she almost orgasmed on the spot.

"Don't forget the game, Harper." He sucked on her earlobe, his breath a sweet pant. "See if you can beat me now."

At what, exactly? She lifted her body an inch and pushed back down on his cock, the sensation so amazing that she did it again. And again.

Her fingers fumbled with the controller, but it was useless. Pleasure had entered the game and it was winning. "I—I can't." She threw the controller down on the sofa and threw herself wholeheartedly into being fucked by this god of ice and fire.

One brute hand gripped her hip, expertly controlling her penetration; the other cupped her breast under the Rebels shirt and rolled her nipple.

"Touch yourself, Harper. Show me how you like it."

She lowered her hand over her clit, the sizzle a shock when she touched the swollen bud. In half a heartbeat, she was upended and pushed to her knees on the sofa with Remy still wedged deep inside her. His strength completely unspooled her.

Kneeling behind her, he pumped long, luscious strokes, each one designed to drive her to the edge and over into mindlessness. Sensation barreled through her, crystalline and hot, and she screamed as her vision blurred and pinpricks of light flashed white behind her eyes.

With the aftershocks of her orgasm still shuddering through her, she panted, "Who won?"

"Christ, femme, are you trying to kill me?"

Laughing, she reached over to the controller and hit the X button to shoot the goal past on-screen Remy into the opposing team's net. "Guess I did."

He withdrew and flipped her over, his body huge and dominant above her. Hastily, he tore off the apron, revealing his dark-flushed cock pulsing through the rubber.

"Apparently I'm not doing a good enough job if you still have enough brain cells to finish the game."

She cupped his jaw and ran a thumb along his lower lip. She loved his lived-in face, how his zest for life showed in every crease and crinkle. She loved this world he'd invited her into.

"I'll concede a draw," she said, chuckling again. "One more night, Remy."

"Love that laugh, minou." In his eyes she saw joy burn bright. He really wanted her here, and that— just the notion of being truly wanted by someone— conjured a dangerous flutter in her chest. She knew her daddy issues made her particularly vulnerable to a man as caring as Remy, so she latched on to a life preserver in the stormy sea:

He would leave before she let him into her heart.

He nuzzled her nose, smuggling unmistakable tenderness into the gesture. "It's not a draw, Harper. Not when we both win." And then he took as his prize a victory kiss and orgasms for all.

TWENTY-TWO

Remy pulled on the collar of his button-down and loosened the tie he'd worn with his game-day suit for the Rebels' annual holiday party. Apparently Harper threw this shindig for the team every year at her house in Lake Forest.

Since Thanksgiving, they'd been taking their chances where they could. During a couple of away games she'd snuck into his hotel room, and on Bren's most recent trip to Atlanta, Harper had spent the night at Remy's. Gretzky adored her and seemed to fart less when she was around. Such a gentleman.

Tonight he had a legitimate excuse to be in here, except she wasn't talking to him.

Scratch that. She was talking to him as DuPre, *her player*, with a brittle politeness he wanted to break in half. Hell, every other bozo in the room was getting quality smiles from the boss, but Remy? He might as well have doused his body in shit spray for all the love it was bringing him.

Most of the team looked to be in *Imma-get-some-tonight* heaven. Callaghan was feeling up his hot fiancée near the fireplace. Jorgenson had turned up with some supermodel who clearly needed a sandwich, but given tonight's selection of finger foods, would be out of luck. Burnett was flirting his ass off with Violet, and this last development was not going down well with Remy's date.

Yep, Remy had a date, a broody Scots fucker who was playing at designated driver. Now that they practically shared custody of the dog, they might as well move in together and turn their act into *The Odd Couple*.

"Should I tell her?" he asked Bren, who had a death grip on a bottle of Coke and was sticking with his usual *glare-Violet-Vasquez-into-the-grave* brand of seduction.

Bren's frown deepened. "Tell who what?"

"That you'd like to ask her to prom? Figure I owe you for the ride over."

"You won't get a ride back if you don't shut your pie hole."

"Such charm. No wonder you're scoring big."

The captain heaved a sigh and turned away from the sight of Violet and Cade huddled together like they were sharing high school secrets. Remy had to admit a certain annoyance, not because he had a thing for Violet but because they seemed to be carrying on a relationship out in the open and no one cared that she was a team owner with a player.

Eager to pile on the misery, he sought out Harper.

She looked gorgeous, her skin glowing under festive lights, her blond hair down in those waves he loved. A strapless red cocktail dress revealed her beautiful rounded shoulders. Didn't she know he loved her fucking shoulders? And now she was taunting him as she played hostess, flitting around making sure everyone was having a fabulous time.

"What's got your jock strap in a twist?" Bren had now moved from eye-fucking Violet to pot-meet-kettle.

"We're professional athletes, right?"

"According to my paycheck and ESPN."

"We are much sought after by women. So what the hell are we doing at a holiday party holding each other's dicks?"

Bren raised an eyebrow. "Not where I thought this night was going."

"You know what I mean. How long since your divorce?"

"I'm not sleeping with you, DuPre." The big guy's mouth went taut with tension. "I can't date anyone until I'm dry for a year."

Well, that sucked. "So you're going to drag me down with you?"

This drew St. James's grin, a crack of light in a darkening storm.

A musical tinkle of steel against crystal cut the bro banter short. Harper Chase, Rebels president, acting general manager, and five feet one and a half inches of sin, commanded the room's attention.

She gave a nervous cough. "Well, Rebels, here we are again."

The team chortled, though it did little to settle her. He hated seeing her look vulnerable in front of anyone. He wanted to defend her from every sling and arrow, keep that soft side of her for him alone.

"The last few years have been lean," Harper continued. "Tough for all of us, but especially for you, our lifeblood. You're competitive, you're warriors, and losing doesn't sit well with you. Fucking hell, it doesn't sit well with me."

Louder laughs greeted that, everyone feeling more at ease joking about the bad old days and hearing sophisticated Harper using language more suited to a locker room. The expletive seemed to open her up, and her voice now rang out clear and resonant.

"I know some of you wanted to bail when my—our—father died." Her gaze slid to Violet, who was barely paying attention, too busy flirting with Cade. No sign of Isobel. "And when we made changes in the front office, you wondered if we'd lost our minds. How were we going to make this work with no GM, morale at its lowest, and the prospect of failure looming? But we've climbed up from the pit since October. Not all the way, not completely out into the light, but we can see glimmers. A few people wanted to bask in the sun sooner and we wish them well. But for those of you who don't mind a little while longer in the trenches breathing coal dust, I thank you—*we* thank you—for placing your faith in us. The ship is turning, and with an organization as huge as this, that takes time. We have faith in you all to make this work, to flip our fortunes, and to touch hardware again." She raised a glass and everyone followed her lead. "I'll allow you all an extra hour to sleep in tomorrow, but then it's back to practice. Tonight, we celebrate the Rebels!"

Everyone cheered, and Remy caught Bren's eye, surprised to find a lack of cynicism there. Hope, the worst four-letter word there is, was doing a number on them all. Who'd have thought Harper Chase could rouse the troops like this?

Something else was rousing. Christ, he needed to touch her so badly. A full hour of sexual frustration ticked over before he saw a chance to make his move.

He found her in the kitchen, instructing the catering staff sergeant-major style to send out more canapés. Isobel stood off to the side, looking sullen. Neither of them noticed him.

"We could announce it tonight, while they're half drunk," Isobel said. "By the time the New Year rolls around, they'll be used to the idea."

Harper curled her elegant fingers around the stem of a champagne flute. "Did you see Deacon's column on last night's game? We're still viewed as freaks, every win as a fluke. Right now, we have this pitch-perfect balance, so why the hell would I upset that by appointing a new coach midseason?"

"You mean a female coach, Harper?" Isobel *hmphed*.

"What happened to grabbing pro hockey by the balls and showing them how bitches get shit done?"

"Maybe it would be an option if I'd found out you quit your last job from *you* instead of from the press."

"They were supposed to keep it under wraps until I was ready to deal with it." Isobel raised her chin, noticing Remy for the first time. "What about you, Remy? Would you have a problem with a woman running skating drills?"

So not getting in the middle of this. "I'm sort of biased, growing up with so many women. Hell, I'm practically honorary in the sisterhood."

Isobel grabbed a beer bottle from the kitchen counter. "You're going to have to realize that this is a joint operation, not just Harper Chase's personal fiefdom." She left the kitchen, a gust of indignation in her wake.

Harper met his gaze, acting all surprised. "Remy! Were you looking for the restroom? It's in the corridor behind you."

"We need to talk."

She blinked at him, panic in her eyes that quickly faded to an indifference he wasn't buying. "I'm pretty busy. Perhaps you could make an appointment with my assistant tomorrow."

He snagged her wrist as she walked by him. "Perhaps I could kiss you senseless in front of everyone at this party."

"Remy—"

"Just a minute of the boss's time." Something on the back counter distracted him. Something both obscene and poorly crafted.

"Is that a ceramic co—?"

"Mug tree? Yep. I know, it's awful, but Violet made it and we're trying to encourage her artistic side. Sculptural version of kids' drawings on the fridge." She laughed softly. "Come with me."

He followed her through a doorway off the side of the kitchen, then farther down a corridor. She opened a door, waited until he stepped inside what looked like a laundry room, then closed it behind them.

Hands on hips, she faced him. "Now what's so urgent that it couldn't wait?"

"This." He gripped her waist and pulled her flush against his full arousal. The heat of her turned his blood to liquid fire. "Have you any idea how hard it's been for me all night?"

"Getting an idea of the extent of your problem."

His lips dropped to her shoulders. "You *know* I love these shoulders."

"You've never told me that."

Surely he had. "If I haven't, which I very much doubt, then I should have. These shoulders are a work of art." He laid a trail of kisses across one, then the other. "These shoulders should be cast in bronze and set outside Rebels HQ so men can worship. They can rub the shoulders and make wishes."

She giggled. "Wishes for what?"

"That their wives and girlfriends had shoulders so sexy."

She laughed again. God, he loved her laugh, and he especially loved causing it.

"So what did you think?" she asked after a minute of rubbing and kissing and soft little moans.

"Thinking's not really an option right now."

She pushed him back. "My speech."

He paused in his exploration of the curve of Harper's exquisite neck. "I think . . . you're doing a mighty fine job of selling hope to a crew that hasn't felt it in a while."

"I'm not trying to sell it. I'm trying to instill it."

He placed a finger under her chin. "You've made some good decisions since you took over. The team sees you working hard. I see you working hard—maybe too hard. We know what you're putting in and we appreciate it. Hope? I'd say we have it."

Had he just said "we"? When did he start lumping himself in with the Rebels?

Something hung in the air between them, the knowledge that he'd crossed some invisible line. Hope—that damn four-letter word again—reflected back at him in those beautiful eyes. Shit, he didn't want this burden. It was one thing to wish her the best, it was quite another to chain his own hopes and dreams to hers.

"Okay there, DuPre?" A slender hand coasted down each button of his shirt, dipped below his waistband,

and settled over where he was most definitely okay. Thank Christ one of them had a head in the game here.

"You know I think you can do anything, Harper. Whatever your father thought, whatever the press throws at you, whatever other team owners say . . . you deserve to be here, running this organization."

A little whoosh of breath left her, and in it he heard her relief. She had her sisters, but he also knew that she felt alone in this. Her father hadn't trusted her. She was carrying an enormous weight on those beautiful shoulders. Every minute he was with her, she needed to hear that he had her back.

At least on some abstract level, because this didn't change his plans. Come January, he'd be out. Tommy was already fielding interest. Remy had given the Rebels his pound of beaten-up flesh, now they owed him a one-way ticket off the island.

She sniffed and her eyes took on a suspicious shine.

"Minou," he murmured. "I've got you. I'll always have you."

He meant his emotional support, nothing else. But every bite of her lip, every blink of those bewitching eyes, every heave of those perfect breasts drew him deeper into her orbit.

"Thanks, Remy," she whispered, and then she kissed him. Soft, sweet, with a breathy little moan that destroyed him. They both pulled back at the same time, recognizing that the terms had changed, but neither of them knowing how to navigate this new path.

She spoke first. "I should get back to my guests."

He nodded, unable to form words that would likely have emerged scratchy anyway.

"Need a second?" she asked.

Only a lifetime.

She rubbed over his significant erection. "I mean this."

"I'll manage," he choked out. Tough as it was, he could turn off his desire for her. His . . . everything for her.

He had to.

Smiling like she knew all his secrets, she opened the door and found her sisters standing outside.

Harper was tempted to shove Remy back, close the door to the laundry room, and pretend that her sisters were not facing her, smirking like finalists in a *well well well, what have we here?* contest.

Womaning up, she stepped out into the corridor. Remy stood behind her, and the urge to lean back against all that solidity almost overwhelmed her. For a moment there when he told her she could do anything, she'd come close to breaking down in tears. Her, Harper Chase, crying! His support toppled her, mostly because she hadn't realized how much she craved it.

"Contract negotiations?" Violet asked with Dad's crooked grin. Isobel stood with fists clenched on hips, looking like she wanted to flay Harper alive.

Strong hands gripped her shoulders and soft lips grazed the top of her head, leaving no doubt that her relationship with Remy was more than boss-employee.

"I'll leave you to it," he said.

She turned to him, gaping. "You're throwing me under the bus?"

"You'd rather I stayed to explain?" His mouth twitched in that wickedly adorable Remy way. "Okay, ladies, here's how it works. When a man wants a woman, a crucial part of his anatomy gets very, very—"

Harper held up an imperious hand. "Be gone, DuPre. Back to your broody Scottish date."

He leaned in and kissed her, a gentle brush of her forehead. "Call me later, minou."

As he walked away, three sets of eyes tracked his long-limbed move back to the party, noting how that charcoal wool clung fondly to his very fine ass.

"Cute flanter, soulful gazing, and min-*noo*?" Violet batted her eyelashes. "That sounds awfully romantic."

"Well, it's not," Harper snapped back. "It's filthy. An insult, really." And just about the sweetest thing anyone had every called her.

Isobel still looked furious. "You've got to be kidding."

Harper's heart thundered violently against her rib cage. "I'm just working off some steam. These last few months have been so stressful and . . ." She waved a hand to fill in the rest.

Violet scoffed. "If you're working off steam, what's

he doing? Because the cooking tells a whole other story."

Isobel's eyebrows shot so high they became one with her hairline. "Cooking?" Said like it rhymed with "puppy beating" or "seal clubbing."

Violet laughed. "He's been using the bartenders at the Empty Net as a delivery service. Remy's cooking for Harper—*actual cooking*—and then sneaking it to her like some sort of food ninja in love."

She could deny. She could insist Violet was imagining things.

"You can't tell anyone." Harper eyed her sisters. "I mean it," she added for emphasis when neither of them spoke.

Isobel frowned. "You mean we can't tell anyone that the boss is banging a player on her team after she expressly forbade her own sisters from doing the exact same thing."

Harper flushed and muttered, "Yes, that."

"And the cooking?"

Another shameful mutter. "Especially that." It was just so damning.

Violet shook her head. "Far be it from me to tell anyone how to conduct their sex life, but I have to say this does not seem like the behavior of Harper 'The Team Is My Life' Chase. I get that the vag can be mightier than the brain, but what about 'the world is watching' and 'our mission is to represent women owners in professional sports'?"

Harper groaned. "I know. Oh, God, no one knows more than me how messed up this is." She'd been doing this alone for so long, and there was comfort in being held by someone. That's all it was. Everyone wanted a warm body to hold on to around the holidays.

"It's just sex and it's winding down. That first flush, the thrill is gone, et cetera, et cetera."

"That did not look like it was winding down," Isobel said. "He was *affectionate* with you. Like he cares. You have to end it."

Harper was already nodding before she'd finished. Of course she had to end it. Not only that, she had to come clean about everything. "He'll be traded out soon."

Isobel's eyes widened. "What are you talking about? We just traded him in."

"About that . . ." Harper filled them in on the bargain she'd struck with Remy at the start of the season.

If she thought Isobel was annoyed before, she hadn't reckoned on how this would fling her over the edge. "I can't believe you made this deal without consulting us! We're supposed to be in this together."

"Isobel—"

"We don't have to trade him," Isobel rushed on, her fury replaced with plaintiveness. "He's holding the team together. We get rid of him and who knows what'll happen?"

"I made a promise," Harper said. "And it's for the

best. He goes, and I don't have to deal with the mess. It's surgical."

"Kind of sneaky on DuPre's part," Violet said, her tone filled with admiration. "He gets a hot time-bounded affair and a decent shot at the champion-ship."

"It's not like that," Harper said, unsure why she was defending him. He wasn't using her. She was using him. They were using each other.

Isobel was back to pissed. "You shouldn't have made this deal with him in the first place, and now we have to get rid of him? Is that what happened with Billy Stroger, Harper? *'You broke my heart, here's your pink slip.'* You can't use the team as your personal harem, and you especially can't make trades because it's awkward for you to be around an ex."

With a frustrated wave, Isobel walked off, leaving Harper stricken.

Violet mouthed *holy shit*. "Don't worry, she'll calm down. You can bang whoever you like."

But she couldn't. Isobel didn't know the whole sorry shitfest that was Billy Stroger, but she wasn't so far off the mark. Yet again, Harper had flown too close to the sun. When you were bathed in a light as bright as Remy, it was all too easy to forget the painful burns of the past.

TWENTY-THREE

Feeling like a kid in a Christkindlmarket, Harper tip-toed through the snow blanketing the ground at Chicago's annual tradition, the European-style Christmas market in the city's Loop. She made it a habit to visit at least once each holiday season, knowing it was the perfect spot to get away from it all and do her last-minute holiday shopping. Productivity had always been the best therapy.

Magic was all around, which Harper acknowledged was about the sappiest thing ever. But one of her happiest memories was when her father had brought her here when she was only six, the first year it opened. It was the Christmas after her parents divorced, but Cliff had insisted that nothing would change. Of course, she didn't know then that Isobel was three months from entering the world with a hockey stick in one hand and Cliff's heart in the other or that this would be the last Christmas he would be truly present.

Shaking off the maudlin, Harper combed the stalls,

looking for stocking stuffers and tchotchkes, trying not to get all gooey-hearted at the sight of couples walking hand in hand and families straight out of Disney Central Casting. That wasn't for her. Apparently she was destined to want guys she couldn't be seen in public with. Any psychologist with a crappy diploma would have a field day.

You are drawn to zee unavailable men, Ms. Chase, her inner therapist said in a heavy German accent. *Zee relationships with zee expiration dates zat are doomed from zee start. Zat way, zey cannot choose to leave you—it is already written in zee stars.*

Self-awareness should have helped, but instead it left her depressed. It was a pattern she gravitated toward because, in patterns, Harper's world and her place in it made sense. Remy couldn't hurt her because he would be gone soon. Their business arrangement kept it clean, a bloodless severance. No fuss, no muss.

One more month.

A cold wind whipped in and sliced through her shearling coat, icing over her soft heart. Perhaps a hot chocolate from the stall she'd passed on the way in would help to warm her up. She turned and walked right into the arms of a heated wall.

"Minou." Said low and husky enough to melt that ice around her weakening love muscle. Remy's blue eyes twinkled in mischief.

"Um—I was just thinking about you," she blurted. *Dumbass.*

"Doesn't surprise me. Once I get in, I'm hard to get out."

Unfortunately true. He wore a faux fur hat pulled down low with hanging earflaps that should have looked silly, but just looked like Remy. His arms had circled her waist and her body settled in against him naturally, fitting into the warm nooks like a desperate limpet.

"Remy," she whispered. "What are you doing here?"

"Holiday shopping. Like you. Like everyone else here."

"We can't be seen together."

He tweaked at her over-the-ears beanie. "Harper, with this headgear, we're unrecognizable."

"So you usually throw your arms around strange women?"

"I mean that we're unrecognizable to the public. My body, on the other hand, would know you in a blizzard."

She'd been thinking something very similar, but she bit back her agreement.

"You're all covered up and I'm wearing this dumb hat that Josette sent me and we're just a couple walking through the Christmas market, doing our holiday shopping and sipping hot chocolate."

A couple. The ice floe in her veins melted while something fractured in the vicinity of her chest. She was having a hard time speaking.

He continued applying the pressure. "If you deny me this, I'll think you're only interested in my body."

"I *am* only interested in your body."

"Jesus, couldn't you try fake-liking my personality for a bit? I'm a professional athlete with a fragile ego that needs constant positive reinforcement."

Feeling overwhelmed—so what was new?—she angled her hip so it brushed against that intriguing ridge in his jeans. "This kind of positive reinforcement?"

His grin lit her on fire. "My ego's feeling better already."

Remy had taken a chance on running into Harper at the market. He'd stopped by her assistant's desk at lunch when he knew Harper was in the weekly scouting meeting, flirted a little, and happened to notice that Harper had Christkindlmarket on her schedule. After he'd Googled it because his German wasn't nearly as good as his French, he headed to the city to do his Christmas shopping. This market was as good a place as any to buy knickknacks and tree ornaments and creepy-looking nutcrackers that he knew his momma would eat up with a spoon.

It was also the perfect place to spend a little quality time with Harper that didn't involve a rush to get naked and a sprint out the door before the sun rose. Don't get him wrong—every moment Harper spent in his bed was amazing. But he liked talking to her, as well. He liked breaking down games, picking her wily brain, listening to her run rings around him in that bombshell gush.

He'd hoped being discovered by her sisters might open her mind up to the possibilities. This woman was the whole package, and but for the fact she was his boss, he'd be making a play for taking this to the next level. If he could get her used to the idea of them as a couple, maybe they could ease into something solid when he moved on in a month.

They stopped at one of the stalls that sold soaps. Remy suspected his nieces would adore them because they were shaped like little gingerbread houses.

"Cute gifts for my girls, maybe?"

Harper chuckled, leaning into his side. "I bet you spoil them rotten."

"Course I do. Little girls should be spoiled." He nuzzled against her neck. "Big girls, too."

"I'm capable of spoiling myself."

He cupped her chin and tilted it up. "It's okay to let someone take care of you, Harper. And I don't just mean between the sheets, because that's a given. You'll always get that from me. But I think you need to be fed and fussed over just as much as you need to be fucked. And you need to be spoiled every now and then to remind you that you deserve the best."

Her big, expressive eyes blinked up at him, those pools he sank deeper into with each new viewing.

"You're the one to spoil me?"

"I'm the man for the job."

Every job, he wanted to say. He'd feed her mind, her body, and show her the meaning of worship.

"You can start by keeping me warm."

He took her hand and interlocked his fingers with hers before popping their joined hands into his jacket pocket. "I'm thinking that the best way to do that would be to check into a hotel."

She nodded her acceptance of that plan, no hesitation. Thank God, because he was fully prepared to throw her over his shoulder and drag her to his lair.

"Harper! Harper!" He turned to find two bright-faced, dark-haired girls in the eight-to-ten-year-old range standing before them.

"Girls!" Harper exclaimed. "It's been so long. Look how big you've grown." She snatched her hand from Remy's pocket and let herself be tackle-hugged by the kids.

The shorter one had her right arm in a cast, and she pointed at her glasses. "I'm a total nerd now, Harper."

"Uh, a totally cute nerd, Franky. Don't forget what I told you: nerds will inherit the earth. How's the arm, kiddo?"

"Itchy. But I was able to get Erik Jorgenson to sign my cast." She pointed at an illegible red scrawl. "It says 'Franky rocks' in Swedish!"

"Awesome! So, where's your dad?"

On cue, Bren St. James appeared like a looming beast out of a Scottish mist, putting his phone into his pocket. A few seconds of silence followed while he read the situation. Remy felt his blood draining to his toes. Something slipping away.

"Franky, Caitriona, this is Remy." Bren put a hand on each of the girls' shoulders. "He's on the team."

Yeah, Cap, thanks for the reminder.

"You're the league leader for power-play goals," the taller girl—Caitriona—announced with authority. Sliding a guilty glance at her father, she added, "But my dad has a better plus-minus than you."

Okay, then. We've got ourselves a future Harper Chase here.

A nervous Harper babbled to the girls, something about the lights and did they like the market and wasn't the Christmas tree festive, while their father's stone-eyed gaze found Remy, not revealing one iota of how this would play out. Thing is, Remy could handle whatever would come. He'd be proud to go public with Harper. For everyone to know he was her man.

Throughout this strange little scene, Remy was struck by something else: Harper was amazing with Bren's girls. No phony adult-to-child condescension, just Harper displaying a genuine interest in their lives. And the girls clearly adored her.

Finally, Harper straightened and backed up so that the three adults now stood like it was some Mexican standoff. Silence ruled for a few seconds.

Harper caved first. "Bren—"

"I need to get these sprites home. We've got a tree to decorate, don't we, girls?"

The girls nodded, oblivious to the tensions in the group. They left, and Remy watched them slip into the crowd that apparently would never be anonymous enough for Harper.

"Shit, shit, shit." The hand formerly warming his now rubbed her forehead anxiously. "There's no way he didn't see that, is there?"

"Harper, it's okay. He won't say anything, and even if he did . . ."

"Even if he did, what, Remy? Even if he did, it'd be okay? Is that what you're going to say?"

"Yes. That's what I'm going to say."

"Are you fucking crazy?" she hissed. "Are you seriously saying that there is an upside to this?"

"I'm saying," he said slowly as he steered her out of the path of foot traffic to a more private location beside one of the booths, "that if it were to get out, the world would not stop spinnin' on its axis. No one would die. There'd be a few headlines for a while and then it'd pass."

Incredulity morphed to anger. "Oh, it'll pass for you, but for me? Not so much. No one will forget how the team's owner couldn't keep her legs closed around her players. No one will remember who I even opened them for, Remy."

They would if they were still together. They would if they took this next level up. They would if they knew that he'd fallen ass-over-elbow for this woman. No one would forget his name then.

Mon dieu, he was in love with Harper Chase.

This sentiment was clearly not returned. The look she was giving him now was the opposite of "in love." It was fear and fury and downright loathing.

"Minou—"

"Don't call me that! Jesus, that's what got me into trouble. I'm so starved for affection I let you in. I let you call me sweet little nicknames and tell me how much you wanted me despite how against the rules it was. But let's face it, you've never had as much to lose, Remy. You've never had *anything* to lose, because I'm just another notch on your stick. A few jokes in the locker room and it's back to business for you."

Whether it was the implication that this was just business as usual for him, or the accusation that he had somehow pushed her into sleeping with him, Remy couldn't exactly pinpoint which was worse. Aw, hell, *both* options pissed him off.

"You think you're just some notch on my stick? What the hell does that even mean?"

She shook her head, as if she had no decent explanation, which he supposed was good. She was merely spouting off in her panic, and he would let her do that because she was afraid. He would let her do it because he was in love with her and that was part and parcel of the territory. You accepted your woman's BS.

"I have to go," she muttered. "I can't do this . . . I have to go."

And then she did.

TWENTY-FOUR

"The sugar content needs something a little drier, don't you think?"

Harper and Isobel stared at Violet because she had just suggested the ideal wine pairing for . . . a Samoa. The Girl Scout cookie.

Perched on stools around the island in the kitchen—in what was increasingly becoming *their* kitchen—the Chase sisters were performing another bonding experiment. Tonight was Violet's turn to choose, and she'd opted for a wine tasting. Not wholly expected, given her inclinations alcohol-wise so far had been mostly of the Pabst Blue Ribbon variety. Then she produced the cookies.

Apparently she had brought a suitcase's worth from Reno and had been biding her time, i.e., scarfing them down solo, the greedy wench, until she deemed her sisters cookie-worthy.

Harper eyed the array of baked treats. "If sugar content is the deciding factor, then wouldn't every cookie need something on the dry side?"

Violet shook her head. "There's also the body."

"Of the wine?"

"Of the cookie." She held up one of Harper's favorites. "Take your Thin Mint, for example."

Isobel plucked it out of her hand and had it in her mouth before anyone could protest. Around her chewing she said, "You did say to take it."

Violet rolled her eyes and raised another, careful to keep it and the entire box out of Isobel's reach radius. "The Thin Mint, despite its contrary name, is one of the more robust cookies in the GSCU."

"GSCU?"

"Girl Scout Cookie Universe," Violet explained. "The chocolate and mint combo could never be compared to the delicacy of a Savannah Smile or even a Lemonade. So it needs something with more oomph."

"Like a Pinot Noir?" Harper ventured, really because there was a bottle of Pinot on the counter.

"Exactly!" Violet seemed pleased with Harper's stunning insight. She poured a measly splash of red—evidently taking the "tasting" aspect of this far too seriously—and nudged the glasses over with one Thin Mint apiece.

They sipped. They nibbled. They sipped again.

"You might be on to something here," Harper said while Isobel chowed down after the initial nibble without any thought to tasting finesse.

"What?" she said when she caught the others staring at her. "Oh, right, the wine." She downed it in one gulp.

"Heathen," Harper and Violet said in unison, then giggled stupidly.

"So where's everyone headed for the holiday?" Harper asked, sipping her wine to cover her unreasonable hope. After her blow-up with Remy at the Christkindlmarket two days ago, she was feeling a touch raw. Not that she expected the girls to change their plans for her—and she would never dream of asking them—but if they were feeling so inclined . . .

"Mom's expecting me," Isobel said. Isobel's mom, Gerry, had moved to Scottsdale after her divorce from Clifford several years ago.

"Same here," Violet replied. "Well, not Isobel's mom, but my aunt and . . ." She paused before declaring emphatically, "My aunt." She turned to Harper. "What are your plans? Kenny-boy expecting you?"

Not likely. She'd made a conscious effort to keep him at arm's length while she was sleeping with Remy. Now that she and DuPre were kaput, using Kenneth as backup to stave off her loneliness wasn't terribly classy.

"Nothing's set in stone yet, but I expect that's what I'll do." She kept her voice as light as air.

Violet studied her. "I bet Christmas in New Orleans is lovely."

"That's over."

Both women stared at her.

"It is!"

Isobel twitched her nose. "I thought you were going to let it die a natural death with his trade out."

"It just seemed like a good time to finish it. That way I don't have to get him a gift for Christmas. Much less messy." She popped a Samoa into her mouth to keep from elaborating.

"You mean less messy than when Stroger left?"

Harper stiffened at Isobel's mention of his name. "It was awkward but . . ." She took a sip of her wine, then a gulp. Then she drained the entire glass.

"But . . ." Violet prompted.

"But nothing." These girls' nights in and out were supposed to be about getting to know each other, just enough to smooth over the cracks and make the next six months bearable. They weren't supposed to be taking a crowbar to the fissures and prying the wounds apart.

"How about I start?" Violet said.

Isobel narrowed her eyes. "Start what?"

"The truth-telling. We all say something we've never told anyone before."

Harper rolled her eyes. Violet threw a Thin Mint at her, and Isobel scooped it up like she was the family Labrador hunting down scraps.

Their youngest sister took a deep breath. "Okay." She cupped her breasts, covered in a *Bitch Please* T-shirt, and displayed them. "These beauties before you? All fake."

Harper and Isobel stared at Violet's breasts. Nicely shaped, perky as shit, breasts any gal would be proud of.

Isobel slid a glance at Harper. "They're lovely, but not all that . . . big?"

Valid point. Harper hadn't given much—or any—thought to Violet's rack before, but wasn't it the rule that if you were going to go fake, you went bigger? Vi's breasts were nice and all, but not anything worth paying for.

"I wanted them to be the same as . . . before."

A slow flush creeped over Harper's skin as realization dawned. "You had reconstructive breast surgery."

"Yep. The big C."

Isobel slapped a hand over her mouth in shock. "Oh, my God. When?"

"Eighteen months ago. When we met"—she raised her eyes to Harper—"when you came to see me in Reno, I'd just been diagnosed. I wasn't ready to deal with you and that and everything to do with Cliff."

The words struggled to be free of Harper's throat. "But we could have helped. We could have been there for you."

"I had friends. I had my mom and aunts. I didn't need a couple of chicks I'd never met, whose only connection to me was a patch of DNA."

Harper understood. If she'd been going through that, she would have clawed at anyone trying to get near her. Unhealthy, perhaps, but it was the Chase family way. That didn't mean they couldn't be there for Violet now.

"Are you okay? Is there anything we can do?"

Violet's expression relaxed. "I'm okay, Harper. Since my diagnosis, I've tried to view my life as a second chance. Trying new things"—she smiled, that blinding grin so like their father's—"new people, new adventures. Like Walter White in *Breaking Bad*, but with less meth dealing. The year of the V, *chicas*."

So that was why she'd agreed so readily to the will's stipulations. She was opening herself up to new possibilities. Harper hoped she'd look at life as a rosy opportunity if she came so close to buying the farm.

"What about you, middle child?" Violet asked. "Spill thy secrets."

Isobel looked uncomfortable. "Harper should go first."

"I already did. About DuPre."

Isobel scoffed. "You just told us that something we already knew about was finished. Hardly a big reveal." Realizing Harper was going to remain tight-lipped, she blew out a breath. "Okay. I haven't had any man action in over two years."

Violet looked less than impressed. "Not exactly earth-shattering. I guessed as much with your ceramic dick that looked nothing like a real, live penis."

Isobel flicked a glance at Harper. "Well, since I got injured, I've been having a crisis of confidence with— well, a lot of things. But guys, mostly. Though it's not as if I was knocking them dead before."

It may have been subconscious, but Isobel's hand touched her hairline. Anyone who didn't know about her injury would barely notice the edge of the three-inch scar above her ear where a skate had sliced into her skull, ending her pro career.

"Is it bumpy?" Violet asked, squinting at Isobel's head. "Your scar?"

"Um, no, it's pretty smooth."

"Can I?" Violet raised her hand. "I'll show you my boob scars later."

With a nervous giggle, Isobel inclined her head, inviting Violet for a closer look.

Vi pushed her hair back. "Wow, you're one tough broad. Isn't she, Harper?"

"She sure is." Harper blinked back tears and reached for the wine bottle.

Iz flushed in embarrassment. "Yeah, well, my tough broad act isn't getting me any action."

Violet looked sympathetic. "I'm not exactly cleaning up myself. Especially as the only guys I meet are hot hockey players who I'm forbidden to fraternize with."

"Believe me, I'm doing you a favor," Harper said.

"Why? Are you saving me from a crapfest between the sheets? Though now you mention it, Isobel *did* say the guy who punched her V-card sucked." She slapped the kitchen island. "I knew it! DuPre's stick-handling skills are lacking."

"No! That was never a problem," she said. A touch smugly, if she was being honest.

Her reward was half a Samoa bounced off the side of her head.

Isobel pointed at Violet, who had thrown the baked-good missile. "Stop wasting the cookies!"

"Jesus wept, Harper," Violet said with much more

passion than the situation called for. "You have a sex-
alicious Cajun on the hook and you're throwing it
away for what? Because 'sex and hockey don't mix.'"
She said that last part in a high voice that Harper
assumed was a really bad impression.

"It's not so simple."

"Isn't it? Think of the poor women starving for
orgasms"—she gestured toward Isobel, who shrugged
in agreement—"while you hog them all. You can't even
appreciate them or the hot piece of ass who's doling
them out!"

"Yeah, Harper," Isobel piled on. "You're so fucking
greedy."

Violet giggled, clearly pleased with herself. "So you
know what this party needs?"

"More wine?" Harper offered, because they weren't
drinking nearly fast enough.

"The musical stylings of . . ." Violet opened up
iTunes on her phone and the soft notes of a guitar
were soon made sweeter by a witchy voice. "Miss Stevie
Nicks."

*One hour, two bottles of Pinot, three boxes of Samoas, and the
entire* Rumours *album later . . .*

"I was once with a guy whose cock head was shaped
like a cauliflower."

Harper squinted at Violet, who had just unloaded that gem. "Dick pics or it didn't happen."

Violet tapped the screen of her phone.

Isobel screeched. "Are you kidding? You actually have a dick pic?"

Their youngest sister held up a hand. "I have never solicited a dick pic, but once it's sent to me, it goes in the dicktabase."

So much to unpack in that statement, and Harper was just a hairbreadth on this side of sober enough to do it.

"Dicktabase?"

"My Tumblr for dicks." A couple of clicks later and Harper was gazing at a scandal in the making. Violet Vasquez, youngest daughter of Clifford Chase, one-third owner of the Chicago Rebels professional hockey team, cataloged pics—and GIFs—of penises.

"This—this—" Harper shook her head as Stevie begged Tom Petty to stop draggin' her heart around. "If anyone ties this to you or the organization, have you the slightest idea how much trouble we're in?"

"Don't be such a prude, Harper. It's just a gallery of cock, and my name is nowhere on the site. Besides, the act of sending it is the equivalent of signing a terms-and-conditions statement—that dick is now fair game."

"Wow, there are a lot of pierced penises here." Isobel had picked up the phone and was scrolling with the avid curiosity of a woman who had not been laid in a very long time.

"Pierced is the bomb. It really enhances the sensations for all involved."

Isobel groaned. "I can't believe my baby sister has so much more experience than me."

Violet blushed, and Isobel grabbed her hand. "Not that there's anything wrong with that! I think it's awesome you're so open about what you want and make no bones about getting it."

"Or boners," an increasingly drunken Harper interjected.

Violet squeezed Izzy's hand back. "I didn't think that's what you meant. I just—never mind." She caught Harper's eye, and while Harper might be ten sheets to the wind, she understood Vi's source of discomfort.

Isobel had called Violet her baby sister, and Violet was trying to decide if she liked that or not.

"So, I could really do with some dating advice," Isobel said, still glued to Violet's phone and the Cavalcade of Cock.

"Dating advice?" Violet exclaimed. "You need a dating intervention. Don't worry, we'll work something out, won't we, Harper?"

"Of course we will. There's no reason why you shouldn't be cleaning up on the dating circuit, Iz. You're a wealthy woman with a badass scar and thighs of steel."

"No hockey players," Isobel said morosely.

"No hockey players," Harper agreed, equally morosely.

Violet chuckled. "This should be good."

TWENTY-FIVE

"Do you think she's going to be all right?"

Isobel frowned as she watched Violet weave unsteadily down the icy path to the coach house. Stumbling slightly, she held her fist aloft and announced without turning, "I've got this, chicas. Go the fuck to sleep!"

Harper giggled, still feeling a bit squishy. "She'll be fine. She's a survivor, that one."

They both waited until Violet was out of sight, then a minute more until they heard a muffled thud—the sound of the coach house door closing.

Isobel shut the kitchen door. "That breast cancer business was pretty wild, wasn't it?"

"Not as wild as the dicktabase." Shaking her head, Harper handed off a glass of water and two Tylenol. "Drink up."

Izzy rolled her eyes but did as she was told. On previous girls' nights in, when Violet left, Harper and Isobel didn't linger alone together. This stranger who had entered their lives played the perfect buffer and, without her, the rubber band's tension stretched between the Chase sisters who had never gelled.

But for once, Harper didn't want the space. She wanted to embrace the raw emotions swirling through the air.

"Look, I'm sor—"

"I should have—"

Nervous laughter ensued. Exercising her privilege as the eldest, Harper started over. "I'm sorry I didn't tell you about the trade agreement with Remy. I wanted to, and maybe part of me thought I wouldn't have to honor it, but then it got so complicated."

"When you decided to have sex with him?"

That. Though everything seemed a thousand times more twisted. "It wasn't so much a decision as an . . . imperative. Maybe I was just lonely."

The excuse sounded weak and pathetic. Exactly what Clifford had despised. But the truth? Her need for Remy was desperate, just as his absence was like a yawning ache.

She peered up to find Isobel staring at her with something like compassion. Her skin prickled under her sister's gaze, and an opening appeared that she could step through. Be honest. Lay it out there. But her guarded heart counted to three and let the gap close. Not drunk enough, perhaps.

Seeming to recognize that Harper Confession Time was at an end—for now—Isobel spoke up. "I should have told you about resigning my coaching position in Montreal. It was just getting tough to be here for the games and be there for the guys. I wish I knew what Dad wanted. He hated that I had to give up playing and go into coaching. I don't want to disappoint him."

"How is that even possible? Have you any idea how proud he was of you?"

Harper would never forget her father's joy the night Isobel won silver for Team USA. He'd broken his ankle before the trip to Sochi and couldn't attend in person, so they watched the games together at his house in Riverbrook. Though it killed her because Harper had never experienced his paternal pride, she still cheered her sister on through every glide, hit, and goal. Harper's baby sister was a champion, not that her envy would allow her a kind word about it.

"I know he was proud when I was winning," Isobel continued, "just like I know he took my injury hard. He wasn't all that tolerant of weakness, was he?"

"No," Harper whispered, tears tightening her throat. "He wasn't."

"I was supposed to be the big success, the one who used those Cup-winning genes. And now . . . I'm not sure what my path is. You've always seemed so sure of what you were meant to do, Harper. You were born to lead this team. I envy your certainty."

Just went to show you could bullshit your way through anything, because Harper had never felt less sure in her life. Neither had she given much thought to how Isobel might have had her own problem living up to the high expectations of her father. Maybe too-high expectations rivaled none at all.

"You gave me a heart attack that night in Buffalo, you know?"

Isobel's gaze shot up. "I didn't even know you were coming to the game."

As if Harper would miss her sister's pro debut, the night she inaugurated the National Women's Hockey League as captain of the Buffalo Betties. Not wanting to pile on the pressure, Harper had told no one she was going. Besides, it was so much fun to blend in with the swaying mass of humanity in the Bayside Arena, all there to witness history.

"I'm all about bitches getting shit done. And that night, Iz, you were getting it done. I was so proud of you. That night, every moment before, and every moment since."

Isobel's eyes were shiny with emotion. "My thirty-seven minutes of glory. That's how long my pro career lasted. One minute I'm celebrating an awesome goal, the next . . ." She curled her hand in a fist on the kitchen island counter, a strategy to stop from touching her scar again, perhaps. "It's hard to get the respect, even in the minors, based on such a short stint."

Maybe there was more to her resignation from Montreal than road warrior woes. Harper wanted to say that they'd find a place for her on the Rebels' coaching staff, but there was too much up in the air to make that promise.

"I'm very drunk and very tired," Isobel said with a sniff and a rusty giggle. "You coming up?"

"In a minute. Just going to load the dishwasher."

With Isobel gone, Harper cleared away the wineglasses and empty cookie boxes, and let her mind wander to a snowy night in Buffalo almost two years ago. The crowd. The cheers. The swish of the blades. The tap of stick-versus-puck.

The pool of crimson seeping from Isobel's head onto the bone-white ice.

At the hospital, her father had been a mess—and even then Harper had resented his concern for Isobel compared to his lack for Harper in the wake of what happened with Stroger. But she'd put her pettiness aside to be there for him. For her sister. And when the doctor said she was out of surgery and her skull would heal in time, her father had cried in relief.

Thank Christ, he'd sobbed. *She'll come back. I know she will. Stronger than ever.*

He'd gone in to see her, leaving Harper to deal with the multitude of visitors. Isobel's teammates, sports media, hockey league officials—

Holy. Hell. How could she have forgotten about *him*?

The Russian.

Harper had met Vadim Petrov one summer eight years ago when he trained with the Rebels as a nineteen-year-old. Instead of taking up a lucrative contract in the NHL, he'd returned to Russia to rule the Kontinental Hockey League, winning every trophy, smashing every record. Five years ago he had finally made his North American pro debut in Quebec, and now Harper was considering trading him in to replace Remy.

But that night—the night of Isobel's first and last game in the National Women's Hockey League—Petrov was in the hospital's waiting room. When Harper emerged to tell everyone about Isobel's condition, he had stalked toward her, his expression so fierce she almost recoiled. Even now she shivered, remembering his words. No small talk, no build up. Just three syllables he appeared to summon from a deep, wounded place.

"She will live?"

Not *"Is she okay?"* Not *"How is she?"* Pure Russian intensity and drama distilled into this singular, charged moment.

Even in the midst of researching Petrov for a possible trade, this memory had stayed buried until now. A night of wine, Stevie Nicks, and sister bonding had pushed it to the surface. Memories, emotions, all the rawness—for so long, Harper had stuffed it down deep, and now her body felt like a live wire, a conductor for masses of inconvenient sensation. Too much was happening at once. Her father's death, her sisters' invasion, the team's haul back from the brink. Her brain could barely keep up and, as for her heart . . . well, it was a good thing she'd put the brakes on with Remy.

He was just one more assault on her senses she couldn't handle right now.

Cade Burnett let loose an orgasmic groan, as well he should. Remy's bouillabaisse was a masterpiece.

"You need to open a restaurant, DuPre. You're better at this than hockey."

"Oh yeah? Then I'd have to charge you to eat, asshole."

Jorgenson coughed. "Yes, much better we eat for free here." He nudged Burnett. "Don't rock the boat, asshole. We have it good."

"So Highlander isn't coming?" Remy checked his phone. No text from Harper, which was not a surprise. He was trying to give her space because he knew her well enough to understand that she wouldn't appreciate being pushed. But he'd texted Bren that the boys would be over tonight and he hadn't responded.

"Don't know. He's been pretty moody the last couple of days." Callaghan looked up from his stew. "Moodier than usual."

Remy had an idea why. They hadn't talked about what Bren witnessed the other night at the market. His girls were in town until today, and Remy hadn't wanted to interrupt, but now the Scot was alone.

"I'm going to knock to see if he's okay."

Burnett shot him a look. "He hasn't fallen off the wagon, if that's what you're worried about."

"Nah. Nothing like that. Eat your bouillabaisse, Alamo."

He took the stairs one floor down and knocked on St. James's door. The dog barked his head off, but not quite enough to muffle Bren's muttered curse, so close to the door that it could only be because he'd seen Remy through the peephole.

"Open up, man. I know you're there."

The door flew open and Gretzky pounced, trying to lick Remy to death.

"Heya, buddy."

Bren pulled the dog back by the collar, and then realizing that he'd only stay if Remy was invited in, he flourished a *come the fuck in* with his free hand. Once inside, they sized each other up.

"You avoiding me, Highlander?"

"Nope."

Remy rubbed his jaw, thinking on how best to play this. Might as well go all in.

"Harper and I were together. But now we're not."

Bren merely stared.

"I'd like to know if you have a problem with what you saw."

"Do I have a problem with the fact the guy who's in line to get my job is fucking the owner-slash-GM, you mean?"

That's what he thought? Sure St. James was on thin ice as far as the captaincy was concerned, but there was never any question of Remy stepping on his skates.

"I don't want your job."

Bren's skepticism was Remy's reward.

"Seriously, Bren, I'm out of here in a few weeks. When I was traded in, I forced Harper's hand. Told her I'd only give a hundred percent if she promised to trade me out to another team by January. One that could go all the way."

St. James blinked. Once. Twice. This counted for emotion with the guy, Remy supposed.

"Who else knows?"

"No one on the team or in the front office. Maybe her sisters, but I'm not even sure of that. We knew how it might look."

"That you're bailing when we need you."

For fuck's sake. "Christ, you can't have it both ways. One minute you think I'm after your job, the next you're pissed because I'm *not* after your job."

"There's a third option. You could stay the fuck away from my job and stay to help us win."

There was that, but that wasn't what he needed to talk about. The plan was still the same.

"About what you saw," Remy started.

"You know that's trouble, right?"

Remy sighed. He knew. "Yeah. I'm crazy about her—"

Bren held up a hand. "I don't mean that, but that's

very interesting and worthy of ball-busting later. I mean it's trouble for Harper. She's gonna be crucified in the press if they find out."

If. Meaning, Bren would never breathe a word because he had Harper's back like she'd had his during his rehab.

Remy offered his hand. Bren stared, squinted, and gripped it while the slightest smile teased his lips. "So you've got a thing for your boss, brother?"

Christ. "Like I said, I'm out of here in a few weeks. And—" He sighed. "I have a thing for my boss."

And then Gretzky farted.

TWENTY-SIX

Harper eyed the package on the kitchen island and contemplated her next move.

Wine. The next move was always wine.

So what if it was nine in the morning. This wasn't just any morning. It was Christmas Day, and she was alone in a mansion, playing at poor little rich girl. No one was here to judge except the ghosts of the past and Harper's chatty conscience, a voice that could easily be drowned out by vino. She poured a liberal glass, toasted no one in particular, and turned her attention to the package sitting before her like it might contain the head from *Seven*.

That seemed unlikely, because it was from Remy. His Riverbrook address was in the upper left-hand corner, her address in Lake Forest was centered in a big loopy scrawl. It arrived yesterday, but as she was spending the holiday alone, she figured she'd open it today.

With wine.

She sliced open the package with a steak knife and removed the more decorative gift box inside it. Carefully, she untied the ribbon as if she might reuse it later. Old habits.

Pulling apart the layers of tissue wrap, she gasped at what she found. The accompanying note was in the same expressive script.

Merry Christmas, minou. I figure this might inspire you to get all that team testosterone under control come the New Year.

Yours, Remy

She burst out laughing. Anyone else would have given her a feminine gift, such as a cashmere scarf (Kenneth) or cashmere gloves (also Kenneth). Only Remy would give her something so perfect it brought a lump of emotion to her throat.

A flash of metal caught her eye. There was something else in the box, wrapped in tissue. She extracted a platinum bracelet cuff, the sort of piece she would wear. But this was no ordinary trinket.

Spelled out in stamped letters was the message she longed to give the press, haters, and the ghost of Clifford Chase: Zero Fucks Given.

Oh, God.

Fortifying herself with a gulp of Bordeaux, she punched in a text message on her phone. *Thank you.*

Her phone rang within thirty seconds. "Am I forgiven?" came that sexy Cajun drawl.

"For what? You didn't do anything."

"That's how I usually start these conversations. Puts a lady on the back foot immediately."

She sighed at how charming he was. "I might have overreacted. But Bren was right there."

"I talked to him, and he's not going to say a word. Listen, Harper, I don't want to fight. I just want to be with you for the time I've got left in Chicago. I've missed you in my bed. Femme, I need you there."

Her entire body swooned. "Should I bring your gift next time? Might make for interesting foreplay."

Her eyes fell on what Remy had sent—a nutcracker, but not just any nutcracker. Undoubtedly custom made, it was a slender figure with long blond hair, a Rebels hockey jersey, and red heels. It was Harper Chase herself.

"My balls are too big for that, minou. It's what you might call symbolic."

A parting gift. Remy was trying to inspire her to stay strong when he had moved on. Tears pricked the backs of her eyelids at the sweetness of the gesture.

"I didn't get you anything."

"Just seein' my nieces' smiles when they opened their presents this morning is gift enough. They sure liked the Rebels jerseys you sent 'em, and Sophie's wrapped herself up in that literary quotes scarf even though it's makin' her sweat buckets. Alexandre and Marie were thrilled with the wine, too." He paused. "That was mighty nice of you to think of them."

"I have an employee discount on Rebels merch and a wine cellar gathering dust." She licked her lips. "Maybe I could give you your totally impromptu present now."

He chuckled, raspy and sexy. "Oh yeah?"

"Are you alone?"

"Nope." Shouting and laughter that made her heart clench with envy bubbled up in the background. He lowered his voice. "For shame, Ms. Chase, wanting to corrupt me in the bosom of my family. How about I call later and tuck you in?"

They said their good-byes and Harper filled her wineglass to the tippity-top. Five, ten, maybe forty-five minutes later, Violet walked in. "What's up, Dictator Spice?"

Harper raised her head from the kitchen island, where she was taking a self-pity break. She sniffed loudly. "Why are you here? I thought you were spending the holiday"—she waved at some point in the distance—"somewhere else."

Violet shrugged. "It fell through. I thought you'd be off at Bailey's mom's exchanging Argyle socks and drinking brunch."

Harper hiccupped. "I'd rather be alone."

"With your creepy doll."

"It's not a creepy doll." She tugged it protectively to her breast. The hair was a little mussed from Harper trying to braid it and create a mini French knot. "It's— it's a nutcracker of a Rebels fan."

Violet drew closer, picked up the note, and read it.

"Well, I'd be drinking, too, if my boyfriend got me this lame gift."

Harper snatched back the note. "He's not my boyfriend and it's not lame. It's perfect. He's . . ." *Perfect.*

Violet pulled a glass from the rack above the island and poured a drink. "I see."

"You don't see anything. You don't see how terrible this is."

"You've fallen for him."

Maybe she did see. She tried a different tack. "This is the worst thing that could happen."

"Is it?" Violet sipped her wine. "Why is it so terrible? Doesn't he make you happy?"

Ignoring that, Harper busied her hands with putting the gift away. It was just a gag gift, really. No reason why she should be reading such significance into it.

Yet she felt compelled to explain. "He makes me feel desired. Wanted. He makes me feel like a kiss could solve all my problems. Like a sandwich can melt all my troubles away. But all those things, they're just fleeting."

"Especially sandwiches."

Especially sandwiches. He fed her, fucked her, fussed over her. But he wouldn't be here when she needed him to skate like there was no tomorrow.

"I've been through this before."

"You said it didn't end well. That Stroger guy got traded out or something?"

Harper went for her glass, but knocked it over instead. "Oh, God, I'm so stupid."

But Violet was already grabbing the paper towels, mopping up, and passing her own glass to Harper.

"It's okay, sis," Violet said, and just that one little word—*sis*—unleashed a fresh wave of emotion. Tears fell down Harper's cheeks, and she belched like a warthog. She wanted to tell someone about the time it all went wrong and her heart had turned to granite.

But she wasn't drunk enough to spill, or maybe the one person with whom she wanted to share every fear and insecurity was nine hundred miles away. "This thing with Remy—it's so dumb of me to do it, but he's very persuasive and he makes me feel special and the fact he's leaving soon—"

"Harper," Violet said, squeezing her shoulder, "it's okay to be upset about trading Remy out. If you feel something for him . . ."

"I can't."

"That's not quite the same thing. Listen, I won't say anything more, except . . ." She looked torn. "Remy is not that other guy, the jerk from Boston, and neither is he Clifford Chase. If you tell him you want him to stay, he'll probably do it. If you want to continue seeing him after you trade him, he'll probably go for that, too. Guys are a lot simpler than girls."

"It's just sex. Really, really great sex."

"And sandwiches. And creepy-ass dolls that look like you."

"Oh shut up."

TWENTY-SEVEN

The blues club on Hubbard in downtown Chicago was hopping, busy with revelers in the city for the New Year, like Remy's parents, who usually visited whichever city he was in around this time of year. Since his poppa was a musician, he also liked Remy to scope out the best blues joints.

Tonight they'd played against Boston for the first of a double-header and won 3–2. The entire team was out in force to celebrate, though they were taking it relatively easy given that they had another game tomorrow night. No one wanted to risk a loss when the season had taken a turn for the better.

Leaning on the bar, Remy eyed Bren, wondering why he chose to come out with them to bars. Did the camaraderie outweigh the risk of being in such close proximity to the drug that had you in its grip? Guess it was his cross to bear, or maybe he saw it as a test of his will.

Speaking of willpower, Remy was trying his utmost

not to look at his parents, not that doing so was a hardship, but because they happened to be sitting with Harper.

"DuPre?" Bren gave him a look.

"Yeah?"

"Cool it."

Just what he needed, an anti-wingman with a Scot's brogue.

Today, while he and his poppa checked out guitar stores, Harper had taken his momma, Josie, and his niece Sophie to afternoon tea at the Drake. He hadn't asked her to do it, but as soon as she'd heard the family would be in town, she'd organized a day out. Shopping, spa treatments, Earl Grey tea. With any other woman, he'd think she was trying to cozy up to his female relatives as a way to him—Lord knew he'd had a few previous girlfriends who tried that and barely lived to tell the tale—but that wasn't Harper's game. She wasn't looking for anything more.

But he sure as hell wished she were.

They hadn't talked much since Christmas Day, since she'd opened his gift. He knew she'd gotten a kick out of it, maybe more, and that she was starting to pry apart in the face of his onslaught. He was in. Inside her head, inside her body, and inching closer to that heart she kept wrapped in barbed wire and pinned with a No Trespassing sign. He intended to trespass. He would invade those borders and plant his fucking flag.

Hauling his gaze away from Harper, he said to Bren, "So almost halfway through the season. In the black for the first time at this point in how long?"

"Happened about seven years ago. Then four years before that."

Bren knew the Rebels' stats inside out, having come up through the ranks starting with the farm team.

"So, 19–16," Remy said, referring to their win-loss record so far this season. "Not terrible."

"Could be worse," Bren conceded. "We're looking . . . viable."

They shared a knowing look. It almost felt like a sacrilege to say it aloud. Less than four months to go on the regular season, but there was a hope in the air that bloomed brighter with every game. When Remy had traded in, players seemed resigned to losing. Now if they lost, they were pissed. Pissed players won games and qualified for playoffs.

Was it possible Harper Chase was onto something?

"Miles to go yet," Remy said, not wanting to jinx it, because if anyone could, the unluckiest guy in the league had that shit down.

"And you won't be here."

Remy eyed Bren, trying to decide how much he wanted to get into this with the captain. He didn't owe the Rebels his shot just because things had graduated from abysmal to decent.

"What would you have me do? This body's not getting any younger, Saint."

Bren just continued to stare with that hollow-eyed look he was expert in. "Your call, brother."

Yes, it was, and no one would guilt him into sticking around because the hard-luck Rebels had the makings of a Cinderella run on their hands. Remy didn't have time for what-ifs, only for certainties, and the Rebels in the playoffs—or further—was a fairy tale. Just like anything beyond a sweaty tangle of limbs with Harper Chase was a fantasy the likes of which Remy should shut down stat. But he wasn't giving up there, was he?

A band had started up on the stage, an outfit with a touch of bluegrass and Zydeco, just like his father played. He chanced a look, and there was Jorgenson leaning over his dad and gesturing to the stage. Like his father needed any encouragement. Poppa was playing it cool in that self-deprecating way of his. That wouldn't last.

When the opening number had finished, the lead singer of the band spoke to the audience. "We just heard that Alexandre DuPre is in the house tonight." Typically, they pronounced it "Alexander," with a hard English *der* instead of a soft French *dreh*. Cheers went up because even in Yankee blues club circles, Remy's dad was well known.

"Alexandre, maybe a song for your fans?"

Remy checked in with his dad, who was waving off requests. Even Harper was on his case, though he could have told her it was unnecessary. This was all part of the DuPre "who, me?" shtick. Finally, he stood and the crowd went wild. *Nicely done, old man.*

Remy caught Harper's eye—first time since forever, it felt like—and that zing zipped, the one that had worn a rut between them since the moment they'd met. They both turned away before they started in with the goofy smiles.

Forget about falling in love. He was already flat on the ice.

~

Harper wanted to spend all evening staring at Remy and all night kissing every inch of his beautiful body. The temptation was almost too much to bear, so instead she turned to watch his father on stage because that was the closest she could get to ogling a male DuPre safely.

Alexandre picked up a guitar and strummed a couple of testing chords. After a quick consult with the band, he launched into a bluesy up-tempo number that had the crowd tapping their feet and up on those same feet before the song had finished. Harper didn't know much about blues music, but she recognized something special when she saw it.

"*Merci, mes amis,*" Alexandre said when the song finished, and that little smidgen of French set the crowd off cheering again. "You might be wondering why I'm here in Chicago. I came to see my son, Remy, play hockey tomorrow night with the Rebels, who are having a pretty good season so far, *n'est-ce pas*?"

More loud cheers led to a healthy buzz as people absorbed the information that Alexandre was Remy's father. "Not a lot of people know this, but as well as being a force on skates, my son also knows his way around a music stage. It's been a long time since we played together." Eyes filled with paternal love sought out his son's. "Remy?"

"I had no idea," Harper said to Marie.

Remy's mom smiled, sphinxlike. "He could have gone into his father's business, but hockey called louder."

The team was going nuts, egging Remy on while the man played it cool, ever the showman. Eventually— not as long as his father took, but long enough—he jumped onto the stage, where he shook his head at his father for putting him in this position. All part of their charming double act, no doubt. Alexandre handed off a guitar to Remy, who slung it around his neck like it belonged there.

The crowd hooted in appreciation. Harper's girl parts gave a little hoot of their own because, Remy with that six string over his shoulder? *Hot dayum*.

"Not expectin' this," Remy said, his accent thicker than ever, "but I sure appreciate the band lettin' us hijack their set for a few."

As soon as he strummed the first couple of chords, the crowd roared, as did Harper's heart.

"Wonderwall."

Maybe it was a coincidence, but Harper knew better. In the early days of the Rebels, when they were the newest sports franchise in Chicago and hope sprang eternal, "Wonderwall" was the team's anthem, played before every game. As the original recording ended, the crowd would pick it up. But when the Rebels' fortunes plummeted, the song was no longer sung—or perhaps the fans who knew it no longer came.

Remy's voice had a rasp to it, the same tone she'd heard when he was inside her body. Deep, melodic, a voice created to draw pleasure from a woman. With each line, his commitment to the song grew, and by the time he hit that first chorus, the crowd had joined in.

Burnett and Jorgenson were on their feet, pointing at the stage in awe of their teammate and this hidden talent. Harper let the music take her somewhere—back to Remy's bed that snowbound holiday weekend, the stolen moments since, and maybe a future she didn't dare imagine.

If Harper had thought one verse and a chorus of "Wonderwall" would make her melt, she hadn't reckoned on Remy's ability to raise the stakes. Now he sang about the things he wanted to say but didn't know how. He never looked her way, but with each additional lyric she felt his attention sear into her.

"Because may-beeee, you're gonna be the one that saves meeee . . ."

He sang the song to her, yet no one in this crowded club suspected a thing.

A rock-sized lump had formed in her throat. Her skin tingled with this strange new knowledge that Remy DuPre was secretly wooing her in front of hundreds of people. The tingle turned into an itch, a panic-laden rash, because she couldn't have nice things. She grasped the glass of wine before her and caught the eye of Remy's mom, Marie.

Ah. So she was wrong about no one else picking up on what was happening. A mother always knew. Marie smiled and looked back at the stage toward her son and husband.

"Thank you for today, Harper. It was very kind of you to take care of us."

Harper nodded, feeling like three layers of skin had been peeled back and someone had taken a blowtorch to her. "Happy to. You were so welcoming to me in New Orleans."

Marie cast another glance at the stage, and this time she kept her gaze on her husband and son while she spoke. "Remy comes off as very laid back, but as a child he was so intense, the most intense of my children. His goals have often clashed with his joie de vivre. Do you understand what I'm saying?"

Harper stared. "Not really."

"Outsiders often dismiss the Acadians as swamp dwellers with little ambition, an insular people who don't have time for material things. All the losses that Remy has endured on the road to the championships have hurt him, but his positive outlook gets him through. For him, there will always be next year. Some people think he is too fatalistic about it, too accepting, too softhearted." She shrugged, a rather fatalistic motion in itself. "He mentioned this bargain he has with you, how you will release him to another team soon. I'm glad of it, especially after this last year with his father's illness. Now, Remy is older and there is no more next year. There is only this year."

A chill crept through Harper. No matter what her heart wanted—her own shot at greatness, her own shot at Remy and the happiness he inspired in her—she would never deny him his true desire.

So what if she needed him to make the playoffs?

So what if his touch was necessary to her very existence?

So what if she had fallen in love with him?

She faced Marie, needing her to know that she meant every word. One strong woman to another. "I'm not going to stop him from going for the Cup, Marie. He and I made a deal, and I intend to honor it."

Remy's mother's shoulders relaxed in visible relief and she reached for Harper's hand under the table.

"Thank you."

TWENTY-EIGHT

Remy watched from the bench, one eye on the forward line that had just gone in, the other on the scoreboard as if it might dare to change without his say-so. The Rebels were up 2–1 on Boston. It would have been 3–1 if they could have capitalized on a two-minute penalty resulting from his old pal Stroger trying to get inside Remy's pants five minutes into the second period. They'd done a little cha-cha, exchanged a few disparaging comments about each other's mothers, and Stroger fell for it hook, line, and sinker. The asshole got called for interference, yet the Rebels had failed to use it to their advantage.

The game had begun auspiciously. Someone had filmed Remy's performance at the club last night and it had gone viral. The DJ played "Wonderwall" when the Rebels skated onto the ice, and every now and then, the crowd picked it up and carried it on a wave to the next play.

He'd only sung it to make Harper feel good, a nostalgic nod to a time when the Rebels were filled with promise. With each line, he'd sunk deeper into it as the words revealed new layers of meaning. The song was for her, but now the fans were co-opting it because it meant all things to all people. To them, it meant hope.

And hope was in full bloom for Remy. Just before he skated onto the ice, his agent had called with the news that Harper was already in talks with both Philly and Quebec to negotiate a trade.

That should not have bothered him because Harper, a woman of her word, was giving him precisely what he'd asked for. Several teams were interested despite the Remy DuPre jinx. Looked like he'd sold the goods a little too well. Played himself off the Rebels and right out of Harper Chase's bed.

He'd give it to her—Harper was a pro at keeping business and pleasure separate. She wasn't the most sentimental woman he'd ever met, a fact he'd sworn was a boon because there would be no tears when he booked out of Chicago. You know what? He might have liked a tear or two. Yep, he wanted to have his cake and eat it, too.

His mind swirled with possibilities. This could work. He'd get a decent shot at the Cup and a decent shot at Harper, because if he was no longer on the team, the conflict of interest that so concerned her would be removed. That sneaky little fucker named hope bubbled in his chest.

Maybe he could have everything he wanted after all.

Back to the game. Stroger was out on the ice pounding down the lane, headed straight for St. James. Both of them were big guys, but Bren was faster and proved it with a deft swerve that left Stroger blinking and puckless. The captain passed to Shay on the left, who unloaded the biscuit and hit it bar down. Score! Thirty seconds later, St. James was on the bench sucking down Gatorade.

"Good move," Remy said, because it was. Remy had never seen anyone as light on his feet as Bren. When the guy was on, he was unstoppable.

Bren nodded but didn't say a word. Likely he was still annoyed after their conversation at the club last night. Screw that. Remy didn't owe the Rebels his soul, and no amount of stink eye and cold silence was going to change that.

"Stroger's more pissed than usual," he said, because while Remy could appreciate silence in others, he wasn't much good at keeping quiet himself.

"Guy's been pissed since birth."

A light went on in Remy's head. Being with the Rebels for most of his career, Bren would've played with Stroger six years ago, back when Harper had "dated" the guy. Would Bren have known about that?

He probed a little. "So his personality has always been shit, then?"

"Aye."

Aye? Remy stewed on that for a few seconds, trying to work his tongue around a query. Bren turned, one eyebrow raised, perhaps assessing Remy's worthiness to be on the receiving end of a confidence.

Remy decided to lay it out there. "Stroger and Harper were together for a while."

"You want to know what she saw in him."

He did, and maybe he wanted to know more. Remy was getting the impression there was a whole lot more to Bren's relationship with Harper than he'd first suspected. They'd known each other a long time, seen the team through more downs than ups.

"Go on."

"Just a little late-blooming rebellion, that's all, stickin' it to her daddy. Women like dangerous men, or so I'm told. Never would have lasted." He sniffed. "Even if he hadn't hit her."

A rushing sound blocked up Remy's ears. His blood turned to an icy-cold slush, then stopped moving altogether. One minute he was present in this world, the next it tilted and crashed.

Fuck—no.

He turned, but Bren was staring at the ice as if he hadn't just blown Remy's universe to rubble.

Jagged pieces that had previously been floating in the air dropped like weights and fell into place. Her reticence in the locker room, that tough-girl act she wore like emotional Kevlar. Stroger had hurt Harper. *His* Harper. Raised a hand to the woman Remy loved and made her afraid. Jesus, how could she bear to be near *any* hockey players? Violent assholes who thought nothing of sorting out their on-ice problems with a fist.

This fucking *fils de putain* had made his woman

fearful. Made her feel less than the amazing person she was. A million questions fought for the right to be asked, and he turned to the man with the answers. But Coach was already calling the captain back to switch out the line, and Bren skated off, leaving that unexploded bomb ticking in time to Remy's hurting heart.

And there was only one way to handle the imminent blast.

It wasn't as if Harper had never witnessed a team snatch defeat from the jaws of victory before. Hockey could turn on a dime. One minute you had a two-goal lead and every pass connected. The next the score was tied after your laid-back veteran center was assessed a match penalty and ejected from the game.

She knew there was bad blood between DuPre and Stroger—there was bad blood between everyone and Stroger—but no one could have foreseen Remy bearing down on the Cougars' defender with the puck nowhere in their orbit so he could pound the snot out of him.

And she meant *pound*.

"Holy shit!" Isobel yelled, jumping up in the executive box. "What the hell is he doing?"

Remy had slammed Stroger against the Plexi, thrown down his stick, and removed his gloves. He meant business, and that business came in the form of a rearrangement of Billy Stroger's face.

So deep in shock was the entire arena that it took a full twenty seconds for anyone to react, which allowed Remy to make several jaw-smashing connections. It was also possible that the delay in pulling them apart might be better credited to the fact that Billy was one of the least popular players in the NHL. Even his own team was slow off the mark. By the time the officials had restrained Remy, Stroger's nose was spurting blood and he was slumped against the boards like a puppet with cut strings.

There was no question of it being game related or accidental, and there was only one possible outcome: ejection for Remy.

Two minutes later, she stood outside the locker room, staring at size five feet that refused to move. Déjà vu all over again, as the great Yogi Berra would've said.

Inside, Remy sat on the bench, skates off, helmet on the other side of the locker room, stick broken in half. That must have happened when he came in.

"Remy."

His head snapped back. "Harper, what are you doing here?"

"I had to see if you were okay."

As she stepped in closer, he stood, his hand raised to hold her at bay. "You shouldn't be here. Someone could see."

She didn't care about that. He was more important, though she acknowledged deep down that the last time she was in this position—the position of entering a locker room to tend to a man she cared about—she'd ended up with a little more than she bargained for. A busted lip to match that broken heart.

She stepped toward him, her body hyperaware of every change in his: the heave of his broad chest, the tic in his jaw, the trickle of sweat taking a lazy trek down his temple.

"Don't come any closer, Harper."

"Why?"

"Because I have a lot of pent-up rage here and I might need to channel it."

"You didn't get it all out there on the ice?" She cocked a hip and backed up a mental moment. "Want to tell me why you did that?"

"Anyone who hits my woman doesn't deserve to walk off that ice."

The words both slammed into her and lifted the weight of six years off her chest.

"Harper," he gritted out. "You should have told me. You should have—" The words died in his throat, though his expression of betrayal remained fixed. He wasn't pissed at Stroger, or at least he wasn't right now. He was furious because he was the last to know. Apparently she owed him this.

"Why should I have told you, Remy?"

His face strained with incredulity. "Because I could have helped you."

"How? With more violence? It didn't happen to you. It happened to me." She struck her breast, anger blazing that he was turning this into some chink in their growing intimacy. Why did men have to make it all about them?

As ever, Remy was evolved enough to realize this. "Harper, I know this is your pain. But if you'd shared it with me, it would be mine, too. I want it to be mine. I want to help you shoulder it. I know I can't make it right, but I can be there for you. Don't you understand that, *minou?*"

Hurt, she turned away from the compassion he wielded like a weapon. Love wasn't supposed to slice ribbons from her soul.

With her back to him, she curled her fist and placed it against the frame of one of the players' lockers. "What do they say? A trouble shared is a trouble halved? Not for me. Sharing this ruined everything."

Sunlight was supposed to be the best disinfectant, but shining a light had cast her into the wilderness. Some secrets were supposed to remain that way.

"That kind of thing isn't supposed to happen to—" *Women like me,* she almost said. Strong, well educated, liberated. She was supposed to be in control of her love life and the men she let into it. "But I wanted to prove to my father that my gender wouldn't matter or I could use it to my advantage. I could corral this beast and be a great leader of men. I don't know. He— Billy . . ."

She heard him move closer, could feel his eyes boring into the back of her head. "He what?"

She faced him. "He punched me and split my lip after a game where he was ejected for starting a fight."

His mouth twitched, the irony not lost on him. "Harp—"

She held up a shaky hand. *Let me say this. Let me surrender this thing you need to carve out of me.* "He was always making trouble. Usually I could soothe him with—with sex, but not this time. He lashed out. At first I thought it was an accident, you know, his fist inadvertently meeting my face. Isn't that crazy?" Her voice had taken on a high pitch, like it belonged to someone else. How stupid to think Stroger might have lashed out unintentionally. Her love-starved heart had given him the benefit of the doubt.

"But he didn't apologize. Not until later, not until his spot on the team was under threat, and I knew then that he needed to inflict his pain on someone weaker. I was convenient. I was weak and I would never be able to live up to my father's standard of toughness. But it was only once."

Fury at that excusing word restarted a tic in Remy's jaw. "You told Cliff?"

She would have kept it to herself for any number of reasons—shame, not wanting to rock the boat, fear of failure in her father's eyes. Women were expert at inventing excuses for men. Look at her mother.

"I didn't want to. It would just confirm everything he thought about women in the man's world of pro hockey. But someone had seen it." Bren, her white knight, punched Stroger, then immediately went to her father. She'd begged him not to, but his anger on her behalf—the anger she couldn't muster for herself—would be appeased only one way. "Dad traded Stroger out, but he was pissed he had to do it. That he had to think of me before the team. He never forgave me for it."

This is why women should not be in charge of a professional sports team. Hormones, Harper. Fucking hormones.

She'd learned her lesson about opening up and exposing her underbelly. No man was worth that feeling of helplessness that rocked her in the split second after Stroger drew blood. For years she had paid her dues, trying to make up for her mistake, her female weakness, only to have her father rip her heart out with his insurmountable hurdles.

But now she was in charge. This team was hers, and *she* made the rules.

Remy stared at her, his expression as anguished as a wounded animal's. She'd had time to adjust to this, and she supposed it would take him a while to return to the easygoing, let-the-good-times-roll Remy she knew and loved.

"You should have told me, Harper."

"So you could defend me? Like you did out there? It's done, and years later, you turn into a caveman and get an ejection for your trouble. For *my* trouble, because you're not on the ice winning, Remy. That's what I pay you to do. We're probably going to lose this game, and that's down to you. That's down to you thinking with your—"

Heart. That dumb, stupid heart she loved so much. She had learned long ago that a heart could fool a brain into the worst decisions, but she'd set that knowledge aside while she let Remy DuPre in. Broken her own rules. No more. "I don't need your defense. I'm perfectly capable of standing up for myself."

He stepped in closer. "And in doing that, you closed yourself off to the possibilities. Built this impenetrable shell."

"I had to! I had to prove to my father that what had happened was a glitch. He'd never give me the team if it came out publicly I'd placed myself in a position of weakness with a player. I worked my ass off for years to prove myself worthy and then . . ."

Remy cupped her face and drew her toward him, his breath a whisper against her lips. "And then Clifford fucked you over when he made you share it."

He had no idea, and she had no intention of sharing exactly how much her father had screwed her with his "playoffs or bust" demand. She wouldn't use that to make him stay. "You don't need to fight my battles, Remy. I've been on my own for a long time and I've figured out what I need."

"Christ, Harper." His thumb swiped her bottom lip. Gently. Roughly. Oh, God. "Have you?"

Yes. At least, she'd thought so before Remy DuPre stormed into her life with his amazing sandwiches and supersized heart and hands that could heal every hurt. She felt it every time they were together, that build to something strong and pure and *more*.

She didn't dare hope. She didn't dare dream.

"Have you?" he repeated, but it sounded like he was pleading. It sounded like he was the one hurting, because he wasn't around then to protect her, because every decision she made since was filtered through the prism of one man's fist. She didn't want him to hurt. Billy Stroger wasn't worth this good man's pain.

She could give Remy what he needed, and in giving him that, she would give him all she had left.

"I came down here to soothe your Cajun werewolf, DuPre," she whispered. "Your Loup Garou."

He pushed her back against the locker, his hand already shaping her ass and aligning her core with his erection. Not even his bulky hockey pants could hide his desire for her.

"Then soothe me, Harper. Make me better."

She kissed him, pretending it was for him but knowing it was really for her. Remy intended to turn her memories of Stroger to dust, to replace horror with reverence, neglect with love, because he valued her. She truly wanted to be worthy of this man who made her feel like anything was possible.

The kiss deepened, reaching a private, closed-off place, telling her stories in the way only Remy could. *This is how good we are. How amazing we could be. Let me take care of you.*

She wanted so badly for this fairy tale to be real.

Fumbling with his hockey pants, she pulled them down along with his boxer briefs and cup to release the cure for her ache. Anyone could enter the locker room, but she was beyond that, existing outside reality. This, only this, was everything she needed, and it trumped the fear of discovery.

"Please," she gasped.

Cupping both hands below her ass, he hitched her up, walked several steps, and pushed through the door to the equipment room. Even now, he was protecting her. Giving them privacy, though she'd have been perfectly happy to let him pummel her to oblivion in the locker room. They could be on the jumbotron, and she wouldn't have cared one iota.

Holding her in the cradle of one arm, he shoved aside a shelf-load of gloves and pads and placed her ass on it. He yanked her skirt up her thighs until it bunched around her hips, pushed her panties aside, and drove deep in one all-consuming thrust.

"Remy," she gasped at the sweet invasion.

He held her still, his hands spreading her thighs wide, his body a piston into her over and over. Pounding away the pain, replacing it with pleasure, and leaving sweetness in its wake, he wiped out the memories and gave her new ones to cherish.

TWENTY-NINE

His body still covered hers, and she had no idea how much time had passed. The period would be over soon, the players on their way back. Sensing this, they quietly parted. He kissed her forehead and fixed her clothing before attending to himself.

"If you can work it out, I'd prefer Philly," he said.

Not your typical postcoital sweet nothings, but nothing about this was typical. An affair with an expiration date, a built-in self-destruct button, and all she had to do was push it.

That's all she had to do.

"Shouldn't be a problem. They have at least two players who would work out for a trade." They'd made a pact. She'd promised his mother, for heaven's sake. She loved him and she would do anything to ensure he got to hold that hardware high above his head come June. If her own heart shattered in the process, then them's the breaks.

With his nod and ready acceptance of her acquiescence to his request, a small part of her died that he would leave without hesitation.

"That's step one," he said.

"Of what?"

"Of the plan. Once I'm off the Rebels, we move to step two."

What was he talking about? "Step two?"

"We go public."

"Go public?" She sounded like a mad parrot.

"You and me. We give this"—he waved between them, because not even Mr. Verbal, Remy DuPre, had words to describe adequately what *this* was—"a chance."

He wanted to give them a chance.

He thought there was something worth nurturing here, and while this should have been a dream come true, why had her heart stopped cold?

You know why. Sure, they were consenting adults, but she paid his salary, and just because he was no longer on the team, the dynamics were no different. Questions would be raised about roster choices and contract decisions, all under the influence of her vagina. "Conflict of interest" and "workplace fling" would be the main thrust of every headline for the rest of the season.

Details, Harper. Stupid little details. You know why this won't work.

"This isn't what either of us had in mind, Remy."

His mouth curved slightly. "Sure wasn't. I was sup-posed to serve my jail time, make myself invaluable, and head for glory. Do not pass go. Do not collect a hot, gorgeous woman who happens to be my boss. Do not second-guess every decision that's brought me to this point."

"That's all good advice. You should listen to it." She put a trembling hand on the door, her ear straining to hear movement outside, which was incredibly difficult when your heart was pounding like a jet engine.

"Harper, I love you."

Oh. That pounding heart cannoned out of her chest, plopped unceremoniously to the floor, and flapped about on the dirty linoleum.

He loved—he couldn't, and even if he did, he shouldn't. She ignored that dumb flapping heart. She *had* to.

"I'm sure your behavior in tonight's game won't have any impact on your trade. Maybe a two-game suspension, but you've been playing well and you're positioned perfectly for the next part of the season. For a run at the Cup."

She knew she sounded hard-hearted, but it was necessary. Inside, she was a hot mess, but outside she was Clifford Chase's daughter, team owner, and acting GM of the Rebels. Her heart would take no part in this decision.

"Did you hear what I said?"

Heard it, enshrined it, am already making Remy ♥ Harper T-shirts and picking out china patterns.

She spoke to the door. "I'm not what you want,

Remy. I'm not this nurturing-mom type who can change diapers while she makes million-dollar deals. You have a plan: the Cup. A family. A happily ever after. I can't give that to you."

I'm broken. No good. I can't trust you'll stay.

"Yes, you can, Harper. You can do anything you put your mind to, baby."

"The championship," she coughed out. "That's what you want."

"And I still intend to get it. But there are greater goals, Harper. There are greater prizes."

That did it, turned her into a little girl again. She had never been a prize before, only the consolation. She heard him shuffle forward, and then his body covered hers from behind, this wall of strength and solace. His lips brushed her temple. Never had she wanted to sink into someone so badly.

"You're sure not what I expected, Harper. You're so much more. You're the woman who keeps me on my toes, who excites me in every moment. You're the person I want to turn to with a dumb joke, when my day's sucked, to get my ass whupped at video games. We can take care of the cookie-bakin' and baby-makin' later. For now, let's just take care of us."

Us. How long had she craved to be a part of something bigger instead of that lonely girl abandoned in the tower? But those were a child's dreams. She'd worked her ass off to become strong, self-sufficient Harper Fucking Chase, and letting her go would undo everything.

She turned in his arms and eased him away before thrusting out her hand. "Thanks for all you've done for the Rebels."

He stared at it for so long she felt foolish and dropped it. "This isn't Would You Rather, Harper. It doesn't have to be an either-or choice, a fulfilling career or a happy personal life." He cupped her face with both hands, searching for Lord knew what. Whatever it was, he wouldn't find it. "I'm asking you to be a little bit brave here. Lean on me. Let me love you. We both get what we want."

"You think that's what I want? Someone to take care of me? I know you're upset about Stroger, but I'm okay. I've had years to become okay. I don't need you to protect me."

"Jesus, Harper, this isn't about Stroger. This is about you and me. This is about wanting more out of life than late nights at the office, poring over game tapes and spreadsheets. It's about wanting more than just okay."

She bristled and withdrew. "You think the team, my career, and this job aren't enough for me because, what? I'm a woman and I'm supposed to want a husband and a family?"

"I think it doesn't have to be one or the other. You're strong enough to do it all because you're the strongest woman I know. Your father tried to break you, and you survived, but you're holding on by your fingernails to this half life, pretending it's the best possible scenario. I'm here to tell you that you can lean on someone. I want to be that someone, Harper. I want to be your person and I want you to be my person."

Oh fuck. That was . . . so perfect. And perfectly impossible.

"We can't—"

He cut her words off with a kiss. A take-no-prisoners, you-are-mine kiss that she'd hold inside her heart as long as she lived. He'd already burrowed his way into each bleeding fissure. Now every kiss was salt, every word a piece of grit.

"We can," he murmured against her mouth, his breath a hot puff of longing. "We can do anything we want. I've never met anyone who needs to be held and loved as much as you do, Harper. Well, it so happens that you've got a man here with strong arms made to keep you safe. With so much love inside him that it's just busting to get out. It's all for you, minou. No one else I'd rather give it to."

In an ideal world where she wasn't afraid, she would say to hell with it and let him love her. But this wasn't an ideal world. It was one where women were held to a higher standard. Where a female team owner and general manager had to be devoid of emotion, sexuality, and weakness.

"Everyone would know I had a fling with one of my players."

His eyebrows slammed together. "It could have started after I left."

She gave that the derisive look it deserved. His cock-eyed optimism was starting to piss her off. "No one would buy that. You tell me how outing this—whatever this is—is good for me."

Hurt flashed over his face. "We get to be together."

But at what price? At the cost of everything she'd worked to achieve.

"It's not worth it."

She backtracked, realizing that sounded harsher on her lips than in her head. "I'd look like a lust-crazed idiot who makes decisions with my vagina. I've traded out a lover because either I want to date him or because he persuaded me to go against my better judgment and give him up to a better team even though we need him here."

He stared, and she knew he wasn't hearing those cobbled-together excuses. He'd already stopped listening at her first snapped reply.

It's not worth it.

They weren't worth the humiliation she would feel after news of their fling got out. Every day the media cracked wise about the Chase daughters and how women didn't have the temperament for high-powered sports franchise management. Too emotional, too sentimental, too weak.

She might feel those things some of the time, but she refused to project that image in her professional life. They'd only just stopped calling her Incompetent Spice; with this news, she'd be relabeled as Hormonal

Spice. Last time, she'd made the wrong decision. History would not be repeated.

"Remy, I'm—I'm sorry. In time you'll recognize you had a lucky escape." She backed up, feeling blindly for the doorknob behind her.

"A lucky escape." He stepped into her orbit, overwhelming with pure maleness and, amazingly still, his love. She could feel his hurt, because it was hers, as well. "I'm jinxed, remember?"

"You don't need luck when you work as hard as you do. This is your year." She placed a hand on his chest. Needing to feel the vital thump of his big, giving heart one last time before her own stopped beating.

"Thought it was," he said. "Thought I was the luckiest guy on the planet for a while."

THIRTY

Harper placed Remy's trade paperwork in the center of the kitchen island. She really shouldn't have brought it home, but she'd been sitting on it for two days, waiting for a sign.

Some might say that the Rebels' loss tonight was a sign that she should keep the player who knitted the team together. His two-game suspension had already adversely affected the dynamic, and while his trade wasn't public yet, the other players knew something was up.

Isobel leafed through the list of possible pickups, her fingers pausing when she came to Vadim Petrov's name. There had been something curious about her attitude when they discussed him with Coach Calhoun in the trade meeting—as if she was waging some internal battle over whether they should trade him in. Please let it not be a problem. Harper was taking a chance on Petrov, who hadn't played well this year, but she knew he had skills that could be cultivated with the right team.

"We're still agreed on Petrov?" Harper asked again, because she was trying to involve her sisters more instead of steamrolling them through every decision.

"He's fast, nimble, a killer in the face-off," Isobel said. "The knee injury is worrisome, but we have his medical records. He has authority issues, though."

"You know him?"

Isobel hesitated before she spoke. "A little. He's got an ego as big as all outdoors."

Violet walked in. "What'd I miss?"

"Just discussing Petrov," Harper said.

"Did you see that naked spread he did in the *ESPN Magazine* Body Issue? Wonder if I can get him in the dicktabase." She fanned herself. "Scots, Russians, Swedes, oh my. We've got ourselves a veritable United Nations of Badass here."

"Except we're losing the Cajun." Isobel held up the contract. "I don't care about the promise you made. We need him."

Harper grabbed the papers and signed on the dotted line. *There.*

So much for letting her sisters in on the decision making. But she needed to do something—anything—to assert control. Helplessness was not a good look on her. Her sisters stared at her like she was mad, and maybe she was a little, slowly spiraling into insanity.

"This is a business decision. He's done his duty and now I'm giving him what he wants. We're in a better position now than we were three months ago, within shouting distance of a playoff spot. I owe him this."

Violet poured a generous glass of wine. "What I want to know is why Remy went ballistic on Stroger. I'd put it down to jealousy, but Remy seems too secure in his manhood to be going off on some guy because you used to fuck him."

"They were nowhere near each other," Isobel mused. "Remy beelined right for Stroger the minute Coach called for the line change. He never gets into fights. He'd rather do a stand-up routine than punch another player."

Violet picked up the contract. "What's going on, Harper? The only reason Remy would go nuts like that is if Stroger insulted you or Remy's momma . . ." She paused, considering, and drew a shallow breath. "Or something."

Isobel said, "Why are you shaking your head?"

Harper hadn't realized she was doing that. She stopped the incriminating behavior immediately, but her lungs had shut down and every breath took immense effort. "I told you before that sex and hockey don't mix. Something always screws it up. Something always goes wrong."

She and Remy were finished.

He said he loved her, and she threw it in his face. *We're not worth it.* She raised a hand to her breastbone and rubbed at the ache. Maybe if she rubbed hard enough she'd get a wish, a do-over, a chance to tell

Remy she was sorry she'd hurt him. He wanted to take a chance on them, to be her person, and Harper Chase had her all-important rules.

"I think she's having a panic attack," someone said.

"I'm not." She was. Heart in chaos, she stood, needing to get away. No one could see her like this. She doubled over against the sink, the pain making her dizzy.

"I'm—oh, God." *Act normal until the panic gets bored. Normal sink. Normal counter. Normal—okay, not-so-normal mug tree.*

She looked down at her curled-up fists, the knuckles popping chalk-white against her pale skin. Her armor had taken a hit these last few weeks, and in its absence, her skin was shedding. But this wasn't some beautiful rebirth. It was her viscera, exposed and bleeding.

"He hit me."

Gasps all around. "Remy?"

"No. Stroger. Years ago. That's why Remy went off on him. He found out." She met the concerned gazes of her sisters. "It was once, and I learned my lesson."

"Harper." Isobel jumped from her chair and put an arm around her. Something broke apart inside her. A rusty sound emerged, and she slapped a hand across her mouth to keep it in. To keep it all in.

It was useless. A sob escaped the prison of tears she'd kept locked up forever.

Violet clasped her hand. "What lesson did you learn?"

"That love and business are gasoline and fire," she choked out around what she suspected was some spectacularly ugly crying. "That a woman has to work ten times as hard for a tenth of the respect."

Violet looked disappointed with that conclusion. "I know the team means everything to you. To you both. So much more than to me. And I know you're afraid of looking weak in the eyes of the world. You say we have to represent women. But what about representing yourself, chica?"

"It's the same thing," Harper sputtered. "I want to get it right. I refuse to let my feelings for Remy DuPre detract from what we're trying to build here."

Isobel squeezed Harper's shoulders harder. "So you love him?"

"Of course I love him! He makes me fucking sandwiches. He gives me dumb, perfect gifts. Behind closed doors, he makes me feel strong, but in the open, I feel weak. I look weak, and perception is reality here. You don't know what it was like when Dad found out what Stroger did. He blamed me for forcing him to give up a key player. And he was right. It was my fault—not getting hit, I know that, but my foolish decision to get involved with Stoger forced his hand."

Isobel was shaking her head in disgust. "I thought I was the one who was completely brainwashed by Clifford Chase. Jesus, being his daughter was like having Stockholm syndrome! We both wanted to please that bastard so much that we were willing to accept this shit? He should have called the police and prosecuted that weapons-grade asshole, Harper, not traded him out. You think he protected you when he did that? He protected himself and the team. And then he made you feel like shit because you fell for a guy!"

Caught off guard by Isobel's fury, Harper could only stare at the sister she had underestimated for so long.

"It doesn't change anything. I can't have a public relationship with a player on my team. Or even a player who used to be on my team. There's too much on the line."

Isobel sighed heavily. "This control thing is all well and good, Harper, but one day you're going to have to recognize that you can't make every call yourself. People want to help you. People want to love you."

Harper's heart shriveled at her sister's words. She knew she'd played fast and loose with some of the decisions about the team, keeping her sisters out of the loop. She'd cultivated a rock-solid independent streak for her own protection, and letting her guard fall was tougher than she'd ever thought possible. Even with these girls. Damn Clifford Chase and his fun-house travesty of a will.

Isobel picked up Remy's paperwork and scribbled her signature across the dotted line. "This wasn't my promise. However, I'll honor the bargain made by a representative of the organization. But no more stunts, Harper, 'kay?"

Harper nodded, but seeing those signatures didn't lift the weight as she'd expected. She would just need some time, that's all. The sooner he left, the sooner she could move on with her life and get back to the business of ensuring that this team made it to the playoffs.

Without Remy DuPre.

"Poppa, you in here?"

Remy stuck his head around the door and let the memory scents of sawdust, wood, and tung oil overtake him. His father's studio might look like a disorganized clutter of parts with bodies, necks, and strings strewn haphazardly, but Remy knew Alexandre had a distinctly organized mind that he only let wander on the stage.

"Ah, *mon fils.*"

His father looked up from his worktable, where he was applying a stain to a Meridian semihollow guitar. Gently, he laid the piece down upright to dry, stepped away, and only then removed the protective mask and gloves he'd been wearing. The potassium dichromate solution was nasty stuff and could burn or blind if not handled correctly.

Remy hugged his father, the man who introduced a Cajun kid to hockey though he knew zilch about it. Of course he had no idea his son would go so far, but he was proud.

Remy wanted him to be even prouder.

They talked about guitars and music and his suspension. His father didn't delve too deeply into Remy's uncharacteristic loss of temper.

"I'm to be traded to another team soon. One that has a real shot of going for the Cup."

Slow nod from Alexandre. "This bargain you made with Harper?"

"Oui. I give them a few wins, light a fire under them, and then I'm out of there."

"Sounds like a good deal."

It did. It was. But now it felt off. Like he was bailing when his boys needed him.

When Harper needed him.

Except she didn't, did she? He was crazy about her, and she had decided he wasn't worth it.

"What about you and Harper?" His father gave him that look, the one that said he'd known before Remy knew himself.

"There is no me and Harper. All she needs is the team."

"Have you told her how you feel? Other than in song?"

Remy felt a smile tugging at his lips for the first time in days. "She knows. Told her I loved her, but she's so afraid. She's carrying the weight of the world, of all women, of fucking feminism on her shoulders." He shook his head in mute apology for swearing. They made a conscious effort not to do that because of the kids always buzzing around. "She's decided that the best way to manage her loneliness is to pretend she doesn't need anyone. I can't break through."

"That doesn't sound like a DuPre."

Remy studied his father, the wisest man he knew. He owed his career to this man who took him to every practice, who cheered him at every game. He wanted his father there when he raised the Cup above his head.

"I thought I knew what women wanted, but Harper's not like other women. She's not looking for the picket fence and two point four kids. She needs to prove herself first, and she'll travel that road alone while she does it. I can't make her see another path."

"You need to speak her language, Remy."

"Poppa," he said with a heavy sigh. "There ain't a dictionary invented that would help me understand Harper Chase."

His dad folded his arms over his chest. "When I met your mother, I felt so dumb around her. She was a brainy college girl, and I was a guy who'd rather hang out in speakeasies playing guitar than read a book. We had nothing in common except our love of music. That was our lingua franca. That is how we found our way to each other." He met Remy's gaze. "Does this woman love you?"

Remy nodded. He knew it like he knew when the puck left his stick it was a surefire goal.

"Then find your lingua franca."

A knock on the door pulled Remy out of his misery and off the ass-dented sofa where he'd parked himself

for the last two days since coming home from NOLA.
There was no reason why he should be miserable at all.
The NHL wasn't going to press for longer than a three-
game suspension, though they would be within their
rights to. One more game and he'd be back, though
whether with Chicago or Philly was still up in the air.
He was getting everything he wanted—the trade to
his dream team was all over but the signatures. Philly
was top of the conference almost halfway through the
season and had looked near unstoppable in tonight's
game.

The Rebels, on the other hand, had not played so
well against Detroit. Remy would be the last person
to claim he was holding the fucking team together,
but . . . he was holding the fucking team together.

Tonight, St. James was nursing a shoulder injury, so
he'd been scratched and placed on the bench. Meanwhile, the rest of the players seemed to have forgotten
how to play hockey. Rumors were no doubt swirling
about Remy getting traded out—maybe even the fact
that he'd been aiming for that all along—and the team
was playing cagey. Sloppy moves on the ice, missed
passes, Hail Mary shots on goal.

He already knew who was knocking on his door,
but the only person he wanted to see was Harper. Sexy,
infuriating, scared-little-girl Harper.

Opening up, he sighed at being right. Bren lifted an
eyebrow, and Remy stepped back to let him in.

"You watch the game?" Bren asked.

"Uh-huh."

The Scot took a seat on the sofa, switched the PS4 on, and remained silent as the game loaded.

"Please. Make yourself at home."

"Not going to be yours for much longer."

So not in the mood for this.

"Only three games on your suspension. Won't affect your trade. Probably will make you more attractive, seeing as how you did what most of the league and the fans have wanted to do to that piece of shit for years."

Remy sat at the other end of the sofa. "Now might be a good time to explain why *you* did it."

Silently, Bren picked up a controller and held it out for Remy. Remy ignored it.

The captain grunted his annoyance. "You've had it pretty easy in your career, DuPre."

Not what he expected. Not even remotely accurate. "How'd you make that out?"

"Sure you've worked some, but overall you've coasted by on your talent. Maybe it's a Louisiana thing. You Bayou boys sure are a relaxed bunch."

"No one's ever accused me of coasting before." That wasn't exactly true, but no way would he admit it to this haggis-eating sheep shagger. Instead he put his energy into *not* picking up the controller and *not* throwing it at St. James's massive head.

"Those championships you lost? You never seemed all that upset in interviews later. You seemed sort of . . . accepting. Like it was fate. Out of your control."

He paused. "Like you believe that shite about being jinxed."

"A lot of the time it is out of your control. Sometimes it's just not your year. But that doesn't mean I haven't been upset about it. I've been mighty fucking upset about it."

He was mighty fucking upset now. He stood, because fuck this shit.

"Where the hell do you get off, St. James? Want to talk about coasting? Want to talk about not working hard? I could—" Lower himself to dirt level and kick the crap out of a man trying to rehab his life, which he would never do, no matter how much of a jerk the man was.

The jerk in question lifted his chin and held Remy's stormy gaze. "We do better when you're on the ice. No doubt about that. We'd do even better if you cared about winning the Cup, not with another team, but with the Rebels." He held up a hand to stay Remy's protest. "Fuck, brother, I know it's a long shot. But if you can pull off that long shot, just think of the rewards."

Why did Remy get the impression they weren't—or weren't only—talking about the Cup here? He did not enjoy being manipulated. "You didn't have to tell me about Stroger in the middle of a game, Bren. In the middle of a game *we were winning*."

Bren's lips twitched. "No, I didn't."

Remy would've dragged him upright so he could

swiftly make him not-upright if the guy wasn't supposedly hurting from that shoulder injury.

"You wanted me to beat the shit out of him in the
middle of the second period."

"I wanted you to get pissed. To think about why
you're doing this. What the true goal is here. Harper
needs you, and not just on the ice. She'll never admit
it. She's got too much pride, too much of her old
man's stubbornness, too much hurt inside her. I
worked for that fucker for eight years, saw the hoops
he made her jump through just to keep her place in
the org. You know what he said when I told him Stroger had hit her? *'Maybe this'll make her pack it in.'* Didn't
ask if she was okay, how badly she was hurt. And he
only traded that shithead out when I threatened to go
public. I would've gone to the cops, but Harper begged
me not to."

Bren shook his head in disgust, whether at Clifford
or himself, Remy didn't know.

"Compare this with what happened when I told
you. The minute you heard what Stroger did to her,
were you thinking about the game or the championship or public relations, or were you thinking that
you'd do anything to protect her and make it right?"

The moment he'd heard, the only thought in his
head wasn't even a thought. It was an instinct, white-
hot, pure sensation with a one-word label.

Harper.

This changed nothing. "She won't give us a chance.

You said yourself the press would crucify her if it got out, and that's all she can think about."

"So maybe she needs to be presented with a different set of facts. Force her hand. Heard you're pretty good at that." The man smirked. "Now let's play."

Remy picked up a controller and settled on the sofa, thinking on what Bren had said. Problem was, he had no leverage.

What was the ideal result here? Win the Cup. Get the girl.

Scratch that, reverse it.

His poppa had said he needed to figure out this woman's language. What made her tick. For his parents, it was music. For Harper and Remy, it was . . . sex, ambition. Hockey. Championship hockey.

He'd told her that taking a chance on them wasn't a case of Would You Rather, that it wasn't an either-or choice. Remy could be on a Cup-winning team *and* they could still be together. What if the two outcomes were halves of the same coin, as inextricable as two hearts that refused to beat without each other?

What if it was Harper or nothing at all?

God hates a coward, Remy. He needed to get off the fence and make a call.

He looked over at St. James, who held a square foil packet and was now eyeing Remy suspiciously. "Do I want to know why there are condoms in your sofa, Jinx?"

THIRTY-ONE

Rumor has it that Remy DuPre is about to be traded for the second time this season, this go-round to Philly. The Rebels' center has been on fire these last three months, largely responsible for Chicago's more-than-respectable 21–19 win-loss record. So that begs the obvious question: Why the hell—pardon my Cajun French—are the Rebels giving up their go-to guy at this stage? Something's rotten in the state of Chase.

—Curtis Deacon, *Chicago Sun-Times*

Something was rotten all right. Harper sat in the Rebels' owners' box, her heart in pulp as she tried to tune out the voices in her head. Pundits, media, her father, even that German-accented inner therapist. Everyone telling her she'd screwed up.

Beside her, Violet sighed heavily. Saturday night at a January home game was the last place her youngest sister wanted to be, and although she was obliged by the will to be present, no one would tell if she slipped away. Of course, Violet was not in the Rebels' box because of the will or even because she liked ogling the players—which she did. She was here because Harper was a hot mess.

The players were going through their warm-up against the visiting team from Quebec, while the DJ played "Wonderwall," as he had played it every game for the last week. Just hearing it made her heart ache. What she felt was raw and hurting, but Harper needed to forget that and put her GM hat on. The player she needed—apart from the one she was about to trade— would be on the ice tonight. Vadim Petrov, the natural left-winger she wanted for the first line.

Lost in her misery, Harper took a moment to notice Violet standing at the window overlooking the rink. She glanced over her shoulder. "So, if it looks like a Rebel and it skates like a Rebel, does that make it a Rebel?"

"What?"

"Take a look."

Tentatively, Harper approached the window. Her heart threatened to bust from her chest, through the glass, and onto the rink to make a bloody mess, because Remy DuPre was cutting figure eights on the ice, passing the puck in his usual warm-up routine.

"What's he doing here? He's still on suspension. He shouldn't even be on the ice." And then he'd be on a plane to Philly before the end of the week. "I need to find out what's going on."

She exited the box to Violet calling her name, and ran into Isobel outside.

"Going somewhere?"

"DuPre's not supposed to be playing. I need to talk to Coach."

"About that . . ." Isobel aimed a glance over Harper's shoulder at Violet, who was looking strangely pleased with herself.

"Can I tell her? Please, pretty, please?"

"Tell me what?"

"The commish cut it to a two-game suspension," Isobel said, smiling in the face of Violet's pout. "They had some new evidence that made them see it another way."

"What new evidence?"

Violet shut the box door behind her and rounded Harper, her expression fierce. "Did you really think we were going to let Stroger get away with what he did, Harper? Isobel had a little chat with that dickweasel. Told him he needed to shine up his story so the NHL knew he'd provoked Remy."

Isobel shrugged as if this was all beyond her control. "I let him know that it was in his best interests to take the blame, or there was a chance his propensity for hitting women might get out."

Harper covered her face with her hands. "You'd make what he did to me public?"

Isobel grasped Harper's arm. "The threat is enough for bullies like that. His career would be over, and he knows it. It was a gamble, but it paid off. Remy's here, playing like he should be."

But not for much longer. His official last game, and she had to watch it like her heart was headed to the gallows.

"If she doesn't like that, she's gonna hate the next part," Violet said.

Harper froze. Her body seemed to be in a fluctuating state of hot and cold, unable to settle on a temperature. "The next part?"

"He really should have called by now," Isobel muttered.

"Who?" Remy? But he was down there on the ice.

Harper's phone rang, and they all jumped. "Spooky!" Violet said in a deep voice.

It was Tommy Gordon, Remy's agent.

Violet grinned. "She's definitely not gonna like this part."

Two minutes later, Harper ended the call, dazed by what she'd just heard.

"Well?" Isobel prompted.

Harper was having a hard time catching her breath, the impact of the practically one-sided conversation she'd just had still rattling every cell in her body. She might have grunted a few replies to Tommy, but she really couldn't be sure.

"He wants to stay. He wants to stay with the Rebels." She rubbed her breastbone. "I don't know why he's doing this. Why is he doing this?"

Isobel's expression softened and she patted Harper's arm—a little patronizingly, Harper thought. "Don't you?"

He loved her. That beautiful Cajun loved her. Sure he'd said it, and she had doubted because she'd lived her entire life trying to turn hope into belief. Men always disappointed, but Remy DuPre was unlike any man she'd ever known.

"But—but the trade. It's practically a done deal. The paperwork has been signed."

"And since torn to shreds," Isobel said. "I signed it under duress. Or at the very least while I was trashed on Pinot."

So not the point. Half of their decisions were made under the influence anyway. "We have a verbal agreement with Philly!"

Violet grinned. "Isobel and I had a conference call this afternoon with the Philly GM—what's his name again?"

"Max Beaudine."

"Yeah, Max Beaudine. Don't you just love that name?" At Harper's scowl, Vi rushed on. "We told him we needed a few more days to think about it. Listen, Harper, you might be the executive branch in this fucked-up system of government, but as long as you're making decisions with your hormones, you really can't be trusted."

Isobel arched an eyebrow and nodded in Violet's direction. "Meet Checks."

Violet thumbed at Isobel. "And my good pal, Balances." She capped that with an evil grin, leaving no doubt that Violet Vasquez was her deceased father's earthly representative.

Hope you're enjoying this from your penthouse suite in hell, Daddy.

Frustration fought against the unfurling emotion in Harper's chest. She'd had this in hand. Why the hell wouldn't anyone cooperate?

Then because that bee-yatch of a universe couldn't leave well enough alone, it started, a low swell of sound building to a twenty-thousand-voice chorus.

"Today is gonna be the day . . ."

Chest-filling emotion overtook her, and she turned on her heel and stumbled away. She couldn't watch the game in company. Every fear and hope churning up her body would play on her face like a movie.

He's still a Rebel. He's still a Rebel.

"You'd better not interfere, Harper," Violet called after her. "Just let this play out."

Just let this play out? Oh, those bitches knew exactly what they were asking.

Isobel caught up with her and placed a hand on her shoulder. Completely overwhelmed, Harper couldn't even turn, but Isobel merely leaned into her and whispered, "Let it go, Harper."

Blinking back tears, she headed down the back stairs to the coaching staff offices, one destination in mind. The moment she stepped inside, memories tidal-waved through her.

This was her father's office, not the one in the front with the fancy mahogany desk and the glass showcase with his three championship rings. This one he used in the early days so he could be close to the players and the coaches. It was filled with old tapes and Isobel's childhood hockey trophies, and its south wall held a framed lithograph that Harper had made in the eighth grade and given to her dad for his forty-third birthday. A quote from the Great One himself, Wayne Gretzky.

You miss 100 percent of the shots you never take.

She sat in her father's dusty chair, thinking about how it had come to this. Queen of all she surveyed, and it wasn't nearly as satisfying as it should be.

A distant roar went up. The Rebels must have scored, and she had no doubt that Remy was there at the center of it, playing his huge heart out. Frustration locked up her lungs. Tears welled and fell. How dare her sisters implicate Harper's hormones in this decision? It was precisely to teach her hormones a lesson that she'd kept her bargain with Remy.

That pulled her up short. She'd graduated from the School of Clifford Chase magna cum laude in Sentiment Is for Losers. In following her father's lesson plan, she'd put her heart in permanent detention and let it become scabbed over for its protection. So used to her loneliness, she had labeled it independence. Turned it into a badge of honor.

Forget what hurt you but never forget what it taught you.
All this time, she'd been framing that mantra in Cliff's
language of bitterness and disappointment. What
Stroger did had hurt, how her father handled it hurt
more. But it made her strong, and strength wasn't
something that came from having it easy. Neither did
strength require she do it all alone. It meant accepting
love when it comes into your life like a wrecking ball.

Little did the bastard know it, but her father's will
bestowed on her more than the second-worst hockey
team in the NHL. He'd also given her three immeasur-
able gifts.

A sister she had underestimated.

Another sister she couldn't wait to know better.

And a path to the man she refused to live without.
And just like that gorgeous man, Harper had a whole
lot of love inside her busting to get out.

She opened her purse and withdrew a dog-eared
piece of paper, which she unfolded. It started with
Harper and ended with *Clifford*, and was probably the
dumbest piece of shit she'd ever read.

> *. . . you've hung in there for so long that I'm going
> to give you one more shot. Maybe this test of your
> mettle will reveal some real balls on you.*

What dipshit had decided balls were the ultimate
signifier of toughness? A pop to those puppies could
incapacitate the biggest, baddest jock and have him

crying all the way home to Mom. Give her a vagina any day—it could take a pounding and still rule the world in the morning.

She tore up the letter and dropped it into the wastebasket.

She let it go.

He won't stay, a voice whispered, sounding remarkably like seven-year-old Harper.

But the response was older, wiser, and remarkably resolute.

He already has.

~

Nothing beat the atmosphere in a home team's locker room after an important win, but as gratifying as it was, it was missing one essential piece. Callaghan was getting most of the attention from the local news media, given the hat trick that capped the 5-0 shutout of Quebec, so Remy was happy to sit back and chill while he waited for his woman to show up.

St. James pulled off his jersey. "What's so funny, DuPre?"

"Just thinkin' about how mad at me Harper must be."

The Rebels' captain shook his head. "You've got it bad, Jinx."

He did, and he prayed to the ghost of legendary player Gordie Howe, Mr. Hockey himself, that she had it just as bad for him. Nothing would stand in the way of how much he wanted her, and he was not above a little skullduggery to achieve his goals. If anyone could understand that, after their sexy back-and-forth for the last three months, it would be Harper Chase.

He had just slipped into his Luccheses when Kayla Jones, the sports reporter for the local CBS affiliate, shoved a mic in his face.

"Remy, welcome back from your suspension. Now, tell the truth. We've been hearing rumors you're about to be traded, and you've made no secret of the fact you want onto a Cup-winning team this year."

He stood and faced the vultures. "Well, I guess, Kayla, that's the kind of thing you media folk latch on to 'cause you ain't got nothin' better to talk about. When the Rebels brought me on, I'll admit it threw me for a loop. I wasn't sure they had what it takes to come together and go all the way. But I think you'll agree that we've played as well as any top-notch team these last couple of months."

Kayla hadn't earned her recent promotion to the field beat for nothing. "What about the Rebels' management? How are you getting along with them?"

"Just fine. They're total pros. They know what it takes to win, and while the ownership circumstances might seem a little unorthodox, it's business as usual on the ice. We have a great coaching staff, a team that's ready to fight for the win, and management that's behind us a hundred percent."

"There's talk that you don't gel with Harper Chase. Care to comment?"

"Think I can answer that."

He whipped around at the sound of his sex kitten's voice. Harper stood behind him, her body thrumming with energy, her eyes bright and fixed on him. His heart stalled, then completely locked up.

She strode over, a queen in his favorite heels and a sexy suit, and stood beside him.

"Like in any new relationship, we've had our teething problems," she picked up, and then the rest was drowned out in the roar of blood in his ears because something so monumental had happened that he was having a hard time keeping a lid on his brain.

Harper Chase had placed her small hand in his, squeezed tightly, and held on.

That dumb ol' heart of his went from locked up to flipped out.

His girl was holding his hand . . . and still talking like this was no biggie. "*. . . Of course, we'll be assessing where we stand in the next six weeks as we near the trade deadline . . .*"

Five seconds passed. Ten. Twenty. All while Harper Chase claimed him for her own, and no one seemed to realize just how mind-blowing this was. So much for the sharp-eyed media.

"*Callaghan and Remy have a good rapport on the top line, and with St. James working his way back to full strength following his shoulder injury, we have multiple options for the forward combinations.*"

He could barely stand it. He wanted to shout to the rooftops that she was his. He wanted to skate hearts on the ice and sing crowd-pleasing anthems to her. Loving the pressure of her fingers in his, he turned his head and watched in awe as she laid out her vision in that all-business way of hers. How could she be so calm?

Time to rock her serenity. He raised their joined hands and placed them over his heart so everyone watching could share in Remy's joy.

Harper's breath caught and she paused in whatever she was saying. She peered up at him, and they stared at each other like idiots while the world distilled to this perfect, crazy, cock-a-doodle-doo moment.

"Wait a second . . ." Kayla did a double take. "Are you saying—"

Harper's beautiful mouth stretched into a grin. "Ready for a scoop, Kayla?"

Kayla slid a look to her cameraman, checking they were still rolling, before her gaze refocused on where Harper's hand was joined with his. The hand that was not slipping away as it had when they were confronted with St. James and his girls at the market. Instead, Remy's femme clasped it tighter and gave him a sly grin.

Kayla coughed significantly. "Are you seeing one of your players, Harper? In a, uh, romantic sense?" *No flies on you, Kayla.*

"I'm seeing Remy DuPre in an, uh, incredibly

romantic sense." The expression on her face was questioning. *Is this all right?*

A little late to be checking for permission, but Remy didn't care. She was his, and he was indisputably hers.

"How long has this been going on?" Kayla gushed, all agog.

"Depends on your definition of 'this,'" Harper said around her sunshine chuckle. Harper was giggling, and he'd never heard a more beautiful sound. "It's been only a few weeks, but we'd rather be adults about it and not hide what's happening."

"Aren't you worried about being accused of a conflict of interest?"

Harper went wide-eyed in a WTF kind of way, and Remy knew Kayla had better watch out if she kept up that line of questioning. He squeezed Harper's hand to tell her she had this and also to remind her not to lose her cool.

"I leave the game-to-game coaching decisions to Coach Calhoun and his staff. Remy's earned his place in the starting lineup, but if his performance starts to slip—"

"Which won't be happenin'," he interjected.

"—then he'll be assessed like any other player. There's no room for sentiment in pro hockey."

Damn straight. He drank in the sight of all Harper's many complex facets coming together and finding peace: strong woman, team owner, passionate lover, keeper of his heart. Guess he'd better make sure he stayed in fighting shape for his place on the team and the privilege of being Harper's man.

Kayla nodded, clearly impressed. "And, Remy, do you have any concerns about your relationship with the team's owner affecting your game? A lot of players might feel a certain pressure to perform or worry about accusations of favoritism."

"With a taskmaster like Harper, there's always a certain pressure to perform." Laughter erupted behind him, and he didn't even bother to turn to his crew, who was no doubt listening in avidly. Shit, he was never going to live this down. "As for accusations of favoritism, I can handle those because, let's face it, I *am* her favorite. Just like she's mine."

Kayla's face melted in appreciation.

"But seriously, Kayla, we recognize this puts us under some scrutiny. As soon as I fu—screw up on the ice, fans and media like yourself will be calling for my head. I trust that everyone will be respectful and let Coach make the calls."

He turned to find Harper smiling, looking lighter and freer than he'd ever seen her. When your happiness was someone else's happiness, then that was love. Unable to resist expressing his joy in as physical a way as he could without getting prosecuted for public indecency, he decided to give the media something to *really* talk about. He drew Harper into the embrace of his body, slapped a hand on her sexy little ass, and joined his lips with hers.

Not even the rowdy shouts of his team could separate him from her, but he recognized that this PDA might be a bit much for Harper, so he stopped after a few blistering seconds.

"Not so fast, DuPre." And then she was kissing him harder, sealing their love in fire and ice, and telling him *everything* along with a few things he hadn't realized he needed. This woman loved him.

Finally. Speaking the same language, right here.

The room was still spinning when he opened his eyes and faced a shocked battery of reporters who had moved in like sharks scenting chum in the water. Harper was touching her lips, a look of wonder on her face, because even she had the capacity to surprise herself.

Remy needed to finish this interview so he could whisk his femme away for a spot of off-ice passion. "Kayla, you asked if my relationship with the team owner affects my game. Here's the only answer I can give you. Every day, I skate for my teammates, I skate for my family, and I skate for myself."

Staring into Harper's dancing green eyes, he spoke from the depths of the heart that belonged to this incredible woman.

"But mostly, I skate for her."

EPILOGUE

One month later . . .

Harper ended the call, jumped to her feet, and fist-pumped the air. "Yes!"

God, that was almost as good as an orgasm with the Chicago Rebels' star center. Almost.

"You get 'im, minou?"

She spun around, rubbing her hands together in glee, knowing her joy was writ large all over her face. "Quebec just signed off. The Russian is mine."

Remy DuPre leaned against the doorjamb of her office, a brown paper bag in his hand, the devil's charm in his grin. "Watch I don't get jealous, now."

As if any other man stood a chance. Still, she couldn't help teasing him. "Well, I have been known to take a liking to my new acquisitions. You'd better start showing me why I should keep you topmost in my affections."

Remy glided over, every smooth stride making his case. Next exhibit: he dropped the bag containing a muffuletta sandwich—extra peppers—on her desk. She gave the food a cursory glance, and though her stomach was already begging for it, other parts of her anatomy were pleading for different sustenance.

"I'm not even going to use my awesome culinary skills to win this battle, Harper. Though we both know I'm responsible for how tight this skirt's gettin'." His palm curved over her ass, which admittedly had filled out some since her man had taken over full-time feeding and fussing. He walked her back until that Cajun-loved rear met the desk's mahogany. Clever, sure hands hiked up her skirt so he could slot his muscular body where he belonged.

"Still need convincing?" He lowered his lips to hers, but at the last moment fiendishly switched direction and nuzzled her neck.

"Most definitely."

"Don't I keep you warm in this cold, cold town?"

"Said while currently removing my panties."

"Now that's so's I can get you hotter, baby. Try to keep up." Her panties had a hard time doing just that as they were dispatched with all the skill of those multimillion-dollar hands. Demonstrating a few skills of her own, she smoothed down the zipper of his jeans, freeing all that hard glory.

"I'm also good at helping you buy shoes." He hitched her thigh up so those red heels he loved could dig into the back of his calf. He groaned, and then she stroked him hard, so he groaned some more. "But mostly, I'm the reason you leave this office at a decent hour."

He had her there. At Remy's urging (read: demand), the team's ownership had made a concerted effort to hire a general manager and had it narrowed down to two candidates. Harper knew who she wanted—Dante Moretti, currently AGM with the Boston Cougars— and she was confident they could bring him on board. Ticket and merchandising revenues were up, and the Rebels' organization was ready to invest in its future.

Harper would always have a say in every aspect of the business, but knowing that Remy was behind her—and over her and under her—when she needed him freed her from the deep-seated compulsion to do everything. He filled all her gaps, put up with her crazy, and loved her for who she was.

"You brought food." She wrapped her hands around his cock and guided him to where she ached. "You brought *this*. Sounds like I'm all set. Sure you're the reason I leave at a decent hour?"

"Just remindin' you that I'm here for you. Loving every facet of you. The tough girl, the bombshell, the ball buster, my minou."

Tears pressed. She'd never been this emotional before she met him, but love had turned her into a basket case. He was the only one who saw it, and she suspected he enjoyed this vulnerability he produced in her.

Eager to regain the upper hand, she said, "We're almost there, Remy. Only a couple of weeks left."

He groaned, just like he did every time she men-

tioned how many days remained to the trade deadline—
and how there was still time to make his escape.

"Only place I'm goin' is here." He drove in hard,
every inch claiming her heart and body and soul.

Her fingers dug into his shoulders as the arguments
to test him found voice. "Even if we make top four—
and that's a moon shot—we can't go all the way, Remy."

"Can't we? That doesn't sound like the Harper
Chase I know, the woman who marched into my house
in Massachusetts four months ago and told me we
were heading to the playoffs. It's with the Rebels or not
at all, Harper." He sucked on her lip as his hips moved
in sexy plunder against hers.

"I—I just don't want you to resent me if it doesn't
happen. If we don't make the playoffs in two months.
If we don't make the finals in June. If we don't—"

He cut her off with a kiss. "Seeing this through with
you is more important to me than the Cup. Loving you
is more important to me than a piece of metal."

"Wash your mouth out, Remy DuPre!"

His grin was all wolf. "I appreciate that you're a
woman of your word, and even now, you're worried
about this call I'm making. This call we're making
together. But haven't you figured it out yet? You're my
ride or die, Harper."

Tears of joy sprang into her eyes at the realization of
what he was prepared to give up to be her true partner
in this. It was one thing to give her his heart, but Remy
DuPre was giving her *everything*.

"I love you so much, Remy," she whispered. "I don't think I could do this without you, and I'm not just talking about the team. I'm talking about my life that's fuller and richer and brighter because you're in it. Loving me for who I am."

She was crazy for the weight of him on her, needing to feel his solidity holding her in place, anchoring her. He wrapped her in the embrace of his big body. He smelled like home and love and the promise of a bright future.

"If we don't win, the press will rake us over the coals," she muttered, not quite ready to give in even as his thrusts exhorted her to let everything go. To surrender to her overwhelming joy and take it as her due.

He paused midthrust, his blue eyes wild and wise. "Only one way to stop that from happening, Harper."

"What's that?"

"We keep winning."

They came together, embracing the miracle of finding each other, knowing that the best was yet to come.

Their season was just beginning.

ACKNOWLEDGMENTS

To the team at Pocket/Gallery, thanks for taking another chance on me, especially my editors Elana Cohen (good luck, lady!) and Kate Dresser (welcome aboard!).

So many awesome people gave plotting advice, answered dumb questions about hockey trades, and read this story when it was in its infancy—particular gratitude goes out to Lauren Layne, Jessica Lemmon, Kelly Jamieson, and Marion Archer.

And thanks to everyone, readers new and old, for taking this journey with me. I hope you enjoy my ice warriors as much as my heroes—and heroines—in the firehouse.

Are you or is someone you know in
an unhealthy or abusive relationship?
The National Domestic Violence Hotline
is available 24/7, 365 days a year,
at www.thehotline.org and
1-800-799-7233 or 1-800-787-3224 (TTY).
No fees, no names, no judgment.

Can't get enough of the Chicago Rebels?

Turn the page for a sneak peek at the next sizzling installment in the series.

So Over You

By Kate Meader

Available in December 2017 from Pocket Books!

PROLOGUE

Hockey is not for pussies. Technically, it's defined as a sport with words like "play" and "game" thrown around liberally to shield its true nature: hockey is warfare with water breaks. In the rink you have over two thousand pounds of brute force clashing with whittled clubs, a rubber disc that could crush a larynx, and knives attached to feet. Let's not pretend there's anything civilized going on here.

—Clifford Chase, three-time Stanley Cup winner,
NHL Hall of Famer, and all-around asshole

Sold out. The arena was freakin' sold out.

On jellied legs, Isobel Chase skated to the face-off circle at the center of the rink in the Bayside Arena, home of the Buffalo Betties. The puck hadn't even dropped yet, but the raucous crowd of twenty thousand was already on its feet in anticipation of history about to be made.

The inaugural game of the National Women's

Hockey League, playing to a sold-out stadium. And she was here! On this night of firsts, Isobel planned to continue her storied career. Winner of the Patty Kazmaier Award for best NCAA player, last captain standing after the Frozen Four, Olympic silver medalist for Team USA . . . she could go on, but she had a professional fucking hockey game to win.

Melissande Cordet, the famed Canadian player and the only woman to get called up for a game in the NHL, hovered, ready to do the ceremonial drop. They'd chitchatted before the game and posed for photos while Cordet told Isobel how far women's hockey had come. How Isobel and her fellow athletes were blazing a trail.

Come back to me with that BS, Mel, when there isn't a salary cap of $270K on each team in the women's league.

Yeah, yeah, Isobel got it. Baby steps. Until they could prove their worth with decent attendance figures, TV broadcast deals, and feminine hygiene product sponsorships, the Great Experiment would continue.

"Ready to make history?" Cordet asked in her lilting French-Canadian accent.

Isobel remained still, her body bowed and tipped toward her opposite, Jen Grady, the captain of the Montreal Mavens. They'd roomed at Harvard together, skated to Olympic glory together, but that meant jack shit now. Tonight Isobel would be the first to touch the puck.

Her father, Clifford Chase, chose that moment to pop into her head for a visit. *Not now, Dad!* But the man always made it his mission to be heard. He was on his feet somewhere in the stands, though with his wealth and renown, he could have easily landed an entire box to himself. Wanting to feel the crowd, that pulsing, living thing as it rose and fell with the team's fortunes, he'd bought a Buffalo Betties cap and planted himself in the thick of it.

When women go pro, you'll be first on the line, Izzy. It's why I'm harder on you than I am on the boys. It's for your own good.

The boys, meaning the pro players on the Chicago Rebels, the NHL team her father owned and ruled with an iron fist. As substitute sons, their success was sporadic, which only served to place more pressure on Isobel's shoulders. She inched those shoulders forward.

The puck dropped.

Grady touched it first.

The night went downhill from there. . . .

ONE

Two years later . . .

"So this is just a flying visit, right? A couple of dances and we're out?"

Isobel's younger sister, Violet, shot slitted eyes of disgust at Isobel. Granted, Isobel had vowed to make more effort in the Grand Plan: get herself a real, live boyfriend versus the battery-operated one she defaulted to in time of need. But six weeks into the year, and she'd gotten no further than a few awkward online chats.

What are you wearing?

A sports bra and— Hello, hello, are you still there? Oh, fuck off, dickbiscuit.

"You're never going to get laid with that attitude," Violet said as they hacked through teeming masses of nubile, tanned, scantily clad bodies packing the floor at Ignite, Chicago's newest, hottest whatever. Most of these people looked like they'd been shipped in from a Pitbull music video.

When Isobel didn't respond, Violet stopped and pivoted. "What did I tell you about showing a little skin?"

Isobel looked down at her nightclub ensemble: black leggings and Joan of Arctic fur-lined boots paired with an Eddie Bauer parka over a black turtleneck. She called it her "French cat burglar" look because it threw off a sixties-beatnik-poet vibe, hugged in all the right places on her six-foot-tall frame, and had the added benefit of protecting her against a Chicago winter. She was nothing if not practical.

"This isn't really a good night to be looking for a man," she muttered.

"It's Valentine's Day. This place is filled with losers who couldn't get a date and now they're on the prowl for the leftovers."

"Like me?" Because she certainly didn't include Violet in the desperate-dateless-leftovers category. Her sister might be currently without an official boyfriend, but she was keeping a few members of the Rebels hockey team—the team they jointly owned and ran with their elder sister, Harper—on the hook. Not exactly principled, but Violet wasn't known for her scrupulous attention to the rules.

"Exactly like you!"

Who was Isobel kidding? Satan would be ice-skating to work before she got lucky, which suited her tonight because she really should be at home, replaying game videos in preparation for tomorrow.

Her first coaching gig with the Rebels. So, she was only a consultant, but it would lead to more. She knew it.

"It's a good thing we're on the list," Violet shouted

over her shoulder as she elbowed her way through the frenzy with sharp jabs, "because there's no way we would have gotten in with you looking like South Pole explorer meets South Side gangbanger."

The list? Now that Isobel thought about it, they *had* skipped a considerable line along with the serious side eye of the club's security. Violet looked like she belonged here with her fabulous gold bustier, a black band masquerading as a skirt, and lashings of colorful ink adorning her gleaming olive skin. Really, she fit in anywhere that was cool and dangerous.

They had only recently started hanging out when the requirements of their father's will threw the formerly estranged half sisters together to manage the team. Two years ago, Isobel hadn't known of Violet Vasquez's existence, as dear old Dad had shoved the result of his one-night stand in the Chase family armoire. On Clifford's death five months ago, Violet had moved from Reno to Chicago and was largely responsible for smoothing over the tension that thickened the air whenever Isobel was in the same room as big sis Harper. Growing up out of Cliff's shadow, Violet wasn't burdened by the Chase legacy. She had a way about her, a go-for-broke attitude, that Isobel envied.

"What list?" Isobel asked just as they reached a short stairway leading to a VIP area. "What's going on, Vi?"

"We're hanging with Cade and the guys."

Awesome! A night skirting ethical boundaries with pro hockey players who worked for her.

Violet was already skipping up the stairway littered with bored supermodels, several "wearing" skimpy cropped tops that barely covered their tits. The poor women were either freezing to death or highly aroused, because their nipples popped like pucks against the thin fabric. The letters VESNA blazed from several surgically enhanced chests. Why was that familiar?

A few more steps, and it became clear that the line of women clinging like sex-starved limpets to the stair's rail was an actual queue with a goal in mind. A mall line for Santa, perhaps, where a deviant Santa was about to have the time of his freakin' life. And here was Isobel blindly following Violet, who now waved at someone behind the velvet rope at the top of the steps.

Shit.

Isobel's heart sank to her club-inappropriate boots. She recognized the head elf pulling back the rope, though Alexei Medvedev was more like a crusty goblin.

Vadim Petrov's right-hand man hadn't changed much in eight years: his age could still be easily placed at anywhere between forty and sixty. Following some ridiculous feudal custom, the man supposedly owed service in perpetuity to Vadim's bloodline. He served as cook, porter, alarm clock, and bodyguard, to name just a few of his jobs. No doubt he picked up his charge's dry cleaning, ushered women out of Vadim's bed in the early hours, and waxed his boy's scrotum for that silky, manscaped feel.

If Isobel had thought Alexei might have forgotten

her, she was quickly disabused of that notion when he let Violet through but placed his Russian solidity in Isobel's path. Seemed she was persona non grata again. They sized each other up, and Isobel was happy to see that she was still taller than him, her six feet besting Alexei by a good four inches. But he made up for it in squat, torpedo-shaped bulk. She was at a clear disadvantage—he could easily push her down the stairs.

He looked like that was at the top of his to-do list.

"What's up, Igor?" He'd *loved* it when she called him that in olden times.

Wondering about the holdup, Violet turned and grabbed her arm. "Hey, she's with me, *tipo*."

After a few seconds, Alexei stood back, his soulless shark eyes boring into her. All he was missing was the two-fingered prong gesture of *I'm watching you*. Fine, they understood each other.

Moving forward into the crowded room—huh, not so exclusive after all—Isobel felt her skin prickle with something like foreboding. As if it knew something she didn't.

She turned and *whoosh!* Sure, she didn't need all that breath in her lungs anyway. Vadim Petrov sat on a chocolate velvet couch, wearing a sharp suit, an icy stare, and a half-naked blonde.

The man had made a bargain with the devil, and the devil had yet to call in his marker. Undeniably beautiful, he sported mountain-high cheekbones that pronounced his descent from an aristocratic lineage, ice-blue eyes as clear as the Baltic Sea, and full lips that miraculously softened the sharp angles of his face. Coal-black hair fell over his brow and past his jawline, its silkiness appearing as otherworldly untouchable as its owner. And don't even get her started on his sculpted, tatted body—currently covered up, thank Gretzky—which he proudly flaunted on billboards as often as his numerous sponsorship deals demanded.

Two days ago, the Rebels had traded him in from Quebec. The plan was to use him on the left wing, but he wasn't quite game fit owing to a recurring knee injury. This gave him plenty of time to indulge his other interests: clubbing and manwhoring.

For the briefest moment she wished she didn't look like a lank-haired, parka-sporting schlub the first time in years she'd been less than ten feet away from him. But then she shot titanium into her spine, cocked her hip a la fuck it, and sidled up to Violet.

Cade "Alamo" Burnett, one of the Rebels' defensemen, had just kissed Violet on the cheek and looked like he wanted to lean into Isobel, but he seemed to change his mind at the last moment. Not a problem. Isobel was all about boundaries.

"Hey, take off your coat, Iz," Vi said.

Isobel felt too warm, too cold, and mighty uncomfortable. "Not staying long."

"Izzz . . ."

"Oh, okay. Keep your bustier on." As she unzipped her parka, she was surprised to feel a tug. After a few seconds struggling with it (*Uh, that's mine . . . I know, I'm trying to . . . back off, lady*) she realized that the woman behind her was actually a coat check person and not a parka thief.

Isobel really should not be allowed out in public.

She hoped Vadim wasn't watching. *Oh, who cares what he thinks?*

Apparently her eighteen-year-old self did, because that's what she'd reverted to. *That* loser's traitorous gaze couldn't help itself, and when it landed on the Russian again, Isobel was surprised to find him watching her with mild amusement. That was different. As a nineteen-year-old, humor had been about as foreign to him as a PB&J sandwich.

A guy who had "PR clown" written all over him was taking a photo of the blonde as she inched her hand inside Vadim's lapel, apparently needing the warmth only those muscles could provide. Poor thing, forced to freeze her ass off at the club. Two seconds later, the blonde was replaced by a redhead who appeared to have similar body heat problems. Santa aka Vadim whispered in her ear, probably inquiring if she'd been naughty or, you know, extra naughty.

The tabloids called him the Czar of Pleasure, a man as well known for his exploits in the bedroom as on the ice. Oh, the things Isobel could tell about this guy's erotic talents.

Eyes bright with admiration, Cade looked around the VIP room plastered with signs for Vesna, which Isobel now recalled was a high-end Russian vodka. "Man, I want a vodka deal."

"You'd be lucky if you got a deal fronting Budweiser Clydesdale piss, Alamo," came a slow drawl behind them.

Remy DuPre, the Rebels' center straight from the heart of the bayou, appeared bearing the most frou-frou drink Isobel had ever seen. Blue with a big chunk of pineapple in the center.

"Is that for Harper?" Isobel asked, knowing it wasn't, because her sister wouldn't be caught dead attending a party with the players even if her boy-friend's presence gave her a good excuse. *Banging one of them is bad enough,* Harper was fond of saying. *I need to at least give the illusion of labor–management boundaries.*

Remy stared at his drink in disgust. "I'm just here to make sure these boys get home by curfew."

Isobel hid her smile. She liked how Remy had stepped up to the position of elder statesman since his arrival four months ago. She also liked how Remy was a calming influence on her older sister. He could have bailed on the Rebels when he had a shot at trading out, but he didn't because he loved Harper and needed her to know that in the clearest terms.

A pang of envy bit into Isobel's heart, but she breathed it away. She wasn't looking for the love her sister had found with Remy, but she wouldn't say no to the obvious fireworks that lit up their bed. Not that it would be happening here.

Excusing herself, she headed over to the bar set off in an alcove. One drink, and she was out. She eyed the offerings behind the broad-shouldered bartender: Vesna vodka as far as the eye could see. A plastic-encased menu listed the cocktail options: Vesna Driller, Vesna on the Beach, Vesna Slap 'n' Tickle . . . you get the idea.

The bartender, who was cute in a swipe-right kind of way, caught her eye.

"Hey," she said, pinning on her I'm-dateable-let's-practice smile. "So what's in the Vesna Bomber?"

"Vodka, grenadine, and passion fruit," she heard behind her in a tone that could freeze a Cossack's ball sac.

Here we go. She turned, the first thing that popped into her head skipping her filter and landing right on her tongue. "Sounds girly."

Yep, pretty proud.

No one would ever describe Vadim Petrov as "girly." Before her stood the most masculine streak of cells Isobel had ever seen, and she lived in a world teeming with machismo.

"Thought you hated vodka," she said.

"I do." A negligent wave of his hand said this was all beyond his control. Who was he, a mere multimillion-dollar spokesman, to counteract stereotypes about Russians?

The gesture might have been casual, but his stare was anything but. "I was sorry to hear about your father."

"Oh. Thanks." It still gnawed, less sharp now but with a constant awareness of the void. Clifford Chase had been driven, difficult, and demanding. He'd expected great things from her, so her failure to make a career in the pros had strained their relationship.

She missed him like crazy.

Vadim had lost his own father about eighteen months ago, and she opened her mouth to offer similar condolences, but they got stuck in her throat with all the other things she longed to say. He'd had a difficult relationship with the elder Petrov, a billionaire businessman with rumored ties to the Russian mob, and a man who didn't want Vadim to play hockey in the United States. Better he expend his athletic energies for the glory of Mother Russia. Sergei Petrov got his wish—his son enjoyed a star-making turn in the Kontinental Hockey League after his visit to Chicago all those years ago.

Isobel might've had something to do with that.

The silence sat up between them, the tension expanding. Vadim seemed to be expecting her to say something, so she happily obliged.

"How's your knee?"

Not that. His eyebrow shot up. "Improving."

She needed to tiptoe around his ego. "There are extra drills you could do to help with your speed. Get you back to how you were pre-injury."

"I'm sure the team will do what is necessary."

"Yes, we will."

Gotcha! That eyebrow became one with his hairline.

She cleared her throat. No nerves, now. "Moretti has assigned me to give you personalized attention. We'll meet for an hour before each regular practice and work on your skating."

Now that injury had forced her out of the game, coaching was all she had left. This morning Dante Moretti, the newly hired Rebels' general manager, had appointed her as a skating consultant with one charge: to get Vadim Petrov into good enough shape so they could qualify for the playoffs in two months. She'd planned to drop this knowledge on the man himself after tomorrow's team practice, but hey, no time like the present.

Now she waited for his predictable explosion.

"There is nothing wrong with my skating," he grated.

"There's always room for improvement," she said with unreasonable cheer. Kill the boy with happy. "Right now, you're placing too much weight on your uninjured leg, and it's thrown off your motion. We'll focus on—"

"Nothing. I can work with Roget, the regular skating coach."

"He doesn't have time to give you the extra attention you need. It's typical for teams to hire consultants, especially for players who are underperforming."

And there was that famous Russian scowl. L'il ol' Vaddy was a touch sensitive about his diminished capacity since that knee injury had sidelined him for half the season. Having battled a career-killing injury herself, she understood what he was going through. The doubts, the questioning. The fear. But unlike her, he was in a position to get back to full strength as a pro.

He snorted. "You are not just any consultant, though, are you, Isobel? You are a part owner of the team. You are Clifford Chase's genetic legacy. And even after his death, you are getting your way."

She understood she'd have to get used to slings and arrows, accusations of using her father's name and her position as owner to get a coaching gig. But that last dig about getting her way? As if she had done that before.

"I know what I'm doing, Vadim."

"Do you?" He leaned in, using his height to overwhelm her. "You can no longer play at the pro level, yet you insist on playing games. With me. And not for the first time. Once your selfishness screwed with my career—"

"That's not what happened."

"Isn't it? Three years—" He cut off, his anger a cloud that practically stung her eyes. "All because you put me in your crosshairs, Isobel. Well, forgive me if I would rather not trust my professional future to you."

She swallowed, her cheeks heating furiously. Of

course, he would see it that way. She had been young, immature, more sheltered than the average eighteen-year-old. All she knew was hockey. It was her life, and then Vadim had skated into it and she'd seen something else. Her eyes had opened to beauty and passion and—hell, she'd been a teenage nightmare.

He was so close, close enough for her to view rings of blue-green fire around his irises as well as a smudge of lipstick tinting his jaw. It was hard being Vadim Petrov.

Regularly bombarded by photos of him in magazines and on billboards over the years, she wanted to think it was easier to look at him objectively now. As a perfectly formed machine of mass and muscle. As a chiseled Renaissance sculpture that was cool to the touch. She wanted to think it, but she remembered too much about the last time she had been this close to him.

Her infatuation. Her embarrassment. Her shame.

She should apologize for how it all went down because it would make things easier.

Well, not exactly *easier*.

They had to work together, put aside their differences for the sake of the team. But she didn't like his assumptions about how she'd landed this job.

Or maybe she didn't like that she half-agreed with him.

Doubts that she had right completely on her side put her on the defensive. "These late nights at the club will have to stop." She curved her gaze around his broad shoulder to the ever-increasing line of women waiting to sit on his lap. "You're going to need your sleep for the extra practice you have to put in."

He didn't respond to that, but if he had, it was easy to guess what he'd say. What every athlete would say.

I know my limits. I know what my body can take.

Athletes were consummate liars.

Vadim leaned in again, smelling of fame, privilege, and raw sex appeal. Discomfort at his proximity edged out the hormonal sparks dancing through her body.

"Does Moretti know that we have history? Does he know you are the last person I wish to work with?"

Before she could respond, someone squealed, "Vadim!" A blond, skinny, buxom someone who was now wrapping herself around Vadim in a very possessive manner. "You said you'd be back with a dwinkie!"

A dwinkie?

Drawing back, Vadim circled the squealer's waist and pulled her into his hard body. "*Kotyonok*, I did not mean to be so long." He dropped a kiss on her lips, needing to bend considerably because she was just so darn petite! Not like big-boned Isobel, who could have eaten this chick and her five supermodel Playmates for a midmorning snack. A group of them stood off to the side, clearly waiting for the signal to start the orgy. And Vadim clearly wanted to give it, except he had to deal with the annoying fly in the sex ointment.

Why did the lumberjack hotties always go for twigs

instead of branches? Did it make them feel more virile to screw a pocket-sized Barbie?

Yep, feeling like a schlub.

But he didn't need to know that. All he needed to know was that she had the power to get him back on competitive ice. This was her best shot at making a difference and getting the Rebels to a coveted playoff spot. Vadim Petrov and his butt-hurt feelings would not stand in her way.

"Do you need to talk about it, Russian?"

She infused as much derision into the question as possible, so that the idea of "talking about it" made him sound a touch less than manly. Big, bad, brick house Russians didn't need to talk about the women who done them wrong.

"There is nothing to talk about," he uttered in that voice that used to send Siberian shivers down her back. Now? Nothing more than a Muscovian flurry.

"Excellent!" *Super-scary cheerful face.* "Regular practice tomorrow is at ten, so I'll see you on the ice at nine a.m. Don't be late."

Pretty happy with her exit line, she walked away.

Far too easy.

A brute hand curled around hers and pulled her to the other side of the bar, out of the sight line of most of the VIP room. She found her back against a wall—literally and figuratively—as two hundred and thirty pounds of Slavic muscle loomed over her.

He still held her hand.

If she weren't so annoyed, she'd think it was kind of nice.

She yanked it away. "Who the hell do you think you are?"

"Who am I?" he boomed, and she prayed it was rhetorical. Unfortunately, no. "I am Vadim Petrov. Leading goal scorer for my first two years in the NHL. Winner of both the Kontinental and the Gagarin Cups. A man not to be trifled with. And you are who exactly? The daughter of a hockey great who was not so great when it came to running a team. The woman who can no longer play, yet thinks she can offer 'tips' to me. To me! You may have pedigree, Isobel, but there is nothing I can learn from you."

This arrogant, douchewaffle piece of shit!

She straightened, pulling herself millimeters from the wall, which had the effect of putting her eye to eye with him. Or eye to chin. Close enough.

Too close.

He was breathing hard, and so was she, the lift of her breasts teasing, tantalizing brushes against his chest.

"One conversation and you're out of breath, Vaddy? We're going to need to work on your conditioning."

More of the dark and broody. More of the nipple pops against her sweater. *Stop being so Russian, Russian!*

"My conditioning regimen is fine."

A glance over to the bar found "Dwinkie" biting her lip in concern, checking in with her gal pals, and possibly planning an extraction with SEAL Team: Boobs Are Our Weapons.

"Getting your exercise with puck bunnies and Vesna groupies doesn't count." Isobel slid her hand between their bodies and brushed his abs. Good God, hard as ice and hot as sin. "As I suspected, a bit flabby with all your time off. We'll take care of that with your recovery program."

He stepped back, as though burned by her touch, and she willed away the ping of hurt in her chest. At least she knew where they stood on *that* issue.

"I will discuss this with Moretti and Coach Calhoun tomorrow."

"You do that, but do it early, because I'm still expecting you in full gear at nine a.m. And, Vadim? I'd suggest you quit with the trail of women looking to sit on your . . . knee. We don't want to weaken it or any other parts of your anatomy. Keep that up and you won't even have a shot at *Dancing with the Stars*."

Then with the reflexes that once accorded her MVP status on the ice, she escaped his orbit and headed back into the crowd.